SNAPSHOT

ebook ISBN: 9781957959108 Paperback ISBN: 9781957959139

Cover Designer: KB. Row

Editor: Brazen Hearts Author Services

Formatter: KB. Formatting

authork.b.row@gmail.com

SNAPSHOT

KB.ROW

Foreword

Snapshot is the first book in the interconnected *Emerson University* series but can be read as a standalone as each book will follow a different couple.

PLAYLIST

Home – Three Days Grace
Gives You Hell – The All-American Rejects
1985 – Bowling For Soup
You Can't Hurry Love – The Supremes
Dirty Little Secret – The All-American Rejects
Juliet – LMNT
L-O-V-E – Nat King Cole
The Reason – Hoobastank
Mama Said – The Shirelles
You're a Jerk – New Boyz
My Girl – The Temptations
Ain't No Moutain High Enough – Marvin Gaye, Tammi
Terrell
Brown Eyed Girl – Van Morrison
You Are The Reason – Calum Scott
Kiss My Slowly – Parachute
Thunderstruck – AC/DC
Cherry Pie – Warrant
Kickstart My Heart – Motley Crue

Out for a Rip (lol) – Shark Tank
Don't Stop Believin' – Journey
Addicted – Saving Abel
Closer – The Chainsmokers, Halsey
Hooked On A Feeling – Blue Swede, Bjorn Skifs
You Had Me From Hello – Kenny Chesney
My Best Friend – Tim Mcgraw
Just So You Know – Jesse McCartney
Sorry – Buckcherry
Burn it to the Ground – Nickelback
Are You Ready – Three Days Grace
I Will Always Love You – Whitney Houston
Chapel of Love – The Dixie Cups

To hot hockey players and the women that love them.

TrIGGer warnInGs

THE TRIGGER WARNING DOES INCLUDE A HUGE SPOILER FOR THE BOOK

- Alcohol use/abuse

- Alcoholic/Abusive parent

- Drug use

- Death of parent

- "Age of consent" sex (mentioned, not on page)

- Violence on page

- Pregnancy & Pregnancy loss (ON PAGE)

Prologue

Reese

"I think sometimes people fight because they don't know how to love."

"I think that's just an excuse."

"Maybe." Winnie shrugs, not caring that I'm arguing with her, and it's not because I don't know how to love. It's because she's wrong.

My parents don't argue because they are in love; they argue because my dad has anger issues and my mom is depressed—or lazy, as Dad often calls her. But Winnie is young, so I don't hold her innocent outlook on life against her. I wish I could still think the way she does, but instead, I have to accept the world for what it is, not what I want it to be.

I fall back onto the rough shingles on the roof outside Winnie's room and stare up at the night sky. Winnie moves, laying her head on my stomach and stretching her feet out perpendicular to my body.

"The stars are so bright tonight."

The sky hasn't been that clear lately, making seeing the stars difficult, but not tonight. They are a stark contrast to the inky sky, and I bet if we wanted to, we could count them all. We've done that a few times. Winnie finds it soothing—I mostly agree.

"They're a good reminder that the world is big, we are small, and our issues aren't always as big as they seem." She drops her head to the side and stares at me with big brown eyes. "Don't you think?"

Winnie's dad always says she has an old soul. He usually tells her that when she's crying about not making friends, but I think he's right. She always says things that sound weird coming out of a kid's mouth.

"Even small issues can feel like big issues if you're close enough."

"True. But it's a nice reminder that not everything is as big as it seems, right?"

"I suppose." It's my turn to shrug now.

Our peaceful moment is interrupted when a door slams. I know that's my front door across the street. I just don't want to acknowledge it. Dad's angry mutters rip through the quiet air. His rusty old truck is loud as it roars to life, and then he's gone, most likely heading to the bar.

Knowing my mom is probably over there crying like every other time he leaves the house pissed is like a brick sitting on my chest. Just once, I wish my parents could pretend to get along. It's exhausting because I know I'll have to go home and try to comfort her. Probably put her to bed, too, since I bet she's popped open a bottle by now. None of my other friends have to deal with parents like mine. I don't know why I had to be born into the family I was.

Why not a family like the Lewises'? Their household is always calm. Our houses might look the same structurally, but they couldn't be more opposite behind closed doors. People in this house actually love and care about each other the way a family is meant to. They aren't looking to argue any chance they get. I mean, I've seen Winnie and Elijah go head-to-head, but it's always over normal sibling stuff. He ate her last snack; she stole his CD player—it's never serious, and an hour after they argue, they are back to normal.

Growing up, I always wanted a sibling like them, but now I'm glad I don't have one. Someone else having to live through our parents nearly tearing each other's throats out on the daily doesn't sound enjoyable. Misery loves company—but not that much. At least not mine.

I wish my parents would grow up and learn how to love each other like Christopher and Sheri do. I've never even seen them mad at each other. Mrs. Lewis has scolded Christopher in front of us for various things before, but usually, he is biting back a smile when she does, and it always ends with him giving her affection until whatever anger she was holding dwindles. That's how I want my marriage to be. No relationship is perfect, but we're meant to fight battles together, not battle with each other.

"How did your parents meet?"

"Uh, college. I think."

College. Two more years and I'm there. Maybe then I'll meet *my* soulmate.

"What about yours?"

My parents? I nearly snort. They were a random hookup, but I won't tell a thirteen-year-old that. I'm sure she hears worse at school—I know I did at her age—but still. I'm not risking her asking weird questions I don't want to answer. Elijah would kill me if she went to him asking what a booty call was.

"I think at my mom's work." It's not a lie. Mom was a stripper, and they did meet at her work. Apparently, he paid for *more*, and nine months later, out popped a bouncing baby boy. The only reason I know all this is because of their arguments. Dad's not quiet when he calls Mom a cheap whore, and she's not quiet when she calls him a drunk, good-for-nothing piece of shit.

Winnie rolls to her stomach and props herself up on her elbows, staring at me expectantly.

"What?"

"Are you coming to the apple orchard with us tomorrow?"

"I can't. I have to work." But I wish I could. Going to the apple orchard with the Lewises every year is one of my favorite memories. It's a tradition, and they have a competition to see who can pick the most. I won last year, but I think that's because Mr. Lewis let me. Picking is fun, but it's all the baking and cooking that I really love. Mostly because Mrs. Lewis is an amazing cook and always asks us to taste test everything.

"Can't you call in?" She frowns, puffing her bottom lip out. She knows I hate it when she does that, and I swear that's *why* she does it.

"Some of us have to work, Winnie." It's not fair to snap at her, but I do. How would she know about struggling? Her dad is a higher-up at the same factory my dad works at, and a few years ago, Mrs. Lewis opened a bakery downtown that is always busy. They probably aren't swimming in cash, but they're comfortable enough, I'm sure.

"I know." Her voice is soft, and I feel like a dick. "I just like when you come."

"Maybe I can stop by after."

Her dark eyes brighten as if that's the best news she's ever heard. This is why I love hanging out with Winnie, even if her brother thinks it's weird. And he doesn't even know about nights like tonight when we simply lie on the roof outside her room and talk. She's always excited to see me, unlike anyone else in my life. And she's a great listener. Maybe a couple years my junior, but she understands most things really well, and even if she doesn't—like my parents' genuine hatred for each other, or me having to work—she's still nice to talk to. The nights I don't want to talk, she finds a way to distract me, always flipping a bad night to good. I consider her as much of a friend as I consider her brother.

"I'll be sure to save you a peeler." She grins and falls onto her back once again, placing her head on my stomach.

I know the world will get to Winnie one day, and her positive outlook will more than likely shift into a realistic one, as it does for most, but I dread the day that happens. Whatever it is that changes her, I'm going to hate it forever.

1

Winnie

PRESENT DAY

Why the hell are there so many flavors of Pop-Tarts? There definitely weren't this many when I was a kid, and that is a crime. I would have loved eating a pumpkin pie Pop-Tart while I watched morning cartoons.

It's no wonder Dad always needed a very specific list from Mom when she sent him to the store. The options are practically limitless. I used to watch Mom toss things into the cart and not think much about it, but now that I'm doing the shopping, I realize it's not that simple. There were many things I knew would change when I moved away from my mom and in with my brother for college, but struggling to decide which Pop-Tarts to buy was not one of them.

I grab a few boxes of new flavors and one of brown sugar cinnamon because Elijah would kill me if I didn't get his favorite kind. They thunk against the plastic basket as I toss them in and turn away, right as someone calls a name I wasn't ready to hear.

Looking over my shoulder, all I can do is blink. *What are the odds*? My first time out in Pinecove, and I run into the only two people I was hoping I wouldn't see. I watch—or listen—to a lot of his hockey games, although I'd never admit that out loud. So I obviously knew he would be around, but I didn't think he would be *around*. And I definitely didn't think he would be linking arms with Zoey the first time I saw him.

Are they together?

It doesn't matter, Winnie. He's *not* yours.

He never was.

I need to remember that, even if seeing him with those hazel eyes I fell in love with so many years ago brings back feelings and memories I've done my best to block out.

"*Never let the enemy see your weakness.*" Dad would always tell Elijah that. He was talking about hockey, but it can be applied to real life, I'm sure. I don't know if Reese Larson counts as an enemy, but Zoey Miller sure as hell does.

I force a smile and head their way, figuring it's too late to take off in the other direction and praying I look as unbothered as I want to. It's a good thing they can't hear my heart, though, because the heavy beating would be a dead giveaway. I'm no longer in high school, and I promised myself I wouldn't be meek in college, but there's something about facing my old bully and the man I thought was the love of my life in the same place—touching—that threatens to bring that trait roaring back to the surface.

The first time Zoey ever approached me, it was to ask about Reese. She wasn't the first girl or the last. I was always around Reese and my brother, and I guess I was more approachable than those two because many, *many* girls thought they could get to them through me. Like I was their door guard or some shit. Either way, Zoey was by far the most persistent. Most of the time, girls would want basic information about them that they could use to connect. It usually worked with my brother, although I prefer to not think about how many girls I set him up with on accident.

Reese, however, never entertained them. I always looked up to him for that, not knowing it was deep-rooted jealousy that made me happy for his rejection of those girls.

Zoey wasn't like the rest, though. She didn't take his blatant uninterest lightly and made my life hell because of it. Like somehow I was the reason he wasn't interested in her.

Couldn't be her horrendous personality or anything.

She tried to befriend me first, but it wasn't long after she first approached me that I caught her talking about me to her friends in the bathroom, and it wasn't nice. They made fun of my hair, my freckles, and the way I followed Reese and Elijah around like a "lost puppy."

I never questioned my relationship with the guys before that, but when I heard them making fun of me for not hanging out with anyone else, I took a step back and wondered if my brother and Reese let me hang around them because they liked being around me, or because they felt bad. It was a real eye-opener and a thought that pricked my mind for a very long time. Even when Reese would knock on my bedroom window after he finished hanging out with Elijah, or when Elijah would call me into his room to play games with them without my prompting.

I guess, in a roundabout way, she's the reason I haven't gotten close to many people. I never wanted to come across as pathetic for being around people who didn't want me there.

2

Reese

Fire alarm—the best sound to hear in high school, especially in the middle of math. As long as it's a drill, obviously. Which I'm assuming this one is, at least until the sprinklers start, and before I know it, I'm soaked.

"Alright, come on," Mr. Hart grumbles. "Everyone outside."

It's the last hour of the day, and with only twenty minutes of class left, this couldn't have happened at a better time. Of course, I hope it's nothing serious and no one gets hurt, but it's still great timing.

Spring hangs heavy in the air, not hot but not winter cold either. Being wet from the indoor sprinklers is uncomfortable, but at least it's a nice day. Things are finally beginning to turn green, which means summer is almost here—my last summer at home. Thank fuck. After graduation next year, I plan on traveling with the money

I've saved from lawn care over the last five years, then head to college. Hopefully with a hockey scholarship.

Someone slaps a hand on my shoulder, bringing me out of my head. Elijah halts next to me, grinning like he usually is.

"You look too happy about our school possibly burning to the ground."

"How sick would that be? Never have to go to school again."

I don't have it in me to tell him that's not how it works, and the school burning would cause several issues for our town, but he's onto a new subject before I can anyway.

"Let's get out of here. I'm starving."

"We can't just leave. They would go looking for us."

He drops his head back and groans as if that's the worst news he's ever heard. There is no way he's that hungry. Lunch was three hours ago, and I saw how high he piled his plate.

Elijah is a nice reminder not to take life so seriously. I'd like to say we balance each other, but I don't think I have any influence on him. He says my "broodiness" is a "sweet personality trait."

Teachers come around, taking attendance; it's not a big school, so it doesn't take long. I know there can't be more than ten minutes left of school now, considering buses have started to line up, so they gotta let us go soon, I hope.

"Let's find Win so when they release us, we can g-t-f-o."

Now, that's something I can agree on. Students are divided by classes, so we wander down to the cluster of freshmen. After a quick scan, I come up empty on a short redhead. Elijah frowns from across the group, twisting my stomach.

I raise my hand in question, and he shrugs, but worry tugs his brows low on his forehead. If there is anything that can make Elijah flip the serious switch, it's Winnie.

"Hey." I grab the shoulder of some lanky kid standing with the freshmen. He looks up at me with wide, scared eyes, but I ignore that. "Where's Winnie Lewis?"

"Uh, I don't know."

Annoyance growing at an exceptional rate, I look for anyone familiar who might hang out with Winnie. She's a bit of a solo bird, but someone has to stand out. Elijah is chatting with Mrs. Duck, most likely asking her since she teaches Freshman English.

Eventually, I find a girl in the sophomore class I think I saw Winnie talking to once and wander her way. Minutes have passed, and I still haven't seen a flash of red hair. I don't think it's a real fire, but I definitely have real worry. Where the fuck is she?

"Hey." I don't grab the girl like I did the dude—that seems inappropriate. But I raise my voice to get her attention. The friends in front of her pause, their mouths open and makeup smeared down their faces from the sprinklers. "Where's Winnie Lewis?"

The girls' mouths snap, and one of them leans closer to the other, whispering in her ear. They both giggle at whatever is said, and holy fuck am I glad Winnie doesn't act like this.

The brunette spins, and her blue eyes widen in surprise. My irritation grows while I wait for an answer.

"She excused herself during class, and I haven't seen her since." She has the nerve to shrug like it's no big deal she's missing.

"How long ago?" I bark, unable to mask my worry but able to shift it into anger.

"Like five minutes into class?" She lifts her shoulders in a shrug, and it's obvious she has no actual clue where Winnie is.

I push by, but a hand snaps out and grabs my wrist before I can pass completely. That same brunette is holding on to me, and I scowl down at her fingers.

"What?"

"I'm Zoey, by the way."

I know her tone and the look in her eye. She's pushing her small tits out, trying to get my attention. Her shirt is white and wet, basically see-through, but it does nothing for me. I don't understand why she thinks I give a fuck about her or her name.

"Great." I pull my arm back and turn to go find Elijah.

My stomach bottoms out seeing bright red hair wrapped up in his embrace. Thank fuck.

"Where the hell were you?" I snap once I'm close enough.

Elijah ignores me completely, used to my anger by now.

Winnie turns her face just enough for me to see. She's waterlogged like the rest of us, but maybe even more so. Her face is clean and free from makeup, unlike her friends. She looks fine and unharmed.

"Shh!"

Shh? Did she just shush me?

I'm about to reem her when Elijah cuts me off. "You getting some young pussy?"

I look around, confused about who he is talking to, but he's looking at me. "Huh?"

"That girl?"

The three of us look over my shoulder to where he nods. That brunette, whatever she said her name was, stands in the same spot, wiggling her fingers in our direction.

"No. I don't even know who the fuck she is."

"Seems like she knows who you are." His voice is light like a tease.

She can know who I am all she wants. I'm not interested in fucking a sophomore—or anyone, for that matter. The last thing I need is a distraction right before I graduate. I've always said once I hit college, I'll think about dating, but until then, I'm not interested in being tied down. I have a goal, and a relationship isn't going to help me get there.

Winnie has pulled away from Elijah and is staring—or glaring is more like it—at the ground in front of her. Using her hair like a shield to conceal her expression. But I know her better than that, and the only time Winnie would hide her face is when she's embarrassed of her reaction. I'm just not sure what she could be embarrassed of in this situation.

The school bell rings, and we are free to go.

"I gotta grab my shit. Meet you at the truck." Elijah runs for the school doors. Apparently, there wasn't a real fire if they are letting people go back inside. It's odd there was a drill at the end of the day and that the sprinklers went off if there wasn't, though.

Winnie hasn't said a word since we got in the truck, and that's not like her. Did my snapping really bother her that much? I try not to get angry with her often, and it's usually not hard because she seems to be the only person in my life who doesn't piss me off.

"I'm sorry I yelled at you. You just had me worried, Win."

A heavy silence stretches between us—something I don't experience often with her.

"You want to tell me where you were?"

"Are you going to date Zoey?"

Huh? Who the fuck—oh, the brunette. "Uh, no? I'm not."

Her ginger hair tumbles behind her when she lifts her head to look at me. Narrowing her eyes, she watches me for an entire minute before sighing.

"She talks about you, you know?"

Why does she talk about me? "I don't even know who she is. I was only talking to her because I thought you guys were friends."

She scoffs at that idea. Apparently, I was way off about the whole friends thing. "The only friends I have are you and Eli, Reese."

I don't know how. Winnie is one of the best people I know; she should have people knocking on her door wanting to be her friend. Honestly, I thought Elijah and I were going to have to beat the shit out of guys wanting to date her, but that hasn't happened yet.

"We're not friends. If you saw us talking it's only because I know you."

Me? What the fuck is this girl's obsession with me? I hope she doesn't become some weird stalker. I can't express how uninterested I am in all that. She couldn't be barking up a worse tree.

"Well, if she bothers you again, tell her I'm not interested."

"Yeah, okay."

I don't know what her attitude is about, but okay. Christopher tried warning us that Winnie would change like a flip had been switched one day. Is this that day?

Mrs. Lewis passed Winnie a tampon while we were out once, so I thought she started her period a few years ago, if that's what he meant. But what do I know?

"But since you asked." Whatever caused her mood to sour slips, and she grins like she has a secret to tell. Winnie's secrets are always unpredictable. "I lit a match and stood on the toilet to set the alarms off."

Like I said, unpredictable.

"Winnie," I gasp. "Why the hell would you do that?"

"Because I heard you and Elijah talking about how you are starting frog dissections tomorrow and that they were delivered today. You know they come in alive? Yeah, me either, and that's so sick. Anyway, when I saw that, I waited until I knew Mr. Stevens had a free hour, set the fire alarm off, and released all the frogs."

There aren't many things Winnie could do that would surprise me, but this definitely did.

"No you didn't."

She bites her lip and nods, a look of pride blossoming on her face. "Yep, I did."

"I cannot believe you did that. You know you can get in trouble for faking a fire?"

"Yeah, that's why I did it in the bathroom where there are no cameras, duuuh."

Smart, but still dumb.

"They will probably just get more frogs."

"Then I'll release those ones too."

I can't stop a laugh from tumbling out of me. Wrapping my arm around her neck, I pull her into my side and ruffle her hair until she pushes away, pretending to be mad. "You are such a softy."

"I *prefer* Frog Savior."

"Yeah, I'm not calling you that."

"Suit yourself."

Someone shouts out, and we follow the noise to find Elijah slapping the back of some random kid and shouting something about a long weekend.

"Oh." Winnie lifts her brown eyes to me. "Please don't tell Elijah what I did. I don't need a brotherly lecture about safety and whatever else."

I don't have many secrets from my best friend, but the ones I do have all involve his little sister.

Elijah hops into the truck and cranks the radio. Drumming on the dash to "1985" by Bowling for Soup. "I heard them talking," he shouts over the music instead of turning it down. "The sprinklers caused a mess, so there's no school the rest of the week to give the janitors time to clean up."

Winnie freezes. It's obvious she didn't consider the cleanup, because she never would have wanted to cause a mess for anyone else. She was only thinking about the frogs.

"That right?" I throw my arm behind Winnie's head to back up, and Winnie shoots me a look that's a mixture of a scowl and regret.

"Yeah. And apparently, there is some kind of frog infestation in front of the school."

A heavy chuckle bursts from me before Winnie elbows me.

"If only there was a frog savior to make sure they got somewhere safe."

3

Reese

Winnie Lewis hasn't changed a bit. Her ginger hair is longer, nearly to her ass now, but everything else is the same as I remember. I can't see much of her face, but her side profile is just as beautiful as the rest of her. I can't help but smile as she debates between the flavors of Pop-Tarts. Her button nose scrunches as she examines one box but smooths at the next. She places that one carefully in the green basket hanging off her arm, and I smirk. She looks so fucking cute shopping. It's easy to think of us shopping together and what that would look like. She would ask for something, and I know the moment she flicked those big brown eyes on me, my answer wouldn't be anything but yes.

Pinecove is a good-sized college town, but I knew Winnie and I would find our way back together once she moved here. I just didn't expect it to be today. Glancing down, I take in my appearance, and a cocky smirk tugs

21

at my lips. Winnie might look close to the same as the girl I grew up knowing—with tits now—but I don't. I've grown another inch or more, got a good haircut, and all the hours I've spent working off my frustration in the gym have paid off. Women yearn for my attention constantly, which is part of being on the hockey team. Winnie's opinion is the only one I care about, though, and I'm not sure how easily she will be persuaded in my favor after everything.

"There you are." Zoey walks up, complaining like always.

Winnie pays us no attention, and after dropping another box in her basket, she turns the opposite way.

"Reese?"

Winnie freezes, and my heart fucking soars. I still have some kind of hold on her if she's stopping after hearing my name. It might not be a big one, and I'm sure once she turns and sees who is next to me, it will probably be even less, but it's there.

Slower than ever, Winnie glances over her shoulder. Everything stops when our gaze collides. All the nights I spent looking into her big brown eyes flash through my head like a train speeding past, here one second, gone the next. The last time I looked into them comes roaring up, and guilt hits me like a brick.

Her focus flicks to Zoey, and that guilt turns to complete dread.

"Winnie Lewis?"

"The one and only," Winnie jokes as she reluctantly saunters our way. She's too nice; normal people would walk away as quickly as possible with our history, but not Winnie.

"Hey, Zoey." She passes a quick look my way, but it doesn't linger. "Reese."

"Winnie." My voice is rough, and I will her to look at me again, but she doesn't.

The navy tank top and light jean shorts do nothing to hide the goosebumps covering her freckled skin. At least she still has some kind of reaction to me. Not that it holds a candle to mine. Fuck, she's more beautiful than I remember. From far away, she looks as she always did, but up close, she's older, matured. Her tank top frames palm-sized tits, and her waist is small but juts into slightly rounded hips. Her eyes are as big as ever. Brown and so warm. Like a cup of freshly brewed coffee. Even her forced smile is beautiful. Flashing bright-white teeth. It's good to see that one crooked tooth on her bottom row. I'm glad her retainer did nothing to fix that.

There aren't many—if anyone else in the fucking world—who cause my heart to beat faster with just a look. Winnie Lewis has always been my weakness.

As a college athlete, I get a lot of—usually unwanted—attention. But I've learned to work with it. Some guys on the team fuck any chick who gives them attention, but I prefer an innocent flirt with no expectations.

Except when it comes to Winnie Lewis. I'd gladly tumble with her—*again*. That night two years ago wasn't what it should have been. I was nervous. I'm not much more experienced now, but confidence goes a long way. I've grown up just like she has.

Treating Winnie how I would any other girl definitely won't get me what I want, and what I want is *her*.

Zoey slips her arm into mine, but I haven't a fucking clue why. I've told her numerous times not to fucking touch me. Still, I don't tell her to get off like I normally might because seeing Winnie's soft eyes fill with rage is like a drug. She's the addict, and I'm the thing she wishes she could quit.

She should hate me. And maybe she does, but I don't think so. Winnie isn't capable of hate—not *real* hate, anyway. She might be scrunching her nose in disgust, and it might be pointed at me, but I've seen her make the same look at bacon. So it really is irrelevant because I know bacon is fucking amazing.

Standing in front of Winnie right now feels like the first time I ever stood in front of her. Like we are five and eight all over again.

Her brother was playing street hockey. Curiosity got the best of me, and I wandered outside to see if I could play too. The neighbors before them were an old couple, and the only time I saw them outside was to get the mail. This was the first time there was someone on my street I might be able to play with.

Elijah gladly accepted my offer, and a little bit later, out wandered a little girl in yellow rain boots and pigtails, holding a camera in her hands.

It's wild to think about how our relationship has changed since then. Constantly twisting, turning, and growing. But it blew up in our faces two years ago.

I hated myself for a while after that night. She was young, and I shouldn't have accepted her advances, but I've never been able to say no to Winnie. Especially when the last thing I wanted to do that night was say no. Though we danced around the tension for a while, a boy only has so much willpower. Besides, the thought of someone else taking Winnie's virginity while I was at college was like a hot knife to the chest.

Same with thinking about who might have come after that night when I left without a goodbye.

"Nice to see you." Her voice pulls me from my head, and when it does, she's no longer in front of me. Instead, she's behind me, heading for the front of the store and yelling over her shoulder. Since she's not looking, I flick Zoey's arm from mine and scowl down at her.

"Don't fucking start with me, Zoey. You know why you're here, and it's not that."

I know my words hurt her. I wish I could say I care, but I don't. Zoey lost any chance for "us" to be a thing years ago, but somehow, she still has it in her head that I'll change my mind. I wasn't into her the first time she came onto me, and I'm not into her now.

The only reason I'm still around her is because her dad is my assistant coach, and it's kind of important I keep the peace with him if I want to continue playing and want any shot at going pro. That doesn't mean pretending to like her when her father isn't around, though.

"It could be," she tries, for what must be the five-hundredth time in the last year since she started college at Emerson U. No matter how many times I tell her no.

"You know how pathetic it makes you going after a guy who would never give you the time of day?"

"About as pathetic as you thinking Winnie Lewis would ever give you a second chance after what you did."

Bitch.

"That's more likely to happen than us ever being anything."

Her arm snaps out as soon as I take a step toward the front of the store, halting me.

"You can't seriously be wasting your time."

"Winnie has never once been a waste of time. Now stop fucking touching me before I have to tell your dad you've been fraternizing with a player. Again." He has a very strict rule on no players dating his daughter—not that anyone would try. Most of us can see through her bullshit. But it doesn't stop her from throwing herself at us—me specifically—for whatever fucking reason.

After glancing around, I spot Winnie at the self-checkout, still scanning her items. A relieved breath tumbles from my mouth, and I pause to take her in for a moment. I can't believe she's really here.

I adjust my hat, then shove my hands into my jeans and approach her. "Hey."

She jumps but quickly recovers, scowling at the box of stuffing in her hand. There have been many times Winnie would eat nothing but a box of stuffing for dinner. I always found it weird, and the same is still true today.

"You still like stuffing that much?"

Her auburn eyebrows twitch as a look of discomfort twists her face. Probably because I remember that detail, or maybe because I'm bringing it up.

"I do." She looks behind her like she's waiting for something. "Why are you here?"

"I go to school here, Win." I smirk, and she scowls.

I'm a confident guy. Good looking enough. Killer in hockey. But Winnie has always been able to see through me. To strip me down—metaphorically, of course. But it's been years, and I'm not used to her heavy stare anymore. The kind that makes me feel like she can see my heart and the contents it holds. Like all my deepest, darkest secrets are on display.

I know she's biting her tongue when her reply is clipped. "Obviously, Reese. I mean *here*. Bothering me."

"Bothering?"

She nods. "That's what I said."

Ouch.

I clutch a hand over my chest where my heart lies below. "You don't honestly mean that. You love me being around."

Her eyes narrow, and I know I fucked up.

"Win." I reach for her arm, but she pulls away. "I'm sorry. I've just missed you, and now you're here. It feels like old times, doesn't it?"

She scoffs an angry huff. "Hardly."

Her familiar sweet smell wafts through the air and straight into my nose when I step closer. The overhead music fades, and I relish being so close. I cup her hand in mine while she scans the item. "It could be."

Our bodies aren't touching besides my hand on hers, but the heat radiating from her small frame is enough to drive me mad.

She shivers, but I don't think it's from the AC blowing above. "Are you on drugs or something?"

I laugh, only because I know she's being serious, and step away. If I stay that close to her, I'm going to end up with a boner I can't hide. "No, I've just grown up, Win. I know what I want." Making sure she sees me look up and down her body, I slap on a smirk. Normally, girls would giggle or flirt back. But I should know better because she's not like that. Easy and Winnie are two terms I'd never use in the same sentence. Unless I was saying loving her is easy, because in that case, it's more than accurate.

She jams her card into the machine, completely ignoring me. Her bags rustle when she grabs them with more force than necessary and shoves past me, and I let her exit, watching the sway of her hips. Conflicted between hurt from her cold attitude toward me and turned on from the same thing, I stare in her direction for a few beats after she disappears through the automatic doors. The expectation of our reunion wasn't high, but Winnie has never walked away from me before.

Shaking my head, I rush to follow after her, but I'm stopped by an older man stepping in my path. He crosses his arms and cocks an accusing eyebrow at me.

"Are we going to have a problem?"

"What?" I say, confused.

He nods his head back. "The girl who all but ran away from you."

Oh. I chuckle and scratch the back of my neck. "Girlfriend. Gets moody when she's hungry."

Whatever tension he was holding leaves his body, and he chuckles. Probably should have asked me more questions, but the longer I'm standing here, the more time Winnie has to drive away before I even make it outside.

"I know the feeling all too well. Go get that girl some food, and remember—happy wife, happy life."

My lips curve up, and he slaps my shoulder on the way by like an old friend.

Imagining Winnie as my wife is bittersweet. I never considered getting married; it's not like I grew up with a great example. But if I were going to get married, I'd want to be standing at the end of her aisle.

It takes a few minutes to find that old blue Bronco after I step outside. I knew she would still be driving it. She will most likely drive it until it quits, and even then, she will do whatever she can to make it run again.

For as long as I can remember, I've dealt with anxiety, but that has never trickled into Winnie. She was the only thing that ever eased it. But now she's back in my life, and what are we? I've never had to question what we were before because we just... *were*. She was my right hand. My shadow. My best friend. When I found out she would be attending EU, it was like a weight had been lifted, but now that she's here—and hates me—that weight is back tenfold.

I jog toward her, not wanting her to pull away before we can talk.

There's a window between us, but it's still comforting being this close. There were a few times over the last two years that I wondered if I made Winnie up in my head; obviously, that isn't the case.

Looking at her isn't enough, though. My hands itch to touch her—hold her. I'll tell her anything she needs to hear to make it right between us again because there is no way I can be in the same town as Winnie Lewis and not be with her. We touched a lot when we were younger, but it was always innocent. Until it wasn't. After that, I knew those innocent touches would never be enough again.

I was *obsessed*.

Then I left.

Shaking those thoughts from my head, I focus on what's in front of me. I've only thought about the past for years, but now it's crucial I focus on here and now. Prove to Winnie I'm not the piece of shit she probably thinks I am.

Winnie flips through the same CD case she's had since she turned sixteen. It's always been important to her to have the perfect songs playing while she drives, even giving herself enough time to pick music for the shortest trips. It's her little quirks like that I've missed the most.

I'm not at all surprised when she slips a disc into the player and "Gives You Hell" by The All-American Rejects blasts from her speakers, rattling the entire vehicle.

She grins, happy with herself, and I can't help but match it with my own at how proud she is of her selection.

Ready to go, she glances around and then screams when she notices me, but it's muted behind her window and the music. The song cuts off as she jams her finger into the pause button and cranks her window down.

"What the hell are you doing just watching me, you freak?"

A couple walks by at the same time, and they tug their son past quicker than before. I have to bite back my laugh because Winnie is obviously pissed, and laughing at her isn't going to help anyone.

"You didn't notice me."

"Yeah, most people knock on the window and don't just stand there like a weirdo."

"Am I a freak or a weirdo? You called me both."

Her auburn eyebrows bunch as she frowns. "Both, probably."

"Hmm." I tap my chin, putting on a show as if I'm really thinking about it. "I don't know if either fit. Why don't you pick a new word?"

Her eyes blaze with anger. And I love it. They say hate and love are neighbors. Right now she is the hate, and

I am the love, but I bet with a little time, I can convince her to love me again. She did once. Surely, she could again.

"How about liar?"

My smirk falls, and any happiness I was feeling follows right behind. I could have predicted this side of things, but knowing that's how she feels about me fucking blows.

She throws the car in reverse, looking behind her as she backs out, and I let her drive away because the truth is, I don't know what to say. I know why she feels that way, and she has every right to, but I really wish she didn't. I'm not so delusional that I thought a smirk was going to make her forget everything. And I'm sure seeing Zoey with me today didn't help anything.

I see Elijah around periodically and have to embrace his glares, but we don't run in the same circle anymore. He quit hockey, quit basically everything, and became a hermit. The only time I see him around people is at parties, and he's not just there for a good time. I see the little bags of whatever he passes around.

The Elijah I knew before would never be doing this shit. He wouldn't be in the corner; he would have been in the center of the room, partying it up with the rest. I was always the recluse, but losing his dad really fucked him up, and he never recovered. Not like he had a best friend to help him through it.

Now Winnie is back on my turf, going to the same stores, maybe even parties, and a friendly hello in passing won't ever be enough for me. I can't ignore her like I can mostly ignore her brother.

I need her. *All* of her.

My mind goes crazy thinking of ideas. Suddenly, the best plan—that I can come up with right now, anyway—pops into my head, and I pull my phone out.

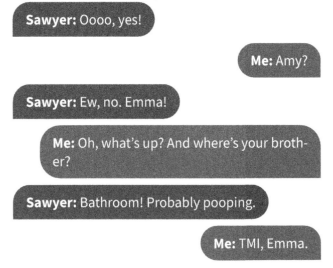

Me: Throw a party tonight.

Message bubbles pop up almost immediately, to my surprise. Sawyer is never a fast replier. If there was an emergency, he is the last person I'd want to call.

Sawyer: Oooo, yes!

Me: Amy?

Sawyer: Ew, no. Emma!

Me: Oh, what's up? And where's your brother?

Sawyer: Bathroom! Probably pooping.

Me: TMI, Emma.

There's a long pause between texts, and my impatience grows more with each passing moment.

> **Sawyer:** Sorry. My sister was using my phone.

> **Sawyer:** But why can't you throw the party?

> **Me:** Can't explain. But I actually need a favor from Emma. Can she text someone for me and invite her to the party?

> **Sawyer:** ...her?

Sawyer is my best friend on the team, but I've never mentioned Winnie or her brother. He caught Elijah glaring at me once and asked about it. I told him he was a druggy and probably cracked out. It fucking sucks lying about a guy I considered a brother at one point, but keeping Sawyer out of my Winnie business is easier than having to admit what went wrong.

> **Me:** Get her to the party and I'll explain.

> **Sawyer:** Send her number.

> **Me:** Idk if it's the same, but I'll send what I do have. Her name is Winnie Lewis. She's a freshman. If the number doesn't work, tell Emma to look her up.

I send the number and wait impatiently for a reply. It takes way longer than I'd like, and I probably look like an insane person pacing the parking lot. Someone even had to honk at me when I didn't notice them trying to back up. This is the chaos she brings to my life. I fucking love it.

Finally, his name pops up, and he's calling me.

"Cute girl."

"Easy," I growl.

His laugh is deep in my ear. "What's the deal with her?"

"Did Emma invite her?"

"Yep," Emma squeals in the background. "She actually picked up when I called. Most people don't pick up random numbers." That is a bit concerning, but not surprising.

"Well, is she coming?"

"Yep! I said something about freshman orientation, and she bought it."

Either Winnie is more naive than I ever thought, or she really wants to go to a party. Neither sit well.

"Okay, sweet. Thanks, Emma."

"Don't mention it! But if you want to pay me back, set me up with your hot roommate."

Rustling sounds on the other end, followed by Sawyer's muffled yells.

"Fucking hell, that girl is a pain in my ass."

"I think sisters are meant to be."

"It was easier when she didn't talk."

"I'm sure. She's into Schmidt, though?"

He groans loudly, and I can picture him dragging his hand down his face, which he does a lot. "She saw him getting the mail this morning, and you know he never—"

"Wears a shirt, I know." Seeing Schmidt with a shirt on is weirder than seeing him without. We are going on three years of being roommates, and in those years, I've probably seen him in a shirt in our place less than five times because it's gone as soon as he steps through the door.

"I heard her telling her friend his abs are *lickable*. So, naturally, I have to kill him."

Having a little sister sounds stressful as fuck. Winnie was the closest thing I ever had, but obviously, the sister feeling didn't stick for long, and I never had to deal with her liking boys who weren't me.

"Fine, but find me a new roommate to occupy his room. Preferably one who can cook."

"Deal. Pick up some snacks for tonight. I'll get the kegs."

"Send Schmidt to get the liquor since he gets a family discount."

"Shit, that's right. Okay, see you soon."

I shove my phone away and head for the store. Winnie might be surprised when she walks into the party and I'm there, but that's fine. She always did like surprises.

4

Winnie

"Where is the party?" Elijah doesn't bother looking away from his game, and he knows how much that pisses me off.

"I don't know. One of the dormitories on campus. It's a freshman thing, Elijah. Not a rager."

"You underestimate freshmen and alcohol." Finally, his brown eyes snap my way. "But fine. You got your pepper spray?"

"Yes." That was my moving-in gift from him—pepper spray. Ever since Dad died, he's taken over his role of head of the family, but unfortunately, he acts more like my dad than my brother anymore.

"Okay. Call if you need a ride."

I pull my phone out and hover over my mom's name. After our dad's accident, she got a little... protective. She never said I couldn't do things, but I could see her anxiety when I asked to go anywhere. It wasn't often, since I never really made any friends, but seeing how distraught my mom would get was enough to keep me home even if I was the most popular person at school.

I don't know if telling her about the party would be a good thing or not. I debate for a little while longer, then decide against it. I don't need her worrying about me all night long. Me not being at home is already hard enough. She's called me seven times since I got into town three days ago. That doesn't count the five times I've called her, either.

"You didn't have to come, Elijah. I'm a big girl, you know?"

He hasn't lost his scowl since I told him the address of the party and he said he was coming. He's always scowling, but it's worse now for whatever reason.

I tried telling him it was a freshman thing, and since he's a junior, he definitely shouldn't come. But he insisted, and once Elijah sets his mind to something, there's no changing it. Now I'm going to be the weird girl who brings her big brother to parties. *Great.*

I climb out of the Bronco and stare up at the building in front of me, my excitement growing now that I'm here. I had always hoped I would make friends in college, like the kind who would stand in my wedding. I'm not off to a great start after seeing Reese and Zoey this morning, but surely there are some decent people somewhere on campus. Like, maybe the girl that invited me in the first place. Although, I'm still not sure how she got my number.

This red-brick building is three times the size of the other dormitories around. I never got to tour the dorms since I always planned on living with Elijah until he graduated, saving myself from paying the room and board fee.

"These are the freshman dorms?" Looking around, maybe I should have toured. The decadent oak flooring and original crown molding in the entryway are impressive.

Elijah presses the elevator button. "No, these are the athletic dorms."

"Why would a freshman mixer be here?"

Elijah slams a finger into the *four* button, even though I didn't tell him which floor. He's right, though.

"I have a feeling I know why."

He doesn't say anything more, and I don't ask, because he's radiating anger, and I'm not interested in receiving the blunt end of it.

The elevators open, and immediately, loud music fills the hallway. I don't know where it's coming from exactly, and suddenly I can't remember the dorm number, but apparently Elijah knows. I should be more concerned about how, but I'm too busy taking everything in around me. Several doors are open, allowing us to see inside the rooms. People congregate in the hallway, red solo cups in their hands and sloppy smiles on their faces. It's not even nine, but I guess this is a party. There are going to be drunk people.

Despite the hallway being crowded, everyone seems to part for Elijah and me. I know my brother is intimidating, but it's hard for me to see him as the broody guy in front of me now and not the thirteen-year-old who used to play Guitar Hero and put on an entire performance during his turn.

Sometimes I really miss his smile. I get it; losing our dad is hopefully the hardest thing I'll ever have to go through, but it didn't change me the way it did Elijah. I try not to take life for granted and live it how I know Dad would want me to. Elijah, on the other hand, completely shut down. It was like I lost my brother the same day I lost my dad. He's here, but it's not the same.

He turns into one of the doors, and I rush in after. But he's bigger, tougher, and apparently more intimidating than me because the crowd is even thicker in here, and they don't part for me like they do him. I end up squished between several people. Sweat, beer, and overpowering cologne assault my nose, and I pray the smells don't sink into my clothes.

One of the guys leans back, and in order to get out of his way, I push into the girl next to me.

"I'm sorry," I shout, hoping she can hear me over the noise. Whoever picked this music needs to reevaluate their taste.

The bouncy blonde turns, and her smile grows even bigger. "You must be Winnie! I'm Emma." She smiles and points to the nervous-looking girl next to her. "This is Laney."

What are the odds the first girl I bump into is the girl who invited me?

"Oh! Hey. This is quite the freshman orientation." I peer at her skeptically, letting her know I know she's full of shit. I'm not mad, though, and with Elijah not being up my ass right now, I'm hoping I can relax and have fun.

"Sorry about that." The smell of alcohol is heavy on her breath as she leans toward me. "He didn't give me great instructions, and I panicked on the spot. I'm not a great liar!"

Wait, did she say *he*? Who is he, and why did she need to lie for him?

I don't get any of my questions asked or answered before a huge guy steps behind her. I wonder for a quick second if it's her boyfriend, but they look way too similar to be anything but siblings. I'm going to believe they aren't both.

"Winnie?" he questions, his deep voice booming over the music.

"Uh, yeah. You know my name?"

His shoulders relax, and his harsh face softens into a half smirk. "I think everyone here knows your name."

"Why's that?"

He leans closer, totally invading my space, but instead of smelling like alcohol, he smells pleasantly like mint. Plus, he's ridiculously hot. "Reese has made sure everyone knows the little redhead, Winnie Lewis, is off-limits."

Shock hits me like a truck, nearly making my eyes pop out of my head. "What?" I screech.

He laughs and pulls back, shrugging. "Don't shoot the messenger."

I don't get another word in before someone yells, "Fight."

Emma dashes away, pulling her friend along with her, eager to see the so-called fight. And her brother—whose name I still don't know—scowls and follows after her, even though at his size, he can probably see clear over the crowd. I push my way through people, following after them until I'm in the front.

Then my stomach drops.

"Stay the fuck away from my sister."

Elijah shoves Reese, and he stumbles more than he should. Elijah and Reese are about the same size, but Reese is staggering and his moves are sloppy, meaning he's probably drunk. Why are they fighting in the first place? And why is Elijah bringing me into it?

Reese stumbles forward, right in Elijah's face, and gives him that same smirk that was directed at me earlier. "You're a little late for that warning." His laugh is mocking, and my stomach twists knowing whatever comes out next is going to make me hate him if I don't already. "Like *two years* too late."

I gasp and throw a hand over my mouth, but it's too late. Elijah shoots a look in my direction, having heard me since the music has cut out, people probably wanting to hear what the two idiots in the middle of the room have to say.

"Eli, let me ex—"

He whirls around and throws his fist, but Reese is looking at me and fails to block the punch from connecting with his jaw. With a loud thud, he drops to the floor like a bag of bricks. A few more guys—bigger guys—move in on Elijah, but he doesn't back down. I'm guessing the guys are teammates of Reese's; they look like hockey players, not to be too stereotypical. That big guy from earlier stays back to help Reese up but isn't shy about his hatred for my brother, aiming a glare in his direction.

I run over, stopping next to my brother while praying these guys are above hitting girls. Normally when Elijah fights, I stay out of it, and even though I know he's tough, I'm guessing Reese has more friends than he does. And as much as my brother is a pain, I don't feel like having to visit him in the hospital—or jail. The big guy gives up on trying to get Reese up and moves in between the standoff, holding up each hand in a different direction.

"He deserved that." *Is he talking about Reese?* "Imagine if someone talked about your sister like that."

That seems to level two of the guys, their heated eyes finding me, then dragging over to Eli. Their jaws tense, but they walk away.

The third guy isn't as easy to convince, but eventually, the big guy is able to talk him down too, and then he turns to face us.

"Elijah. Always a pleasure."

"Fuck off, Sawyer."

Elijah shoves by me, only stopping for a beat to show his disappointment. It's heavy, and I hate the feeling curdling deep in my stomach.

Embarrassment, hurt, and anger all take their turns ripping through me like a dull knife. I don't want to go after him, because I don't know what I would say. I can't deny it; Elijah knows when I'm lying, and I'm not ready to admit everything to him just yet. I don't know if I thought I could keep that night between me and Reese from him forever, but I definitely am not ready to deal with it now. Maybe I thought he would find out at one point, but Reese and I would be happy and in a relationship, and he would be forced to get over it. We couldn't be further from that place right now.

I turn my attention to the pathetic man groaning on the floor, having not yet found his balance to stand. Wiping away whatever angry tears fell, I step in front of him. The shirtless guy trying and failing to help him up lifts his head just enough to look at me through his round-framed glasses. He uses his middle finger to push them up, and I don't know if that was meant for me or if he always does that, but it's not like I'm the bad guy here, so he can kick rocks for all I care.

"Get up, Reese."

His head whips up, and he has the audacity to smile at me like I hang the stars. If I didn't think he was drunk before, I know for sure now. His jaw is swollen, but his eyes are dilated, and I'm not sure if he's really looking *at* me or *through* me.

"You came."

"Tricking me into attending your party? Stating I'm *off-limits*?"

He takes his time climbing to his feet, stumbling and swaying the whole time. The guy holding him doesn't let go, and it's a good thing because if he did, I'm convinced Reese would fall on his face.

"You are, *baby*."

My shoulders tense hearing *baby* from his lips. The same term of endearment he grunted in my ear *that* night. Memories threaten to flash through my head, but I don't let them. "Don't call me that."

It's not lost on me that we have an audience, and when he reaches for me, I take a step back. He whimpers like a puppy that was just denied a bone, and my anger surges. Growing up, I always saw Reese as untouchable. Even during those late nights on my roof when everything would catch up to him and he would cry, cursing his parents, his life, and anything and everything he could, he always felt invincible. A hard exterior protecting the charming insides not many got to see. Right now, I wonder where that man went. Because this pathetic, blubbering man saying things that aren't even coherent isn't the Reese I know. In fact, he's reminding me a lot of his dad.

It wasn't often, but on a few occasions, I would catch Mr. Larson on his knees, begging Reese's mom for forgiveness. And that scares me because right now, his son looks exactly like him.

Not wanting to look at Reese any longer, I glance around the room at the various forms of shock written across so many faces, and it hits me. None of these people know *my* Reese. They know whatever version of him he has been fronting since he moved here—a version I have no interest in getting familiar with.

He falls onto his knees in front of me and wraps his long arms around my body, pressing his head against my pelvis. If I wasn't so unbelievably turned off right now, I might've had flutters from having him so close after so long, but they couldn't flap even if I wanted them to.

"I'm sorry, baby. I'm so sorry."

He clings to me, and his weight tugs on my loose-legged pants. The material shifts before slipping over my ass and onto my thighs. I blow out a rushed breath, but I'm not able to get him off me no matter how much I struggle. Gripping the waist with everything I have, I urge them to not slip anymore. But he weighs close to double what I do, and when he slumps to the ground, my pants rip from my grip and go down with him.

I'm in shock, standing in front of a room full of people with both my pants and a drunk slob around my ankles. The same guy who was holding him rushes forward, as well as the big guy I think Elijah called Sawyer. It takes both of them to rip him off me so I'm able to pull my pants back up.

The embarrassment from before is nothing compared to how I'm feeling now that everyone saw my ass and thong. I guess I should be glad I wore underwear at all, but no, that's not the point. The point is Reese

Larson is an ass. Whatever tie I had to him before is completely gone.

I feel nothing—well, maybe disappointment, sadness, and hurt—when I look at him now. But no conflicted feelings other than those.

"I'm sorry, Winnie. He doesn't usually—" Sawyer says while the shirtless guy stares.

"Don't apologize for him."

Reese reaches for me again, but the guys hold him back, and he doesn't like that at all.

"She wants me to touch her, don't you, *Pooh Bear*?"

My eyes fly open hearing my childhood nickname from his mouth. He knows my dad was always the one to call me Pooh Bear, and ever since he passed, I've only heard it a few times from my mom. It was a special name between me and my dad, and he just spit it out like it was nothing.

"Just like old times," he adds, slurring the words.

I wish I could smack that smirk off his face. My fist won't do much damage, but I know where to hit a guy with as little or as much force as I want and drop them at any given moment. I pull my leg back and thrust it forward, right between his legs. The guys let go when he cries out, and he falls onto his face with his hands holding his aching dick.

"I wouldn't want you to touch me again if you were the last man on earth."

"You love me," he shouts after me, his voice strangled.

I pause in front of the crowd and glance back, seeing him still rolling around and holding his dick. "Whatever I felt for you died the moment you threw *that* night in my brother's face. All I see in you now is a—" I bite my tongue only for a second because I know it's going to crush him. But maybe Reese needs a wake-up call, and this will be it. "Younger version of Robert."

Whatever alcohol he had in his system seems to disperse for a single moment of sobriety. So many bad emotions push to the surface, but I don't stick around to see or hear anything else.

I don't let the tears fall until I'm out of that room. People in the hall stare, but I don't care. I back up against the wall, unable to support my weight any longer, and drop my head to my hands.

Someone touches my shoulder, and I jolt and pray it's not Reese.

"Sorry, sorry." Emma frowns. "I—we..." She looks behind her to Laney, Sawyer, and that shirtless guy.

"I had no idea Reese had it in him to act like that," the shirtless guy mutters. "I'm Schmidt, by the way."

"Schmidt?" A weak smile tugs on my lips. "That's an odd name."

He pushes his glasses up and chuckles. "It's my last name."

"Don't bother asking his first," Sawyer gruffs. "No one knows it."

How do none of them know his first name? Whatever, not my business.

"Winnie." I slip my hand into his, surprised at how soft it is.

"You can hang out still," Emma offers. "Reese went to bed, so you won't have to see him."

"Thanks, but knowing that entire room just saw my ass makes me never want to step foot in there again."

"Why? You have a great ass."

Even though the last thing I feel like doing right now is laughing, it tumbles out of me anyway. Sawyer rests a hand on his sister's shoulder and gives her a disapproving look.

"Er, thanks, but I just want to go home." That's not really true, though. I don't want to deal with Elijah either.

"Yeah." Sawyer scratches at the back of his neck. "You need a ride or anything?"

"Thanks, but I'm go—"

"Well, well, well. I didn't think I would see little Winnie Lewis at a college party."

This night just keeps getting worse. To my pleasure, no one else seems excited to hear Zoey's voice either.

"Zoey, always a pleasure." I take a step around her, but she grabs my arm, just like I saw her do to Reese outside the school all those years ago. I hated it then, and I hate it even more now.

She puffs her bright-pink bottom lip out into a fake pout. "I just got here! Let's catch up. It's been far too long."

I'd rather eat dirt. "No, thanks." I pull my hand away and step around her before she can grab me again. "Sorry if your boyfriend can't get it up anymore, though. That's my bad."

I don't look back, even though I really want to, and I don't let out the breath I was holding until I'm in the safety of the elevator. I'm not a confrontational person, but Zoey has always brought out the worst in me.

What a great fucking start to freshman year.

I drop my head back, enjoying the silence before deciding I need to text Elijah. I can't leave him here.

> **Me:** I'm leaving. Where are you?

> **Eli:** Just go home.

> **Me:** Don't you need a ride?

> **Eli:** I'm not there anymore.

Me: So you left me at a party all by myself? What the hell, Eli?

Eli: Figured you were in the hands you wanted to be in.

Me: You don't know anything.

Eli: Yeah, no shit, sis.

I groan and drop my head back, wishing the hard wall would knock some sense into me. Getting involved with Reese is not what I need. Not that I was aware I would be getting involved with him tonight. I knew he went to college here, but I'm not here for him. I'm here because they have a great photography program, and it's where my brother is.

The door dings, and I wipe my face and suck in a deep breath. When I walk out of here, everything between Reese and me is done. He's a junior, I'm a freshman. I don't know what he's going for, but whatever it is will probably be the complete opposite of my classes. The campus is big enough that I bet I won't even see him around.

Everything is going to be fine. I'm going to kick ass in my classes, meet some real friends, and it'll all be good.

How many times do I need to say that for me to actually believe it?

5

Reese

Who the fuck is playing drums in my head? Everything hurts, and I think my dick is broken. *What the fuck happened last night*? The last thing I remember is drinking and staring at the door, waiting for Winnie to arrive.

I shoot up and instantly regret it when my body cries out against the sudden movement. My head spins and my stomach swirls so much that I'm wondering if I need to head to the bathroom or if I could even make it there before it all spews out of me.

"Well, good morning, sleeping beauty."

I jolt at the voice next to me. Not realizing how close to the edge I am, I fall off the mattress and groan when my back hits the floor. Schmidt pops his head over the edge.

"Rough night?"

"What the fuck happened?"

"You were a dick." Sawyer sits up from the floor at the foot of my bed.

Emma pops up next to him. "A huge one."

"Why the fuck is there a sleepover in my room right now?" I lie back down and rub my aching temples. "And why is my jaw sore?"

"Not just sore, bruised. Same as your dick and probably your dignity. At least it should be," Schmidt says as he steps over me. I don't open my eyes, but a second later, his piss stream can be heard from my bathroom.

"Shut the fucking door, there are girls around," Sawyer demands far too loudly, and I have to shush him.

"Girls?" Is one of them Winnie? But if so, why would she not be in bed with me?

"Yeah," an unfamiliar voice squeaks. I peek one eye open to look at who the voice came from. A petite girl with warm-blonde hair, big blue eyes, and a nervous smile waves from the other side of Emma. My eyes snag on the scar across her nose, directly under her eye. "I'm Laney. Emma's friend."

"Best friend." Emma squeezes Laney's face between her thumb and fingers.

"Great. Why are you all in my room?"

"To stop you from escaping—again." Schmidt wanders back into the room, rubbing his eyes.

"*Again*?" I ask.

"Yeah," Emma giggles. "I woke up to you in the hall, shouting about how you had to go get a frog."

What?

"You insisted on going to the pet store to get a frog, but they didn't have any," Sawyer tells me. "So you got a turtle."

I follow his pointed finger across my room to the small cage and the turtle inside it. *What the fuck did I drink last night?* Jack and Coke hasn't made me black out in a long time. I rarely even drink, but the nerves of waiting for Winnie got to me.

"Well, how much was it?"

His smirk is enough to make me want to hurl. "Only seven eighty."

"You're shitting me."

"Nope," the three of them reply simultaneously.

Unable to stand, I crawl over to the cage with the turtle inside, and the others move next to me.

"He's cute at least," Emma's friend—whose name I forgot already—offers, I assume trying to make me feel better about the entire situation. "Did you decide on a name?"

"I don't know, did I?"

My friends look at each other and swap grins. "Uh-huh. You named him Eeyore."

Fuuuck me. I named a turtle after the cringey nickname Winnie used to call me just to annoy me? *How pathetic am I?*

"Yeah, you tried calling it Winnie, but the pet store owner said something about it being a boy." Sawyer chuckles.

"Well, did she ever show up? Winnie, I mean?"

They swap looks again, but it's not with a grin this time.

"Yeah, she showed up." Sawyer flattens his lips, meaning whatever went down isn't good. "With her brother."

Really not good.

"He punched you," Emma blurts as if it was killing her to hold it in.

That's not surprising. And not the first time I'm sure he's wanted to do that, but what pushed him over the edge?

Seeing my questioning gaze, Schmidt slaps my back. "Why don't you get cleaned up, and then we will fill you in."

Good idea. Alcohol's oozing from my pores, and it's making me more nauseous than I already am.

"The entire room saw her ass?" My voice booms over the apartment—probably clear down the hall too.

"They did," Sawyer says. "Amy is going to be pissed I saw another woman's ass. No one tell her." He eyes each of us individually with a wannabe-threatening glare.

"Yeah, because we want to hear her insufferable crying," Emma grumbles, and he shoots her a frown.

I once heard Amy crying for two straight hours, and Sawyer's apartment is across the hall from mine. Beckett—our teammate and Sawyer's roommate—ended up sitting at our place because it was so loud. I don't know what her issue was, but whatever Sawyer did, I hope he never does again because it was brutal. She must have a pussy made of gold for him to stick with her as long as he has. She's nearly as bad as Zoey, and if Amy wasn't so jealous all the time and Zoey wasn't such a skanky bitch, they might be good friends. So I'm glad Emma said something, because we were all thinking it.

"Back to last night. What else happened?"

Schmidt sighs and glances at Sawyer in a way I don't like. The first half of this story was bad enough. What the fuck else could have happened? I can't imagine Winnie handled being pantsed in front of a room full of strangers all that well. Some kid pantsed her in middle school, and she was mortified.

"She kicked you in the balls." Emma giggles.

I'm glad I was drunk for that. The soreness I'm feeling now is painful enough. I've never been kicked in the balls, so the fact Winnie was the first is both surprising and also not. She's the only girl I would ever piss off enough to lead to that point.

"Was it hard?" That should tell me how mad she was.

"You should check to make sure you can still have kids, bro." Sawyer cringes.

Damn. I heard everything they said. Mentioning that night together in such a casual way to her brother was uncool, and pantsing her was worse, but that was an accident. So there must be something more they aren't telling me.

"Then she left?"

"Yeah." Schmidt shrugs. "She said something about you acting like a young Robert, but—"

I stop listening. She compared me to my *dad*?

What the actual fuck, Winnie?

If anyone knows how much that would bother me, it would be her, and she just threw it in my face in front of everyone. Like I did about our night together... but it's not the same. My dad is... fuck, there's not a word to describe that man. He's the worst. A drunk asshole with anger issues.

A drunk asshole with—

Fuck. *Am I my dad?* Did I really spend so much time hating him only to turn out just like him? Maybe not entirely, but I know Winnie, and she doesn't say anything she doesn't mean, even when she's upset. Meaning if she saw my dad in me, she meant it.

Her saying that wouldn't make sense to anyone around, because no one at college knows my dad's name. The only thing I've ever said is he's never been in the picture and that he died because, in my mind, he did.

"Was Eli around when she said that?"

"Eli?" Sawyer's eyebrows pinch. He knows who I'm talking about, but it's probably surprising hearing me call a guy who hates me by a nickname. Old habits and all that. "But no. He left after punching you."

I fall back into the chair and groan inwardly.

I fucked up. Big time. Convincing Winnie to be mine after I walked out on her two years ago was going to be hard, but after last night... it's going to be damn near impossible.

"I feel like it should also be mentioned that she thinks you're dating Zoey."

"Oh, yeah. Good point," Emma tells her friend. I don't know how Emma and Laney got involved in all of this, but whatever, I guess. Maybe having female opinions could be useful.

"Yeah, you wanna tell us what that's all about?" Sawyer suggests.

"No. I was stupid and bumped into Winnie at the store yesterday morning, right before I asked you to throw the party. Anyway, Zoey was up to her same shit and was acting all cuddly with me, and I didn't put a stop to it."

"Bro," Schmidt groans. "I just fucking got her to leave me alone. Don't tell me she's going to be here all the time now."

"No." I sigh and drop my head to my hands. My temples are pounding, and as much as I want to blame the hangover, I have a feeling it also has to do with everything I was just told. "Fuck no. You know me better than that. But there is a history between Winnie and me—"

"Obviously," they say in unison.

"Yeah, well, I liked how jealous she looked." After all this time, I still had her. But is the same still true? There's a pit in my stomach that says it might not be.

If there is anything in this life I'm sure of, it's Winnie Lewis.

"Newsflash, dumbasses." Emma scoffs. "Making a girl jealous is never cute and only pushes us farther away. If you want to show us how much we mean to you, do something *nice*. Thoughtful, even. The whole being mean when you have a crush is so 2007."

Nice? Thoughtful? I can be those things. At least when it comes to Winnie. I'm not the most approachable guy to everyone else, but she's my girl.

"You fucked up." Sawyer slaps me on the shoulder on his way to the door. "Don't forget we have an open practice tonight. Coach says it's not mandatory, but we both know it is. Especially for captains."

Fucking shit. I did forget. I'm in no state to skate around a rink for four hours, but Sawyer is right. If I want to be a captain this year, I gotta go. Even if it kills me—and it just might.

I guess it'll be punishment for last night.

6

Reese

There's something about untouched ice that settles my nerves. This is the first practice of the preseason, and it only pumps me up for the season to come. Playing hockey has always been the one thing I've never fucked up. Everything I'm carrying falls away like forgotten memories, only to be remembered again after the four-hour practice.

It's my entire life.

Despite my head spinning and my body feeling like I've been hit by a fucking bus, I've never been more ready for practice. Everything from yesterday, last night, and this afternoon completely fades, and the only thing left right now is me, my team, and the ice.

The gliding of my skates is the only thing that allows my head to clear, and I soak it in because I know it will be an entirely different story after practice. I spent the better part of the day coming up with ideas to do for Winnie. I could have asked for help from Emma and Laney, but they don't know her like I do. No one does, and after I was able to wash down the rest of the alcohol from my system, it didn't take long to come up with something.

She should be getting my delivery in the next few hours. I'm sure she's still pissed, and the odds of her caving after a bouquet of yellow flowers and falling back in love with me aren't great. I'm expecting—or hoping for—a pissed-off text, because I can work with anger. What I can't work with is nothing.

"Larson! My office, now."

Fuck me. What now?

With my head hanging low, I skate to the edge and head for Coach Swanson's office. I've pissed him off a few times since he first scouted me and offered me a spot on his team. He said he saw a lot of potential in me, and now I consider him to be sort of a father figure, like a lot of the guys. So hopefully whatever I did to piss him off this time isn't too bad.

Stepping into the room and seeing the athletic director, Mr. Kinnon, with Coach Swanson and Coach Miller has my stomach dropping to my ass. *What the hell did I do?*

Miller gestures to the chair in front of the desk, and I wander over. My pads are like a fucking hot box right now.

Immediately, my attention snags on Coach's desk, and all the color drains from my face.

There's one thing about this school that I will always hate. The fucking EU Student News is the worst decision anyone has ever had, and right now, I wish I knew who was in fucking charge of it so I could put a stop to it. But it's a secret who runs it, and it's fucking annoying, but usually, it's other people I'm seeing humiliated on the cover. Never me.

"Go ahead, pick it up," Coach orders.

I swallow the lump and rip my glove off to grab the newspaper with Winnie's ass on the front.

My entire body cringes seeing me and her pants wrapped around her ankles. It's likely nobody would even know who it was if my name wasn't in big, bold letters right underneath the stupid photo.

It's not appropriate, but Winnie's ass looks fucking perfect. I'm pissed I wasn't sober enough to see it in person. More pissed that others did. And fucking livid it's on the front page for anyone and everyone on campus to see.

At least it doesn't say her name.

PHOTO OF EMERSON'S ELITE CENTER FOR THE TIMBERWOLVES, REESE LARSON, CAUGHT ON HIS KNEES. BUT WHO'S THE LUCKY (OR UNLUCKY) GIRL WHO WAS ABLE TO BRING HIM THERE? GOOD QUESTION. SADLY, THAT'S FOR ME TO KNOW AND YOU TO FIND OUT—OR NOT.

AS FOR REESE, WOMEN USUALLY LOVE MEN ON THEIR KNEES... BUT NOT LIKE THAT. BETTER LUCK NEXT TIME!

The paper disappears from my hands, and Coach slams it on the desk between us. I don't react, and I don't need to look up to see the disappointment; I can feel it.

"You want to tell me what the hell is happening in this photo, Larson? I'll give you one chance to tell me this isn't some weird sex thing."

I wish it was a weird sex thing. "No, sir. It's, uh, just a normal party. I had too much to drink and…" And what, Reese? Made an ass out of yourself in front of the most important person to you? I glance at the clock on the wall, knowing she's probably received the delivery.

"Who's this girl?" Miller steps forward, eyeing the photo for longer than I would like.

"Someone from my past."

He dips his chin. "Is she going to be a problem, son?"

A problem? No, Winnie Lewis has never been a problem a day in her life.

"More so, are *you* going to be a problem with this girl around?" Mr. Kinnon asks, with a sharp eyebrow angled at me.

"No, sir. Bad night, that's all. It won't happen again."

"You're damn right it won't." Coach huffs. "Fix it, Reese. Whatever you've got to do, but I don't want to see you or any of my other players on this fucking paper again, you got me? Athletes are held to a higher standard than others here. Treated better than anyone else on campus. You boys need to remember that and not take advantage of it. The basketball team might fuck around and make this school a laughingstock anytime they walk out of their dorms, but not my boys."

"Of course, sir. It won't happen again. I swore off alcohol this morning after I threw up in the shower."

His face contorts with disgust. "TMI, son. Now go warm up."

"Yes, sir." I stand and dip my head to Mr. Kinnon and Miller. Before I turn, I pause. "Oh, sir, you should be aware your daughter is telling people she's dating someone on the team. So, if you hear that, just know it's a rumor."

Maybe that will keep her in her lane from now on. It's never worked before, but one can hope.

Coach stops me just before I disappear out the door. "Spread the word that the next player to end up on this paper in a bad light will be responsible for washing the team's pads by hand the entire season."

Fucking gross. I definitely don't want to be the guy stuck doing that. "Got it, sir."

"Fix whatever you fucked up, Larson," he yells after me. "I don't want your head up your ass—or anyone else's—all season!"

Yeah, yeah. I'm working on it.

7

Winnie

"Win," Reese complains for, like, the tenth time. "We've been at this for hours. You gotta almost be done."

"I need to get the best photos, Reese. Your mom is trusting me to take your senior photos. That's a really big deal." I lower my camera and puff my bottom lip out. He hates it when I give him this look, but it always gets me my way. "And you promised I could send one in for that competition."

"Last I checked, I said maybe."

"Yeah, but we both know you're going to say yes." I flutter my eyelashes and cup my hands together under my chin, really laying it on thick.

He rolls his eyes but sighs, and I know I've got him. "Shit, Win. Why do you make it so difficult to say no to you?"

"That's the charm." I grin and wiggle my eyebrows. "Now smile, pretty boy. Let's see those missing teeth."

He's not actually missing teeth, but I still think it's funny to say.

"Not all hockey players lose teeth." He groans. "You keep saying that shit and you're going to jinx me, and it's you who will have to see it all the time, not me."

Lately, Reese has been saying things that make my stomach flutter. Like he is hinting at there being something more than friends between us. I know he's not, but my mind sure likes to put ideas in my head. I don't know when I caught feelings for Reese—when our relationship shifted in my head—but it's been a real bother reminding myself that he is seventeen, going to be a senior, and is not interested in me in that way. Like at all.

But every so often, when we are alone on my roof, or like right now when his smile is just right. I wonder if maybe someday I won't just be his best friend's little sister.

Oh. My. Freaking. Gosh! Reese is never going to believe what I just got in the mail. I hope he's as excited as I am. I jump out of Dad's truck before he pulls to a stop. "Reese!"

A few of his coworkers stop their work and glance my way, but I'm looking for one in particular. I've never bothered him at work before, but I couldn't wait any longer.

"Reese," I shout again, and some guy points across the large yard toward a group of five guys. They're all wearing the same thing, but I immediately spot Reese among them and take off running. It's a hot summer day, and it's not long before a thin sheen of sweat coats my body. I cannot imagine working outside all day in this. No wonder he's the first to pass out when he stays over.

"Win? What's wrong?" He jogs in my direction, but not as quickly as I am, so I reach him first.

"I—" I pause and bend at the waist, unable to speak. Maybe I need to start going on those morning runs with Dad and Eli after all.

He pulls his sunglasses off and leans down to see my face. Blades of freshly cut grass are stuck to various places on his exposed skin, and it makes me want to grin, but there's a lump in my throat. He's had this job for a couple years now, but by the time I see him, he's showered any remains from the day off. He looks... well, he looks hot. "What the hell is going on, Win? Are you okay? Is Eli?"

I wave him off, hoping he understands that's my way of saying nothing is wrong. After a few minutes, he's tapping his work boot at me. I suck in another breath and stand, allowing a grin to contort my face.

"Winnie Lewis, tell me—"

"I got it."

He pauses, his eyebrows furrowing before quickly jumping up his tanned forehead. Is he using sunscreen? "You got it?"

I nod vigorously. "I just got the letter. They loved my photo and—"

Reese wraps his strong, sweaty arms around my body and spins me around without needing to hear the rest. We've been waiting for this letter for what feels like weeks but has really only been days since they said they would start sending them out. I was beginning to think I didn't get it, but Reese made sure to do his best to erase any thoughts like that from my head.

"Holy shit. You're going to be famous!"

That's a little extreme. But winning a national photography competition and getting to fly out to New York and sit in on a real-life professional photo shoot is super cool, so I don't correct him.

He sets me down but keeps his arms around my waist. I wonder if he realizes, though I'm certainly not going to tell him to move them. He's so warm, and it bleeds from his hands through my shirt.

"Well, it was your face that helped me, so I guess I should thank you."

He drops his head and flashes my favorite boyish grin. "My good looks might have caught their attention, but it was your talent that convinced them. Not me, Win. That's all you."

"I can't believe I'm going to get to sit in on a real photo shoot. They didn't say who it would be with, but what if it's, like, Boris Arcadia or something—it probably won't be, but whoever it is, I get to see them in real time!"

"I'm so fucking proud of you, Winnie." He pulls me into his body once more and squeezes tightly. I bury my nose in his chest and suck in a deep breath, inhaling his intoxicating scent of freshly mowed grass and sweat. I kind of love it. Maybe it's gross, but I've been stuck between him and Eli in the car after hockey games, and nothing is worse than that.

He lets his hands fall when we release this time, but mine stay planted on the smooth planes of his chest. He's still smiling, but it's sharing the spotlight with confusion as he looks down and sees I'm still touching him.

Reese and I have always been close. We touch a lot, but usually, it's not so... intimate. I'm only touching his chest, but something feels different, and I think he feels it too.

"Thanks, Reese." My voice is hushed—full of nerves. Whatever I've been feeling for him is back and raging full force. My eyes drop to his lips like a bee seeking honey. I think I want to kiss him. Without thinking about the consequences of kissing my brother's best friend, I lean forward, jump, and smack my lips against his. They touched for less than a second, yet it was still the best moment of my entire life.

I kissed him. I actually kissed Reese Larson.

Holy crap, I can't believe I kissed Reese Larson.

I don't think he can believe it either. His mouth is parted, eyebrows furrowed, and he looks... oh. He looks kind of mad.

I drop my hands and take a step backward, putting space between us. "I, uh..." I retreat, the repercussions of what I just did weighing heavy on my feet, but I push against them so I can get the frick out of here.

His coworkers are huddled together, staring at the catastrophe that just occurred. I can't believe I just kissed him while he's at work. I can't believe I kissed him at all, but especially in front of a bunch of guys who will no doubt make fun of him for it. I'm sure they know he doesn't have a girlfriend, and I probably look like some weirdo stalker now. That's if they didn't hear our conversation, which I'm guessing they did since it's now dead silent outside, not a single lawn tool running anymore.

Embarrassed tears burn the back of my eyes. Reese takes a step toward me, but I turn and book it to my dad's truck before he can say anything that's going to make it worse between us. I hope I didn't just ruin our entire relationship. Reese and Elijah might be best friends, but I've always considered Reese my best friend too—at least the closest thing I have to one.

I slam the door behind me, but Dad makes no moves to go, and I know he must have seen everything. This couldn't be any worse.

"Can you drive, please?"

He throws the truck in drive, and I let out a small breath. The tears I was holding back streak down my cheeks as Dad's stare burns into me.

He lays a heavy hand on my leg. "Oh, Win..."

"Please don't tell Eli. He's going to be so mad at me."

Dad chuckles. "I'm not going to tell your brother about your first kiss, Pooh Bear."

The truck falls into a heavy silence. My stomach is in knots, and I can't find the humor anywhere in this situation. I drag my arm under my nose and across my stiff cheeks. "I can't believe I did that," I mumble.

"Sometimes we do things without thinking." To say the least. "I'd much prefer if you didn't do that anymore, though."

I peek over his way. He's scowling, but there's amusement in his warm eyes. At least someone thinks this is funny, because Reese definitely did not, and I don't think I could laugh right now even if I were at a comedy show.

"At least not until you're older."

"I don't think you have to worry about that, Dad. Did you see the way he looked at me after?" I groan just thinking about it. I hope this is something I can laugh about in a few years—or forget about altogether. If I had my choice, it would be the latter.

I pull my feet onto the seat and drop my head between my knees. Dad moves his hand to my back, and it's comforting, but it does little to get rid of the embarrassment burning a hole inside me.

"He probably hates me now." My voice shakes with emotion. "I think I just lost my best friend, Dad." It's beyond pathetic that I consider my brother's best friend my best friend when he probably doesn't see me as anything but Elijah's little sister, but that's the cold hard truth.

"I don't know about all that, Pooh."

I lift my head just enough to rest on my knee. "Why? You couldn't see his face. He looked mortified. Betrayed even, maybe. Whatever he was feeling definitely wasn't good, Dad."

"Why'd you kiss him?"

"What?"

He repeats the question, even though I heard him the first time. I just don't know the answer.

"I don't know. I thought..." My brows furrow as I look out the window. Houses pass slowly, and I realize Dad isn't heading home. These houses are on the opposite side of town to ours. "Where are we going?"

"I thought you could use a little time before we go home."

I scoot across the seat and buckle into the middle one, leaning my head on his shoulder and breathing in his comforting scent of pepper and those cigars he doesn't think we know he smokes behind the garage.

"I just wanted to kiss him, so I did. No real reason, I guess. I obviously completely misread the situation and am never going to kiss anyone ever again."

Dad's body rumbles with a low chuckle. "As much as I wouldn't mind that, I think you just need to give it time. You're still so young, Pooh Bear."

I don't tell him that I think I'm the only one in my grade who hasn't kissed someone, but it's true. "Well, older, younger, all I know is the next time I kiss a boy, I'm letting him initiate."

I can feel his smile when he kisses the top of my head. "Smart girl. But remember what I said, not for another ten years."

"Daaad," I groan, a hint of a smile ghosting my lips.

He grins down at me and pokes my nose. "Okay, five."

Right now, I don't care if I ever kiss anyone again, so five years doesn't sound too bad. "Deal."

"That's my girl. I love you, Winnie."

I really lucked out in the dad department. Most girls' dads, at least according to movies and stuff, aren't cool to talk to about kissing or boys in general. Maybe it's because he and Mom are so in love. I hope one day I can find a love like my parents'—a love that grows each day. A part of me hopes it's with Reese, but I'm not sure if he's ever going to look my way now, let alone marry me eventually.

A girl can dream, though.

8

Winnie

PRESENT DAY

No one is better at the silent treatment than Elijah. Probably helps I've seen him go weeks without uttering a single word. I, on the other hand, struggle to go minutes. At least Mason isn't ignoring me, but he's usually at his girlfriend's, and when they are here, they are locked away in his room doing God knows what.

I sigh for probably the thirtieth time in the last twenty minutes. Mason glares at me, then at my brother, and after the next time, he drops his spoon in his bowl with a clang.

"Dude. Fucking answer her."

"What, Winnie?" Elijah snaps.

I smile at Mason, but he doesn't return it. "I could really use my big brother's help with hanging my photo wall." Cupping my hands, I bring them under my chin and flutter my eyelashes, but Elijah rolls his eyes, not paying any attention.

He pushes from the table. "Let's go. This better not take long. I got shit to do."

I don't know what he has to do at four p.m. on a Thursday, but whatever. Things haven't been the best between us since that party. I think we're avoiding talking about it, and that's fine. But he won't talk to me about anything else, either, and it's killing me. I can only call Mom so many times during the day. The last time I called, she told me I needed to make up with Eli because I was interrupting her day too many times. My mother should always have time for me, but apparently, that's not the case. I guess she is adjusting well since my first few weeks here when she was calling me constantly. She might even be doing more now than she has since Dad died.

Seems everyone has an exciting life besides me.

We walk into my room, and I immediately start with the directions on where I want everything. I have three different corkboards full of photos from over the years; some I took, others I didn't, but they are all great memories for me. They are the same boards that hung on my walls at home. Elijah even smiles at a few of the photos, but then he sees one that involves Reese, and it swipes it away like Swiper from *Dora*. But instead of stealing items, he is stealing good moods.

Reese was involved in almost everything growing up, so yeah, he's in a lot of the images. Photographs are my favorite keepsake. People might forget why other items are sentimental, but they'll never forget the moment surrounding a photo.

Like the one Elijah is looking at now. It's the three of us in bathing suits from the time Mom and Dad took us to a waterpark. I'm probably twelve, so they would be fifteen or so. Big smiles on all three of our faces. We look so happy, and I remember just after this photo was taken, we went down the largest slide there, and Eli and Reese had to hold my hand the entire way down because I was terrified.

He doesn't say anything when he turns away, and neither do I.

I step back to eye the third board, and after some adjustments and lots of arguing from Elijah, we get it hung. I consider telling him it's off-center but figure it's probably for the best I don't ruffle his already ruffled feathers.

"What else?" he asks as he heads for my bed, where I have a handful of photos laid out.

"Nothing, I can get those ones."

"I'm already here. Just let me help."

He's not going to like what he sees. And I know the moment he finds the photo of Reese and me because his jaw locks. It's one of the few photos we took after the kiss. His arm is tightly wrapped around my body.

He's smiling at the camera, but I'm looking at him with so much love in my eyes it makes me cringe.

"It was so obvious, and I was blind to it."

I don't think I was meant to hear that, so I ignore it and head his way.

He picks up another photo, this one of just Reese.

As much as I would love to say the photo isn't great, which I wouldn't like at all since I took it, I couldn't even if I wanted to. It's a beautiful picture of Reese, and it won me the trip to New York. No matter how I feel about him, this snapshot gave me one of my best life experiences.

It's black and white, which I don't really care for usually, but it works in this instance. The harsh contrast between light and dark brings out every pore, shadow, and highlight so beautifully. It's perfectly imperfect. And his smile is huge. I caught him off guard, and it's obvious it's a real smile and not forced for the sake of the photo. I still remember the essay I wrote to go along with it. Something about how even when all the flaws are visible, it takes a special eye to see the perfection. I guess that's how I used to feel about him.

If I were to write the essay today, it definitely wouldn't be like that. But seventeen-year-old Reese was different from the man he is now. He was sweet and kind and—

"You're basically drooling," Elijah growls and drops the photo. "I'm leaving, so if you need me, don't."

"Eli."

He pauses in my doorway but doesn't turn.

"I'm sorry, you know? That's not how you should have found out."

He pauses for a long beat before saying, "There should have been nothing to find out, Win. Not after everything." He takes a step and mumbles, "I love you," then disappears without letting me reply.

Reese is... Reese. And Elijah has every right to be mad at him right now for the other night, even without me telling him what happened after he left, but we will never agree when it comes to his hatred. He blames Reese for everything when in reality, he was a casualty of a really bad circumstance. It's not Reese's fault he was born to the worst person I've ever known. I'll never be able to hold that over his head, and I wouldn't want to anyway. Maybe there is a part of me that is protecting him, even now, but there was also a time when Reese was like family. As weird as it is to say. I can't just erase him from my memories when he's damn near a part of them all.

Ross and Rachel were on a break, and I don't know why this is even a debate. That's not an excuse for him to be a sleaze bag, but it's the facts. What the argument should be over is whether or not they should have ever gotten back together. I would love to say absolutely not, no. But I'm weak and love them together. It's not like it's real life, so I can say that, but I also love those few episodes with Rachel and Joey. Though I'm not sure if I would have liked them ending up together. I don't know, but what I do know is my mom ships Rachel and Pablo, and that's the worst duo in the entire series, so at least I'm not like my mom.

Elijah left hours ago, and not too long after, Mason headed to his girlfriend's house. I've been sitting on the couch with a pint of ice cream and a bucket of popcorn watching *Friends* ever since. This is my life now. Maybe I'll gain the freshman fifteen and finally grow some boobs. If only I could be so lucky.

I'm in the middle of shoveling a handful of popcorn into my mouth when the doorbell rings. Frowning, I pause the TV, move all my snacks, and head for the door. It's a little late to be having visitors. At least that's what I think until I glance at the clock and see 8:01 p.m. It's official, I'm lame.

I really need to get out and make some friends. Class starts Monday, and I'm hopeful I'll meet some in my classes. I mean, we are in the same class, so we have to have something in common.

I peek through the eyehole but come up short when the only thing I can see is a giant stuffed animal sitting in the middle of the floor. Rolling my eyes, I tug the door open and look around because I'm not a complete idiot. This is the fifth night something has shown up on my doorstep, and I don't have to guess to know who the giant Eeyore is from. If he wasn't so annoying, I might smile. He always hated that nickname, but if I was going to be Pooh Bear and Eli was Tigger, Reese had to be something. It's funny because now he and Elijah could switch nicknames since their personalities seem to have flipped completely.

The stuffed animal is honestly a little creepy, and I have no idea where he found a life-size Eeyore. Sighing, I take a step forward and pray this thing isn't as heavy as it looks. But then I swear the leg moves, and I freeze.

My heart slams against my chest at an accelerated speed, but I take another step because I know it's just my mind freaking me out. At least that's how I feel until his arm moves as I'm looking right at it.

A blood-curdling scream rips from my throat, and I look around for anything to hit it with. Coming up empty-handed in the hall, I sprint inside and grab the first thing I can reach, which happens to be Eli's guitar from Guitar Hero. He's going to be pissed, but I start swinging, ramming it into the doll over and over, not caring if the damn thing breaks over this weird, possessed Eeyore.

"Fuck, stop! Winnie, stop. It's me!" The head is ripped off, and I scream again. Reese stares up at me with wild eyes.

I'm tempted to continue to wail on him but figure I don't want to go to jail, so I drop the guitar to my side.

"What the hell is wrong with you?"

He climbs to his feet, still wearing the stupid costume. "I thought you would drag me inside, and then you'd have no choice but to talk with me."

"You thought I would be able to drag your two-hundred-pound body, not including the weight of the costume, into my apartment?" I deadpan, giving him a look like he's an idiot—because he is. "Are you drunk?"

"You're still wearing your pants, so no."

I think he's trying to make a joke, but I don't laugh.

"Too soon? Okay."

"Go home, Reese."

I turn for the door, but he beats me to it, blocking the entire thing with his stupid Eeyore body. "Come on, Win. I just want to apologize."

"Go on, then. You don't need to come in for that."

He drops his head and looks down his nose at me. I think he's trying to do my puppy-dog face, but he's failing miserably.

"Fine. As long as you never, ever make that face again. It's creepy."

He moves, and I push open the door, letting him go first. I grab the Eeyore head and the guitar from the ground before following him in. Somehow, he's already ditched the costume on the floor and is nowhere to be seen. I don't have to guess to know where he probably found himself.

Stopping in my doorway, I try not to focus on how natural it is seeing Reese wander around my bedroom again. Maybe it's the hockey shirt and gym shorts he's wearing, or the shagginess of his medium-brown hair poking out from under his backward cap that is confusing me because, from behind, he looks so much like he did in high school. From the front, he's more angled and sharp. A dusting of facial hair.

I drop my head forward and close my eyes. *But he's not, Win.* This *isn't* my Reese. It's just so hard to remember.

"Your room looks the same. Except you're missing the yellow walls."

My parents somehow convinced me that my favorite color is yellow. It worked, because it is, but they laid into the *Winnie the Pooh* theme hardcore, all because my dad's name is Christopher.

He stops at my corkboards and takes his time looking at every photo. Making comments about a few of them and smiling at others.

When he gets to my bed, he pauses, and I cringe, knowing what he's looking at.

"This one started it all," he mutters, then flicks his gaze up at me.

"What do you mean?"

"Everything, Win. The moment this snapshot was taken, our fates were set. It led to you kissing me. Which led to a year of turmoil fighting the feelings it brought to the surface. Led to the night we finally took *that* step."

My stomach fills with a thousand flutters, as if ten thousand moths were floating around in there. I can't tell if it's a good thing or not. No, it's bad. *Remember the other night? He pantsed you and threw that night he's referring to in your brother's face like it meant nothing at all, and wasn't the most special night you remember it to be.*

"A night that never should have happened." I reach across the bed and try to snag the photo from his hand, but he pulls it away before I can.

"Awe, baby, don't say that."

"Stop calling me that."

He has the audacity to look confused by my request.

I rip the photo from his hands and glare down at it, my emotions swirling behind my eyes, but I'm not going to cry. "This photo didn't set our fate, it altered our timeline. Without it, I never would have kissed you, you never would have gotten confused, we would have never hooked up, and that's how it should have been. We messed it up, Reese. I messed it up."

Reese walks around the bed and stops behind me. He's not touching me, but he might as well be for how his body heat is warming my backside. With each passing moment of awkward silence that stretches between us, my stomach tightens to an uncomfortable degree. He's so happy in this photo, and as much as I love it, I also hate it. I wish I could go back and take back that kiss. "Don't do this, Win. Don't tell me you regret anything, because it'll kill me."

It's not fair for him to guilt me. It's not fair for him to be making me the bad guy right now.

And yet, all I want to do is cry, let him pull me into his body, and accept what he is calling our fate.

But I won't. I straighten and drop the photo onto my bed like I don't care about it.

"Why are you here, Reese?" I spin to face him.

"To give you—"

"No. Why are *you here*? What do you think is going to happen from these weird gifts I've gotten all week?"

Hurt beats across his sharp features. "Do you not like them?"

"That's not what I said." I shake my head. "But answer the question. Why. Are. You. Here?"

"School starts Monday. Hockey season starts soon after, and I'm going to be busy with practice a lot. I won't get the chance to send you stuff or drop by in costumes anymore." *Darn.* "But I don't want you thinking I've given up."

"It would be easier on both of us if you did." I wrap my arms around my waist, wishing it would make the ache low in my chest disappear.

With a hesitant hand, he tilts my chin up so I'm forced to meet his warm honey eyes. "I can't give up on us, Win. I have to prove to you that we are it. You and I are the goal, baby."

Why does he have to sound so sure about it? I force my eyes closed, unable to stand looking at him any longer. Tears trickle down my face.

I gasp when his hot breath dusts over my cheeks. He kisses each side, soaking up any wetness. Then he brushes his lips over mine, and I'm frozen solid in a trance. It's not quite a kiss, but it's the closest thing I've had since that night.

"I'd wait an eternity for you. But please don't make me."

Fall might be my favorite season. Something about the crisp mornings without having to shovel snow and the fallen leaves that brush the ground with each step. My closet full of sweaters also comes in handy. Mom never understood why I would come home with a new hoodie or sweater whenever I went shopping, but I don't get how she doesn't understand there isn't a more comforting piece of clothing than a large sweater that warms your body.

"Winnie?"

My feet falter, and I look behind me to the voice. Not many people, if any at all, know my name, so who is...

Emma and her friend from the party wave excitedly before making their way to me.

"Hey."

"You know you are, like, one of the few people on campus with red hair. I swear I've only seen, like, five."

I giggle but nod. "Yeah. It's like that most places I go. We stand out a lot."

Emma hooks her arm through mine like it's a totally normal thing to do to someone you met once for five minutes.

Laney trails on the other side of Emma but smiles at me. "Hey, Winnie."

Before I can respond, Emma scrunches up her face and asks, "What are we doing at the library?"

"Am I missing where people go to the library for things other than studying?"

Laney giggles. "That's what most people do at the library, Em."

"I can think of a few things that don't involve studying." She grins, big and wide.

Like she manifested them, a group of guys walks in front of us, taking their time to check each of us out and not being shy about it at all. One of them whistles, and Emma wiggles her fingers in their direction. Mortified, I tug on her arm, dragging the girls completely around the group of guys and hurrying toward the library.

"Absolutely not. I'm here to study, and that's it." My heart pounds in my chest, and I glance over my shoulder, happy to see the guys have moved on.

"Bor-ing. What are we doing *after*?"

I lift an eyebrow at Emma. "We?"

She drops her head back as if I'm exhausting her. "Come on, Win! You're a college freshman and it's Thursday night!"

Thursday night? Aren't Friday and Saturday the party nights? "Since when is Thursday a party night?"

Her eyes blow wide. "You've never heard of thirsty Thursday?"

"Uh, should I have?"

"Even I have." Laney nods.

"See?" *Not really.* "Anyway, I'll make you a deal. I will study as long as you do, but after, you have to come out with us."

"I'm not really a going-out type."

"Me either," Laney throws out.

"I need new friends," Emma grumbles. I guess making my first college friend wasn't that hard after all. Even comes with a bonus friend. *Sweet.* I've failed miserably at making any in class. There are a few people who are friendly, but it's mostly a *hello* and *how are you.* Not much more than that. "But I can ease you—both—into it. Pleeaassee? I promise no shit-faced guys trying to take your pants off." She pauses and pulls me to a stop too. "Well, no. I can't promise that, because men are pigs. But it'll be fun turning them all down."

I've never been one to give in to peer pressure, but going out kind of sounds fun. My first party experience was taken from me. Maybe tonight will be better.

"Why are you so adamant about going out, anyway?"

Laney leans forward and gives me a timid smile. "The guys are busy with hockey practice tonight, so there's no one around to tell her no."

Oh, that's right. Her brother is on Reese's team. It's been a week since Reese stopped by the apartment, and he was right after all; I've not received anything after the weekend. I'd be lying if I said every day I get home from class, I didn't hope there is something on the doorstep, but there never is. It's not fair for me to wish for that when I'm the one who told him to give up. I'm only getting exactly what I asked for, so why does it suck so bad?

Emma nods, agreeing with whatever Laney said. "Sawyer is a bit overprotective. He doesn't like me going out without him, and I can't drink and flirt with boys like I want to when he's around."

"She still totally does, don't let her lie to you."

Emma grins, not bothered at all that her best friend just threw her under the bus. "I do, but he is such a cock block. I had to basically throw my virginity at the first guy I saw when he left for college."

Oh my. Elijah is protective, but nothing like that. I'll still probably let him know where I'm going to be, but he most likely won't even reply. Our relationship still isn't great, but it's better. Though I didn't tell him about Eeyore showing up.

"Are you a virgin?" she asks me.

I speed ahead of them, hurrying toward the library, but they jog after.

"Are you?" she asks again.

"No, I'm not."

Emma squeals. "No way, who did you lose it to?" She gasps as if just remembering something. "Was it Reese? Is that the night he was talking about?"

Damn him. There's no point in denying it. My face is probably close to matching my hair with how hot it feels. "Yeah, it was that night."

She squeals again, and I'm tempted to plug my ears because she's so loud. "Are you guys—"

Nope, not even entertaining that question. "What about you, Laney? Virgin or no?"

Emma snaps her mouth shut and turns to Laney.

"Uh, yeah." Her voice is soft like maybe she's embarrassed, but she shouldn't be. Me giving my virginity to Reese, only for him to turn around and disappear for two years the next day, is way more embarrassing.

I don't have a lot of homework or studying to do since it's only the first week of school, but I take a little longer than I need just to drive Emma a bit crazier. She's been bouncing in her seat pretty much the entire time. I doubt she got any studying done, so really I could back out of the night, but I'm a little excited.

Emma mentioned dancing, and I love dancing. I'm not really good at it, but I'm banking on everyone else around me being drunk enough that they don't notice my two left feet.

"You guys can wait here or come up, but I'll warn you, my brother isn't friendly like yours."

"Oh, we know all about your brother," Emma says, shooting Laney a sideways look I don't understand.

"What do you mean?"

She shrugs her thin shoulders. "He's known around campus. That's all."

Elijah is *known* around campus? What the hell does that mean? Known for what? I don't get a chance to ask because Emma jumps out of my car, and when I look at Laney, she scurries out after her. Well, okay then.

Elijah is sitting on the couch shirtless, his hand shoved down his pants. Thankfully, he's not watching porn, but it doesn't make it any less awkward when Emma and Laney trail in after me and he scowls at them. Making no move to remove his hand.

"The fuck, Win? I told you no girlish slumber parties."

"Don't be rude, Eli. We're just stopping by so I can change." I don't bother introducing them because he's already gone back to watching *The Walking Dead* and ignoring us.

I wait until we are in my room before turning to the girls. "See, I told you he wasn't friendly."

"I can fucking hear you, shithead."

"That was the point, dickface," I shout back, then slam the door before he can reply. I flick my lock and face them, plastering on an obviously fake smile. "Charming, isn't he?"

"I like him," Emma says, her blue eyes wide as if she just met Santa Claus.

"Trust me, you don't." I head for my closet, and they fall onto my bed. It's weird how normal this feels. I've never had girls in my room. I've had guys—or the same two guys—numerous times, but one of them is my brother. It's weird I've never had a girl friend, though. Someone to gossip and paint my nails with. Not that I paint my nails... but maybe if I had a girl friend, I might. I never really tried to make friends in school. I always had Reese and Eli, and after they were gone, I had lost my dad and wasn't interested in making friends. Mom needed me, and truthfully, I needed her just as much.

"What do we wear to go out?"

"As close to nothing as legally possible," Emma states.

"I think a cute dress," Laney offers, probably reading the mortification I'm feeling. Laney seems more my speed when it comes to this kind of stuff.

"Well, considering half the campus probably saw my ass, something that makes sure that doesn't happen again."

"You mean the whole campus?" Emma snorts. She gets up from my bed to look at my photo wall. "Wow, you and Reese really were close."

I swallow the lump and nod, even though she can't see it. "What do you mean whole campus? I know there were a lot of people there, but unless there were thirty thousand people in that room…"

Emma and Laney once again swap faces. It's mildly annoying how they converse without actually speaking.

"Did you not see the post from the EU Student News?" Laney's eyebrows furrow.

"Student News? What's that?"

My stomach sinks and my head swims with the possibility of whatever they are talking about. Surely, my ass can't be posted anywhere, right? That would be illegal. I think. Laney drops her eyes to her phone, and after a second, she holds it up.

Forget my stomach sinking, it nearly drops out my ass now. I scramble across my room and grab the phone from her. I gasp loudly, then remember my brother is next door, and if he saw this, he would go ballistic.

"What the hell is this?" Most of it is shit about Reese and the team, or the party in general. My name isn't mentioned anywhere. Not even in the comments under the post. A lot of them are guys giving heart eyes or laughing faces. Some compliments, but they do nothing to stop the mortification from suffocating me. My ass is on a website. If my name gets attached to this in any way, there goes any future career I might want.

Emma walks to my side and sighs. "EU Student News. I can't believe you've never heard about it. It's like the Pinecove version of *Gossip Girl*. A bunch of anonymous posts of things happening around campus, mostly gossipy things that make people look bad. It's the worst, but it's even worse that they now have a printed version."

Wait... *printed*? "You're telling me my ass is printed on the front page of some kind of weird newspaper?"

"Uh, yeah? Haven't you been around campus at all this week? There aren't many newsstands, but you should have seen one." Her brow knits. I walked past a few newsstands that had the school colors on top, but they were all empty when I saw them. Either my ass sold out, or they weren't in the ones I saw. I guess if they weren't there, then maybe they weren't everywhere like Emma said.

"I am not going out tonight." I toss Laney's phone back to her, and she catches it.

"Noooo," Emma cries. "This is a good thing, Win. Think about it, your ass is out there being complimented by basically everyone in a fifteen-mile radius, and no one knows it's your ass. Your ass is famous!"

Emma's a little bit delusional, but she's good at making a drastic situation—like my bare ass being printed on newspapers—seem small.

"A new story always comes out after the weekend, and there will be another ass for people to chat about. So I say enjoy your time in the spotlight."

Maybe she's a lot bit delusional. But right now, delusional works for me. "Fine, but I'm not wearing anything that could lead to me flashing anything."

"Boring, but okay." She grins. "And we can get drunk enough you won't even care if you do."

I've never gotten drunk before, but I just might tonight.

I'm sure this night is going to end *super well*.

9

Reese

"Alright, ladies. Hit the showers."

Thank fuck. If Coach would've said "lines" one more time, I think I would have quit. Preseason is such shit. It's mostly conditioning and not a lot of playing. It sucks big time.

"I never thought that practice was going to end," Beckett grumbles from my left. "He's got a stick up his ass this season."

Gavin slaps him on the shoulder. "Nah, he just wants to win. I heard Mr. Kinnon is putting a lot of pressure on him this season."

"I'd like to see Kinnon get his old ass on the ice," Sawyer growls. He's the biggest out of us and is also the guy who sweats the most during conditioning practices, so he tends to be the one who gets the most pissy about them.

Hot water burns against my chilled skin, but I welcome the sting. Coach prefers we take cold showers to help with muscle recovery, but none of us listen to that suggestion. Nothing feels better than a hot shower after four hours on the ice. Except maybe a massage.

When Winnie was little, Eli and I used to trick her into massaging our backs after hard practices by telling her we would buy her a roll of film. I wonder if that would still work... I haven't seen or spoken to her since I showed up at her place. Can't lie, I was hoping she would cave and call me by now, maybe even confess her love, but that has yet to happen.

I'm still holding my breath, though. I wasn't lying when I told her my life would get hectic once school started. Who knew lawn care classes were hard? Not me. I kind of thought they would just be, like, what kind of blade do you cut grass with? I had no clue science went into it and shit. But I'll graduate next year with a degree I can put to use almost right away. My old boss has been looking to pass his business down for a while, and when I saw him last and mentioned my degree, he promised he would save it for me.

Going pro is still the dream, but having a career ready for when my playing days are over was really important to me. Growing up listening to my parents scream about money scared me straight. As soon as I could, I got a job, and I've been saving my money ever since. Even got a few investments that have already doubled my savings.

I jump into Sawyer's passenger seat, and Beckett and Gavin climb into the back. We stop off at McDonald's and order nearly the entire menu before heading home. I only have two classes tomorrow, and then it's the weekend, and I can't fucking wait. Preseason weekends are great because Coach leaves us alone, unlike weekends during the season. I gotta think of something to do for Winnie this weekend, though. I considered standing outside her apartment with a boom box, but I'm not interested in fighting with Eli again. Getting rocked in the face by an infamous underground fighter isn't exactly fun. But the flower bouquets aren't cutting it. I need something big, but not too big. Something medium. Something perfect. It'll come to me, and if not, then I'll resort to a prank call telling her I'm in the hospital. It was Schmidt's idea; I think he was kidding, but I'm getting to the point of desperation.

I toss what's left of the food on Sawyer and Beckett's table before crashing onto their couch. Bad move, because I'm not sure I'm going to be able to get up now.

Gavin falls next to me and rips a piece of his burger off. "I heard you got rocked at the party." He just got to school, so he missed the whole ordeal.

"I did."

"That's embarrassing for you."

Not as embarrassing as everything else that happened that night. "Yeah, well, what can you do?"

"Probably not mention fucking someone's *underage* sister right to their face."

I turn and glare at him, but he shrugs and stuffs the rest of the burger in his mouth.

"Just saying."

"Have you guys seen Emma?" Sawyer emerges from his room, a frown on his face.

"No, where is she?" Gavin asks.

I slap the back of his head, and he complains. "He wouldn't ask if he knew, dumbass."

Much to my dismay, he barks at us to get up and help him look. The athletic dorms are big, but not three-guys-looking-for-one-girl big. If he didn't find her, we're definitely not going to.

"Maybe she finally moved into her dorm?" It's late, and the last thing I want to deal with is a worried Sawyer. I've never seen anyone worry about their sister the way he does.

"No, maintenance said it would be another few weeks before it was ready."

I lift the several McDonald's bags in case she left a note, and ah-ha! Bingo.

"Saw!"

Went to bed early! Don't bother me!!!

-Em

He snatches it from my hand, and his frown deepens.

"What's wrong? Isn't she in her room?"

"No."

Beckett saunters back into the room, carrying the other half of this note, by the looks of it, and Sawyer tugs it from his hands like he did to me.

> *Okay, I lied. I'm out. But I'm totally safe, and you do NOT need to come get me. I'll be home before two. I love you!*
>
> *PS. Please, please do not ruin this night for me!!!!!!*

I'm not sure what I would do with a sister like Emma. Probably have a stroke from all the stress she causes. Elijah really lucked out by getting the sister he did. Winnie was always content just chilling with us.

"Fuck, that girl." He tosses the papers down. "Where do people go on Thursdays?"

"Wayside, maybe? I don't fucking know."

He snatches his keys up and heads for the door, pausing once he reaches it to look at me expectantly. Lucky Beckett, who peaced out after bringing the note out, and Gavin, who ducked the moment Sawyer turned his back.

I truck forward, grumbling under my breath, and follow after him. We hit the parking lot, but on the way to his truck, I pause, narrow my eyes, and gaze at the blue Bronco parked a few spots away. Winnie is obviously not the only one to drive a blue Bronco, and if this were hers, it would have a small dent in the back where she backed into my truck years ago. I step back, and my stomach tenses when I find exactly that. I look up to the dorms, but I know she isn't inside. I don't know how I know, but I do. I jog over and throw myself into Sawyer's truck.

"What are you in a hurry about all of a sudden?"

"That was Winnie's Bronco."

He glances my way curiously. "And?"

"And she's probably out with your sister." My voice is a growl. The words *out* and *Winnie* don't go together in my book.

Eighteen minutes later, Sawyer and I come to a stop just short of the bar at Wayside.

Emma, Laney, and *my* Winnie all stand on the countertop, moving to the beat of some shitty throwback from high school dance days.

"I'm gonna fucking kill them," Sawyer growls before stalking through the rowdy crowd that's gathered around the girls.

I've only been to Wayside a few times, but it's the hoppin' place on campus. Lots of alcohol and little security checking IDs. Everyone knows it; hell, I bet the police even know it.

Thank fuck Sawyer and I are fucking huge, because the crowd is nearly impossible to get through, and without our size, I don't know how we would. I shove past faceless people, and a few of them throw me glares until they see my size and who I am.

There's a reason I'm called *The Rapture* in the rink. As soon as I touch that ice, everything logical leaves my head, and my only focus is hockey. I'm known for wrecking people when they are in my way. Usually, it doesn't bleed off the ice, but when Winnie is involved, anything is possible.

We finally get to the front, and Sawyer argues with Emma to my left, but I'm more interested in what's on the other end of the bar. I storm over until I'm directly under her swinging hips. Winnie has never been a good dancer, and the alcohol no doubt pumping through her body doesn't change the fact. Still, she's never looked so sexy. Thank fuck she's not wearing a dress like the other girls on the bar, or I'd be able to see everything, and if that were the case, I'd have to pluck out every guy's eyes in this place.

Winnie's jeans are tight, showing every small curve on her body, and when she turns around, I nearly black out. Fuck, her ass. So round and perky, even with the ugly fanny pack sitting on top. I hate every guy here tonight. Her tank top is tiny and white, and her nipples are damn near visible through it. Hair pulled into a floppy pony, she's so fucking beautiful it hurts.

"Winnie," I shout, loud enough she can hear me over the music.

Her movements halt, and she whips around to look down at me. I see alcohol doesn't make her like me any more than she does sober.

She rolls her eyes. "What are you doing hereeee?"

Yeah, she's definitely drunk.

"Get down and I'll tell you."

The faintest, most mischievous smile pulls on her plump lips. "No, thanks. I'm good."

She brings the drink in her hand to her lips and wraps them around the tiny straw, sucking back whatever is in that cup. What I would do to have her lips wrap around my cock like that.

"Come on, Win. Get down."

She shakes her head.

I glance in Sawyer's direction and snort seeing him with Laney draped over one shoulder while he attempts to reach for his sister, who is just out of reach. Thank fuck I only have one to worry about.

And if she won't come down. Then I'll just come up.

I plant my hands and jump with ease on top of the sticky bar so I'm upright next to Winnie. These girls have to be short as hell to not worry about the hanging lights that are swinging in my face.

"Reese!" She turns and gasps at finding me on the bar with her.

My shoes stick to the surface, but I grin. She stumbles a few times while heading for the edge, wanting to get away from me. She looks down at the ground and then back to me.

"Pick your poison, baby. Me or the floor."

As disappointed as I am when she stumbles off, I'm not surprised.

My feet hit the floor with a loud thump as I jump after her and grab her arm before she can get away from me. I spin us, caging her between my arms against the bar.

Our heavy breaths mix, mine smelling of mint and hers smelling like apple liquor as she sasses, "I chose the floor, so that means back off, Reese."

"I backed off for two whole years, Win. I can't anymore. Not when you're right in front of me."

"Exactly." She slips under my arms before I can stop her. "You had no problems ditching me for two years *after* you took my virginity. So do it again."

I let her get a few feet away before I charge after her. Soft denim brushes against my palms as I grab her waist and pull her against my body. *Fuck.* Her ass pressed against me was a bad fucking idea if I want to keep this semi-appropriate for public. I'm not risking being on the front page of EU Student News again.

"You're not the only one who lost their virginity that night, princess. So stop acting like it was easy for me to walk away. Because it wasn't."

Her body tenses, and she turns her head in my direction. "What?"

I don't know if she will remember this or how drunk she actually is, but I let it all out. *All on the table now, Win.* "I was a virgin too. I felt that connection just as hard as you, but I was also eighteen, and you were barely *sixteen*, Win. Come on, you're smart enough to know we couldn't 'play house.' Your brother would have killed me."

"Can't play house but can sneak into my room, fuck me, and leave without a fucking goodbye? Fuck you, Reese Larson."

"I wish you would," I growl, but she pushes from my arms, and I let her walk over to the bar, order two shots, and throw them both back. Glaring, she storms onto the dance floor. The next song blasts from the speakers, and I swear Winnie must be the one in control of the music. "You're a Jerk" by New Boyz blares around us while she stares at me with a smug expression, and fuck if my dick isn't throbbing for her.

The DJ mixes it, and girlish screams fill the air at the new song. Sawyer stops next to me, his arms crossed over his chest and his jaw tight while watching Emma drag Laney onto the dance floor next to Winnie.

"You give up?"

"They're fucking slippery. When I would grab one, the other would disappear. Fucking children."

I bite back my laugh because I know he's not in the mood. "Come on, Saw. You remember what it was like to be a freshman? That first taste of freedom."

"I wasn't basically naked," he growls.

He's got a point there. Emma's and Laney's outfits could be combined and still not be appropriate for every day. Thank fuck Winnie isn't dressed the same. I don't think I'd be as relaxed watching her dance if she were.

"Amy is going to fucking kill me for being here."

"She can't be mad. You're here for your sister."

He dips his chin, but we both know that's not true. Amy will always find an issue with anything Sawyer does. If he's not at home or with her, he can't do anything right. When she transferred schools, I thought they would break up because she couldn't have a tab on him constantly like she could before, but now she just calls him three hundred times a day.

"Shots" comes up next, and I slap Sawyer's shoulder. "Since I'm not driving." I order a shot of Jameson and throw it back. I'm not going to get drunk, but if I have to stand here and watch Winnie dance without being able to touch her, I'm going to need some fucking alcohol.

"You okay with that?" He nods at the dance floor toward the girls.

I drag my eyes over, and a smirk tugs up one side of my face. Winnie tilts her head back, her ponytail swaying and her arms in the air.

"Yeah. She looks happy, doesn't she?"

He eyes Winnie for a moment, then nods. "Yeah, I guess. What's the deal with you two anyway?"

Now *that's* a loaded question if I ever heard one. "It's a long story, but basically, we grew up together. Elijah and I were best friends, and she was just always... there. I probably hung out with her more than him a lot of the time, honestly. To put it short, she kissed me when she was fifteen, and the rest was history. I stayed away for a while, but eventually, I couldn't anymore. I was leaving for college and—" I shrug and blow out a breath. "It just happened. I know I should have never fucked her when she was underage, but I don't know, man."

"I can't lie, bro. If that was Emma, I'd do a lot more than punch you."

I snort. "Yeah. I know, and so would I, but I can't explain it or why because I knew it was wrong then. It hit me that I was leaving for college and—" I pause for a moment, unsure what to say, then sigh. "I just wanted to strengthen our connection before I left."

It's a shit excuse, but not a lie. Our relationship had been weird since she kissed me. I hated how it felt awkward when we were alone, and I didn't want to leave for college feeling that way. Winnie came on to me that night, in her own subtle way, and for once, I gave in to what we both wanted, even though I shouldn't have. It killed me having to leave the next day, but I had to. She's right, though. I should have said goodbye, and then maybe she'd be grinding on me right now instead of with her friends.

"I get it," he mutters. "The pull, I mean."

I eye him curiously because there's no fucking way he's talking about Amy right now. "Who?"

His focus drifts over to the girls.

"Laney?" I guess, assuming it's not his sister he's talking about.

He gives me a tight nod, still watching her. "She always had a crush on me, and I took advantage of that one time and kissed her. It was a dare, but still. It never should have happened, but I liked Laney's attention. I liked knowing she wanted me, but I didn't want her back. The kiss wasn't meant to be more than a kiss, but." He shrugs. "Something changed." He clears his throat and bunches his eyebrows. "Anyway, Amy was there, but that was before we were serious. It didn't take long after for her to demand we make it official."

"Fuck."

As if she knows we're talking about her, Laney looks our way. Her head tilts, and her blonde hair tumbles to the side. She stares at Sawyer for a moment until she sees me watching, and then she quickly turns away.

"She still wants you?"

He shrugs. "I don't know. Sometimes I think so, others I don't."

"But you want her to."

He doesn't answer—not that he needs to. I see it all over his face that he does.

"Fuck, man."

His eyes flick back to me, and he lets out a deep breath. "I like teasing her. I like the deep pink that stains her cheeks when she sees me without a shirt. I like how she gets goosebumps when I say her full name."

"But you say you don't want her? Because it sounds a lot like you do, Saw."

He finds her once again, but this time, she's not dancing with her friends. A random guy has his arm snaked around her waist, holding her to his front. Anger burns deep in Sawyer's eyes as he watches, yet some-fucking-how, he doesn't go pull her away. If that was Winnie... *Fuck*, I would kill him for touching what's mine. It's like he likes the pain it causes.

"I'm with Amy."

"You don't look at her the way you look at Laney."

He might kill me for saying it, but it's true. Now knowing what I do, I can see it. The want, the need to be near her. He's a hell of a lot stronger than me, that's for sure.

"I love Amy. We make sense, and our families have been planning our wedding for years."

"That's not a good enough reason, Saw."

He ignores me. "Now you know why she acts psycho sometimes. And why I just deal with it, because I caused her to act like that. I know she sees the way I look at Laney—as hard as I try not to. It's there, and Amy hates it. Rightfully so."

Maybe, and if I were Amy, I would hate Laney too. I can't imagine how I would be if Winnie had a boyfriend, so I get it to a point. "Wouldn't it just be easier to break up instead of both of you being miserable?"

He finally looks away from Laney and drags a hand down his face. "Maybe. But we do have good moments. I know you guys only see the bad, but when it's just us, she's not that bad and Laney won't always be around."

"*Not that bad*? Saw, you hear yourself, right? That's *not* a relationship." At least it shouldn't be. Not one I would want, that's for sure.

Emma runs up to us, and he shrugs, not having a chance to answer.

"Do you have a condom?"

Sawyer looks as if his head is about to explode. "Are you fuc—"

"Not for meeee, for Laney!"

Oh *fuck*. His anger doesn't dwindle at all, and I follow his sharp gaze to Laney standing with that same guy down the bar now. He's smirking, and it's obvious he's trying to get in her pants, but she is smiling equally as big. My heart beats harder for my best friend as he watches the woman he really wants be propositioned by another man.

"He looks familiar," I mutter, mostly to myself.

Sawyer gives a sharp nod.

"No, and you need to get your friend away from him." Sawyer shoots me a curious side-eye.

"What? Why?" Emma's eyebrows pinch.

"I think that's the guy I saw in the clinic getting tested." I don't know where I've seen this guy. Definitely not at a clinic, but anything to get him away from Sawyer's girl. He might not realize it now, but Laney is his girl just like Winnie is mine.

"Tested for what?"

"An STD, Em," Sawyer snaps, losing his patience.

"Oh!" She gasps before heading toward her friend on a rescue mission. She whispers in Laney's ear, and her eyes widen. I can hear her weak excuse without actually being able to hear it as they stumble away.

Sawyer lets out a deep breath. "Thanks."

"No problem. But that won't work forever. You either gotta take the plunge or let go." Rich coming from me, because I'm the king of not letting go, but it's not fair to either of them for him to keep a hold when he's still got one foot out.

The complete opposite of Winnie and me. I've never been more into anything.

"I know." His voice is low, bitter even.

Knowing what I do, it's so easy to see the tension between them, and now I wonder how I ever missed it. Her eyes widen a beat as she looks to him and gives him a hint of a smile. All of Sawyer's tension releases, and he dips his head back. And I know there's not a fucking chance he's ever letting her go. There's going to be a blowup at some point, and I just hope I'm there to see it.

I don't know how long it's been before Winnie finally stumbles my way from the dance floor. Technically, toward the bar, but I move in the direction she heads, so it might as well be toward me.

"You're like a lost puppy. You know that, right?"

"So why don't you claim me?" I reach for her belt loops with a grin, but she swats my hands away.

"*Unwanted* lost puppy, Reese." She orders another drink, and I step behind her and throw down the money for it before she can dig into that ugly fanny pack resting on her ass.

"Come on, Win. We both know you'd never turn down a stray."

"Thanks," she shouts to the bartender, throws whatever drink she ordered back, and spins in my arms. A glare already melting into her pretty face. "You are the definition of pathetic, Reese Larson."

"Keep going, I love some degradation."

Her eyes widen before she rolls them. "Stop it."

"Stop what?"

"Trying to make me like you."

She pushes by me, and I trail after her. "Why? Is it working?"

Winnie shoots me a scowl over her shoulder, but she doesn't answer, and I take that as a *yes*. I stop before the edge of the dance floor.

"You still don't dance?"

I lift an eyebrow. "No, but I can think of a few different ways for us to *move* together."

I love the way her chest heaves when I say stuff like that. I mean everything that comes out of my mouth. If only she would let me prove it to her and stop being so damn difficult. Then she would see how good things could actually be between us.

She snatches my hat from my head, places it on hers, and backs away with shaky legs, and I don't think it's from the liquor because she hasn't taken her heated gaze off me. I'm so close to getting her to crack. And maybe it's the alcohol pumping through her system, but if Winnie being tipsy is what it takes for her to cave, then so be it.

"I love this song!" Emma blurs past me, grabs ahold of my girl, and spins.

I forgot how nice it is merely being in Winnie's presence. She's so beautiful, and not just physically. The light aura she gives off is like a drug. It makes me fucking happy to see her happy. I've never seen her with friends who weren't Elijah and me, so seeing her, Emma, and now Laney singing and dancing like nothing else matters, well. Fuck, it's a good sight.

Sawyer stops by my side, still sporting a scowl. "They are going to be trashed tomorrow."

"Better them than me."

He snorts. "Maybe this is where she pantses you in front of everyone."

"Fuck, I wish."

He slaps the back of my head and shakes his. "Who knew you were so twisted?"

"She makes me crazy." I'd pay Winnie to take my pants off if I didn't think that would offend her. "But I'm not me without her."

After she downs a few more shots, her movements relax, and my hat hardly hangs off her head anymore. She's more drunk than I would prefer her to be. Maybe we won't have sex tonight, but sleeping next to her will be almost as good. Big emphasis on *almost*.

"I'm gonna piss, and then we should probably get them home," I tell Sawyer before heading for the bathrooms. Being sober in a club is annoying, but being sober in a club bathroom is fucking nasty. There's a couple in the corner, and the guy is getting head, while another dude is passed out across the room. I pay no attention to anything else, doing what I need to do and hurrying out.

I find Sawyer leaning against the bar with his head hung between his shoulders.

"You good?"

"Our talk is fucking with my head. And watching her dance..." his jaw clenches. "When we were kids she was always dancing. Em and I used to beg our driver to take us to her recitals, but once I got my license I'd sneak into her practices and just watch her. The way she moves—"

His mouth clamps shut and he doesn't say anything more.

"You know, they say dancers and figure skaters are one in the same."

"Yeah, I know."

I clap his back. "You're right."

He glances at me and furrows his brows.

"You're fucked. Now let's go get our girls and get the fuck outta here."

The place has only gotten more crowded as the night has gone on, so it takes longer than I'd like to find the girls, and when we do, everything inside me revolts at the sight.

"You gonna go get her?" Sawyer asks, stopping by me and glaring at the scene in front of us.

I take a step but pause. My chest burns with the need to get to her and push away the same guy from earlier, but not yet.

"No," I tell him simply, even if everything inside me hates myself for saying it. "Not until she needs me to."

It doesn't take long. Winnie throws her hands in the air, spins to the guy, and rips into him. I wish I was close enough to hear, but her pissed-off face says enough.

Sawyer chuckles. "You got a feisty one, Reese. Sure you can handle her?"

She shoves a finger in the guy's chest, and he holds his hands up in defeat and steps back.

I grin. "Yeah, I can handle her just fine."

Winnie glares at him for a beat more before turning and throwing her hair over her shoulder to join her friends again. Sawyer and I tense when the guy doesn't move. It's like a switch goes off, and his wide eyes tighten as he zeros in on them. His jaw locks, and I don't wait another second. Sawyer is right behind me, ready to back me up if I need it. The guy might be close to the same size, but I'd bet money I can hold more anger than he can, resulting in a meaner punch. He doesn't get a step in before Sawyer and I block him from getting any closer.

"You were so close." I tsk.

"Close to what?" he bites back.

"Not making me do this." I pull my arm back and slam my fist into his nose. My knuckles pop, but I hardly feel it. Elijah was always the one who liked to fight, but there were several times I had to step in and help him out when he would take on too many or someone bigger than him. The guy drops, holding his nose. He makes a move to get up, and Sawyer places his foot across his chest.

"I wouldn't."

It takes longer than it should for the guy to make the right choice. There's not a single way he thought he would take both of us, and there's no one around him, so I'm guessing he's alone. After a minute, Sawyer pulls him up. He tugs him close and mutters, "Think of touching our girls again, and I'll break your hands." Then he shoves him away. He scowls at us but eventually turns and disappears into the thick crowd.

Sawyer drops his eyes to my hand. "You good?"

"Yeah, I'll ice it when we get home. Let's get out of here."

10

Reese

Drunk Winnie is a handful. I don't know how many of those little test-tube shots she had when I was in the bathroom, but enough to be a giggling mess. It's like she's a child again, and her dad is chasing her through the house, trying to get her into the tub. Except it's me chasing her around the car, and she's not naked. *Unfortunately.*

I get her in, grab my hat back, flip the child safety lock, and slam the door in her face before she can jump out. *Again.*

Sawyer rolls down his window and cocks an eyebrow at me.

"Yeah, yeah." I brush him off and head around to my seat. "Go," I tell him as soon as my door is closed. "Before she tries to jump through the sunroof."

Winnie leans forward, and Sawyer floors it.

"I'm hungry."

"I have something you can eat." I grin, but she doesn't. Instead, genuine confusion etches across her face, and Sawyer barks out a laugh.

"Trust me, you don't want what he's got. But there is a Subway on the way home."

Winnie makes a gagging noise, and he frowns.

"Not a fan of Subway?"

"No. But I do like pizza. Is there pizza?"

The other two girls lean forward and squeal in happiness, wanting pizza too, and no matter how many times we tell them no, Sawyer caves and turns down the road that leads to our favorite joint.

It's the definition of hole-in-the-wall, but they stay open until three a.m. for all the college kids to grab a slice after the bars, and their pizza is fucking amazing. Best in town, and I've tried them all, several times. But we keep coming back to Max's Slices because it's just that damn good. I'm glad I get to show Winnie it for the first time. I know she's going to love it.

That is, if she is sober enough to remember how good it is. And if not, I guess I'll have to bring her back when she is. I jump down from the truck and wander over to Sawyer's side to pull open her door since she can't do it herself. As soon as it opens, she tumbles out right into my arms. I steady her and try not to focus on how close my hands are to her ass. Or how she's breathing on my neck and it's fucking erotic as shit.

Her teeth chatter together, and I push her away to see her face. "Are you cold?"

I don't wait for her to nod before I'm pulling off my sweatshirt and slipping it over her head. It hangs off her narrow shoulders like a dress. The sleeves are too long, and it hits her mid-thigh, but fuck it all if she doesn't look so damn sexy in my clothes.

"Let's get you some 'za." *Before I do something I shouldn't.* Like fuck her against Sawyer's truck.

The best part about Max's is the pizza by the slice. Any kind you want, and they have a ton that are ready after a quick run through the oven.

"It smells so good in here." Winnie sucks in a deep breath with her nose in the air. "What do you normally get?"

"I like the pulled pork. But I think you'll like the macaroni."

Her eyes widen with excitement, reminding me so much of a young Winnie. "They have macaroni *on* pizza?"

"Yeah." I chuckle. "It's really good too."

"I love it here." She spins to face me. Tilting her head to stare at me—or my lips, mostly. Losing all train of thought, I take in her lips, so soft, so pink, so wet from her dragging her tongue across them, and so begging me to take them.

My heart races. I lean down, she closes her eyes, and—

"Next!"

She jumps, ramming her head into my chin. We groan at the pain, and I feel around, but there's no blood. Fuck, she has a hard head, though.

"Well, look what the cat dragged in."

I kiss the place Winnie is rubbing on her head before greeting Tony. He graduated from college within the last ten years and is a really cool dude. His brother Max, who he named the place after, is the biggest Timberwolves fan—specifically hockey—and Coach is cool enough to give Max and Tony season passes every year.

"Thanks, man." I scowl, seeing his shitty grin because he knows what he just interrupted.

"Anytime, and who is this?" He leans on the counter between us and eyes Winnie with interest.

"Winnie." Her voice is almost too sweet. Without a second thought, she offers her dainty hand to the big man behind the counter. He takes it, shakes, and brings it toward his lips to press a kiss.

"Alright, alright. He punched one dick tonight, we don't need to make it two." Sawyer pushes between us, making him drop Winnie's hand.

"That right?" Tony lifts an eyebrow.

I shrug it off, not wanting to get into it. I order our food before stepping aside to let Sawyer get his, then lead a bouncy Winnie over to a booth and let her drop onto the squeaky seat before sliding in after her.

"Are you excited, or are you cold and trying to stay warm?"

She giggles the sweetest sound. "Excited. I haven't had good pizza in so long."

Shit, that's right. I forgot the pizza place back home closed a few years ago.

"Well, it's the best. You can't beat it besides the help."

She giggles again and falls into my open chest. For as long as I can remember, Winnie has smelled of raspberries and vanilla. I broke down once and asked what the smell was, and she said it was her body wash. I'm glad she still uses the same stuff; the smell is so comforting. There were so many nights we would sit up on her roof, and I would catch whiffs of the sweetness. It brings back a lot of good memories.

I drop an arm on her back, and she sighs.

"I'm going to regret letting you hold me like this."

"Guess I need to appreciate it while you do, then." I pull her closer and kiss the top of her head. "You don't have to regret it, though, Win. I'm right here, and I'm not going anywhere."

She doesn't reply, not that I expected her to. The others join us after stopping off at the arcade games in the corner, and she sits up but stays close. Sawyer shoots me a look, and I shrug. I don't know what's happening. All I know is I'm enjoying holding her.

"Sawyer! Reese," Max cheers when he sees us.

"Hey, buddy. What's going on tonight?" Sawyer pulls him in for a bro-hug.

I stand and do the same across the table.

"Pizza, pizza, pizza."

I can't help but match his laugh. It's contagious. "All the best things, then, man."

Tony passes out our slices and rests a hand on his brother's shoulder. "Don't be rude, Max. Greet the pretty ladies these two chumps are lucky enough to court around."

"Pretty! Pretty!"

"You remember my sister, Emma, and her friend, Laney?"

Max nods excitedly. Then he looks at Winnie, and his eyes get big. *Me too, buddy. Me too.*

"Red! Red!"

"Whoa, hold on there. This one is taken."

Winnie slaps my hand wrapped around her body. "I'm Winnie. It's nice to meet you, Max."

"Max! Max!" He points to himself, so happy that she knew his name. Then he begins to sing the theme song of the *Winnie the Pooh* movie, and a laugh falls from my lips. Winnie slaps me again. Her smile is friendly, but I know if it were anyone else, she wouldn't be smiling. She hates the comparisons, especially after losing her dad.

"Yeah, just like the bear." She giggles.

"Alright, kid. Let's let them eat."

Max complains, but Tony promises he can check on us in a bit, which seems to soothe him enough.

"He's sweet," Winnie says.

"Yeah, he is. Their parents passed away years ago, so Max was left to Tony to care for and raise."

"Oh, wow." Her lips puff out a small amount. "That's so sad."

I look over the booth to the two brothers now behind the counter. Max jokingly snaps Tony with the towel, and he pretends to get mad. It can't be easy, doing what Tony does and knowing there's no end to the care Max needs, but I commend him for it. He mentioned there being a few times he's caught people making fun of Max, and he's kicked them out, but if it were me heads would roll. How can you make fun of someone just because they are different than you? I'll never fucking understand.

"They make the best of it."

Winnie nods, seeing the same thing I am.

"Dig in." I squeeze her shoulder to turn her back around.

After the pizza, she seems even more sober, but she's still leaning against my chest, and I'm too afraid to bring attention to it. Sawyer stands and collects all our garbage with the help of Laney, and they carry it over to the trash cans across the room. Emma is hardly awake on her side of the table. How she hasn't noticed the tension between her friend and brother, I don't know. Maybe it's because I know what I know, but when Laney accidentally bumps into him, she jumps away—way further than necessary—and her cheeks bloom a deep red. They share a quick look, but she is gone and heading for the door before anything can be said. It's so painfully obvious now.

He stares after her for a long time, and his chest rises and falls as if he's letting out a deep breath.

"Emma," I call out, and Winnie jumps in my arms. She must have been sleeping, too, because now that she's awake, she quickly removes herself from against my body, leaving behind a chill.

"Ready?" Sawyer asks, only getting nods in return.

"Later, gators," I holler, waving to Max and Tony in the back.

"In a while, crocodile," Max shouts before he starts singing the *Winnie the Pooh* theme song again.

Winnie smiles and waves. "Bye, Max!"

I open my wallet and grab a twenty. Sawyer paid for the pizza, and it's a rule that whoever buys the food, the other is responsible for the tip, so I drop the cash on the table. Moving to fold up my wallet and put it away, I falter when Winnie snatches it from my hands.

"If you need money, baby. All you gotta do is ask." My smile falls when she doesn't pull out cash. Instead, she pulls out a photo.

Shit.

"What the hell is this?"

11

Reese

FLASHBACK

"What the fuck is happening in my house right now?" Elijah pushes open the door, and the music we could hear from outside blares louder.

The house isn't filled with people, and I don't think they would be playing The Supremes if they were having a party. I've come to love oldies, thanks to Mr. and Mrs. Lewis always blasting it when they cook, but I'm not sure "You Can't Hurry Love" is a party song, though maybe I'm wrong. I don't know what old people parties are like. I'm assuming they don't happen at four p.m. on a Tuesday, though.

"Tigger! Eeyore," Winnie shouts as soon as we step into their living room. I groan internally hearing that stupid nickname. Winnie hates when we call her Pooh or Pooh Bear like her parents do, so in order to get back at us, she gave us those nicknames. Eli doesn't seem to mind his, but I hate mine, so it worked. I don't call her Pooh, and she doesn't call me Eeyore—usually.

She throws herself at us in a double hug.

Mr. Lewis grins as he turns down the music. "She's still a bit loopy from the anesthetics."

Oh, that's right. I forgot she was getting her wisdom teeth out today.

"How you feeling, Win? Less wise?" Eli jokes and squeezes her.

She lets go of us and scowls, but it's a lost cause with how swollen her cheeks are. The white headband around her face isn't easy to take seriously.

Mrs. Lewis walks back in and kisses my and Elijah's cheek one at a time. Then she slaps the back of his head. "Be nice to your sister."

After wrapping his arms around Winnie, Mr. Lewis belts out "My Girl" at the top of his lungs, replacing "my girl" with her name.

Elijah joins his family in singing and dancing around, and I take my seat on the couch. I'm not going to sing and dance, but I can't lie and say I don't love being here to witness it. The Lewises are everything I want in a family. They remind me that true love exists, and with the right person by your side, all the happiness in the world is possible.

Winnie drops next to me and leans her head on my shoulder when the song is done.

"How you feeling, Win?"

"Tired. Hungry." She tilts her head up to look at me, her eyes glassed over and distant. "I love you, Reese."

That's the other difference between our families. I've only heard my mom utter those words once when she thought I was sleeping, and I've never heard my dad say them. It's not a common phrase in my house, but the Lewises say it all the time. It feels like any time someone leaves the room, they say it. It may be excessive to some, but I think it's nice to know how someone feels about you.

"Me too, Win." But it doesn't make it any easier to say, even when you feel it.

We settle into the couch and watch her parents put on a performance to "I Got You Babe," and eventually, she drifts to sleep, her head still on my shoulder.

Elijah drops onto the side chair and slides me a plate with a sandwich and some chips. Without moving Winnie too much, I grab it and bring the sandwich to my lips.

"Oh, look," Mrs. Lewis cries with a smile. "Stay."

Like I have a choice.

A second later, she returns with their old Polaroid camera.

"Smile like you like being here, son." Mr. Lewis chuckles.

They let me swallow, and I listen, leaning my head on top of Winnie's and smiling.

Mrs. Lewis shakes the photo out and shows Mr. Lewis before handing it to me. "You can keep that one. I think Winnie would be upset if I hung it up."

It's not the greatest photo she's ever taken, but I think it's cute.

"I'll put it in my wallet. She'll never see it."

12

Winnie

"Reese?" I repeat when he doesn't answer me the first time. "What is this?"

"What does it look like, Win? It's a photo."

"Why—How? Why do you have this in your wallet? How did you even get it?" I have never, ever seen such a horrendous photo of me. Even with the faded quality of the Polaroid, there's no denying it's the worst. Granted, I was thirteen and had just gotten all four wisdom teeth out, but still. Mouth hung open, cheeks swollen beyond belief, and that stupid wrap around my head. It even looks like Reese's shirt is wet with my drool.

He looks cute, at least. His sandy-brown hair is shaggy and plastered to his forehead from his backward cap pushing it down. His smile is wide, and blue braces stick to each tooth. I can't deny this is a cute photo, even if I look awful. I just don't understand why he has it in his wallet, and judging by the prominent folds in it, I would say it's been here a while. Like since it was taken.

Why does he make it so hard to hate him?

"Your mom took it," he tells me. "She told me to keep it somewhere you wouldn't see. I thought my wallet was a safe place, and it was. Until now."

I can't pull my eyes away from the image. It's a terrible angle, but it's not the photo itself that is making my heart beat a little faster and goosebumps erupt across my body. It's the fact he kept it this entire time.

I head for Sawyer's truck, but I don't get in. Reese stops behind me, not touching me, but he might as well be for the nerves bouncing around inside me right now.

"I can't believe you haven't gotten a new wallet in nine years."

"I have."

I pause, looking over my shoulder. Reese pinches at the back of his neck. A boyish, almost nervous grin tugging on his full lips.

"What?"

"I have," he repeats. "Like three times. I just put it back every time."

Damn it all. *Damn him.* I turn, and he drops his arm. His face is indifferent, and when I step closer, he stiffens.

I tried to be strong and stay away. I really did.

"I really hate you for not letting me hate you."

His grin is back, and before he can say something cocky, I throw myself at him. He grabs my face and pulls our lips together. The moment they meet, I throw everything to the wind. His lips are soft but demanding. And he kisses me like he can't get enough, which is exactly how I feel. I crawl up his body, and he lifts me with ease and pushes me against the bed of the truck.

"Fuck, Winnie."

Fuck indeed. If we weren't in public right now, and I didn't want to end up in jail, I think I would fuck him. And that's scary.

Ignoring the red flags blaring in the distance, I wrap my arms around his neck, making sure not to knock off his backward cap, and press myself into his hard body.

His tongue dives into my mouth, battling with mine until I give in and let him do whatever he wants with me. The air is cold, but my body is on fire.

Reese pulls away but keeps our heads together. Our heavy breaths creating a fog between us. "How drunk are you right now?"

"Drunk enough to want to fuck you in this street. Not drunk enough to not remember this in the morning."

He groans and leans back in, murmuring, "that's the perfect amount," against my lips.

Slipping his hand between us, he tugs his sweatshirt up enough to tease the top of my jeans, but he doesn't get any further. "Fuck, why are you wearing a belt, Win?"

"So I couldn't be pantsed tonight." I pull away and scowl, but it's not easy when all I want to do is kiss him again.

"Smart girl. But now you *want* to be pantsed, and I can't."

I unwrap my legs and drop back to the ground. "Speaking of... I saw the post."

His eyebrows knit with confusion. "What post?"

"On EU Student News. Laney showed me. Emma mentioned they also have a newspaper, but I didn't see those."

Realization hits, and a cycle of surprise, anger, guilt, and back to anger flicks across his handsome face. "Fuck, I forgot they post online. Shit. I'm sorry, Win. I'm sure you could press charges for posting your nude ass without your permission."

"Reese." I grab him, noticing him starting to spiral. "It's fine. A new post goes up Sunday, and me and my ass will be forgotten."

"I highly doubt that. But let's get home, I'm fucking freezing."

Oh, shit. I totally forgot he gave me his sweatshirt. I go to pull it off, but he grips my arms. "Don't even think of taking that off—or giving it back. I want you to keep it." He drops his hand into mine and drags me around the side of the truck.

"Reese, I have a million sweatshirts. I don't need—"

The cold metal bites through my layers as Reese pins me against the truck door. The heat burning from his body is quick to balance it, though.

"You don't have any of mine, Win."

Well, that's not true, but he probably doesn't remember all the ones he used to lend me and I never gave back. I know of at least four of Reese's sweatshirts hanging in my closet right now and another two at home under my bed.

"And besides"—he tugs open the door and helps me up, which he doesn't need to do since there's only a small lift on Sawyer's truck, but I think it's an excuse to touch my ass—"you'll need something to wear to my games."

He shuts the door in my face, not giving me a chance to reply. Not that I know what I would say anyway. I don't know what we are right now, and I hadn't thought about going to his games at all. Okay, that's not exactly true, but I figured if I wanted to go, I would sit in the back so there wouldn't be a chance of him seeing me. Eli and Reese's hockey games used to be my favorite things to go see. I never cared that they were every weekend and always looked forward to going. I haven't been to a game since before my dad died, and I would love to see him play again, but if I go, especially if I wear a sweatshirt with his name and number on the back, what is that going to tell him?

What is that going to tell *me*?

Reese helps me out and tucks me into his side. I don't know if it's for his pleasure or if he's using me for heat, but I don't mind either way. Tonight, I'm not going to think too hard about anything. I'm going to enjoy what's left of the night and deal with all the regret, guilt, and whatever else comes tomorrow when I wake.

Sawyer, Emma, and Laney all move in close to me until I'm surrounded entirely.

"Uh, guys, I know it's cold, but the door is right there."

"Shh," Reese mutters and quickly drops a kiss to the top of my head before tugging his hood over my face.

"Hey, Mark," Reese chimes, but he has such a tight hold on me that I can't even see who Mark is.

"Good evening, kids. Have a good night?"

Emma and Laney groan some kind of answer, and the man laughs.

"Oh, to be young again."

"Have a good one," Sawyer calls next.

The elevator dings, and Reese pulls me inside.

"The five of you have a good night, too."

Reese's arms relax. He and Sawyer chuckle, and I'm able to finally see the security guard grinning at us.

He offers a wave, and I give one back before the doors close.

"We're not meant to bring people who don't live here in after midnight," Sawyer answers my unasked questions.

"I can go home?" I offer, even though I really don't want to, but it might be the smart thing to do before I do more than kiss Reese. "Catch an Uber or something."

Sawyer shoots a look at Reese, and he frowns.

"You're not going anywhere."

"I don't want to get you in trouble."

Reese moves forward, crowding me against the steel elevator wall. "The only trouble I'm planning on getting into anytime soon is you, baby."

"Awe, you guys *are* cute," Emma says.

Reese and I reply at the same time.

"Not cute."

"Extremely cute."

Reese's hand cradles my back during the walk from the elevator to the apartment. Apparently, it was Sawyer's apartment I was in the other night. Reese sets me on the couch and promises to be back in a second before disappearing across the hall. I don't know why he didn't bring me to his place. Maybe he's trying not to pressure me? Unfortunately, I think the low tingle in my belly is disappointment. Do I *want* him to pressure me? Maybe. It wouldn't be pressure if I wanted it, though, would it? I sort of wish someone could make decisions for me. Tell me yes, sleep with Reese. That's a great idea. Or ask, are you completely stupid? Do you want your heart broken again?

Ugh.

I'm still too drunk for this decision, even if I don't feel very drunk anymore.

The couch bounces, and when I open my eyes, I meet the green orbs of a stranger.

"Uh, hi?"

"So you're the ass."

"Excuse me?"

"On the newspaper."

Oh. Right. Okay, there is one point for not sleeping with Reese. If I'm permanently known around campus as "the ass," I'm going to kill him. "Well, I prefer Winnie, but yeah, that was me."

He dips his chin casually. "Nice ass."

"Er, thanks..."

Sawyer falls on the opposite side of me, breathless. Emma and Laney must have drank more than me for how exhausted he seems right now. However, I think they have the right idea about going to bed. *Where the hell is Reese?* And where the hell am I sleeping? In his bed? Or did he put me on the couch as a way to say this was my bed for the night? Maybe he's getting blankets. Hopefully a sheet, too, because this is a boy's apartment, and I'm not about to lay my face on a couch that looks like it's been through hell and back. Sitting, okay. Sleeping without a sheet? No, thank you.

"Leave her alone, Boog. Reese catches you complimenting his girl's ass, and he's going to release The Rapture on you."

He called me "his girl," like as in Reese's girl. Neither of the guys seem surprised I'm here, and I saw the hint of a smile on Sawyer's face after we climbed into the truck after kissing. Reese must have been talking about me. Okay, one point pro-sex.

This is going to be difficult.

"What's *The Rapture*?" I ask, hoping changing the subject from my ass and the whole *his girl* comment will help clear my head. And calm down my beating heart.

Sawyer cocks an eyebrow, and the guy whose name I still don't know whistles a low sound. "You're in for a treat, eh, Saw? What you say we crack on some old film?"

But Sawyer's too busy looking at his phone to reply. Not that I am trying to snoop, but I can't help but look to see who he is texting at this hour.

> **Larsy:** I need you to distract her for a few minutes.

Her? Me? It's obvious Reese is texting him. I've heard him be called Larsy by hockey friends before. What I don't get is why Reese is asking Sawyer to distract me.

My head swims with the different possibilities of why he would need me distracted. What is he doing over there? Maybe it's something as simple as showering, or maybe he's trying to clean his room, but Reese was always a clean guy, so unless that has changed, it doesn't really make sense.

"Yeah." Sawyer drops his phone to his lap after typing out a reply I didn't see. "Let's show her The Rapture."

Apparently, "The Rapture" is Reese destroying guys on the ice. I remember him always being more aggressive than others, but this is a whole new level than what I'm used to seeing. He's throwing guys around like they weigh nothing and ramming into them at full force, and it's so... *hot.*

The way he uses his powerful body against his opponents for one goal and one goal alone is like foreplay. I wish he would throw me around like that. Okay, maybe not exactly like that, but if he can rock two-hundred-pound men, surely he could toss me around a little. He held me like I weighed nothing when we were kissing, but I didn't even realize it. Seeing this, I have a whole new respect for his beautiful body.

The guys *ooh* and *aah* and make their comments about different parts of the game, but I can hardly pull my eyes away from Reese long enough to notice what else is happening. Despite the aggression, he's so graceful. He makes skating look easy, and I know it's not. He and Eli used to drag me to the local pond every winter, so I know how to skate. I'm just not very good, and considering it's been years since I've touched ice at all, I'm guessing I'm even worse than I remember.

By the time Reese walks through the door, I'm shifting in my seat, the need for Reese between my thighs getting worse each passing second. To feel him touch me, hold me, and hopefully toss me around.

He's breathing hard, but he zeros in on me and tilts his head. "What's wrong? Your face is flushed."

Shut up, Reese! "Uh..."

The couch shakes as the guys next to me chuckle. "The effect of The Rapture," Sawyer comments, a hint of knowing in his voice.

Reese continues across the room, eyeing me curiously. His gaze snaps to the TV, and the biggest grin stretches across his face. And just like I wanted, he lifts me, takes my seat, and sets me on his lap like I weigh *nothing*. I think if he offered to carry me everywhere for the rest of my life, it would be extremely difficult to say no.

We watch in complete silence for a few more minutes, and my squirming only gets worse feeling his hard dick under my ass.

Reese and I have had sex, but I didn't pay attention to his dick size when we did because I was so nervous. I honestly don't remember a lot of it because I was so wrapped up in thinking "is this really happening" the entire time. But the rod under my ass is *huge*. I have no clue how it ever fit in my body—or how it's going to again.

Reese pulls me against his chest and drops his hand to the inside of my thigh while kissing the base of my ear. "If you keep squirming, I'm going to give you something to really squirm about."

I'm certainly willing to try.

13

Reese

Winnie's whimpers are the best sound I've ever heard. Her hand flies to her mouth, and she shoots a desperate look back at me.

I flick my eyes to Sawyer, and seeing the heat behind mine, he dips his chin and makes a scene about being tired and how he has to get to bed. I felt the same until I walked in here and saw Winnie looking like she just ran three miles. Turns out my girl was just horned up from seeing me dominate.

The guys have always mentioned how girls thought it was hot, but I never cared because they weren't Winnie. Knowing she thinks me wrecking guys on the ice is hot makes me want to throw down with my friends right now. See how horny I can make her without even touching her. But my dick is hard and throbbing, and I'm not giving either guy the opportunity to see her come.

"Ready for bed. What about you?" Sawyer's asking Beckett, but I answer as if it's directed to me.

"Nah, not yet."

Winnie shimmies her ass, and I clamp on to her hips, halting her movements. The need to come burns low in my back, and if she doesn't stop, we are going to have a mess on our hands.

"Beckett," Sawyer snaps.

"What? Nah, man, the game is just getting good."

Fucking hell, Boog.

I knock my knee into his. It's not a secret to Winnie that I'm trying to get rid of them. I think she's at the point that if I didn't make them leave, she would.

"What?" Beckett looks back at me, and I nod toward Winnie, who is pretending to watch the game, but I can feel the heat radiating from her pussy. It's driving me mad. He looks up to her and then back to me. His eyes drop momentarily to my dick pressing against my shorts, and his jaw slacks. "Actually, yeah. Bed. So tired."

He trails after Sawyer, only dispersing when they get to their rooms.

Winnie sags against me, and her legs fall open on either side of me. I drag my hand from her thigh up to cup her pussy over her jeans.

"Fuuuuck, baby. Your jeans are soaked."

"I'm so horny."

Fuck. Me.

What I wouldn't give to plow into her right now, but I've been waiting for this moment for so fucking long, I can't just jump into it. She might have worked herself up watching me play, but I didn't get to partake in any of the fun of making the mess in her pants.

And that's not okay.

Winnie

Forget the point system. If Reese stops touching me right now, I'm going to explode.

"Take these jeans off, baby. Let me see you."

I scramble off his lap because, right now, I don't care how desperate I look or sound. I turn so I can see his face and am happy with how desperate he looks too. His dick is hard as he strokes his hand up and down over his shorts.

"Now, Winnie." His jaw tenses, and he flicks his heated eyes to me. "Please."

I work at my fanny pack, belt, and, finally, jeans until I'm able to push them down my thighs.

"I appreciate you being a nice guy, but right now, I want you to boss me around and—" I bite my lip, not believing what's about to come out of my mouth, but when he leans forward, lifts his sweatshirt off my body, and drops a kiss to my bare stomach while still looking at me, I blurt it out. "I want you to use The Rapture on me."

His lashes flutter, and he pulls back, a smile on his face that tenses my stomach. His usually hazel eyes are nearly black when they meet mine. "You really shouldn't have said that, baby. I'm not the boy I was when we had sex the first time." He pushes to his full height, now towering over me. "I'm a man—a hungry one. And the only thing I want to eat right now"—his gaze drops down my body—"is you."

14

Reese

She takes off running, and for a moment, I'm stunned, wondering if I said something wrong and scared her, but she looks over her shoulder and smiles once she reaches the door.

Need burns inside me as I prowl toward her. Right when she's out of arm's reach, she throws the door open and slips into the hall. I glance back at her stuff on their floor, but I'll grab it later. Right now I have to catch a bear cub who wants to play with the big bad wolf.

The guys are going to regret being home tonight for how loud I plan on making Winnie scream. And I hope the guys on my floor got their beauty sleep already because if I can help it, we will be at this for hours.

Winnie is nowhere to be seen when I throw the door open, but Schmidt and Gavin stare at me with wide eyes.

"Having a good night?" Gavin asks.

"It's about to get a lot better." I grin. "You two might want to crash across the hall tonight."

"Roger that, captain." He offers a sloppy salute. "But in the morning, I want to officially meet the half-naked girl running through my dorm."

"Deal, now get out."

They both groan, but Schmidt slaps my back on the way by. "Don't forget a condom." The door slams behind me, and the place falls silent.

I hadn't been thinking about wearing a condom. I was going to, though, obviously. *Right?* Of course. We're still young, and Winnie just started college. We're in no place to bring a baby into the world.

But...

The cutest giggle rings out from the hallway, and I shake the thought away. Condom or no condom, what's it really matter when we start a family? Because I knew it was always going to be Winnie.

I trail across the room to the hall. Winnie stands in the middle, playing with the hem of her tank top and biting her lip.

"I didn't know which one was your bedroom."

"End of the hall."

She bobs her head a few times and takes three steps backward until her ass hits the door. It creaks open, and her bottom lip disappears between her teeth before she dips inside. Out of sight.

I suck in a shaky breath and prowl forward.

Winnie Lewis lying in my bed, half-naked and wet for me, is everything porn should be made of. She's like the wettest of wet dreams, and the best part is it's not even a dream. I know that because my dick is painfully hard in my shorts, and there's no pain in dreams.

I drop a knee on the foot of my bed, tug on my shirt, and pull it over my head. My hat drops to the ground behind it.

Winnie's eyes fly to my bare chest, then dance around my abs while I crawl up the bed. With a hesitant hand, she brushes over my pec when I'm in reach. I shudder at her cold hands, and she giggles a breathy sound.

"Sorry."

"Please don't ever apologize for touching me."

Her fingers are like ice, but they're burning my skin in the best way. Up and down my abdomen. She traces each dent in my abs, but when she skims the band of my shorts, my dick fucking leaps, and her eyes blow wide.

"Sorry," I grunt. "It's been a while."

She swallows hard but nods. "Me too. I, uh... I haven't done *this* since... you know."

I don't let my hopes rise just yet. "You haven't had sex since we did?"

She shakes her head.

Thank fuck. I knew there was a chance Winnie would move on and find another guy. Maybe even get into a relationship, and that would have really blown.

"That's good." I lean down but still support my weight as I brush my lips over her soft ones. "Me either."

Winnie's hand stiffens on my stomach, and she pushes me to sit back. "You haven't had sex in two years?"

I shake my head.

"At all?"

"No."

Her brows knit and her hand falls from my body. "Well, why not?"

Is she really asking me this? When will this girl understand? "Isn't it obvious, Win? It's you. It's *always* been you. Why would I fuck around, waste my time and other girls' time, when I knew this"—I grind my hips against hers—"was inevitable."

When she doesn't reply, I take that as a sign to move on from this conversation and continue down the road we were on. I lean down and press my lips to hers, but she doesn't kiss me back. I pull back and scowl.

"What's wrong now?"

"You," she blurts. "You're just, I don't know. I just." She lets out a frustrated breath. "You have sex with me, then you leave me. Two years later, you're here claiming your love for me, and it's, I don't know. A lot, I guess."

I push back onto my knees and pull her to sit up with me. "Hey." I take her chin and tilt her head up. "I know, okay? I know it's a lot. But, Win, I didn't *want* to leave you two years ago. It doesn't make it better, but I've thought about you every day since, and when I saw you in the store, it was like no time had passed."

"But it did pass, Reese. A lot of time. Time I spent crying myself to sleep because you weren't picking up my calls, answering my messages, or visiting like you promised. You say you thought about me for two years, but why couldn't you send me a text? Anything so I knew you felt what I did that night."

She's right. I was a coward, but that's not a good enough reason, not that there is one. "I don't know, Win."

She scoffs, but I don't let her pull away.

"I know that's a shit fucking answer, but it's the only one I have. I don't know why I ghosted you without so much as a text. I guess... I guess I was scared."

"Why were you scared?"

"I didn't know what love was. When you grow up with parents like I had, any big emotions scare you because you don't know what they are. I knew I loved you, but I didn't know what that meant. I always thought I would go to college and meet my soulmate, but after that night, that didn't seem like a great plan anymore because my soulmate was right there in front of me. I don't know why I walked away without a goodbye. Maybe because I knew I wouldn't be able to give you one."

Her eyes bounce between mine until, eventually, she sighs and tugs me back on top of her. "I don't know if I believe you. I don't know where we go after this night. But I do know that if I don't come in the next ten minutes, I'm going to start crying."

A hesitant grin tugs on my lips. "Now, *that* I can manage." I drop onto her body, still not giving her my full weight but enough she grunts with the pressure. "You might not be sure yet, but I am. I love you, Winnie. Always have, always will."

Her eyes close, and she doesn't answer, but she pulls my lips to hers and I soak in the words she doesn't say. I know nothing I say is going to make her believe me, and I appreciate her hesitancy to trust me. It shows how smart she is. If it takes a month, two, or the entire school year to prove to Winnie that I love her, then fuck it. That's what I'll do.

Starting with fucking her how I should have two years ago.

Winnie

A million different thoughts zip through my head like angry hornets but are silenced at once by Reese's lips. He watches my expression with a dark look as he drags feverish kisses down my throat, cleavage, and lower.

I lift my hips, craving any kind of friction, and find his thigh. Better than nothing. I grind up and down, and he grunts, hitting low in my ear and adding to the dampness between my legs that is no doubt leaving behind a spot on his green shorts.

He tugs on my tank top, and I help him remove it and toss it to the ground.

Stiff peaks on the end of my small breasts beg for his attention, and he gives it to them. First with his fingers, and then he clamps his lips over one of them, and I gasp. I've never had anyone play with my nipples in this way, but the sensation is almost too much.

His name falls from my lips before I can help it, and he sucks on my already sensitive skin.

"You have no idea how fucking good it sounds hearing you moan my name."

"Probably not as good as it feels when you do that." I arch into his touch.

He rips a whimper from me when he pinches my nipple. It stings, but it's good.

Nerves bloom as he moves down my body, and my skin pricks. He pauses at my thong, and I suck in a ragged breath before nodding, answering his unasked question. My heart thunders in my chest, waiting.

With painstaking slowness, he hooks his thumbs into my thong, drags the damp fabric down my legs, and drops it next to the other discarded clothes on the floor. I cross my ankles, but he pries them apart to move between them. Hard eyes drop to the V between my thighs, and he groans. Loudly.

"Fuuuck, Winnie. Of course you're fucking bare." He drops onto his hands and lowers his face. Darkness swirls as I pinch my eyes closed and squirm, waiting for his touch, but it doesn't come. I peek an eye open to find him scowling at my pussy.

"You're making me self-conscious, Reese."

"Why are you bare?"

Huh? "What do you mean *why*? I shaved."

"Today?"

"Obviously."

"When you knew you were going out?" His eyebrow lifts in a challenge. "Why the fuck did you shave to go out? Who did you plan on seeing your pussy?"

I stare at him because what the hell else am I meant to do when he sounds crazy? I have to admit hearing the word *pussy* from his mouth is sexy, though.

"You know women shave for more reasons than just sex, right?"

Apparently, he doesn't because his harsh stare doesn't budge.

"Basic hygiene... Comfort...?" *Nothing.* "What if I tell you I shaved because I was worried someone was going to pants me again?"

That seems to do the trick. He rolls his eyes and lowers his body onto mine, then kisses me, hard.

"I'm the only guy who gets to see your pussy. Tell me, Winnie."

I'll tell him anything if he keeps kissing me how he is.

"That depends."

He nips at my lip and then laps at my neck. Stinging bites soothed by deep kisses. "On what," he growls.

"If you leave me again."

"Never. Fuck." He thrusts his hips, and I gasp when his dick—still behind his shorts—rubs against my pussy. "I'm yours for life, baby."

Reese's thrusts feel good, but it's not enough. Need burns deep in my body, and I know a little dry humping isn't going to be enough to curb the appetite only he can satisfy.

Dragging my fingers down his hard body, I slip one under his smooth gym shorts. He breathes a shuttering breath against my face, and I pull his lips back to mine. "Take them off, Reese. Please."

"You keep begging like that and I'll do fucking any-thing."

He shifts off me and climbs off the bed, hooks his shorts, and pushes them down his legs. My mouth gapes.

His laugh booms in the small room. "I want that reaction every time I disrobe around you."

"I don't remember it being that big."

As he climbs back onto the bed, I can't take my eyes off the thing swinging between his legs. "I don't think it's going to fit, Reese."

He presses his lips to mine and grins. "Mm-hmm, keep going."

His eyes are half-mast, but he's watching between us as I get closer to touching him. I brush a single finger against the tip, and he grunts with pleasure. Swallowing down the knot in my throat, I wrap my hand around the shaft.

"Shit, Win." He hisses.

"Does that feel good?" My eyebrows pinch; I'm hardly touching him. I've not watched much porn, but I've seen enough to know that when guys jack themselves off, it looks painful. Like they are fighting with it. Yet all I'm doing is holding it, and he has that *look* in his eye.

"So *fucking good*."

Well, okay then. I wonder if I—

He clamps a hand around mine. Teeth clenched. "Seriously, Win. Two years."

Two years? Oh. *Oh*. It feels *good*, not just good.

Giggling, I pull him down and kiss his cheek. "Did you mean it when you said you haven't been with anyone besides me?"

He blows out a sharp breath against my face. "Of course I meant that, why?"

I shrug. "It's hard to believe you went two whole years with nothing."

"Hey, now. Don't disrespect my hand like that. He's not the best worker, but he tries really hard."

I snort a laugh and drop my head to his chest. "Maybe it's not that hard to believe."

He nips at my chin, and then it's his turn for his hands to explore. With my legs already parted, it's easy for him to slip a finger into my pussy. I whimper at the unfamiliar pressure. Not only have I not had sex in two years, but I haven't had anything else in my vagina since then either. I am able to come on clit stimulation alone, and the feeling of something inside me is... euphoric. But it's also tight, and knowing his dick is at least twice the size of his finger, I know it's not going to be easy.

"You're so fucking wet, Win. I bet I could just slip right inside."

Well, I don't know about that...

"I'm nervous," I admit. Reese pulls away to read my face, confusion knitting his brow.

"Why?"

"I've not had anything in there since. I'm basically a virgin again."

He breathes out a low, almost relieved breath. "I can work with that."

Reese flips us by falling to his back and tugging me on top. My head is spinning, and by the time I settle, there's a new pressure between my legs. Reese's dick is settled under me. His angry cockhead poking out. I swallow hard and look up to meet his eyes. He watches me with a hard, hungry stare.

"Okay." His voice is tight. "Now move."

"Like? With it like this?"

It's obvious Reese is struggling to stay in the moment, lost in how good it feels without us even moving. His dick is warm, long, and hard, and pressing perfectly against my clit.

He nods and breathes out, "Yeah."

I plant my hands on his chest and roll my hips. His lashes flutter closed, and the sound that erupts from deep in his throat is enough to push me to the edge of an orgasm. I don't remember him making many noises the last time because we had to be quiet, but I'm a huge, huge fan of this.

He cups my hips painfully hard but lets me control the movement while grunting out a mix of cuss words and my name every few seconds. I know he has to be close, and so am I, but we're not even having sex.

Wetness grows between us, a mixture of mine and his. I bet he would so easily slip in now. And with that thought in mind, I lean forward and press my lips to his eager ones. He eats me like he can't get enough.

I lift just enough to let his dick tease my entrance.

Desire rushes through my veins, but he grips my hips and halts me from moving any more. "Baby," he begs. "You are testing every single fiber of what little self-control I have when you're around."

"Sorry," I breathe, not really sorry at all. It's so hot how he's struggling. I tease him a little more by pushing just the tip inside. It hurts, but it's not unmanageable.

He groans, dropping his head back and opening his neck for me, and I take the opportunity to suck on his tender skin. His moans deepen, and until now, he's let me have control, moving how I want, but his hips flex, and he pulls out and lets out a sharp breath.

"Winnie," he growls. "I'm a twenty-year-old man who hasn't had his dick wet in two years, and my dream girl is sitting naked on my lap and playing just the tip. I promise if you keep teasing, it's not going to end well for your pussy."

I pull back and stare into his honey eyes, his pupils so big they almost look black. I half expect to see his usual crooked smile, but he's never looked so serious. Almost like he's in pain.

"Show me." I shimmy my hips a little, and he slips in a centimeter more. I know I'm not even close to taking the entire length of him.

He's hesitant to take the lead, probably worried about how I'm going to handle it when he finally breaks, but I want it. I want everything Reese Larson can give me.

I bring my lips to his ear. "Fuck me, Reese. *Please.*"

15

Reese

If I were a better man, I would take it slow with Winnie since it's been so long and she's still unsure about us, but I'd like to meet the man who could say no to a naked and begging Winnie Lewis. I take in her beautiful body—red nipples hard and begging for attention, and how wet her fucking pussy is—and know even pretending I'm going to say no is a waste of time.

I hook her waist and throw her onto the mattress, falling on top of her in the same motion and taking her lips. Gripping my dick, I line back up with her opening. I pull back just enough to watch her face because I'm not going to miss a fucking second of it.

Inch by inch, she takes my dick like it was made to be inside her. I know I'm not a small guy, and hearing Winnie's whimpers, moans, and grunts until I'm seated inside her makes me feel like a fucking king. Balls deep, I don't move, even if my body is tingling for me to fuck her senseless. I know Winnie needs a moment to get used to the invasion.

I've spent two years fucking my fist and pretending it was once again her pussy, and now that I'm inside her, it doesn't even hold a candle. It's not just the feel of her tight little body squeezing me but the look of adoration on her face and the way my chest is squeezing knowing I finally have my girl back. Maybe not completely, but if Winnie didn't want anything to do with me, she wouldn't be in my bed right now. Call me selfish for taking advantage of her draw to me, but no other guy in the world will treat her as good as I will.

My love for Winnie runs deep. Sex will never just be sex between us.

When her tense body relaxes, I pull almost all the way out and slowly sink back in. I nearly black out from how good it feels being inside her again. I had no clue what I was doing two years ago, and I might not be any more experienced, but I know what feels good. Plus, I can read Winnie's body like an open book. She likes my slow thrusts, but they aren't getting her where she needs. Which is good, because me either.

"I'm going to fuck you how I should have two years ago, and you're going to take every inch of me, okay?"

She nods quickly. "Okay."

I pull out, and this time, I slam into her tight body with everything I can. She slips up the soft sheets, and her gasp is loud as she takes all of me. Her short nails dig into my back, but her legs wrap around my waist, holding me deep inside of her.

Breathing in her heady need is enough to make me want to come already. I've waited two years for this, so it's not like I was going to last long anyway.

Thrust after thrust, I pound into her, and her nails sink further into my skin. It's a good thing I sent my buddies across the hall because, fuck, Winnie is loud. Next to her yelling and our hips snapping together, there was no way anyone would be able to sleep or concentrate on anything but what is happening in this room. Guess my roommate's fucked-up sleep schedule is finally coming in handy.

"Reese, I'm gonna... gonna..."

Her pussy flutters, and the tingle I've been fighting off rises to the surface. "Come for me, pretty girl."

Not a second later, Winnie buries her face into my neck and cries out as she comes all over me.

Fuuuuuck.

"Winnie, I have to come. Where do you want it?"

She's breathing hard, her eyes closed, and I'm not even sure she's awake anymore. Then she mutters, "Inside me. Where else?"

I drop a kiss on her shoulder, then open my mouth and sink my teeth into the same place I just kissed. My body burns with the need to cum. Thrusting my hips forward, I sink as deep as I can inside her tight body and let go.

She squirms lazily under me as I collapse on top of her and press a gentle kiss to her pouty lips. "I love you, Winnie Lewis."

Eyes still closed, she smiles and tightens her hold on me but doesn't reply. Not that I expected her to.

Who knows what morning will bring, but right now, still balls deep inside my girl, I roll us to the side and drift to sleep perfectly content with life.

16

Winnie

Morning comes way before I'm ready for it. I didn't look at the clock after we got to the apartments, but I swear the sun was rising when my eyes finally drifted closed. Now looking at the clock on his nightstand, it's ten thirty. My first class isn't until one today, and it's my photography class, so I actually don't want to skip it, even though I feel like absolute ass.

Why do people continue drinking if this is how they feel when they wake up? I didn't even drink that much, but my head is throbbing. Reese's heavy arm is pinning me to the bed, but I slip from it and immediately shiver from the temperature difference of Reese's body against mine and the cool air of his apartment. I pad to the bathroom attached to his room with the sudden urge to pee.

As soon as I cross the threshold, I meet my reflection in the mirror and cringe. It's good to know I look as bad as I feel. Gathering some water in my hands, I splash it onto my face without making too much of a mess. My hair looks like it hasn't been combed in days, and I'm guessing Reese's hair isn't long enough for him to have a brush, so I pull the hair tie from my wrist and toss it up. It's a problem for later.

Sighing, I drop my hands to the sink and stare at myself again. Despite feeling and looking like shit, something makes me want to smile. Maybe it's the fact I had an actual girls' night last night and experienced my first club, or maybe it's the snoring man in the next room.

I close my eyes and shake my head, but there's no denying my happiness when I think about Reese—more so all the things he said and did to me.

It's you, Win.

I spent so many days wondering what Reese was doing at college. *Who* he was doing. As much as I tried not to think about it, it was always in the back of my mind. Reese is hot. No, hotter than hot. And he plays hockey and looks so sexy doing it. So who knew this whole time, the answer was the same as me—no one. He could be lying; I'm not completely naive. But Reese has never lied to me before, and I'd like to believe that's still true.

The question comes, though. What are we? I know what he wants—*everything*—but what do I want?

Of course, it would be easy to accept what is and be together, even if there is still hurt here. I trust him when he says he's sorry. Does it make it better? No, nothing can ever take away that heartache, but I would be lying if I said there's no chance of us being together. I missed Reese, plain and simple. And spending the night with him last night reminded me just how much. But there are a few things that need to be discussed before any relationship talk. One being my brother.

I'd love to say his opinion on who I date doesn't matter, but it does. Especially if that person is Reese. He would see it as a personal attack.

Maybe I'm foolish for thinking of my brother's needs over my own or Reese's, but he took our dad's death really hard. It wasn't easy on anyone, but I saw a complete shift in character with him. Mom still hasn't fully recovered either, but the soulless look in Elijah's eyes is something I'll never get used to.

After our dad died, he was really distant from the entire family, and we are only now getting back to a place even close to where we were before. The way he reacted after finding out Reese and I slept together in the past will only be a blip of what it would be if he found out about last night. Sex is one thing, especially in Elijah's head, but admitting to real feelings? I worry I would lose my brother forever.

Feeling something slick between my thighs, I look down, worrying that maybe I started my period. And what unfortunate timing that would be. But there's no red; it's just clear. And that's when the rest of last night comes crashing back.

He didn't wear a condom. And he didn't pull out.

Where do you want it?

Inside me. Where else?

I cringe. How could I think that was a good idea? I'm going to blame the alcohol and sex brain, because I'm not on birth control.

I got off it a year ago because I wasn't having sex, and it wasn't doing me any favors. My body didn't like it, and since my sex life was nonexistent, I didn't feel the need to get back on. My stomach rolls, churning the pizza and alcohol from last night.

The thought of us getting pregnant never crossed my mind in that moment. I was so worried about the act itself and him fitting that I forgot what can come from sex. A baby.

Holy shit, what if I'm pregnant after the second time having sex?

What is Reese going to say? Of course, he seems sure about us now, but will a baby change that? I wish I could force myself to throw up just to get rid of the sick feeling in my stomach.

I really wish I had a friend I could talk to about this right now.

Emma and Laney are right across the hall. We're not that close, but the only other people I would talk to about this is the possible dad, and I'm not ready for all that. My brother—that's not even an option. I could call my mom, but I've been at college for less than a month. Calling to tell her I could have possibly gotten pregnant last night isn't something I really want to do, even if I oddly think she would be happy after the initial shock. She loves Reese and admitted to me once before that she wished we would get together because she would love to have him as a son-in-law.

Reese's homelife bothered Mom more than she let on. She doesn't know as much as I do, but there was one night I broke down and spilled just how awful his parents were. He doesn't know I ever told her, but I think after that night, Mom hugged him even tighter than usual.

I quickly wash my hands and sneak back into Reese's room for clothes, praying he's still sleeping. I grab his shorts and a shirt off the floor because they are the closest and tiptoe out of the room and into the hall.

I don't know how heavy of sleepers his roommates are or when they have classes, but when I round the corner into the open living room and kitchen, I find it doesn't matter. They are both sitting at the table eating cereal while scrolling on their phones—or they were until I walked out.

Schmidt, I think I remember his name being, leans back and grins. "Good night?"

I assume his comment is directed at my clothes and the fact neither the shirt nor shorts I have to hold up are mine and praying it's not because he heard us or anything. Reese kicked them out, but I don't know when they came back.

"Uh, yep."

I walk to the door, hoping I don't look how I feel, but the other unfamiliar guy stops me.

"I'm Gavin. The third and best roommate."

"Winnie," I blurt out before pulling open their door and stepping through it. I lean against it, catching my breath before moving any further. *Calm down, Win. You're not pregnant. Probably not. There's a chance you're not. Maybe he's sterile.* No, I won't wish that on him, but if he were, then my heart wouldn't be threatening to beat from my chest.

Music plays from down the hall, and before someone comes out, I rush over and pray the door isn't locked. Relief washes through me when the handle turns, and I push through but make sure not to let the door slam behind me.

Sawyer sits shirtless on the couch, a plate on his lap and some kind of food held halfway to his mouth. He flicks a look at the TV, and I follow his gaze.

"Shut up, Winnie," he says before I have a chance to say anything about him watching *One Tree Hill*.

Biting back my smile, I ask, "Is Emma or Laney here?"

"Emma's not. But Laney is in the shower." His jaw clenches before he shoves the food into his mouth, still scowling.

"What are you eating?"

"Spaghetti." He doesn't bother chewing before answering; luckily, I grew up with Elijah and am used to that.

"On... toast?"

He shoves the rest of the toast and spaghetti into his mouth and nods.

"Okay..."

An awkward moment passes between us while I wait for him to finish chewing and swallow. The room is completely silent until the theme song of *One Tree Hill* breaks it. I fight back my smile, but I know he can see it growing on my face, and he's not happy about it.

"I like to fill up on carbs before conditioning days, and since conditioning is outside today, I know I'll need all I can get."

They have conditioning today? Why didn't Reese tell me that? I wouldn't have stayed out so late. I wouldn't have... kept him up till early morning.

"I'm guessing Reese is going to need all the carbs he can get too?" he questions, eyes dropping to my outfit.

Heat blooms up my neck. "Uh, I guess?"

A knowing smirk tilts his lips up. "Sex burns a lot of calories. More than you would think he will need to recharge. How late were you guys up?"

"I don't know. Like, sunrise?"

His eyes widen, and he whistles a low sound. "Damn, yeah. He's going to need more than carbs. Our practice isn't until five, though, so he's lucky."

Lucky indeed. The bathroom door creaks open, saving me from this conversation.

"Sawyer? Are you still home?"

He shifts and grunts a reply.

Laney pokes her head out, her wet hair dripping on the floor. "I, uh, forgot my clothes. Oh! Hey, Winnie."

"Hey. I can grab you something if you want? I'm here to talk to you, anyway."

"Okay! Yeah, if you wouldn't mind. My clothes are in the cow-print luggage in the back room. Just any shirt and shorts, please."

I make haste finding her clothes, which isn't hard, and it's easy to see which side of the room is hers. For some reason, it makes sense that Emma's side looks like a bomb went off and Laney's is nearly bare. Emma gives off chaotic vibes. It's what makes her so entertaining.

I knock on the door, and when she opens it, I rush inside and close it behind me. She stares at me with wide eyes. At least she's still wearing her towel and I didn't just force her to flash me.

"Hi, sorry. I really need to talk to someone."

"Um, okay. Like…" She glances down. "Now?"

"I'll close my eyes."

"Are you dying or something? What's wrong?"

I suck a breath in. "I may or may not have gotten pregnant last night, and I'm freaking out."

17

Reese

Stretching my arm out, I find cold, empty sheets instead of a warm body. Panic trickles through me as I sit up and look around. Winnie's tank top and panties are still on the ground. I reach down, grab the silky material, and shove them into my bedside drawer.

It's obvious she didn't leave completely, so she has to be around here somewhere. My bathroom is empty, but there is water splashed on the counter, and my shorts and shirt from last night are missing, so I throw on some new ones and head out.

Schmidt is working on his laptop when I walk out of my room, rubbing my eyes. "Hey, you see Winnie?" A pit forms in my stomach thinking maybe she left. Like she woke up regretting everything.

Or maybe she fucked me and left like I did to her as payback.

"Sawyer just texted the group chat saying she was in the bathroom with Laney."

"What?"

177

He shrugs without looking up from whatever he is doing on the computer. "I didn't ask, but maybe if you hurry, you'll catch them."

The thought of her with anyone—even a girl when I know she's straight—makes me wanna punch something. I storm across the hall. Sawyer stands in the middle of the room and shoots me a murderous glare when I step through the door.

"Are they still in there?"

"Yes," he growls.

What's got him so pissy?

"What are they doing?"

He throws his arms out to the side. "I don't fucking know. All I know is she walked in and said she needed to talk to Laney, but she was in the shower. Next thing I know, she's closing the door behind them."

Ah... it's not anger. It's *jealousy*. The same thing burning a path through me. How I never saw the way Sawyer is with Laney before fucking blows my mind. It's so obvious now.

"Well, what the fuck do you think they are talking about?"

He storms over and drops onto the couch, and I do the same.

"I don't know."

"Are you pissy because she's in there with a freshly showered Laney and you aren't?"

His eyes flick in my direction, and his jaw tenses. But he doesn't answer, not that I thought he would. It must be really shitty not to be able to admit your feelings out loud because you are in a relationship with another girl. *If he would just end that relationship*, but whatever. That's his deal.

My deal is figuring out why my girl was over here, needing to talk to someone instead of in bed with me.

"How long have they been in there?"

"Twenty-eight minutes." He pauses. "Now twenty-nine. What the fuck happened last night?"

I spill everything but leave out the intimate details I don't think Winnie would appreciate me sharing. Like how tight her pussy is. And it only takes me a few minutes to fill him in, not fucking thirty.

"If it was good, why is she over here?"

Exactly. It was good, right? I didn't miss some blaring red flag or something, right? There has to be a reason she would need to speak with a girl she hardly knows, but I can't come up with what it could be.

Another two minutes tick by before the doorknob twists. Sawyer and I have to look like lunatics sitting on the edge of the couch and staring at the wooden door.

They are laughing until they see us, but Winnie's smile doesn't fall, so I guess that's good? She tilts her head and watches me for a passing minute, lost in a trance.

But then Laney nudges her, and Winnie shakes free from whatever thought she was lost in.

"Thanks, Lane." She squeezes her hand before sauntering my way. You'd think she was in the tightest little dress for how my body is reacting to seeing her in my clothes. She's holding the top of the shorts to keep them from falling, and the shirt is barely holding on to her shoulders, but her sleepy eyes and messy hair make her look fucking perfect.

I wrap my arms around her, and she burrows into my chest.

Sawyer looks between us, a frown deepening his brow with each passing minute. "Well, do we get to know what that was all about?"

Winnie giggles, tickling my chest with her breath. "Girl talk. Sorry."

He rears back, shock coloring his face. "You're being a real *Peyton* right now."

I don't fucking know what that means, but Winnie pulls back, mouth open, and is obviously offended. Sawyer looks proud of himself, though.

"Yeah, well, you're a Lucas. Not a Nate."

Sawyer's eyes narrow, and I'm so fucking confused about what is happening.

"Get this traitor out of my face."

To my surprise, Winnie grabs my hand and is the one to lead me to the door.

"Gladly." She scowls at him. Before the door closes behind us, she yells a thank you to Laney and something else I don't understand to Sawyer.

Wanting to get her back to my room where she should have been all morning, I don't pin her against the wall and demand to know what the fuck is happening like I'm tempted. Instead, I let her lead me wherever she wants.

The door slams shut behind us, and Schmidt stands and follows us to the hallway, then cocks an eyebrow at me. I shrug, not knowing how to answer his unasked questions.

"You get any sleep?"

"Nope."

I'll never understand how he runs on basically no sleep. It's not even because I kicked him out last night. Schmidt just doesn't sleep.

Winnie tugs me to my bedroom, but she doesn't stop there. Instead, she turns and walks backward, shimmying her hips in the sexiest way until we are standing in my bathroom. Then she lifts her other hand, and my shorts drop to the ground.

I swallow hard. Going years with no contact ramped up my horniness tenfold. I've never been so quick to catch a boner. I drop my hand and absently stroke over my shorts, attempting to calm my aching cock. Need bubbles inside me, waiting for the go-ahead.

Winnie pinches the hem of my shirt and tugs it over her head. Somehow, she looks even more beautiful in the morning light streaming through the window.

"You're beautiful."

A sexy pink creeps up her neck and colors her cheeks. Winnie reaches over and flicks on the shower, then grips the band of my shorts and pulls me close.

"Join me?"

"Winnie, if there is ever a time I refuse a shower with you. Call 911."

If I showered with her every day, we would cause a drought. My skin would shrivel up from being over moistened and still, I'd regret nothing. She pads around me, touching and teasing different parts of my body, familiarizing herself and causing my skin to prick. She grabs my soap, lathers her hands together, and sniffs deeply, sucking in the scent before raising her hands to drag down my back.

I lift my hands to the wall in front of me and drop my head between my shoulders for some stability. Fuuuck, this is almost as good as sex. My tense muscles loosen automatically for her like she has some sort of code to get them to relax. Someone's touch shouldn't feel so good, but hers is perfect.

Her feet splash in the water that hasn't drained yet as she tiptoes to my front, ready to give my chest the same treatment as my back. I force my eyes open and find her studying me with the cutest look on her pretty face. Her deep eyes are focused on where her hands are skimming, and the faintest of smiles graces her lips like she's enjoying this as much as I am. It's surreal having her here with me right now. So many times I dreamed of this exact thing, and here she is.

The steam floating around her from the hot water almost makes it feel like a dream, but her touch is very much real. She lowers herself to the ground, sitting on her knees in front of me, and fuck. Me. She reaches up and grips my dick, watching me expectantly as I shudder against her touch.

"Is this okay?"

Okay? No. Fucking fantastic? Yes. "It's good."

She smiles. Turning her wrists in opposite directions as she strokes me, and it's an out-of-body experience. Trembles rack through my body, and I'm happy my hands are braced against the wall because I could collapse right now and end this godly experience.

"*Winnie.*" Her name is a prayer that tastes so sweet on my lips.

The moment her lips wrap around the tip of my cock, I'm a goner. She's uncertain as she takes my dick deeper, and I fight not to come instantly with her hot tongue pressed against the underside of my dick. Wanting to reassure her, I drop a hand from the wall and place it on the back of her head, smoothing down her drenched hair as I do. Not pushing her, just resting it there. It's mostly so I know this is really happening and I'm not so delirious I'm imagining it.

She takes me deeper yet, then gags, and my balls draw up. *Fuck*.

"You can do it, baby."

Her eyes brighten, and she does it again.

"Good girl, Winnie. Gag on my cock."

Fuck. The more I encourage her, the deeper she takes me.

Seems my girl has a praise kink.

"Look at you go." My voice is breathless, amazed at how good this feels. My buddies talk about blow jobs often, but I could never relate.

"I'm going to come. Swallow it all for me, okay?"

Her eyes pinch and she makes a whimpering sound, but it's muffled with my dick down her throat.

I press against the back of her head, holding me deep in her mouth as my balls draw up. She gags and chokes as my cum shoots down her throat, and she's never looked better.

The second I release her, she falls back and gasps for air.

"Fuck, Win."

She tilts her head, looking at me expectantly.

"Did you swallow it all? Open your mouth."

She climbs back onto her knees and sticks out her tongue for me to see. If I didn't just come, I'd be hard again.

"Fucking beautiful. Now get on the bench and open your legs. It's my turn."

Her eyes widen, and she scrambles to the seat. Hot water pelts my back as I lower myself to my knees. Fuck, how did she do this? The floor is not easy on the joints.

She's barely opened her legs, but that's not going to work. I grip her thighs and spread them wide, lifting them into the air as I give myself the perfect angle to her pussy.

I've not seen a lot of pussies, or any besides hers, but Winnie's is the prettiest. Pink, swollen with need, and fucking beautiful.

I kiss her thighs, close to where I know she wants me, but not quite *there*. Teasing her. I want her so edged she's ready to burst when I finally take her pussy in my mouth.

"Please, Reese."

There we go.

"Please what, Win?"

She swallows hard, an unsure look pinching her eyebrows. "Please lick my pussy."

Atta-fucking-girl.

Diving in, I'm not gentle. I eat her like a starved man. Lapping at her pussy, sucking on her clit. Her screams bounce off the shower tiles when I do that. I bring my fingers up, wanting to fill her, and she gasps when I shove two inside. But she takes them like a champ.

People always say you are what you eat, and I know my girl loves honey. And I'll be damned if she doesn't taste like it. Sweet, earthy, fucking perfect.

She's close, tugging on my hair and riding my face. She chants my name, only encouraging me to fuck her harder. I curl my fingers, hitting that perfect spot, and tease her clit with my tongue.

She's thrashing so much I worry she's going to slip, so I bring her thighs to my shoulders for more security, then finish the job until she's whimpering for me to stop.

Winnie slumps, and I tug her off the bench and fall back against the wall with her on my lap and her head on my shoulder. Her breathing is steadying out, but her heart is pounding and loud in my ears.

"Good?"

"Mmm."

I chuckle and kiss the side of her head. "Good girl, Win."

Winnie is walking around my room when I exit the bathroom toweling my wet hair. She's found another one of my shirts, and this one might look even better than the last with my name across her back and my number, seventeen, below it. I laid it out so it would be ready for conditioning tonight, but that's even better because at least it will smell like her—before I sweat in it, anyway.

She pauses at my bookshelf that holds my collection of movies, tilting her head to read the titles. I cross my arms and lean against the doorway, enjoying her snooping when she doesn't know I'm here.

When she loses interest in those, she moves away, stopping at the cage holding Eeyore.

"That's Eeyore."

She spins with wide eyes. "Eeyore? You hate that name."

I snort. "Yeah, I know. Drunk Reese named him. Apparently, after the party, I got it in my head that I had to get a pet frog." It dawns on her why I would insist that, and her hand flies to her mouth, concealing the growing smile.

"No you didn't."

I reach for the back of my neck and grin. "Yeah, but they didn't have any frogs. So I got a turtle instead, I guess."

"I cannot believe you, Reese Larson. You really are a sloppy drunk."

Her soft, warm skin presses against my body as I tug her against me and kiss her head. "Even as drunk as I was, I knew I fucked up. Apparently, I thought a frog would win you over."

"It just might have."

"Yeah, but turtles are cool too, right?"

She turns in my arms to eye the turtle crawling around on a bed of leaves. "You know Eeyore's not a turtle, right?"

"What do you mean?"

She pulls away, reaches into the makeshift cage, and pulls him into her hands. "He's a baby tortoise."

"And the difference *iiisss*?"

She places him on my floor and kneels, so I do the same on the other side of him.

"Well, first. He needs a way bigger cage. An outside cage would be better, but obviously, you can't have that here, so. Yeah, just a bigger cage and daily walks outside. I will get you a list of what they eat. And third." She flicks her eyes up to me. "He can live to be over a hundred and be, like, a hundred and twenty pounds."

This little turtle, who is no bigger than two of Winnie's hands and one of mine, is going to be a hundred and twenty pounds? "What the fuck am I meant to do with a hundred-and-twenty-pound turtle?"

"Tortoise," she so kindly reminds me. "But didn't you know what you were getting yourself into? These guys are usually expensive. Didn't you wonder why your turtle was, like, five hundred dollars?"

Seven, almost eight hundred, but I'm not telling her that. I feel stupid enough. I'm glad she seems to find amusement in all this because I definitely am not.

We play with my pet *tortoise* for a while before Winnie is anxious to continue her snooping of my room. She leaves him out, letting him wander the room the same way she does. I make sure to keep an eye on him so we don't lose him. Not like he will be hard to find when he's a hundred and twenty fucking pounds. Fuck.

I drop on my bed, and she stops next to my desk, looking through the stack of sports magazines.

"No porno magz?"

I tuck my hand under my head to see her better. "No, those are under my bed."

She shakes with a giggle. "Remember when I found your stash when we were kids?"

"I told you, those weren't mine."

"Sure they weren't, perv."

I don't have it in me to tell her those really weren't mine. They were her brother's. Her mom found them under his bed once while she was cleaning. She didn't say anything to him, I guess, but they were in a different place than he left them, and he was mortified. He asked me to hold on to them, and it wasn't like my mom was going into my room to clean. No one ever went into my room besides me. And one of the few times Winnie did, she saw them in my closet. She swore she was looking for something, but I know she was snooping exactly like she is doing right now. She's never been shy about butting into my business.

Stopping in front of my closet, she looks over her shoulder at me. A teasing look on her face.

"So if I look in your closet, I won't find any porn?"

Oh, she will, but not what she's thinking. My closet probably wasn't the best place to hide the newspapers if I didn't want her finding them, because I know how nosey Winnie is, but it was a last-minute decision when we got back to the dorms last night. "Go ahead and check."

The closet doors are shitty, and they complain—loudly—as she opens them. As soon as there's a gap, the pile of newspapers tumble to the ground at her feet. She's frozen for a moment, looking around at the three hundred or so newspapers with her ass on the front.

"Why?" She kneels, picking up a paper in each hand and eyeing them. I can't see her face, but her voice is small.

"Why what?"

"Why do you have so many?"

I climb from the bed and settle behind her with my legs stretched outright aside her. "I didn't want anyone else to have them. It's an invasion of your privacy, and

I'm a selfish fuck who doesn't like to share. Now, I know I didn't get all of them, but pretty damn close."

"You, Reese Larson, could make anyone in the world fall in love with you."

I wrap my arm around her waist and tug her to her ass, then drop a kiss to her slender neck. "I don't want anyone. I just want you."

Winnie's back hits the door, and the moan she lets out is enough to make me demand she stays, but she has class, and I have conditioning, and it would be nice to possibly get a nap in before it. Coach is still pissed at me about the article, and if I'm slacking at all today, he will keep me late and make me run double. Which I have no interest in, so I kiss her hard, a silent way of claiming her, then pull away. But I keep her caged in my arms.

"You know I'm only letting you leave because you are forced to come back for your clothes?"

She gives me my favorite smile. "And if I didn't, would you keep me here like a prisoner?"

"Mm-hmm. My very own sex slave."

She gasps and slaps my chest. "You're such a perv."

I lean forward and nip at her ear. "I told you, I like it when you degrade me."

Her giggle is so fucking sweet. I don't know how I ever went without hearing it.

"I gotta go."

"I'll see you later?"

Without thinking about it, she nods. "But not tonight. Eli is probably already wondering where I am, and if I start spending too much time out of the house, he's going to get suspicious."

Fucking Elijah. "Fine. But call me tonight."

"Deal."

I know this is where I let her go, but it's fucking hard. Things aren't set between us. We don't have any official title or commitment, as far as she knows. She could walk out this door and never speak to me again—or try, at least. I don't want to worry about losing her when I just got her back.

"Reese," she whispers, her voice full of unsaid words. "I really have to go unless you want me wearing this to class?"

She knows I don't. The only reason she's allowed to leave in nothing but my sweatshirt and a pair of my black briefs is because I know she's going straight home.

Sighing, I back up enough to let her open the door. My heart beats hard as I watch her step out, but before she turns and leaves, she grabs my neck and pulls me down to her level to place a deep kiss on my cheek.

"I'll talk to you later."

I nod because I know if I were to try and speak right now, the only thing that would come out of my mouth would be I *love you.*

18

Winnie

"Where the fuck were you last night?"

I thought I lucked out when Elijah was gone this afternoon and I had the place to myself. I said it would give me time to come up with a good excuse, but him jumping down my throat the moment I walk in the door after class leaves me floundering.

"I told you I was going out?"

"Where did you stay?"

I walk past him, my head low, pretending to mess with something on my keys so he hopefully can't see the lie. "The girls'. You saw who I was with, Eli. Why are you so pissy?"

"Because I thought we were closer than this."

The pain in his voice is the only reason I lift my stare to meet his cold one. Jaw tight, eyes narrowed, and his arms crossed over his chest, he looks so much like our dad, but a meaner version.

"Eli..."

"Were you with Reese?"

Oh, come *on*. How am I meant to lie right to his face when he asks me outright like that? I can't.

"You know what, forget it. I know you were, so there's no point in lying."

"I wasn't," I whisper.

"Wasn't what? With him? Really? Because I saw photos, Win."

Photos? My eyebrows crease. "What?"

He rolls his eyes and pulls out his phone, then flips it my way. A photo of Reese kissing my forehead this morning fills his screen. *What the fuck?* Reese couldn't have taken this because it was shot from down the hall, from the looks of it. Like someone was sneaking photos of us. My blood runs cold. If they got this photo, what else could they have? We didn't do anything in the hallway... I don't think.

"Who sent you these?"

"Does it fucking matter? You lied to me, Win."

"Yeah, Elijah, it kind of matters that someone was invading my business and sneaking photos of your sister." It's not even a question of whether or not it matters.

"Calm down, it wasn't some fucking stalker. It was Zoey."

That's so much worse than a stalker. "What the hell is she doing taking photos of me and sending them to you?"

He kicks off from the counter and stops on the other side of the island from me. "Answer my question first, and don't lie, because you know I have proof. Were you with Reese last night?"

"Yes, but—" He storms from the room without letting me get another word out, but I follow after. "Elijah, wait. It's not what you think." It's not? Really? Because I'm sure it's exactly what he is thinking. In fact, it might be worse than that.

"Then tell me. Tell me my baby sister wasn't fucking with the one guy I hate most in the world. Tell me that, and I'll drop it."

What the fuck do I do? Be honest and risk Elijah doing who knows what? Or lie and hope he never finds out the truth?

"Reese was there, but I wasn't *with* him. Not like you think. I went out with the girls, and Sawyer came looking for his sister. He brought Reese with. They took us back to their place after a while. I was drunk, so I crashed there."

"And the photo?" he snaps before I'm even able to get to that point.

"The photo is of Reese comforting me. That's all." Knowing he's going to ask for what, I come up with the most ridiculous but hopefully believable lie I can imagine. That Reese was kissing my forehead because Sawyer and I slept together last night, and I woke up to find out he has a girlfriend. That's why I'm wearing a hockey sweatshirt. *Thank God he can't see the name or number in the photo.* "Reese caught me leaving Sawyer's place. I was crying, and he was just helping me."

The lie is heavy on my tongue and in my heart, but when Elijah's shoulders relax the smallest amount, I know I made the right decision. Even if it hurts having to lie to my brother, I'd rather lie than have him do something that will permanently damage our relationship.

"I know it's probably not what you wanted to hear, but that's what happened. He was just being a friend, Eli."

"A friend." He scoffs. "Reese doesn't know the first thing about being a friend. He probably turned around as soon as you left and went and laughed with Sawyer about it all."

He turns again, heading back out to the living room, and this time it's my turn to ask him the hard questions. I get why he hates Reese. I don't agree, but I know how Elijah thinks. What I don't get is why he considers him a bad friend. As far as I know, Reese was always there for him. Even after their falling out.

"What happened between you two? And don't tell me it's because of Dad, because we both know that's bullshit, E."

His jaw clenches. "Drop it, Winnie. You won't like the answer."

"But if you tell me, then maybe I can understand why you hate him so much. Because right now, I can't, Eli. It doesn't make sense for you to blame him for Dad's death when he wasn't even in the car. Or that night between us. We were both there and, like it or not, I came onto *him.* So what is it? What happened?"

"You really want to know? You're going to hate your *friend.*"

I roll my eyes at his condescending tone. I highly doubt anything he could say would make me hate Reese. "Go for it."

And he does. He tells me everything. About the party they attended the night they came home for Thanksgiving break. How he had lost Reese at some point during the night, and how Zoey never came to bed with him. So the next morning, he went looking for her and found her naked in the place he never would have expected—in bed with Reese.

When Elijah is done telling me, I excuse myself to the shower, and he lets me go, no doubt sensing my desperate need to cry. Elijah hates crying—or any sort of emotion.

I didn't think he was going to say something to actually make me hate Reese, but I was wrong. He knows I hate liars, and yet he lied right to my face, multiple times. I texted him that weekend, asking why he didn't come home if Elijah did, and he said he was catching up on schoolwork when he was most likely across the road the entire time. Maybe even with Zoey.

That. Fucking. Blows. I don't know if that's worse, or that he lied about it yesterday. Why would he tell me he's only ever been with me when it's such a blatant lie? I didn't want to ask if he had slept with anyone else because, truthfully, I didn't care if he had. I was here now, so anyone after me the first time didn't matter.

But he lied. And why? To protect me since he knows I hate her and that would be a line in the sand for me? Or to protect *her*?

Emma said they weren't dating, even though Zoey said they were. But he didn't push her away when she slipped her arm into his at the store. Maybe that doesn't mean anything, but it's all the small things that are jumping out now.

I'm such a fucking idiot for ever trusting him again.

Well, not anymore. I've cried over Reese Larson one too many times, and I refuse to do it again. After today.

I'm going to need the rest of the night to get it out, but come tomorrow, I'm moving on with my life, and I'm not looking back ever again.

Even if I am pregnant.

The talk with Laney left me feeling good. She made some good points about how Reese was obviously into me and how he would make a good dad, along with so much other bullshit that I left that bathroom truly believing that if I was several hours pregnant, it would be okay because Reese was a good man.

I could laugh. Does she know anything about him and Zoey? I'd think if she did, she would tell me instead of encouraging me to have a baby with him, in a round-about way. If Reese and Zoey are some kind of weird fuck buddies, I want no part of that. I'm not getting with Zoey's sloppy seconds, even if she would have gotten mine first. Unless he lied about losing his virginity that night too.

"Ugh." I drop my head to the back of the shower. I really should have removed my clothes before I got in because I hate the feeling of wet clothes, but the water was cold when I stepped in, so it made sense to leave them on.

A knock raps on the bathroom door.

"Win?" Elijah asks. "You okay?"

No. I feel like my heart has been ripped out of my chest and stomped on right in front of my face. "Yeah."

"I gotta piss. Can I come in?"

"Go ahead."

Elijah does his business, and I wait to hear his zipper before pushing open the curtain. He looks down at me, a new kind of frown on his usual scowling face.

"I hate seeing you cry over such a dick."

"I know."

"Sawyer too. The next time I see him, I'm going to punch him."

Poor Sawyer. Hopefully he doesn't bump into Elijah anytime soon. Should I even feel bad? He probably knows all about Reese, Elijah, Zoey, and whoever else. I can't help but feel like an idiot for trusting people I don't even know so easily, but I guess that's what happens when you make your first friends. A *learning curve*, I bet Mom would say.

"It's fine."

"It's really not." He flops down outside the tub and takes my hand in his rough one. "But it will be. I got you, and you got me, Win. That's what's important."

I smile at my brother, and for the first time, it feels like old times again. Sucks it took getting my heart broken—again. But it's nice to see a glimpse of my old brother, even if it's only for a second.

"Get out and get changed. We can put on a movie and eat popcorn until we're sick."

"Can I pick the movie?"

He chuckles as he climbs to his feet. "Absolutely not."

Yep, just like old times.

"Oh, Win,"—Elijah looks over his shoulder from the door—"never let someone lie to your face twice." He says, using the same advice Dad used to tell us. Advice I never needed before now.

19

Reese

FLASHBACK

I don't think I ever want to drink again. Fuck, my head is swimming. My mouth tastes like cotton, and I could really use some water, but I don't want to open my eyes because I know the morning light trying to pierce through my eyelids is going to hurt like a bitch when I do.

I reach a hand out, but instead of water, I touch something soft and warm. I bolt up, and through burning eyes, I look at the bed next to me. Dark hair drapes across the pillow.

There's no memory of me talking to any girls last night, let alone falling into bed with one. The last thing I remember is playing foosball with my buddies, but there's no denying there is a girl in bed next to me. Her back is bare, which isn't a good sign. Running my hands down my body, I realize I'm naked too. That's a really bad sign. Pushing the girl's hair away, I jolt back.

I fucking know this girl, unfortunately.

My best friend's girlfriend.

"Zoey." I shove her shoulder before scrambling from the bed.

With a grumble, she flops onto her back. I look away, not only because I don't want to see her tits but also because I need to find clothes and get to the bottom of whatever's going on. I know I didn't fuck his girlfriend. One, I would never do that to Elijah; he's like my brother. But two, I can't fucking stand the girl. Didn't the first time I met her two years ago, and the feeling is the same today.

"Zoey." I walk around the bed and shake her, still looking for my shorts. Yes! Finding them on the floor on her side, I ignore how bad that looks for my situation and step into them.

The door across the room flies open, and Elijah steps in.

"Bro." He laughs at me, holding a hand up to block my dick as I finish tugging my shorts up. "Sleeping naked at someone else's house is a little weird, ya know?"

I shoot a look at Zoey, who's still asleep, and he follows my eyes before his round. "Holy shit. You had sex?" he whisper-shouts, probably trying not to wake the girl. The girl he has no idea is his girlfriend yet.

When he finds out...

As if she knew what I was thinking and wanted to make my life even worse than she already has, Zoey yawns and sits up, pushing her hair from her face. She smiles at me, and my stomach fucking rolls. "I had a good night last night."

Fuck.

I wait for it to click with Elijah. He's still staring, his face a mask of indifference as he takes in the scene in front of him.

"You fucked my girlfriend?"

Oh shit. I shake my head. I didn't. I know I didn't. "I know it looks bad, E. But I promise I didn't fuck her—"

"Yes," Zoey says with her head down and fake sadness in her tone. "I'm so sorry, Elijah. It just happened. We... we've been sneaking around behind your back for months."

What? What the hell is this girl on?

"No the fuck we have—"

"Just tell him, Reese." She stands, at least having the decency to wrap a sheet around her.

"E." I turn for him, but it's not the eyes of my best friend I meet. It's the eyes of an enemy. Cold and distant, and I know he wants to punch me. I've seen this very same look on him more times than I can count, but it's never been directed at me. "You know I would never." I take a step toward him. "Especially after everything."

He flinches. "Don't fucking bring my dad up, you back-stabbing piece of shit."

"I didn't fuck her! I fucking swear, Elijah. I know it looks bad, but I swear to God we didn't."

"Swear to whoever the fuck you want, but it doesn't change shit. You woke up in bed with her, right?"

"Yes." The answer tastes like acid in my mouth.

"Naked?" His jaw clenches. Mine does the same, and I nod because I can't bear to mutter the words out loud.

"So tell me, Reese." He spits my name like it's dirt on his shoe. "If roles were reversed, what would you think?"

I say nothing because we both know the answer, and the answer sucks. I didn't fuck her; I know I didn't. I just need to get to the bottom of whatever the fuck is happening. How she got in here, and why I was naked. Why she was naked, because I refuse to believe it was sex.

"Thought so," he mutters, a humorless laugh slipping past his lips. "Do me a favor and stay the fuck away from me." He storms to the door and slams it behind him.

I stare at it for a long time. Too long. And by the time it hits me what just happened, the only thing I can hope is that he doesn't tell Winnie. She's mad at me for a very legit reason already; I can't give her a second one. Especially when something isn't right. I don't sleep around. The last person I fucked was Winnie, and I planned to keep it that way until we fucked again.

And I hate Zoey. There's not a single fucking chance I would ever take her to bed; sober or shitfaced.

Turning, I glare at her with a brand-new hatred, maybe more anger burning inside me than ever before, and I so badly want to hit something.

205

She eyes her nails, not an ounce of care that she just ripped my best friend's heart out and stomped on it.

"I don't know what actually happened last night, but when I find out, you're going to regret ever coming between me and the people I love."

She saunters my way and reaches a hand out, but I shove it away. She fakes a pout. "Pushy for the guy begging me to fuck him last night."

I spit out a laugh. "Not in a million fucking years would I beg you to fuck me when I can have the best pussy around."

Hurt slashes through her eyes, and she crosses her arms. "Who?"

I scoff and move across the room to find my shirt.

"Who is it, Reese?"

I'm not telling her it's Winnie. She would only make her life more miserable than it already is.

I find my shirt and wallet, thank fuck. Opening it, I pull out the photo and stare down at it, wishing I could go back to that moment. I wouldn't make so many fucking mistakes if I could.

Zoey sneaks up behind me and snatches the Polaroid from my hands. "Well, well, well. Look what we have here."

"Give it back, Zoey."

She pulls her arm away when I reach for it, and since the only thing covering her naked body is a sheet, I'm not going to fight her and risk it falling.

"Is Reese Larson *fucking underage pussy?*"

Technically, no. I Googled the age of consent—which is sixteen in this state, and since Winnie is sixteen...

Zoey doesn't need to know that, though, so I keep my face unreadable. "Mind your fucking business, Zoey."

"Oh, he is. Well, I have to admit. I thought you were a good boy. I'm a bit surprised."

"You don't know shit, Zoey."

I reach for the photo again, and she lets me have it this time. I place it back into my wallet to keep it safe and then shove it into my pocket.

Carrying my shit, I head for the door. I need to get out of here. Before she pushes me to a point of no return. She might not care about what she just did to Elijah, but I do. I saw the last bit of life he was holding on to since his dad died dwindle, and it fucking scares me.

Things between us have already been rocky since everything with his dad, but now? I don't know how we come back from this unless I can somehow prove we didn't fuck. Which I don't know how to do.

"And to think I thought I had to wait until I turned eighteen to get with you. Silly me."

"Shut the fuck up," I growl. "I haven't admitted to anything."

"You don't have to say anything when I see the way you look at her. I saw the way you held her at her dad's funeral. That's not brotherly or friendly. It was love."

I shoot a glare over my shoulder. "So I love her. That doesn't prove anything?"

Her mouth gapes like she didn't expect me to say that. I've always loved Winnie; that wouldn't be a surprise to anyone close to us.

"Just watch your back, Reese. It only takes a small inkling in a cop's ear about underage sex, and you know my mom's husband is a deputy..."

I slam the door behind me because I don't care to hear her threats. They don't mean shit to me. I didn't admit to anything, and no one knows about Winnie and me besides us. And I know she wouldn't say anything even if Zoey is crazy enough to go to the police.

At least, I hope not, and if not, the scummy age-of-consent argument has my back.

Fuck, what a mess.

Elijah is probably home now, blabbing everything to her. I should go home and wait for the fucking police cars to line up my driveway, ready to carry me away and murder any future I planned.

20

Reese

A week of fucking agony. I knew the pit in my stomach when Winnie left my place wasn't something I made up. Somehow, I knew something would happen and I wouldn't see her again.

I just don't know what changed, and it's fucking killing me. I've texted her more times than I can count. I've called. I've sent flowers and other gifts to her place, but they get sent back every time.

I even considered going over there, but the last teddy bear I sent had its head cut off, and I know that was Elijah's doing. He's probably sitting at home, sharpening his pocket knife and waiting for me to show up so he can test it out. As much as I want to get to the bottom of whatever is going on, me getting stabbed isn't going to get me anywhere but the hospital.

Maybe if I was in the hospital I could set her as my emergency contact, and then she would come see me.

Holy shit, I need to go outside.

The only time I've left the house this week was to take Eeyore on those walks Winnie told me he needed. As far as my teachers know, I've been "sick" all week. I've been so bored I even did the assignments they sent me.

My roommates are doing their best to not pay my bad mood attention, but I can tell my moping is getting on their nerves. I don't know what else to do. I could drop by her class, though I don't know her schedule. We didn't get that far, but I do know what her Friday afternoon class is. I glance at the clock across my room. It's nearly twelve thirty, so I have about an hour to get showered and head over. Which is something else I haven't done and another reason my roommates are miserable. The smell isn't pleasant, but it's nowhere near as awful as the weight in my chest.

The worst part of this all is not knowing how to go about it. I don't know what could have possibly happened after she left here that caused her to block me on everything. I tried sending her money through an app with messages telling her to unblock me so we could talk. But she never did, and I was losing too much money to continue if I want to be able to buy us a house one day.

"What's that smell?" Schmidt sniffs into the air when I step into sight. He slaps Gavin's and Sawyer's chests, making them do the same thing. "Did Reese finally wash his ass?"

"Funny," I grumble on my way past.

"We're just kidding, man. Where are you heading? Conditioning isn't for another few hours."

"Out."

I catch them giving each other the side-eye.

"I gotta see her." I allow the vulnerability to shine through for just a moment before I shut it back down.

Sawyer stands from the couch and wanders into the kitchen where I am. I've not eaten shit this week, but if I'm going to survive conditioning, I gotta get something in my system.

"You really wanna do that? After she ghosted you?"

These guys don't get it. No one gets it. Winnie wouldn't ghost me if there wasn't a real reason—or something she thinks is a real reason, anyway. They think she ghosted me like I did her, and no matter how many times I tell them that's not something Winnie would do, they don't listen. Sure, the thought occurred to me, but Winnie doesn't have a revengeful bone in her body. I saw the way she looked at me. I felt the love pour from her during sex, and I know when she kissed my cheek and promised to talk later, she meant it. So something had to have happened after she left.

"Elijah is her brother, and he hates me. It wouldn't surprise me if he said something that made her do it."

He blows out a long breath. "Is she really worth it, Reese?"

I whip around from the microwave, and he holds up his hands.

"Listen before you go all 'Rapture' on me."

I don't think I could even if I wanted to with how weak my body is feeling. Pizza rolls are probably not what I need to give me energy, but I can't be bothered to make anything else.

"Even if Elijah gave her a legitimate reason, you sure you want to get involved in all that? A girl who is going to take her brother's word without even letting you explain what you need to?"

If Sawyer knew the extent of everything between Elijah and me, he wouldn't be questioning me right now. In fact, he might hate me as much as Elijah—okay, probably not, but I might not be far off.

"She's everything to me. You met me without Winnie, but you don't know me when I'm with her. Everything is better. She makes me want to be the best version of myself. To you, I'm the hockey guy. You think that's the one thing in life I love, but it's not. Hockey is my life, but she's my world, man." I shudder. "It's fucking me up. I know Winnie seems flakey to you, or whatever, but I'd bet money that she's in worse shape than me."

Famous last words.

"Well, okay. I just want to see you not so messed up. I'm meant to be the miserable one. It's my thing, and you are stealing my thunder."

I chuckle as best as I can and slap his shoulder on my way by. "Give me a few days to get to the bottom of whatever the fuck is happening, and then you can have your miserable title back."

Winnie

"Turns out, the flash wasn't on." Oliver laughs, and I force one out as well. I don't know if what he said was actually funny, though. I wasn't listening.

"So, uh, before you go, I was sorta hoping to ask you something."

Oh, God. Is he going to ask me out? I've never been asked out before. Not, like, officially or anything. I think some kid in eighth grade tried to ask me to the movies, but it was a movie Elijah and Reese had been talking about seeing, so I agreed to go, then invited them. It was weird, and I didn't know it was meant to be a date until Elijah told me after. Then he told me I wasn't allowed to talk to that kid ever again, which wasn't a problem since I brought my brother and his best friend on what he thought was a date. He mostly avoided me after that day. As did most guys in school. I guess word got out about the weird date, and they figured it wasn't worth even asking.

Oliver is nice and handsome enough, with his swoopy blond hair and bright blue eyes, but I'm in no place to even consider dating.

"Sorry, Oliver. As flattered as I am, I'm just really not interested in dating right now."

He was in the middle of saying something, but he freezes. Mouth still half-open and his eyes wide with surprise. Geesh, has he never been turned down before?

"I was just going to ask if I could copy off you on the test on Monday..."

Oh.

Kill me. "Uh, yeah. Sure, that's fine."

He takes a step away, and an awkward pause stretches between us. "Well, I'll see you Monday, then."

"Yep."

Then he turns and books it out of the building like he can't get away fast enough. "Way to go, Win," I mutter to myself.

But someone else answers anyway.

"He was definitely asking you out."

I spin, clutching my chest, and gasp at Reese leaning against the wall outside of the door.

"What are you doing here?"

"You blocked me. You won't talk to me and—"

Mr. Hudson steps out of the classroom directly between Reese and me. With his nose in his phone, he doesn't seem to notice, but then he presses the power button and drops it into his pants pocket. Noticing me, he smiles. "Hello, Winnie. Did you have a question for me?"

Oliver is cute in the boy-next-door way. Mr. Hudson? He is hot in the "I'll bend you over my desk and make you call me daddy" type of way. Not my type, but not a sight for sore eyes, for sure.

"Uh, no, sir."

"You're doing amazing in class, by the way. If you ever have a question, my door is always open."

Pride blooms inside my chest, and I smile. "Thank you, Mr. Hudson, but no questions." I take a hesitant step back, not realizing Reese has moved behind me and bump right into his warm chest.

Mr. Hudson flicks his focus from me to Reese and cocks an eyebrow.

"And you are?"

"Her boyfriend," Reese bites out.

I gasp and shoot a look at him. He glares down at me as if to say *don't push it*, but I don't care what he's saying.

"No he's not." I clench my teeth. "Sorry, Mr. Hudson. Would you excuse us?"

He seems far too amused with whatever is happening in front of him, but I can't even blame him because, from the outside, it probably is entertaining.

"Of course. I will see you next Friday, Winnie."

I offer a smile and a small wave before grabbing Reese's hand and forcing him to follow me outside. It's not easy trying to drag a two-hundred-pound man, but eventually, we break into the cool autumn air.

"What the hell is your problem, Reese? We are not dating. Don't tell people that."

"You sure couldn't wait to tell that prick we weren't, too," he bites out.

My mouth drops open as I rear back, dumbfounded that he has the audacity to be jealous right now. "You're joking, right? That 'prick' is my teacher, and he was just being friendly."

"Please, Winnie." He scoffs. "Don't be so naive. He was hitting on you, and we both know it. If I wasn't there, would you have fucked your teacher?"

My eyes blow wide, and I stumble back as if he hit me. "How *dare* you."

I spin on my heel and head for my car. Reese catches me around the wrist and spins me to face him again before I get too far. But, thankfully, he drops my hand before I have the chance to pull it away.

"Fuck, sorry. I'm not sleeping well, and that guy really rubbed me wrong. Sorry, none of that is your fault."

"No, it's not," I repeat, just so he gets whatever is going on is definitely not *my* fault.

He drags a hand over his face and sighs. He does look tired. Deep bags rest under his usually bright eyes that are now a dull hazel. A black cap sits backwards on top of his head, hiding what I'm sure is messy hair. What the hell is happening to him? He said he wasn't sleeping, but why?

"I know."

"Okay." I spin, continuing to my car.

"I think that teacher is a scumbag, though."

Of course he does. "Thanks for the warning." Sarcasm drips heavily from my voice. "Why didn't you step in when Oliver was asking me out?" I ask, narrowing my eyebrows as I look over at him.

"It was painfully obvious you weren't listening, and he knew it. That's why when you turned him down, he lied about not asking you out." He shrugs. "You weren't into him."

"And you think I am into my teacher?"

His smile slips and his jaw clenches. "No, but I think the power balance, or lack thereof, could lead to situations you don't want to be in."

My stomach turns at the accusations he's making. "I'm a big girl, Reese. I don't need you looking out for me like when we were kids."

We're at my car now, but he's standing in front of my door, blocking me from getting in.

He tilts my head back with two fingers, and his eyes fall to my lips. "Maybe, but you'll never be too old for me to look out for you, Win. I care about you."

My stomach clenches, but it's not bad or good. I wish it were bad. I wish his words had no effect on me.

"I don't want to hear this." Tears threaten to burn my eyes, but I close them, refusing to let any fall. I said I wasn't going to cry over him anymore, and I've done a good job.

That's a lie. I've cried basically every night, but it's been in the privacy of my own room when everyone else is asleep or out. I can't risk Elijah seeing me cry again.

"Why are you here, Reese?"

"You blocked me. On everything." He drops my chin and pulls his hat off to scratch his head underneath, something he does when he's anxious. "You left me no choice but to show up to your class. Just be happy I waited until it was over."

"I'm not thanking you for not disrupting my class when you shouldn't be here anyway. I blocked you for a reason, Reese. I need to move on. We need to move on. We're not good together."

Reese moves closer, not touching me but my feet are frozen to the ground, holding me in place. "You don't mean that."

"Yes I do." My voice shakes. I slip around him to move in front of my door now. "I'm tired of getting hurt by you, and I can't be with someone I don't trust."

Agony rips through him, and he stumbles back. I think seeing his genuine pain hurts most of all, but it doesn't make sense because how can he act so surprised by what I'm saying?

"What the fuck happened when you left, Win? We had such a good night, and you promised to call but didn't. Why?"

I can't believe he's doing this to me. He knows why, and yet he's acting so innocent. I bet this is his way of waiting to see what I say instead of having to own up to what he did.

I cross my arms over my chest. Gone are the sad tears, and in their place is anger. "You tell me."

His jaw clenches. He flattens his hands above my head on my car and leans toward me. "If I knew, I would have fixed it a fucking week ago because this"—he gestures between us—"is *killing* me."

Not as much as it killed me hearing you lied.

"You lied." I wait for any kind of reaction, guilt maybe, but it doesn't come. Only confusion.

"About what?"

I open my mouth but am cut off by his phone ringing. He digs into his pocket and mutes it. The third time it rings, he sighs and puts it to his ear but keeps me trapped so I can't leave.

"What?"

His eyebrows furrow at whoever is on the phone. It's a deep voice, and as much as I wish that doesn't send a shot of relief through me, it does. "Why? Yeah, okay. I'll be there soon." He ends the call, then crowds me even closer than before, our bodies just barely touching. "That was Sawyer. I gotta get to practice early, but I'm not leaving here until you tell me what I lied about so I can fix it."

"There's nothing to fix."

He slaps a hand against my window, and I jump. "Don't play that fucking game. Tell me what happened. Did Elijah say something?" For the first time, a hint of guilt crowds his brown irises, and my stomach twists. If he's feeling guilty when it comes to Elijah, then what Elijah told me must be true. Not that I didn't believe him. I was just really hoping he had the situation wrong or something.

Apparently, it wasn't. "I can't do this with you, Reese." My voice is small. "Please let me go."

"I can't." His voice comes out equally as broken as mine, and I wish it didn't affect me, but it does. Hearing Reese so torn up only reminds me of when we were kids, and that same little girl who would hold him while he would cry begs to reach out and grab him now. But this time he's the one responsible for the tears that are refusing to fall.

"You have to try, Reese." I grip his sweatshirt. I don't know why, but this feels like goodbye, and I didn't know the last time I got to touch him would be it. "I'm tired of crying myself to sleep over you."

21

Reese

"Elijah! Put that spoon down. Your dad is going to be back from picking your sister up soon, and if you eat all the ice cream before she gets to have a float, she's going to be so upset."

Elijah groans but drops the spoon into the sink and grumbles. "My birthday celebration and I can't even have my ice cream when I want."

I chuckle and clap his back. "Yeah, but your mom is right. Would you rather wait or listen to Winnie whine the rest of the night?"

He seems to ponder, then nods. "You're right. I knew I kept you around for a reason. So, what did you get me for my birthday?"

I cock an eyebrow. "I gave you your gift last week, when it was actually your birthday, and we've been playing it every night since."

"Yeah, but I figured since we are celebrating tonight, you'd get me something else." He's grinning, but I know he's serious. Asshole.

"You owe me, like, twenty gifts. Christmases and birthdays alike."

Elijah's face splits even more with a guilty grin. "Call us even?"

I roll my eyes but take his extended hand. "Yeah, whatever. One day you're gonna owe me something big, though."

"Just say what and it's yours, man."

Oh, this could be good. I better save it for something really big. By the time I'll cash it in, he's going to owe me a shit ton of stuff, or something really big, anyway.

We're playing the birthday gift I got Elijah when someone lets out a blood-curdling scream. If I was at home, I probably wouldn't even react, and for a moment, I forget where I am because that's not something I hear at the Lewis household.

Elijah jumps out of his chair and runs for his mom, and I'm not far behind.

My feet halt at the bottom of the steps seeing the flashing red-and-blue lights and two police officers with their heads hung low outside the front door. Elijah drops by his mom's side.

"Mom, what's wrong?" He shoots a panicked look at me, then up to the cops still standing there.

One of them, the one I recognize from seeing him drop my dad off a time or two, is eyeing me. Almost like he's judging me, and it's making me uncomfortable.

"There's been an accident, son," the cop who isn't glaring at me says.

My heart slams against my chest.

An accident.

Mrs. Lewis crying.

Winnie.

Fuck, please don't be Winnie.

"W-what do you mean?" he asks. "Mom, what's he mean?"

Mrs. Lewis wipes her face, but there's no point since the tears are still falling. "Your dad was in an accident, and..."

And...

"He didn't make it."

Elijah doesn't move. I watch as the life drains from my best friend right in front of my eyes, and all I can do is stare at him.

Mr. Lewis is... dead? But, if he was in an accident, does that mean—

"What about Winnie?" Elijah thankfully asks, his voice hollow.

She shakes her head, and it takes everything in me not to throw up.

"She's fine. She's still at the airport. She doesn't know." The Lewises collapse together, their sobs filling the small room. It's suffocating. On one hand, I'm relieved Winnie wasn't involved, but I loved Mr. Lewis. I loved him more than I could ever love my own dad, and now he's... gone.

I don't know how long passes, but eventually, Mrs. Lewis pulls away and stands on shaky legs. She turns to me, but I keep my head down because it's not fair for me to cry when I'm not the one who lost my dad.

She cups my face and tilts it up to look at her. "Can you do me a favor, Reese?"

Anything. I say the word in my head because I don't trust myself to say it out loud.

She nods as if understanding. "Can you go pick up Winnie? The police officers offered to do it, but I think it would be best for one of us to do it, and we are in no state to drive."

"Of course." My voice is hoarse and hurts from biting back my emotions.

"We have to head to the hospital." Another sob rips from her, and she cups her mouth. And, finally, my dam breaks. I wrap my arms around the woman who's always been like a second mother, and I hug her soft body as tight as I can without actually hurting her.

I can't imagine the pain she feels. I've never seen someone as in love as the Lewises, and now... now she has to go through life without him.

A *few minutes pass, and then she pulls away, once again calmed down enough to speak. She wipes my face before I get the chance.* "I love you, Reese. You know that, right?"

"Yes, ma'am."

"Never forget it, okay? Promise me."

I don't understand why she's telling me this now, but I guess it's one of those things where you hold your loved ones closer after a tragedy; I'm just glad to be considered one of them.

"Promise, Mrs. Lewis."

She taps my face and lets me go. "You better get going. She should be landing anytime now."

"Okay." *I reach into my pocket and pull out my keys. Keys I was so excited to hold a few days ago when I finally saved up enough money to fix up my truck. It's a piece of shit, and the gas mileage is ass, but it's mine. I don't have to fight with my dad to get him to let me borrow his, and that's the best part about it all. I texted Winnie a video of it finally running, and she said she couldn't wait to ride in it. Sucks the first time she gets to, I have to tell her that her dad died.*

"You can just come back here. We shouldn't be too long, and she doesn't need to see anything." *Her lips wobble, but she doesn't let it out this time.* "Elijah, you might want to stay—"

"I'm coming," he snaps. He hasn't moved from the floor. Hugging his knees and leaning against the wall.

I'm not used to seeing Elijah not smiling. He smiles more than anyone I know, but right now, he looks so lost, like he's never smiled before in his life.

I crouch next to him on my way out. Unsure what to say, I rest my hand on his knee. He looks up with lost eyes and lays his hand on top.

"Brothers," I mutter. It's been something we've done forever. Usually when one of us is pissed at the other and we need a reminder that, even though we're pissed, we are still here for each other.

"Yeah." He lets out a long breath and winces. "Drive safe, please."

Winnie

"Wooowie. Listen to her!"

Reese leads me to the truck that's been sitting across the way, unable to move for so long. "It sounds even shittier in person," I joke, but he doesn't smile. I think he's trying, but it doesn't work. He's been quiet since he met me at *baggage claim. I was expecting my dad, but I'm also happy to see Reese. I just wish he was happier to see me.*

The ride home is awkward. I thought we were getting past the awkwardness after I kissed him a few months ago, but I guess not. Needing a dose of comfort, I pull my feet up, assuming he doesn't care if they are on his ripped seat, and tuck my chin. I want to blab about my time in New York because it was absolutely amazing, but it doesn't seem like the time anymore.

Right now, I'm wishing my dad was the one to pick me up.

After a while, Reese pulls up outside my house, and I frown at the darkened windows. "Is no one home?" I look over when he doesn't answer, finding him shaking his head. "What? Why not?" I thought we were celebrating Elijah's birthday today since I missed it last week.

"Winnie..." His voice is soft in a way I don't hear often. Something inside me sinks, and that feeling you get when something bad is about to happen is overwhelming. I shoot a look back to the house and push open my door. He calls after me, but I don't stop. His door slams, and his feet are quick behind me.

I shove open the front door and flick on the light. Everything looks okay. A little messier than normal, but maybe they have been busy. Moving to the kitchen, I peer at the ice cream tub sitting on the counter, melting all over the place and onto the floor.

The pit opens.

"Reese... what's going on?"

He steps behind me, and his chest shakes. I close my eyes because I instinctively know whatever he's going to say is going to destroy me.

Reese wraps his arms around me and kisses the top of my head. "I love you, Win. You know that, right?"

I did, but he's never told me outright like that before. "Reese," I whisper, scared of my own emotions swirling inside me.

"Let's go sit down." He grabs my hand and leads me into the living room. Taking a seat next to me, he keeps my hand in his and rests it on my lap. His eyebrows are pushed together, and I want to smooth that stress line between them.

"Your mom and E are at the hospital."

My chest aches with how hard my heart is beating. "Why?"

Tears burn the back of my eyes, but seeing Reese fighting with his own causes them to flow. He swipes one away and drops his focus back down to our hands. "Your dad."

Please don't.

"He, uh, he was in an accident on his way to get you, and..."

No. No. Please don't say what I think you're about to, Reese.

"He... didn't make it. I'm so, so sorry, Winnie."

Reese

Winnie hasn't stopped crying since I told her. I've been holding her for forty minutes, and I don't know what else to do. The front door clicks open, but she doesn't react, having not heard it. Mrs. Lewis walks into the room, looking even more run-down than before. She looks absolutely defeated.

She regards me with a thoughtful look, her eyebrows pulled together as she looks to her daughter in my arms. "Winnie." Her voice is weak, and she clears it.

Winnie sits up with a blotchy face and looks to her mom, who is waiting for her with open arms. Everything inside me revolts hearing Mrs. Lewis and Winnie crying for their husband and father.

Wanting and needing to give them space and get some fresh fucking air, I push to my feet and head for the entryway but stop when I notice Elijah on the front porch still, staring across to my house.

I head out and stop next to him, looking at whatever he is seeing. But there's nothing.

"I'm sorry." It sounds so fucking lame saying, but I don't know what else to say.

He dips his chin.

"If you ever wanna talk—"

"I don't."

I snap my mouth shut at his aggravated tone. "Okay."

Mrs. Lewis calls for Elijah, and he flinches, but he turns, only pausing to glare at me before storming inside, slamming the door in my face.

I know death can affect people in different ways, but I don't understand why he seems to be mad at me.

I don't move for the door, still staring at my house and wondering what he saw that would make him so angry, but I don't see it no matter how hard I look.

The door opens, and I hope it's him so he can fill me in on what is going on, but it's Mrs. Lewis. She sets my shoes down next to me.

"You better head home, sweetheart."

But I don't want to go home. I feel like they need me here. Like I—

"Reese," Mrs. Lewis cuts off my thoughts, and I drag my eyes over to her swollen ones. "It was your dad who hit Christopher."

My entire world comes crashing down with seven little words.

"What do you mean?" I regret asking as soon as I do, but I need to know exactly what she's saying because it sounds a lot like it was my dad who killed the best man I knew.

"Your dad had been drinking. He swerved into Christopher's lane, and..."

No. No. It couldn't have been my dad who killed him. God wouldn't be so cruel to put that guilt on me.

"Is he dead?" I choke on the words, even though I hope she says yes.

"No." Damn him. "But he's not doing well. The police were trying to get ahold of your mom, but she didn't answer when they called."

Yeah, she's probably already taken her drugs and passed out. I clench my fists. "Okay."

"Reese." Mrs. Lewis grabs my shoulders and forces me to look at her, brushing a piece of my hair behind my ear.

"I'm sorry." It's word vomit, and seemingly the only thing I know how to say tonight.

"You are not to blame for your father's actions, you hear me?"

I don't think Elijah feels the same; his anger toward me makes sense now. I'm angry at myself now too. Why was I given to such shit parents at birth? Why couldn't I have been born into a nice family like the Lewises'. If I was actually family, there would have never been a weird moment between Winnie and me, and my dad would have never been the cause of all of this.

"Did you tell Winnie?"

She nods her head slowly. My heart threatens to jump from my chest, and right now, I wish it would. "She asked what happened. I had to tell her, sweetheart. I'm sorry."

"You don't have to apologize." *You're not the one who killed someone.*

If anyone should, it should be my piece of shit father who is possibly lying on his deathbed. I hope he dies. I've never felt that way before, even through all the bullshit, but right now, I wish—no, I pray for my father to die.

He took away the best man, father, and friend from the best family I know. Mr. Lewis didn't deserve to lose his life. He's going to be missed by so many, but no one would miss my dad. The drunk. The murderer.

"Winnie wants the night alone, but she asked me to ask if you would meet her on the roof tomorrow."

I shoot her a sideways look. *I didn't know she knew about that.*

A gentle smile that doesn't reach her eyes graces her face. "Christopher and I knew the first time you climbed up there all those years ago, Reese. You left the fire ladder down."

Well, I didn't know that either.

She grabs my hand and squeezes. "My family is going to take some time to heal, but I don't want you pulling away. We all love you so much."

The guilt weighs on me like a boulder, but I don't want to abandon them after they've lost so much. "I'll be around as much as you need."

"Thank you. You better go wake your mom and tell her."

Fuck, that's the last thing I want to do. So I don't. Mom won't care. She's going to be too high to know what I'm saying anyway. Instead, I climb in my truck and head for the hospital.

22

Reese

I don't know why I put a leash on Eeyore every time we come outside. It's not like he can escape me.

"Is that a turtle?" A feminine laugh fills my ears from behind me, but I don't look back.

"I'm not interested." My voice is flat, but she decides to jog up to my side anyway.

"In what?" Her head tilts in fake innocence, and my insides turn.

"Whatever you're offering, I'm not interested."

She huffs and yet still doesn't go away. I knew puppies were chick magnets—babies too—but who knew a tortoise would be as well. It's fucking annoying. A guy can't even take his tortoise for a walk in peace.

"Look, I'm flattered, but I can't make it any more clear how uninterested I am in whatever you're offering."

Anger pinches her face. "You got a girlfriend or something?"

"Or something," I grumble. Something like the love of my life avoiding me for three fucking weeks. I'm not any closer to figuring out what happened, but I'll think of it. In the meantime, I've been following her around campus when I don't have class or hockey. I'm totally stalking her, even going as far as hiding in a bush when she looked my way. That was only once, but it doesn't make it any less pathetic.

"Well, whatever the deal is. Get my number, and I can help you forget."

Ha. If only it were that easy. Jennifer Aniston could proposition me and I still wouldn't forget about Winnie Lewis. She's a part of my entire heart, mind, and soul.

The girl holds out her hand with a fucking business card pinched between two long nails decked out in jewels. I stare at it, hoping I look as bored as I feel.

After an entire minute of me just staring at her, she scoffs and storms away. Thank fuck.

I lift Eeyore and tuck him into my side, feeding him the last of the lettuce I brought. We've been walking for a while. Despite Winnie pretending I don't exist, she still got me the information she promised on tortoises. And you know how she sent me the nine pages of information? My fucking school email. Addressed to my whole-ass government name and signed by hers. As if I wasn't balls deep inside of her just a few weeks ago.

With a heavy sigh, I lift the turtle to eye level. "Your mom is being a real pain in my ass."

He opens his mouth and snaps it shut. I roll my eyes and shove him back into my side. Even the fucking turtle is on her side.

"Larson," Coach booms from the side of the rink. "My office, now."

What the fuck is it this time? I know I haven't been on the EU Student News. I haven't even left my house more than necessary, so that's not it. Unless, of course, someone caught me stalking.

Fucking hell.

"Sit down, son."

At least he doesn't sound as angry as the last time I was in here, but his bushy gray eyebrows are pushed together behind his glasses.

"Something wrong, Coach?"

"Who's the girl, Reese?"

I blink. "Excuse me?"

"Don't offend me. I know puppy love when I see it, and you've been bitten hard by your puppy. So... who is she? The girl from the photo?"

I guess you gotta give the old man props for knowing his players as well as he does, but I was just starting to get Winnie out of my head. That's a bald-faced lie, but a single second went by during warm-ups when I didn't think about her.

"Yeah, it's the same girl."

He leans back and crosses his hands over his round stomach. "Well, go on. Tell me what happened."

"You want me to tell you about my relationship struggles?"

"If that's what will pull your head from your ass, sure. Now spill it, Larson. We haven't got all day. You might be having relationship struggles, but my wife of thirty-nine years is making her infamous chili, so I'd like to be home as soon as I can."

See, that's the issue because that's what I want. I want thirty-nine years with someone. No, not *someone*—I want Winnie. It fucking blows she won't even give me five minutes. Deciding there is nothing I can lose from telling Coach—besides a bit of my dignity—I spill everything. From the very start to the last time I spoke to her outside her car. He listens intently the entire time, doesn't interrupt, and waits until I finish to say anything.

"Boys these days are idiots." He huffs. "You've known this girl for how long?"

"Since I was eight, Sir."

"Then what the hell are you doing? You know well enough to know what she really wants. Yes?"

"I thought so, but every time I think I'm on the right path, it's a dead end."

He leans forward and lets out a long breath. "Because you're going about it all wrong. This girl sounds like the sentimental type. She liked that you carry a photo of her around. So you need to do something sentimental. Your gifts sound decent, personal, but they aren't sentimental. Reach into your past and figure it out."

Easier said than done, old man. If I knew what to do to get Winnie to speak with me, I would have done it weeks ago.

But maybe it's not a gift she wants at all.

What does Winnie love more than almost anything? Easy, photography. But what can I do with that? I could get her a new camera, but I don't know shit about cameras and would probably end up buying the wrong one. Maybe I can sneak into her place, steal her film, and get it developed. But the odds of me getting in and out without getting caught by someone probably aren't high.

What the fuck can I give her that deals with photography?

I don't know how long I sit there, but Coach gives me the time to think without saying anything. Looking around his office, I take in the several team photos, and something dawns on me. I don't know if it's possible or even a good idea. But it's worth a shot.

"Sir." I lean forward and lick my dry lips. "What would you think about hiring a team photographer?"

"Explain what you mean."

"I mean hiring someone—Winnie, specifically—to take photos for the team. I don't know what we will do with the photos, but I'll figure it out. I'll even be the one to pay her, but it can't come from me."

He steeples his fingers, deep in thought over my proposition. "I'm proud of you, son."

"So, is that a yes?"

His face gives nothing away, and the pause he's making me suffer through is frustrating beyond belief. "This would be a trial. If she gets in the way or becomes too big of a distraction, she's out. I can't have my guys acting a fool because there's pussy around."

Not a fan of the way he's referring to my girl as *pussy*, but he's an old-time bastard, so I let it slide.

"She won't. My high school coach used to always say I played my best when I had someone to impress. There's no one I want to impress more than her."

"I will need to speak with Kinnon and the board, because if she's going to be a part of the team, she will need a badge to tag along for games. But when I have an answer, I'll get ahold of you."

Fuck yes. "She's really good, Sir. I bet she could grow our social media shit with the right help just by making us look good."

He snorts an ugly sound. "Ain't no one making you boys look good. But I will pass along the word about social media. Mr. Kinnon was just telling Coach Miller and me that we need more press. Basketball is getting a lot of traction from bringing in some infamous player, and our numbers are down." He waves me away, lost in thought now. "Go. You'll be hearin' from me."

Sweet. I have a good feeling about this. Winnie can say no to me all day long, but she loves photography too much to ever say no to an opportunity like this. *I hope.*

23

Winnie

"Daddy, what's that?" I point to the weird thing in his hands. He's been playing with it since he found it in a box Mama said he's meant to be putting away, but he's been messing with it for a long time instead of playing with me. It looks cool, though.

He picks me up and sets me on his lap. "This is a camera, Pooh Bear. You take pictures with it. Like what Mama takes with her phone, but better." He laughs. "Don't tell her I said that."

"Why do you need a camera? What are you going to take photos of?"

"Well." He sits back. "I don't know yet. I used to work for the newspaper, you know?"

I didn't know that. "What did you do?"

"I took photos. I would go around town and take photos of cool things that would get to go in the paper."

"That sounds fun. Can I do that?"

I love it when Daddy smiles.

"Sure, sweetheart. Here." He wraps his arms around me and pushes us across the room on his wheely chair. Then he reaches into an old box and pulls out something that looks like his camera but smaller. I reach for it, but he holds it just out of reach.

"We will consider this an early birthday present, okay?"

I nod excitedly.

"This is a disposable camera, which means your photos are limited. So make sure you only take photos of the cool stuff, okay? Once you can't take any more photos, we will take it to the store and develop your film so we can see what you find cool."

He places the box camera thing in my hand. It's lighter than it looks, and I smile. I love it already.

I jump from Daddy's lap and bound for the steps.

"Be careful and have fun, Pooh Bear."

"Will do, Daddy. Thank you," I shout over my shoulder.

I thought it would be easier to find something cool enough to photograph, and I've come close to taking my first one a few times, but none of them have felt right. The sound of Elijah hitting slap shots into the net outside travels in through the windows, and I turn for the front door. Maybe Elijah will be cool enough for me to photograph.

I stop on the edge of the step when I realize he's not alone. Another boy who looks to be his same age is playing street hockey with him, but he's not wearing roller blades like Elijah. I wander over, my camera ready in case anything cool happens. As if the boy knows what I'm doing, he picks the tennis ball up with his stick and starts doing all these cool tricks I've never seen Elijah do before.

I pull the camera up to my eyes, focus on the boy, and snap my first photo.

My first snapshot.

He shoots the ball into the net, then turns to look at me. "Did you just take a photo of me?"

Uh, am I meant to ask first? Well, it's too late if I am. "Yeah, I'm going to be a photographer one day."

"Sweet." He shrugs. "I'm Reese. Your new neighbor."

"Like the candy?"

He rolls his eyes. "Yes. What's your name?"

"Winnie."

Reese smiles a really pretty smile, and I quickly snap another photo before it slips.

"Like the bear?"

Ugh. "Yes, but don't call me that. I only like my daddy calling me Pooh Bear. Unless I can call you Eeyore."

He scrunches his nose. "Why Eeyore?"

"Elijah is already Tigger."

"No, I'm not." Elijah says. "We can call her pain-in-the-ass because that's what she is."

My mouth drops. "I'm telling Mom you cussed. And I am not." I huff, crossing my arms over my chest.

"I don't think you're a pain."

I meet Reese's eyes again, enjoying the way the sun above makes them look like melted honey. "No?"

He smiles and shakes his head. "Nope, you seem cool."

Elijah skates up to his side and frowns at me. "You just met her."

But Reese shrugs, not caring about that fact. And neither do I. I think I like Reese.

A lot.

24

Winnie

There are lots of photographers in the world. The people who get paid and others who simply enjoy a good snapshot. But every one of them will be able to tell you their favorite subjects to photograph. Mine is humans. Particularly action or candid photos. When the person is being a human and doing normal things.

For the past few weekends, I've been finding myself around campus, snapping photos of innocent bystanders. Sometimes they will catch me, others not. But I haven't gotten in trouble yet. It's not like I'm doing anything weird with the photos. We have a project due in a few months that's worth 33 percent of our grade. The kind of project was up to us, but it had to involve photography, obviously, and be able to tell a story or a lesson of some kind without us actually *telling* it. I'm not sure what my story is just yet, but I'm hoping all these photos will work for it, or I'm screwed.

With the camera held up to my face, I turn in a half circle, changing my direction. A couple walks by, and I snap their photo, but they are too busy smiling at each other to notice. Cute. *Gag me*. I turn again but come face-to-face with a familiar man right in my lens.

"Mr. Hudson." I jump, startled to see him.

"Hello, Winnie. What are you doing out here?"

"Taking photos." *Obviously*. "What are *you* doing here?"

A crooked smile tilts his lips. "On my way back from a meeting. One about you, actually."

Surprised, my eyebrows shoot up my forehead. "Me? What about me?"

"Why don't we head to my office to discuss it?"

Mr. Hudson is the most intimidating person I've ever met. I don't know why, but being in a small office alone with him sounds... dangerous. Not that I think he's going to do anything inappropriate. It must just be Reese's warning getting to my head. Mr. Hudson has never been anything but professional. In fact, I'm pretty sure he's married. Unless he wears a wedding band for fun.

"I'm sorry, *what*?"

Mr. Hudson dips his chin. "They were very adamant about wanting you, and I can't say I blame them. You have a real gift, Winnie."

My cheeks burn at his words. I get compliments from my mom, used to from Reese and Elijah back in the day, but none of them know anything about photography. Mr. Hudson has a degree in it, teaches it to students for a living, and is an infamous photographer around the area. He's known for *eclectic* tastes. I saw some of his work before, and most of the subjects were naked or close to it.

"But why don't they hire a professional? Why not you?" I can't understand why the college hockey team specifically asked for me. Of course, I have an idea, but that would be crazy for Reese to get his coaches and the athletic director to meddle in... whatever is going on between us.

"You are cheaper," he states, but I'm not offended. He's right, after all. "The team has been lacking in their number of fans attending games. They are hoping with your skills and the help of a social media manager, their fan base will grow. You'll send the photos and videos to the manager, and they will post them as a form of marketing. Apparently, it is quite popular right now."

It almost seems too good to be true. I'd be making money—not a lot, but some change—*and* doing what I love most? Of course, that's always been the goal, but I'm only a freshman. Only a few weeks into the school year, at that.

"And they saw my work?"

"I showed them, yes."

My eyebrows furrow, but I push it away. I'm sure he has my application on file. "Well, I don't really have any reason to say no."

"No, you don't." He chuckles, then folds his hands together on top of his desk. "This is a great opportunity. It would be foolish to turn it down."

I lean back and sigh. "Well, when do I start?"

A bright smile splits his face. "We all agreed that a trial run would benefit everyone. They can decide if you are the right choice—which I have no doubt you are—and you can decide if you even like taking their photos."

I don't know why I wouldn't. Sure, Reese will be there, but I can put everything between us aside for the sake of this amazing opportunity. If I do well for them, my dream of photographing professional teams doesn't seem so unrealistic.

"They have morning practice on Saturday. I will come with you and assist in anything you need until you are comfortable enough on your own."

That's only two days away. I don't have much to prepare, but I'll need to make sure my cameras are fully charged and I have a few empty memory cards. I'm sure the store in town sells cards, so I won't have to delete anything I currently have.

"Thanks, Mr. Hudson. I'm really excited."

"You should be. This is a great opportunity. Especially if you would like to make a career out of sports photography, which I saw on your application that you do."

"That's right. I've always liked the action sports bring."

"Anyone in your life help encourage that?"

I wonder if he's hinting at Reese, but surprisingly, he wasn't the reason. Not the biggest, anyway.

"Yeah, my dad. He was a photographer too. Not professional, but he worked for the local newspaper in my hometown until me and my brother were born and he needed to make more money."

"Does your dad still photograph?"

I swallow against the lump in my throat. "No, he unfortunately died a couple years ago."

"I am sorry to hear that, Winnie."

A beat of awkward silence passes before I say, "Thanks. But the reason I like sports specifically is because he played hockey in college, and he used to coach my brother's team growing up. He always let me tag along, and I would snap photos the entire time. I don't know." I shrug. "I just really liked it. Men are sort of beautiful when they are doing something they love, you know?"

No, Winnie, he probably doesn't know. Why did I say that out loud?

"Humans are extraordinary," he concurs, unaffected by my weird comment. But I suppose someone who takes nude photos of people would probably agree.

I twist my lips, debating if I should bring up his work, but might as well. The conversation is already awkward enough. "I looked you up. When I was researching the school, I mean."

He settles into his chair, not at all bothered. "And? What did you find?"

"Your boudoir shoots. Specifically the one with that pretty blonde with the heterochromia eyes."

"Ahh." He chuckles. "Yes, I was in college and trying to make some side money. Boudoir was the popular thing. Big money-maker."

"They were beautiful photos."

"Yes, they were." He dips his chin. "I don't photograph boudoir for anyone but my wife now, but I enjoyed it at the time. Nothing is sexier than a confident woman. I assume you feel the same about men, as confidence is appealing in either gender. Men are confident during sports, which would be your appeal."

I never considered it lustful, but I suppose, in a way, me photographing men in the state I do is similar to him photographing women in the state he used to. I do think it's sweet that he no longer photographs any other woman besides his wife, though.

"I never thought about it like that, but I suppose you're right."

"I usually am." He grins, and I laugh.

"Now I feel dirty."

He flashes his bright teeth and throws his head back, laughing. "Photography is intimate no matter the circumstance. Do not be embarrassed by that, or you will struggle to get anywhere."

I narrow my eyes. "How did you meet your wife, Mr. Hudson?"

"On a photo shoot."

"A boudoir one?"

He dips his chin. "That's right. She was getting photos done for her boyfriend at the time, but I looked into her eyes, one blue, one brown, and that was it. I was infatuated with a taken woman."

My eyebrows shoot up my forehead. "No way, that girl is now your wife?" I'm not into girls, but I can admit when a girl is hot, and the photos I saw of her were *hot*. Like she was making love with the camera. "That's a bit scandalous, Mr. Hudson."

He chuckles darkly. "He was a lame excuse for a man. Didn't deserve the photos anyway."

"Well, what did you do? You know, to make her yours?"

He smirks before meeting my eyes with a distant look. "What any lovestruck man would do. Anything it took."

Someone knocks on my bedroom door, and I call for them to come in. It's probably Elijah. He mentioned that he was going out tonight and would let me know when.

I've been in my room most of the day, having woken up sick. Even had to miss my photography class, but Mr. Hudson said it was fine in the email he sent and offered to fill me in tomorrow at the rink if need be.

I'm just hoping I wake up feeling better tomorrow. It would be miserable taking photos with how I'm feeling.

"You look like shit."

Brothers. Always there to humble you.

"Yeah, thanks."

He steps in, his eyebrows furrowed, and walks over to place a hand on my forehead. "You're not warm. What's wrong?"

"I don't know. Just a stomach bug, I think. I've thrown up, like, three times since breakfast."

Worry etches over his harsh face. "Do you want me to stay home?"

"No, I'm a big girl."

He seems to think it over, then sighs. "Yeah, but you'll always be my baby sister. If you want me to stay home, I will."

"No, I really don't want you to. I want to curl up on the couch and watch *Friends*, but I can't do that with you breathing down my neck."

He matches my smile and ruffles my hair. "Fine. But call me if you need anything. I might not answer right away, but I'll call you back."

I'm half tempted to ask where he's going. Where he disappears to every Friday and Saturday night since I moved in, but I know he won't tell me. The first time I asked, he ignored me. And the second time, he told me it was a need-to-know situation and I didn't need to know. Asshole.

"Yeah, go have fun. Or whatever."

He smirks and kisses my forehead. "Get some sleep, too."

"Okay, *Dad*. Go."

We freeze, and I swallow hard. "Eli..."

But he's already storming from my room. A haunted look across his face.

My already-upset stomach rolls, and I sprint to the bathroom.

I don't know what is making me sick, or at least I'm trying really hard not to think about what it could be.

25

Reese

The first time I came to The Underground, I was drunk and don't remember much, but ever since that first night when I saw my old best friend getting the shit beat out of him, I'm stone-cold sober when I walk through those double doors. I don't come every weekend, and I haven't been here since the start of school.

I don't even know why I'm here tonight. On the off chance Winnie tagged along? Elijah would never allow her to come here, and for good reason. It's a shithole. I mean, what else would an illegal underground boxing ring be besides a shithole?

Girls are practically naked, and I've seen guys do unthinkable things to the workers carrying drinks. Yeah, this definitely isn't the place for Winnie.

Sawyer leads us across the large room to a couple tables in the back. It's not a great view, but I don't particularly like seeing Elijah nearly kill guys. I just know he's imagined them as me a time or two.

It's hard for me to accept the person Elijah is these days; he's so different from when we were kids. He was always the happy one. Constantly cracking jokes and teasing. He loved his family more than life and was really good about making me forget my shitty homelife. I never told him much, but it's not like I had to tell him my parents argued when you could hear it clear as day most of the time.

Elijah loved hockey almost as much as I did, and then his dad died and everything changed. He only played because he knew his dad really wanted him to, so when he died, he quit. But he was good. He would probably be playing next to me instead of fighting in cages to get an itch scratched if my dad had never killed his.

That's not an easy pill for me to swallow.

Brogan drops three beers and a coke for me onto the table before taking his seat. "Word is Ace is in a mood tonight. They are saying this is going to be a good fight."

Mood? What the fuck does that mean? "Who is he fighting?"

Schmidt pulls up the paper he grabbed by the door to read the lineup. "Lincoln."

Shit. Lincoln is another good fighter. I get why people are saying it's going to be a good one. Still, my money is on Elijah—or *Ace*, as he goes by down here. Even if I knew he was going to lose, I couldn't stand myself not to put my faith in him. He might hate me, but I don't think I could ever find it in me to hate him.

Before the main event, there are always a few smaller fights. Some women fighters, others just rookie guys who haven't earned a proper name yet.

The night passes slowly, and each minute closer to Elijah's fight, my anxiety fucking spikes.

Finally, his name is announced over the intercom, and Lincoln's follows. Cheers and boos alike sound from all around us. Lincoln is loyal to The Underground. Elijah is a wild card who won't commit to anywhere. So, by default, Lincoln has more fans, but Elijah can hold his own without the screaming crowd.

Normally, when the guys move closer to watch, I stay back, but tonight I slip from the chair and trail after them. Taking our place on the far end.

It's obvious Lincoln is out for blood tonight. He's more savage than usual, but whatever mood Elijah is in is helping him meet each of Lincoln's punches with his own. It's like a game for Elijah. Growing up, he would pick fights with kids just to tumble. He found joy in it, and this is no different. Even with blood dripping down his face, he's still smirking. This is the only place he looks genuinely happy.

The third round starts, and both guys are stumbling around with looks of determination across their bloody faces. I wish I could tell who is going to win, but I can't. Lincoln took the first round, but Elijah came out on top with the second. If he loses, I'm only losing out on a hundred bucks, so it's not going to break my bank. But I was hoping to walk out with more than I walked in with.

I'm going to have to start paying Winnie to take our photos—why I stupidly offered that, I don't know. But Mr. Kinnon, Miller, and Coach took me up on it. Fifty bucks every game, and fifteen for practices. It doesn't seem like a lot, but it adds up. My savings are heavy, but I'm saving for my future and would like to keep it that way. Paying the girl I love to take photos of me wasn't in that plan, but hopefully all that money will one day end up in our joint account.

The crowd is going wild. Shouting unintelligible things, and the guys are feeding off it. Lincoln stands taller, and Elijah looks ready to kill. Which wouldn't be the first time. It's never on purpose, I *think*, but with a fucked-up place like this, death can happen, and I've seen Elijah kill before. Not something I enjoy remembering.

I would never want Winnie to know about this side of her brother, and I'm guessing he feels the same.

Elijah ducks and dodges every punch thrown his way. He has speed on most of the guys he fights, but usually, the other guys pack more of a punch. Lincoln is huge, with arms probably double the size of Elijah's, and I know every punch he takes fucking hurts.

Elijah ducks under him and comes out behind. He kicks him in the back, and Lincoln stumbles forward.

Elijah uses that time to jump on his back, then jabs his elbow into his neck three times until Lincoln drops to his knees. Then Elijah pulls his knee back and slams it into his face.

When Lincoln drops to the ground and they call the fight, my mouth is hanging open.

"You're buying the 'za tonight." Schmidt slaps my back on our way out of the building after I collect my money. Everyone else bet against Elijah, like every time, but I bet they are regretting it because I'm five thousand dollars richer than them currently.

"Fair enough." I grin.

We head for Sawyer's truck but stop when the sound of gagging fills the air around us. It's hard to see anything with it being so dark, but there's a small light from the end of a cigarette, and without going to look, I know who is getting their dick sucked.

"Let's go," I mutter, not really wanting to hear Elijah get off.

We just get to Sawyer's truck when he calls after us.

I freeze with the door handle still in my hand.

"Lose some money tonight?" he asks bitterly.

"Actually—" Brogan starts, but I cut him off with a harsh stare. If Elijah knew I bid on him, he'd be pissed.

Turning, I stand face-to-face with the guy I once considered a brother. He's still shirtless, covered in even more tattoos than the last time I saw him, and puffing on a cigarette.

"Good fight," I comment.

His jaw tightens, and his eyes flick over my shoulder. "You." He nods in Sawyer's direction.

"What?" Sawyer asks, probably as confused as I am.

"Yeah." Elijah walks around the truck, stomping on the cigarette as he does. As soon as he's in arm's reach of Sawyer, his fist bolts out, and he smokes him in the nose.

"Fuck!" Sawyer cups his face, but he's on Elijah a second later, slamming his fist against his face. Elijah slips from under him and backs away, breathing hard and looking around at the four of us as if we are the enemy. I guess right now, we are. I wouldn't willingly fight Elijah, but he just socked Sawyer in the face for no reason.

"What the fuck?" I bark out.

"That's for fucking my sister." Elijah spits a wad of blood onto the ground, and I realize he's not looking at me. And it wasn't me he punched—this time.

"What the fuck are you talking about?" Sawyer snaps, still holding his nose.

What the fuck *is* he talking about?

"She told me about the night she went out. You fucked her without telling her you're not fucking single."

She told him *what*? Sawyer darts a look at me, but I don't have the answers for him.

"What else did she say?" I ask, hoping to find out what the hell is happening right now.

"Does it matter?" he barks before turning the opposite way. "Oh, by the way, if you were wondering why she hates you." He spins but continues walking backward. "I told her how big of a piece of shit you are."

"What did you tell her?" I growl and step forward. He's down the street, but I can see him shrug from here with the help of the streetlights bouncing off his pale skin.

"Only the truth. Night, boys. Stay the fuck away from my sister."

Then he's gone. Around the back of the building. Sawyer turns, no longer bleeding, but his face is fucked, no less. He's for sure going to have two black eyes.

"Why the fuck did your girl tell him we fucked?"

That's a good fucking question. It wasn't Sawyer's bed she was in that night. It was mine, so why did she lie? The obvious answer is Elijah despises me and only hates Sawyer, but that still doesn't make sense why she is telling her brother who she fucked anyway. Not unless there was a reason she had to, but that doesn't make sense either.

Pinching the bridge of my nose, I shake my head. "I don't know. I'll figure it out, though."

"If Amy hears, she's going to lose her fucking shit, and I'm letting you pick up that call."

Fucking thanks, Win.

"Let's get some ice and 'za. Practice is going to come around early."

I jump into my seat, and Sawyer takes his. The other two guys already loaded into the back.

"What's he mean about you being a p-o-s?" Brogan asks. "How do you know him?"

I've done my best to keep my old life and this one separate, especially from someone like Brogan, who I'm not that close to. He's on the team, but he's sort of a dick. The only time we hang out is during fight nights.

I should have known Winnie being in town would dig it all back up and expose me to the people I have been close to for the last two years. That it would be impossible to keep everything separate anymore.

"We grew up across the street from each other." Bright lights flash and blur as Pinecove's nightlife passes by outside the window. "There was a point I considered Elijah a brother."

"What happened?" Sawyer asks, glancing in my direction.

I could blame my dad, and it would probably be true, to a point. But a few weeks after Christopher's death, Elijah caught me outside practicing slap shots and joined me. We didn't say anything, but after that night, things were better between us. Not great, but better. We probably would have made a full recovery if it wasn't for the night of that fucking party.

"Zoey happened," I ground out.

"Zoey? Like, Zoey Miller?"

I nod. "She was into me back in high school—"

Schmidt snorts. "You say that like she's not still."

"Yeah, well, my feelings for her never changed. I have never liked her or felt remotely the same. Eventually, she and Eli started dating." My fists tighten. "Long story short, she set me up. Made it look like we slept together and had Elijah catch us."

"Crazy bitch," Sawyer gasps.

"I told you." I warned them all to stay the fuck away from her as soon as her dad mentioned her coming to school here after she graduated from high school.

"But how did she stage it?" Brogan asks.

I shrug. "We were all at a party. I drank a lot and found a room to sleep in. Sometime during the night, she snuck in, took off all her clothes, and crawled in with me. Elijah walked in the next morning and saw us."

I'll never forget the look on his face. So much hatred. We were just getting back to normal, and Zoey ruined it all.

"Are you sure you didn't actually fuck, though?" Sawyer glances my way.

I nod. "Yeah. I hated her. I would have never, even drunk."

The truck falls silent, and I sigh. "My heart has always laid with one girl, and it's not Zoey. I've never slept with anyone other than Winnie, no matter how drunk I get."

Each guy takes a turn questioning me on my two-year celibacy and how it was possible, but I don't have an answer for them. It was easy because none of the girls who showed interest were Winnie. Simple as that.

"None of that makes sense as to why he thinks *we* fucked, though."

No, it doesn't. Sawyer's right. "I don't know, man, but I'll find out."

"You don't think Zoey, like, jumped her when she left our place and filled her head with crazy stuff, do you?" Schmidt asks.

My stomach threatens to expel everything I've eaten today. The thought of Zoey filling Winnie's head with lies is something I could have seen coming. She's crazy enough, but I hadn't been thinking about her.

"Maybe Zoey saw you two together and threatened to tell her brother," Sawyer offers.

"And because Elijah hates your guts, she said it was Sawyer," Schmidt adds.

"She should have said me. I'd never let that dick punch me."

Sawyer and I swap looks because we both know Brogan is the biggest pussy on the team.

At a red light, Sawyer tugs down his mirror to eye the damage. "How am I meant to explain two black eyes to Amy when we video call tomorrow?"

"Hockey," the three of us say. It's more than believable. I don't know one hockey player who hasn't had a black eye or something close at some point. Brogan is missing two teeth, for fuck's sake, so I know he has been hit in the face. Injuries are more than common.

Sleep doesn't come easy to me. My head is spinning with everything I learned today. Everything we talked about makes sense—too much sense—and just imagining what Winnie is thinking about me right now is enough to drive me insane. I drop my arm over my eyes and urge sleep to come. The quicker I can get to sleep, the quicker practice will come, and I can hopefully fix things with Winnie.

26

Reese

I remember the first time I ever got jealous of Winnie's attention being on someone other than me. Elijah was having his fourteenth birthday at their house like he did most years. It was a pool party. His mom always went over the top for parties, and looking back now, it's not that there was a lot of expensive shit, but I remember there being so much food. Mr. Lewis would make their cake, even though his wife is a professional baker—it was always their thing. I even got a cake on my birthday when it rolled around.

A bunch of us were in the above-ground pool, and a game of chicken broke out. It was one of those rectangle ones, so it was big enough for the twenty or so people who were there. A random girl from our grade was on my shoulders, and I remember being in the middle of playing when I saw Ryan Thompson swim up to Winnie. I couldn't hear him, but whatever he was saying was making her smile, and it irked me. I didn't understand what the deal was or why I was so pissed when she climbed onto his shoulders, but looking back now, I was jealous. I think in my head, I've always known Winnie was mine. The meaning shifted over the years, but I've never enjoyed when I wasn't the one making her smile.

The same can still be said today as her teacher grins and she giggles into her hand. If you didn't know their dynamic, you would probably think they were together, but they're not. And apparently, rules don't mean shit now because I'm pretty sure he shouldn't be standing so close to her. If that's not in the rulebook, it should be.

"Who's the suit?" Gavin stops next to me.

I answer with a tight jaw, and his eyebrows inch up his forehead.

"He's a little close for being her teacher, nah?"

It's worse knowing he notices it too.

I'm across the ice from her, but I knew when she walked in. I could feel her in the building. What I didn't expect to see with her carrying her camera shit was this prick.

"Yes."

He claps my back before skating away. "Good luck with that one, bro."

I don't need luck; I *need* Winnie.

Knowing the issue between us, I know I can save it; I just need to get her away from Mr. Flirt. I don't care about spilling everything in front of him, but I doubt Winnie wants her teacher in her business.

"Larson," Coach booms.

Winnie and whatever the fuck his name is look toward the ice. We meet eyes for the first time, and she stiffens. I continue staring at her until she looks away; then I drift my eyes to the teacher and narrow them. He looks unbothered, and that pisses me off more.

Unwillingly, I skate over to the team but keep Winnie in my sight.

"Alright," Coach snaps. "It's obvious you guys have noticed the pu—girl in the rink. She is here in hopes to make you sorry saps look good. I expect you all"—he locks eyes on me—"to be on your best behavior. She's here on a trial basis," he reminds me specifically.

"Make us look good for what?"

"To grow our numbers. Ms. Lewis will be taking photos, videos, and whatever else she needs to at practice and games, and they will get posted wherever it is kids are into these days. A way to gain attraction and foot traffic."

Winnie takes her first steps onto the ice looking so similar to the peewees we sometimes help coach. She used to be good at skating, but I guess Eli stopped, and she had no reason to skate anymore since I was hardly around.

With her arms held out to her side and her feet shuffling in her skates, she makes her way toward the group.

"Christ almighty," Coach grumbles, followed by a few snickers.

Her teacher steps onto the ice, and I will him to be shit at skating, but of course he's not. He reaches her in no time and makes a half circle around her, stopping when he is in front of her and holding his hands out.

Fuck no. Without another thought, I'm off and stopping at her side. I must startle her because she gasps, and the next thing I know, she's going down. I grab one arm, and the stupid teacher grabs the other, stopping her from falling on her ass.

"Holy shit," she breathes, pink creeping onto her neck. "Sorry, Neil."

Neil? Did she just call her teacher by his first name? *What the actual fuck?*

"It is not your fault you almost fell." His harsh eyes flick to me, and I glare right back.

As if just noticing her arm in mine, she pulls away from both of us, but me first. *I'm going to kill this dude.*

"Nice to see you again." He dips his chin, but we both know it's not.

"Can't say the same." I grunt as Winnie throws an elbow into my gut, shooting me a warning look, but I roll my eyes because I don't fucking care what she says, I hate this guy.

She wobbles again, but when I reach for her, she shoos my hands away. "I'm fine."

I fucking hate that this prick is watching her be cold to me, and even more that he seems amused by it.

"We need to talk."

"No we don't," she hisses, shooting me another look that I ignore.

I lower my eyes to her feet and frown. "Why are you so bad at skating? You were never this bad."

"Thanks, asshole, but it's been a while. I just need to get used to it again." Hopefully she gets used to it soon so this fucker can back the fuck off my woman.

Coach calls for her, but she doesn't let me help her up in front of the group. As soon as she's out of earshot, I look over to her teacher since he's still standing next to me, watching her struggle to the front.

"She's taken, you know?"

He smirks but quickly wipes it away, and I want so badly to throw a punch in his pretty-boy face. "That is not what she told me, but nonetheless, I have no interest in being a stereotype and starting something with a student."

"Could have fooled me," I murmur.

He chuckles as if I said something funny, but I didn't. "Winnie reminds me a lot of my baby sister."

I eye him, waiting to call his bluff, but my attention is pulled away when Coach speaks.

"This is Winnie. Everyone say hello."

Her cheeks bloom a bright red at the team's attention and them all saying her name.

She stumbles, and he grips her shoulders, holding her steady. "You sure you're going to be able to stay on your feet and not your ass?"

"I'm a fast learner," she assures him, but I'm almost positive he can see through her bullshit. Winnie is a fast learner, but it's easy to tell how nervous she is waiting for a skate to kick out or something.

"Prove it," he gripes before turning on his heel and walking away.

We know what to do without needing him to direct us, and while the guys head to start warm-ups, I skate up to her, making sure not to cause her to fall this time.

"You need to warm up."

"I will."

Her chocolate eyes flick up to me, worry resting deep in the depths. "I'm on a trial basis here, Reese. I can't have your coach getting mad at me because you're distracted."

I know she's right, and maybe this wasn't the best idea I've ever had. Having Winnie here might be more of a distraction than I expected. Especially with Mr. Flirt following her around. "Why is your teacher here?"

She rolls her eyes. "He's coming to the first few practices in case I need help. Which"—she gestures to her pigeon-toed skates—"I'm obviously going to need."

"Stay after practice today. I can help you get back into skating in no time."

She eyes me curiously, and I wonder if she's going to say no, but she must have decided better because she nods her head, and I let out a deep breath.

"Fine, but only for skating lessons. I don't want to talk about anything besides hockey, skating, and ice."

I don't know how realistic that is for us, but I'm willing to try anything, so I agree, and we shake on it. Winnie and I have never had a surface-level relationship. Even as kids, I was constantly catching myself spilling my deepest secrets.

The moment Coach releases us, I drop my gear on the bench and hurry over to Winnie. She stayed off the ice most of practice after I saw her struggling to get anywhere. I actually preferred when she wasn't out here because it allowed her teacher to back the fuck off, at least a small amount. He was still around, looking like he was directing her at some points, but at least that didn't require him touching her.

"Ready for your lesson?" I butt in on their conversation, not giving a shit.

Winnie shoots me a dirty look, but he has the audacity to smirk.

"Sorry, Neil."

I fucking hate her apologizing for me as if I'm some kind of inconvenience in her life. And I hate her calling him Neil.

"It's not a problem, Winnie. I need to get home anyway. I promised my wife we would head to the pumpkin patch today."

Winnie's eyes light up, and my jaw clenches.

"Oh, I love the pumpkin patch. Have a great time."

He smiles and turns in my direction. "See you both Monday."

I grumble, and he chuckles before walking away.

Winnie zips her bag up and spins to me, placing her hands on her narrow hips. "Stop being rude to him."

"Why? He's a douche who is flirting with someone who is not his wife. That should bother you."

"He's not flirting with me, Reese. He's helping me so I don't get sacked by your coach. He actually cares about my future."

"So do I, Win. Who do you think got you this opportunity?"

She pauses while reaching for her skates, and I reach down and lift them to her frozen hands.

"No one cares about your future more than me, Winnie, because *I'm* going to be a part of that future. Remember that."

Winnie

I can't believe Reese did that for me. No, I *can* believe it, and that's the worst part. Reese has always gone out of his way for me. Any opportunity he thought I would enjoy or that would benefit me, he got it for me. Like when I was in middle school, and the local animal shelter was looking for volunteer dog walkers. I was too young, and even with Reese's convincing, they weren't budging on that, so he asked if I could help as long as he was there. We spent the summer walking dogs, even though Reese is allergic. He showed up to help every day simply because he knew I would enjoy getting to be with dogs. And he was right. Dad always said we were too busy to have one, and he wasn't wrong, but like most kids, I always wanted one.

It wasn't hard being around Reese during practice. I was distracted enough trying to get the best shots and basically just staying on my feet. But now that it's just us on the ice, it's a lot more intimate than I am ready for. It's not like I can move away from him, either. I can hardly move at all.

"I can't believe how bad you are."

I scowl, but he's not wrong, and I can't believe it either. I didn't grow up on the ice like Elijah and Reese, but I was on it enough I shouldn't suck so bad.

"You were never good, but you could at least let go of the wall."

I'm only holding on to the wall because I don't want to hold him.

No matter how mad I am at Reese, my body doesn't seem to agree, and watching him today didn't help any. Mr. Hudson's words were loud and clear in my head during the entire practice to the point it was like foreplay watching Reese, and I worry if I touch him now, he will somehow be able to sense the heat for him between my thighs.

"I thought you were here to teach me, not make fun of me?"

"I'm going to need you to let go of the wall and look at me if I'm going to teach you, Win."

I turn my head enough to see his weary smile. He grips the back of his neck, and I'm able to see the veins in his forearms, still bulging from his workout. Why does he have to be so ridiculously hot? It's so unfair. His light-brown hair flops over his forehead, and his smile is crooked. His honey eyes look more golden than ever despite the shitty fluorescent lighting over us.

But he fucked Zoey and lied about it.

"Start teaching. I have plans tonight."

I don't. I have no plans or anyone I would even have plans with. I've gotten a few texts from Emma wanting to hang out and explain, but I don't think I want to hear it. Seeing Reese here is enough. I don't want to risk seeing him at his place, too. Or Sawyer. I saw the black eyes, and I'm sure those are from my brother. And I'm not interested in explaining any of that to them. Laney has also messaged me a few times, but she's asking questions I don't have the answers to, nor do I care to find out.

It's occurred to me that there could be something growing inside me, but I'm not willing to find out for sure just yet.

"With who?"

"Myself." There's no point in lying; he would know I was anyway.

His shoulders relax and he nods a few times. "I was planning on grabbing a bite after. I thought maybe we could talk?"

"There's nothing to talk about."

"Yes there is, Win. I know Zoey got to you, but what-ever she said was a lie."

I tense hearing her name fall from his lips. Everything Elijah told me comes flooding back full force, and it takes everything inside me not to cry. "I can't do this." I look around for the closest door and head for it.

"Win." He catches my arm, and I wobble but don't fall. "Please, you gotta believe me."

"Do I?" I whip around now that I'm on solid ground. Dropping onto the bench, I quickly rip my skates off as fast as the stupid laces allow.

"I love you," he blurts, and if I wasn't sitting, I would have fallen over. "I know I've fucked up—a few times—but I do, Winnie. Zoey and I have never been anything. The only reason you saw us at the store together was because her dad had to stick around here after a summer practice, and he asked one of us to bring her back to the dorms. She needed to stop by the store, but that was it. We've never been together and we aren't now."

It takes everything for me to lift my eyes to his. Reese is a lot of things, but a liar isn't one of them. At least I never thought so. "Why does Elijah think you fucked?"

"Because he caught us in bed together."

"Naked?"

His head falls, and he nods.

"And I'm meant to believe you didn't fuck?" I snort a humorless laugh. "Come on, Reese."

"I know." His voice is low, and I have to force my body not to tremble from his deep, masculine tone. "I know how it sounds and how it looked to him, but I fucking swear, Winnie."

I stand, making sure not to get too close to him because his natural, manly scent is potent and not helping with the dampness down below.

"Believe it or not, Reese. But I don't really believe your swears anymore."

"I don't have anything else, Win. If I had proof we didn't other than my word, I'd give it. But it's not as easy to prove we didn't as it would be to prove we did. All she had to do was strip and it was believable."

The thought of Reese naked with another girl, especially Zoey, isn't a nice one. Anything I was feeling during practice is gone. The only thing I feel now is my heart breaking. He seems genuine, but it could be guilt. "I'd love to believe you, Reese, but I can't."

He slumps forward, crowding my space, and cups my cheek. I want to push him off, but I don't.

"Please. I lost my best friend because of her. I can't lose you too."

A battle rages inside me. A part of me wants to believe him, because I've known Reese for over half my life and used to believe everything he said, but there is the other part. The part that remembers how heartbroken I was after he left for college without a goodbye.

How I felt seeing him and Zoey at the store.

How I felt that night in Sawyer's apartment when he pantsed me.

And how I felt when my brother told me the story.

If I believed Reese, what would that tell Elijah? That his word means less than Reese's? I can't do that to him. Elijah is the only family I have here. We've only just gotten close again, and if I don't take his word, it would crush him. He wouldn't show it, but I know him well enough, and he would probably never speak to me again. He's already not happy about me being here in the first place.

I step away from Reese, and his body shakes.

"I can't do this to him. Even if I did believe you, Elijah never would. He knows what he saw, and no one can convince him otherwise. I'm sorry, but I can't lose my brother, Reese."

"I can't lose *you*." His voice cracks, right along with my heart. "I'll do anything, Winnie. I'll fucking swear on a Bible. Take a lie detector right in front of Elijah."

The faintest of smirks tilts my lips as I back away more. "I don't even think God himself could convince Elijah he didn't see what he thinks he saw."

27

Reese

I already regret this, but I need the one person who might be able to convince Elijah and Winnie. The only other person who was in the room that night and who I *know* knows what actually happened. Elijah is going to be the hard one to convince; Winnie looked like she maybe already believed me, but her brother thinks less of me than she ever could. If I can get Zoey to tell them the truth, maybe, just maybe, that will fix everything.

I just hope meeting with Zoey doesn't do more damage than good.

"What's good here?"

Is it possible to clench your jaw so tight it may never open? Because right now I feel like it could happen.

"Just fucking decide," I growl, hoping my harsh voice urges her to order, but the waitress comes by, and Zoey shoos her away for the second time.

She's going to make me rip my fucking hair out. I tug my cap off and drag my hand through my hair before shoving it back on.

"But I want to like what I get." Her pout has to be the most annoying thing I've ever seen. It's in close competition to the annoyance I felt when she walked in wearing a dress that barely contained the breasts her daddy bought for her last year. That was a glorious time because Zoey disappeared for the entire healing process.

I picked this hole-in-the-wall diner for a few rea- sons—one of them being it's definitely not a place I'd ever bring a date.

Fed up, I wave the waitress over and order two club sandwiches.

"I don't eat meat!"

The waitress pauses her pen, but I assure her it's fine and send her on her way. Folding my hands on the table, I narrow my eyes.

"Then this will be quick because you'll be hungry." If I come home with an extra club, one of the guys will eat it. Or I could swing by Winnie's on the way home and give it to her, she loves sandwiches. Maybe if her brother wasn't like a fucking bodyguard set out on keeping us apart.

Zoey puffs her lips out and crosses her arms over her chest. "If you didn't ask me out for a date, what the hell am I doing here, Reese?"

"I want something from you." Seeing her eyes light up, I regret the words immediately. "Not like that." My jaw clenches for what feels like the hundredth time in the last twenty minutes since she sat down at the table.

"Well, what else could you want from me?"

It's almost sad she thinks sex is the only thing she has to offer. Then again, maybe it is. Whatever, not my problem.

"The truth."

Her eyebrows knit. "What do you mea—"

"I need you to tell Elijah and Winnie the truth about that night."

Her lips flatten, and any smugness she was holding deflates, along with her shoulders. "What truth?"

"You know what truth, Zoey. The only fucking truth there is—we didn't fuck."

Her eyes shoot around the room, I'm guessing looking for listeners, but another reason I picked this place is because it's on the outer part of campus and is hardly ever crowded. Their milkshakes are the best, though.

"We were both naked, Reese." As *if I don't already know that.* "How else do you explain that?"

"I have a pretty good idea," I say through clenched teeth. The waitress sets our plates down and leaves after asking if we need anything else. Zoey looks at her sandwich and snarls before shoving it across the table and reaching for her drink instead.

Opening up the second sandwich I take the bacon on top and slap it onto mine. I rip off a piece of my club, not bothering to swallow before speaking. "I think you had a crush on me, but I wasn't interested, so you dated Elijah." It's an awful fucking accusation because only a monster would date the best friend of the guy they really wanted, but this is Zoey. "I think you were looking for any chance you had to make Elijah and Winnie hate me. You found me in that room and set it up to look like we fucked, and it was just dumb luck on your part that we got caught."

Silence stretches between us. I finish half my sandwich and chug down most of my drink, waiting for her to say anything, but for once, she's silent until her lips flick up.

"You know how crazy that makes me sound?"

"Yeah, unfortunately, I do."

Her eyebrows drop. "You've always been so rude to me. Why?"

"We're getting off topic." I slam my drink down a little harder than I meant to.

She leans forward, resting her breasts on the table, but I don't look like she wants me to. "Answer me, and then I'll answer you. Why do you hate me?"

I know there's a chance she's wasting my time. That she will never answer. But I have half a sandwich left, so if I answer her and she doesn't give me the same by the time I finish, I'm walking out and will be forced to find another way to convince Winnie and Eli of the truth.

"The first time I ever spoke to you, you threw yourself at me while simultaneously talking bad about one of the most important people in my life," I deadpan.

She rolls her eyes. "Can you blame a girl for making it known what she wants? I've never been one to play games."

"No, I can't, but it doesn't mean I have to be interested. That's your issue—you've made me some kind of unreachable target. *You've* made it a solo game, and that's why you're still persistent. But—" I pause and lean forward, making sure she can hear everything I'm about to say. "There will never be anything between us."

"Because of her?" she scoffs.

"Me not wanting you has nothing to do with Winnie and everything to do with you." I hold up a hand, stopping her from asking anything else. "Your turn. Answer my question."

She leans against the back of the booth and averts her gaze. If it wasn't Zoey I was talking to, I would probably feel bad for being so blunt, but she needs a reality check, and if I have to give it to her, so be it.

"So?" I press. Ready to get the fuck out of here.

She doesn't look my way, interested in something across the small diner. Following her eyes, I find out why. *What are the fucking odds?*

I meet Elijah's hate-filled stare first but am quick to look behind him into Winnie's. Standing in the doorway, she's frozen and gazing in our direction. Her mouth is partially open, and with each passing moment, I notice her chest deflate.

I'm frozen in my seat, that is until Zoey leans forward and drags her hand up my arm. I snap my eyes to her and rip my arm away as fast as I can.

"Don't," I growl.

Winnie, Elijah, and some guy I don't recognize head our way, needing to pass by our booth to get to the rest of the diner.

Much to all of their dismay, the waitress sits them at the booth directly behind me. I wait for them to order their drinks before I can't handle it anymore and slip from the booth. I grab Zoey's arm and drag her with me to their table. As soon as we are in front of it, I let her go.

"Tell them. Now."

She shoots a fleeting look at them, then back to me and tilts her head with fake confusion. "Tell them what?"

A growl rips from my throat. "The truth."

"Reese," Winnie whispers. I glance down at her, and she shakes her head, but unshed tears catch my eye, and I know I can't just let it go. It's now or never.

"Now, Zoey."

"Go the fuck away," Elijah snaps. "Or you'll end up worse than I left Sawyer."

I ignore him, boring my eyes into Zoey, who is making it a point not to look at any of us.

"Zoey," I warn for the last time.

Elijah shifts from the corner of my eye, and I know if it wasn't for Winnie blocking him in, he would be in my face, ready to drop me.

"We didn't sleep together." The moment the words leave her mouth, a weight lifts from my chest. Even if neither of them believe her, I know the truth. I guess there's always been a part of me that wondered. I knew we didn't, but a small part of me questioned if I was so drunk and just didn't remember. "I found him passed out. I was going to leave but saw his clothes on the ground and got the idea to make it look like we fucked."

If I didn't feel so relieved, her shrug as if it was no big deal would've sent me over the edge.

"Why?" Winnie whispers.

"Who the fuck cares?" Elijah cuts off anyone from answering. "It doesn't fucking matter if you did or didn't."

I shoot a look to Elijah and find Winnie looking at him with pinched eyebrows as well.

"What the fuck do you mean it doesn't matter?" I ask.

He scoffs and rolls his eyes. "Maybe that's why I started hating you, but finding out you fucked my sixteen-year-old sister put a nail in that already-decomposing coffin."

One step forward, three steps back.

"E—"

He slams a hand on the table, and I snap my mouth shut. If Winnie wasn't here, I would be in *Elijah's* face. He's given me hell, called me names for the last couple years, and when I prove the reason he hates me to be faulty, he doesn't care. Classic Elijah.

"Don't fucking call me that. In fact, get the fuck out of here. I have no interest in hearing your pathetic excuse for sleeping with someone so young, you sick fuck."

"Elijah." Winnie winces. "Please, stop."

"It's fine," I say, and they both look up at me. I meet her eyes and can feel the battle raging inside of her. Her heart speaks to mine, a silent dance neither of us can hear, only feel. "He's right, Win. I should have never slept with you while you were so young. I'm sorry to both of you, but you heard what I wanted you to. I needed you to know that there never was and never will

be anything between Zoey and me. It's always been you."
I whisper that last part, even though I know Elijah can
hear me. I need Winnie to hear it.

Zoey scoffs. I didn't realize she was still here, but that
must be enough for her because she turns and storms
away.

Elijah clamps his jaw, but Winnie is on the verge of
tears, and the only reason I don't pull her into my arms
right now is because I know she doesn't want her brother to know what is happening between us, if anything
even is. I honestly don't know.

"I'll leave you to your dinner."

Winnie lifts her hand as if she's going to reach for me,
but Elijah grunts, and it falls.

I drop money onto the table, and instead of getting a
box for the untouched sandwich, I grab it and slide it in
front of Winnie.

"Bro, don't you get the fucking hint?"

Ignoring Elijah, I wink at Winnie. "Club. No bacon."

She whispers a small thanks, and Elijah calls after me,
but I don't pay any attention.

Tonight didn't go as planned, and I didn't get to say
anything I wanted to say when I drug Zoey to Winnie
and Elijah's, but at least my name is cleared from ever
sleeping with her. I saw the look in Winnie's eyes. She
wanted to reach out to me, but now I gotta figure
out how to deal with her brother so we can finally

be together. Forever is the goal, but nothing serious can happen between us until her brother is on board. She would see a relationship between us as a betrayal because that's what he would see.

Fuck me, this is a lot more difficult than I expected. Why does Elijah have to be such a pain in my ass?

28

Winnie

"You look tired." Mr. Hudson shoots me a sideways glance.

I drop the hand rubbing my eye and shrug. "Long weekend." That's not really a lie. After bumping into Reese and Zoey at the diner, Elijah was beyond pissy the entire weekend. I tried to talk to him about what Zoey confessed, but he quickly shut it down, saying it doesn't matter. I don't know how it doesn't, because that was what led to their entire falling out. But apparently, I don't know what I'm talking about. It's like anytime Reese gets brought up, Elijah shuts down. So I stopped trying to bring it up.

There will always be a part of me that wants to see the good in Reese, and maybe a part that wants to see the bad in Zoey. And although there was a point I doubted him, I think deep down, I wanted to believe what Elijah told me wasn't true. It makes sense she would do something crazy like that, but I don't understand why she ever had to bring my brother into her little games. She could have just not agreed to go out with him when he asked her out. She knew she was into Reese and still agreed. I guess that's where I'll never understand her. I've been into Reese longer than I knew what that meant, and in that time, I've never even looked at another man longer than a few beats. It's messed up since we've never even officially dated.

Besides the drama with Elijah, I've been nauseous the last few days. Elijah mentioned me not eating, and I blamed it on the diner food, which is quite believable, honestly. But I know that's probably not it.

I told myself I would buy a test this week. It has been long enough now, but I don't know if I'm ready. If it is positive, what do I do? I think Reese would oddly be happy, but that alone scares me. Am I ready for a family with a guy who isn't even my boyfriend? And what about Elijah? What do I tell him?

"Winnie."

I stop and look up at Mr. Hudson. His eyebrows are furrowed.

"Yeah?"

"You're muttering to yourself. Are you sure there isn't anything I can assist with?"

I wish. "Sorry. No, I'm fine. Just some drama with my brother, is all." To put it lightly.

His eyes narrow behind his glasses, and just when I think he's going to press, someone speeds by us, music loud enough it would be hard to hear Mr. Hudson if he said anything. I don't have to look to know who it is.

Mr. Hudson glances toward Reese's truck and chuckles. "Let's get inside and get set up."

"Winnie!"

Sawyer and I look toward Coach.

"The girl." He rolls his eyes before turning for his office, I guess expecting me to follow.

"If he keeps you on, you gotta find a new nickname," Sawyer tells me.

"It's not a nickname. Winnie is my *name*."

He angles his body away and taps his shoulder that reads Winnifred across the back in bold letters. "Not in the rink, it's not."

"We can call her honey," Brogan offers, throwing an arm over my shoulders and grinning. Reese skates over like he does anytime one of the guys gets too close.

"Hands off," he growls and shoots me a harsh look. "And no. You're not calling her honey."

Brogan drops his arm but noogies me before skating around to the small crowd of guys.

"So, then what?" I ask.

The lot of them tilt their heads.

"What about Snapshot?" Reese offers, and my tummy flips.

The guys think it over, then nod. "I like it. We can call her Snaps," Gavin confirms.

"Or Snappy when she's PMSing." Brogan winks.

"Anything is better than using *my* name." Sawyer nudges my back as he skates behind me.

"It was given to me at birth," I shout after him, and he flips me off.

"Don't care."

Reese skates forward, a timid smile playing on his lips. We haven't really talked much this week. I've been at every practice, but I duck out right after, not wanting to get roped into talking to him. My skating has organically gotten better. So I didn't need much of his help.

"You better not keep Coach waiting."

Coach Swanson is sitting in his chair when I walk into the room. Miller, the assistant coach, stands off to the side and smiles at me. I've not interacted with him much, but he seems like a nice guy—surprisingly, considering who his daughter is. I was tempted to ask if she was biologically his, but I figured that would be inappropriate—just like mentioning how hot he is. Definition of silver fox.

"You wanted to see me?"

"Yes, sit."

I take a seat in the green chair in front of his desk. Nerves bubble up inside me, and I shift awkwardly.

A few strands of hair shift from the breeze as he drops a manila folder in front of me. "Here's your team badge and some paperwork I'll need back on my desk first thing Monday if you want to go to next week's games with us. Which you do, because if not, what the fuck are we paying you for? I believe there is some other Timberwolves stuff, but that's not from me."

I shoot a look at Miller, and he smiles.

"What is this for?" I pick up the thick folder, surprised by the weight of it.

"You're hired. Officially," he says.

My eyes pop open. "Really?"

"Why would I waste my time with a joke?" Coach deadpans. "Of course, really. Kids these days," he grumbles, but I'm too happy to care how pissy he is. I got it. I kind of hoped I might get hired, even though I told myself it didn't really matter. The pay is not great, and while it's a great opportunity for me, it's not the easiest being around Reese all the time.

But none of that matters now. I pull out my badge and smile at my name followed by Team Photographer. I wish my dad were alive to see this. He would be so proud.

"Get out of my office before you start crying."

I grin as I pack my stuff away. "Thank you, both of you. I can't tell you how amazing this is."

Coach waves me off, already focusing on something else, but Miller offers me a friendly nod.

"It's our pleasure. You are very talented."

"Yeah, you're great. Now get out."

Miller chuckles, and I grin as I back out of the room. Holding the folder to my chest, I let the door close behind me before I let out a soft squeal. Mr. Hudson stopped coming with me two mornings ago after making sure I could handle it on my own, but I wish he were here right now so I had someone to share the news with.

My eyes snag on the guys on the ice, one in particular. Watching Reese skate shows just how much he loves the sport. I think that's why I love shooting him; he's so animated while he plays. Even now, just watching him push the puck around, I know there is nothing he would rather be doing than this.

He shoots the puck, and it sails over Sawyer's right shoulder and hits the back of the net. Reese pumps his arm and makes a crude gesture toward his friend. And I can't stop the laugh from bubbling up from my stomach. He glides around the net and glances in my direction. My heart thunders in my chest, and I offer a small wave as well as a smile. I've been civil with Reese, but I haven't gone out of my way to be overly friendly, so when he slows to a stop and tilts his head, I know he has to be wondering what is going on in my head.

Before I think too hard about it, I bounce down the steps to the opening, unable to hide my grin as I wave the folder in his face.

"What's that?" He pulls his gloves off and tosses them onto the ground at my feet so he can open the folder. He pulls my badge out, and a smile as cheesy as my own stretches across his face. "You got it."

Something passes between us, and suddenly, we're just Winnie and Reese, and it's years ago. I lunge, and he catches me around the waist, spinning us on the ice as he holds me to him.

"Thank you." I hug him tighter, knowing if it wasn't for his meddling, I wouldn't be here.

"As much as I love this, you don't need to thank me, Win. It's your talent that got you here."

He lets me down far sooner than I want but doesn't move his hands from my waist, keeping me balanced on the ice.

"Did you really doubt you would get it?"

I shrug. "I don't know. Your coach doesn't seem to like me, so I wondered."

Reese grins. "He doesn't like anyone. You'll get used to it."

"I guess I will." I have a whole season to get used to it. A whole season to spend with Reese. Long bus rides, away games... we really need to address what we are. What is—or isn't—happening between us.

But first, I need to take a test.

29

Winnie

I love the library because there's only so much to be distracted by. That's why I come here to study. Unfortunately, it has taken nothing to steal my focus these last three days. All the distractions are in my head or stomach.

Three days since I took the test and two very dark pink lines popped up almost immediately. It didn't even take the full five minutes.

I'm pregnant.

Preg. Nant.

Just thinking about it makes me sick. Surprisingly, not in a disgusted way, but in an uneasy way. I've always wanted kids; at least two, because I loved growing up with a sibling. But I thought I would be graduated and stable in my career, or at least be married. And if not married, at least in a steady relationship with the dad. I am none of the above. Eighteen—nearly nineteen—first year in college, and not even through the first trimester. *Damn Reese and his super sperm.*

Thank God Coach told me to take the week off because it's an away-game weekend. Plus, there are only so many photos I can take at practice. We decided on one or two practices a week unless more are needed, but I'll be at every game. Which works well for me, especially right now when the last person I want to be around is the dad of the baby growing inside me. Honestly, telling Reese doesn't seem that scary because I know him, and weirdly enough, he's going to be ecstatic. That's the part that scares me. I don't know if I'm ready for everything yet. There are still so many variables, and my feelings for him are complicated, to say the least. Especially now.

"Winnie?" A soft, feminine voice sounds behind me.

I turn enough to see who it is, and Laney smiles back at me, holding a few books to her chest.

"Hey, Laney."

"Oh, good. I thought it was you, but I also thought the redhead I saw two weeks ago was you. It was awkward for everyone. Anyway! How are you?"

I don't know what happens, but I burst into hysterics. Poor Laney looks mortified as tears and snot pour down my face.

She sets her books on the table next to me and throws her arms around me, squeezing as tightly as her small frame can. We might not be that close, but right now she feels like a friend, so I hug her back.

"Winnie, are you dying? You're scaring me."

Unable to help myself, I giggle. She pushes away to see my face, worry still prominent on her light eyebrows. I glance at the scar across her face before quickly looking away. I am curious how she got it, but that's not something you can just ask someone.

"No." I shake my head. "Not dying, but there is something I need to tell someone, and I guess you're the lucky one who gets to hear it." I take a deep breath and then blurt out, "I'm pregnant."

As scary as it is admitting it out loud, since this makes it really official, it feels good to get it off my chest. That first weight has been lifted.

She takes the seat next to me but stays close so we don't have to talk loud.

"Are you sure? You took a test and everything? Have you been to the doctor?"

I reach into my bag and pull out the test, just enough so she can see; then I drop it back inside. "I've not been to the doctor, but I'd say that's pretty positive."

She nods her head quickly. "Like, the most positive. Maybe you're having twins."

Oh, God. "No, let's not put that into the universe, please."

Giggling, she says, "Well, have you told Reese?"

I twist my lips. "Uh, no. Not exactly, but that's why I have three pregnancy tests hanging out in my backpack. I planned on going to his place and showing him, but... ya know, I haven't."

"I mean, I can't say I really blame you, but Reese is going to be so happy, Winnie. We don't live there anymore, but we still see the guys here and there, and anytime we do, Reese mentions you at least once."

My heart flutters. "Really?"

She nods quickly. "Yes, really. He is in love, like more than I think I've seen anyone be in love."

Love. When he told me he loved me the first time, I was drunk on alcohol and sex, so it was easy to ignore. The second time felt like a punch to the gut. He was right, though. I wasn't ready to hear it. Now... I don't know, maybe I am. I still need to deal with Elijah, but if I'm going to have Reese's baby, he's going to have to accept it if he wants to be in his niece or nephew's life.

"I plan on telling him after the weekend. I don't want to distract him before the first game of the season."

"Oh, right. Yeah, us too. I take it you are riding with the team?"

"Yeah. Got my own badge and everything."

"I heard, that's such a good opportunity, Winnie!"

It really is, and I wouldn't have it without Reese. In fact, Reese is to thank for a lot of the best moments in my life. He's been a part of every big, special occasion for as long as I can remember. It's only fair he should be a part of this one too.

"Are you up for being my support while I tell the father of my baby I'm pregnant?"

Her eyes round, but eventually, she nods. "Okay. Right now?"

I wanted to wait, but now that I've just admitted it out loud, I don't know how I can wait to tell him. This is a huge thing, and I know Reese would want to be aware. Knowing him, he would want to be holding the stick I peed on if I allowed it. I gather my stuff in a hurry and eye her anxiously. "Yeah, I don't think I can wait."

"Well, alright." She follows my lead and stands, and I think she's kind of excited too. "Let's go make Reese's day."

Gosh, I hope she's right about him being happy.

Reese

"You're fucked if you think Ross wasn't in the wrong."

Sawyer rolls his eyes. "She broke up with him."

A sudden knock on the door pulls us from our debate. I straighten from the foosball table and lift my hands in a truce while I head for the door. "She called for a break. You know what?" I tug the door open, my eyes still on

Sawyer. "I'm not getting into this with you. Just know you're wrong."

"Wrong about what?"

I whip my head in the direction of the sweetest voice. Winnie stares at me, a curious eyebrow lifted and a nervous smile on her face.

"Uh..."

Sawyer stops by my side and slaps my shoulder. "He thinks Ross was in the wrong for fucking that bar girl after Rachel broke up with him."

Winnie's smile falls, but mine grows. "And you think Ross was in the right?"

Sawyer nods, not backing down at all. What he doesn't know is Winnie is the biggest *Friends* fan I know, and she feels very strongly about Ross and Rachel.

"Of course you do."

"What's that supposed to mean?" he scoffs, crossing his arms over his chest. She mocks him by doing the same thing.

"It means I'm not surprised *you* feel that way."

I can't help but chuckle at Winnie's vagueness and how Sawyer is handling it. I never noticed before, but Sawyer is like the male version of Winnie. No wonder he's my best friend and they butt heads.

I flick a look to Winnie, still smiling. "What are you doing here?"

"Um..." She chews on her lip in the cutest way. "I kind of need to talk to you."

Is this where she breaks my heart and tells me she can't do it? Whatever it is between us? We've been dancing around it after she jumped in my arms. I catch her looking at me more than not, but anytime I try and talk to her, she runs away.

She seems happy, though. Nervous but happy. So maybe she's here to say she finally gives in. I hope it comes out better than that, but I'll take anything if she's telling me she wants this between us.

"Fine, but you can't do it in my apartment," Sawyer huffs from somewhere behind me.

"I wouldn't want to step foot in your apartment if someone paid me."

"Good. Go be an Emily somewhere else."

Winnie's eyes round, and when Sawyer barks out a loud laugh, she storms forward. I catch her around the waist and tug her into my arms. "Easy, killer. He's just pulling your leg. Everyone knows you're my Monica."

That seems to settle her, but it doesn't last long because Sawyer doesn't know how to keep his big mouth shut.

"More like your Janice."

"Ugh! You're the *worst*."

Sawyer winks in her direction, but she spins and storms from the apartment. I glance back, and he grins.

"You really are the worst. You know she's going to marinate on that all night."

He gives me a salute. "Good luck, brother."

I follow after Winnie but stop when I notice she's not alone.

"Laney? Are you here to see Sawyer?"

Her eyes round. "Uh, n-no. Why would I be here to see Sawyer?"

I shrug, pretending not to notice her stutter. "Just wondering."

"No, I brought her for support."

I cut my eyes to Winnie. "Why do you need support?"

They share a look I don't understand, and my impatience grows.

"Actually, he's probably right. You don't need to sit in with us. I'm sorry I dragged you all this way."

Laney doesn't seem bothered that Winnie changed her mind. She offers to call her an Uber, but I have an even better idea.

"Why don't you go hang with Sawyer? I was playing him in foos. Maybe you can take over crushing him for me."

Before Laney can say no, Winnie jumps in. "Oh, yeah! Then we can get pizza or something after."

I don't know how my girl does it, but she gets Laney to agree, and once she's disappeared through Sawyer's door, Winnie grabs my hand and drags me across the hall to mine. I can't get a read on her right now. Something is different.

Memories of the last time I followed her into this apartment flash through my head, but I do my best to keep them at bay. I still don't know why she's here, and I don't really want to have a boner if she plans on breaking up with me.

Not that I will let her, but it'd be awkward for everyone involved.

Instead of sitting inside, she decides she wants to take Eeyore on a walk. I don't tell her that I already did earlier because I heard there might be some bad weather later. Whatever keeps her here longer, the better.

We walk in peaceful silence. At least *she* seems peaceful. I, on the other hand, am freaking out over what would bring her all the way to my place. It has to be big for her to show up randomly. I can't imagine what it could be, though.

"So, you wanted to talk?"

She sucks in a sharp breath. "I did."

Okaaay.

"Do you remember when Dad's Bronco rolled down our driveway and hit your truck?"

"Uh, yeah. I guess." Not sure what that has to do with us now. Unless she hit my truck again. "You hit my truck again?"

She giggles and nudges my arm with hers. "No. And I didn't hit it the first time, so stop it."

"Sure, you didn't."

Every time Winnie smiles, it's like a time machine. It's so easy to remember the first time I ever saw it. She was missing teeth, but so was I, and I remember thinking she had the best smile. I didn't want to go another day not seeing it. It feels good that she's happy again. I've seen enough tears from Winnie to last me a lifetime.

"I've missed you, Win. Not just lately, but the last couple of years. Life without you isn't the same as when you're in it."

"Me too, Reese," she whispers.

My annoying text tone cuts through the moment, and I think to ignore it, but it's Coach's ringtone, so I pull it out.

Coach: Possible storm tonight. Not sure games will be happening this weekend, and no practice. Will reschedule games if they don't happen, but spread the word and tell everyone to get home.

Me: Will do, Coach.

I slip my phone back into my pocket, and Winnie glances back from a few feet ahead with Eeyore in her arms.

"Girlfriend?"

"Nah, she wouldn't be texting me right now."

Her eyes blaze before I add, "Considering she's right in front of me."

Winnie's cheeks pinken, and she lowers her face to the ground. "You're impossible."

I nudge her shoulder. "It was Coach. We're meant to get some bad weather tonight. Might not have games this weekend."

"That sucks. What kind of weather?"

"I'm not sure. Let's get back so I can warn the rest."

While Winnie is putting Eeyore back in his new and improved cage, I head across the hall to Sawyer's place. Not worrying about knocking, I throw open the door. Laney jumps away from Sawyer, and he shoots me a murderous glare.

"What?" he barks angrily.

I don't know what was happening or why they were standing in the middle of the room looking like they were about to kiss, but Laney's cheeks are on fire as she tries to avoid my eyes.

"Coach texted me. The weather might stop games from happening this weekend. Practice is canceled."

"The season is already starting late as it is."

I shrug. "I know, but what can you do? I just checked the weather. They are talking about high winds and possible flooding. Unheard of for this time of year."

He huffs and rakes his hand through his hair. "Where's Emma?"

I assume he's not speaking to me, so I leave to talk to the others.

No one is excited about our first game being possibly delayed, and I can't blame them because neither am I. Practice is great and all, but games are where the magic really happens. I'm itching to play, to fight, and to win. But our playing season was already delayed because they were having issues with scheduling or something. I'm honestly not sure; I was zoning out when Coach was telling us about it because Winnie was wearing green that day.

I *fucking love when she wears green.*

Winnie is stepping out of my apartment when I round the corner, and she smiles when she sees me. Fuck, she's pretty when she smiles.

"I thought I lost you."

"Had to warn the rest of the team about the weather and games."

"Oh, okay."

An awkward beat passes between us before I move closer than I've been since that night. She lets me, and

I take that as a good sign. Her eyes bounce from mine to my lips.

Just before our mouths meet, she says my name.

"Yeah?"

She licks her lips and sighs. "I'm—"

"You have an apartment right fucking there, you know?"

Groaning, it's my turn to glare at Sawyer for being interrupted. "This payback or some shit?"

He shrugs. "I gotta go get Emma. You guys mentioned something about pizza?"

"Pizza, yes!" Winnie slips under my arms, excited over the mention of food. A little too excited, I think.

What did she say before Sawyer came out? Fuck, I can't remember. I guess whatever she was going to tell me will have to wait. It's obvious she doesn't want to say it in front of someone.

I'm going to run through the hints like this is fucking *Blue's Clues* in my head, though. She brought someone as support, she mentioned when she hit my truck, and she seems genuinely happy... those don't fucking connect to me.

Women and their mind games.

30

Winnie

Reese didn't give me the option of not staying with him. When Sawyer mentioned Laney and Emma would be staying with him, Reese demanded I stay with him too. He claimed it was so he didn't have to worry about me in the storm, but I think that's just an excuse. I don't mind, though. I still haven't told him about the baby, so this should be the perfect time to drop the news.

Should be, being the key words.

"We have to get alcohol." Gavin grabs a case of beer and drops it into the cart.

Reese wraps an arm around me. "What do you like to drink?"

"Oh, uh, no. I'm good."

"You sure?" He eyes me for a beat, and I wonder if he knows, but then he shrugs and reaches for a few different boxes full of a variety of drinks into the cart. "Just in case you change your mind."

If I could drink right now, I *would*. Maybe then it would rid me of my nerves. Or make them worse.

Stay vigilant for falling trees and flooded roads. If you don't have to go out—don't. Emergency workers are advising people to stay indoors. Check back for updates.

"Well, shit." Schmidt looks out the window at the darkened sky. "Yeah, it looks nasty."

"I can't believe our games might be canceled for some rain."

Reese scoffs at his teammate. "Not canceled. Rescheduled. And it's not just fucking rain, Brogan. There's a flood warning, if you weren't listening."

"Well, whatever. It's fucking dumb."

I grab Reese's thigh resting aside mine and stroke it, hoping it calms his irritation with Brogan. If we are going to be trapped here all night together, I'd rather there not be any weird tension. All afternoon, I've watched each of the guys roll their eyes at something Brogan has said, and he's deserved it each time. The guy is obnoxious, for sure.

Reese slips his fingers in between mine and kisses my head. We've still not had time to talk, but it's been nice having a lazy afternoon together.

Sawyer's phone goes off for what feels like the fifteenth time, and I guess he's had enough of not answering it. He picks it up and, with slumped shoulders, stalks over to the kitchen. Everyone else disperses, some leaving the apartment, Brogan thankfully being one of them, leaving only me, Reese, Sawyer, Emma, Laney, Schmidt, Beckett, and his girlfriend, Avery. This is my first time meeting Avery, but she seems sweet. She's, like, model pretty, too. Dark curly hair, deep skin that glows like the sun is shining directly on her, and wide set eyes framed by thick eyelashes.

Beckett lifts her up and drags her back toward his room. "Let me know if the building starts falling down."

"That's not funny." Emma swats at his ankle, and he chuckles.

Laney has been visibly uncomfortable all afternoon, and when I asked her about it, she just said she doesn't like storms. It seems more than just not liking storms, though. I don't think she's uncurled her arms from her body since we sat down. Every time the wind makes too much noise, she winces, too. Must be a really bad fear.

"I don't know what you want me to do, Amy." Sawyer's voice is low, but we are only separated by a doorway.

She's not on speakerphone, but I'm pretty sure I can hear screaming on the other end. She must be very unhappy.

"I'm not driving in this. You know how I am with storms."

I glance back at Reese since we are the only ones close enough to hear him, but he just shrugs.

"He doesn't talk about it."

Huh. I wonder what that could mean. "She sounds really mad."

"She's always mad, but I would be too if you were bunked up for the foreseeable future with some guy you had a history with."

I shoot a look around the room. The only other girl besides me is his sister, his roommate's girlfriend, and Laney.

"Laney?" I keep my voice a whisper, making sure Reese is the only one to hear me.

He nods a few times. "Yeah, don't you see the way they look at each other? I didn't either until he said something, but now I don't know how I missed it."

They look at each other? Just then, Sawyer walks back into the room, and exactly as Reese said, his eyes lock on Laney right away. *Holy shit.* He looks physically uncomfortable standing in the doorframe, like he can't decide what to do.

"What happened?"

Reese shrugs. "I don't really know. I guess she's always had a crush, and one time they kissed."

"But he's been with Amy for, like, ever, right?"

"Sure, but it wasn't that serious until a year or so ago. Then she flipped and has been a crazy girlfriend ever since, but now I kind of don't blame her. I still don't like her, because she treats my best friend like shit, but at least I mostly get why she's an insufferable bitch."

I would have never guessed there was anything between Sawyer and Laney. Reese said she holds the crush, but watching him look at her like he would protect her from the world, like her suffering is killing him, is enough for me to wonder how one-sided that crush really is. If that crush is even still there. I drift my eyes across the room to Laney. Emma is showing her something on her phone, but her eyes keep drifting to Sawyer, and there is definitely a moment shared between them. *Huh.* Now that I'm thinking about it, they would make a really cute couple, and it seems that Amy makes him miserable, so I don't know why he stays with her. There must be more to the story.

Wind blows outside, and something hits the window. It doesn't break it, but it was loud enough that I'm surprised it didn't, and I shoot a quick look at Laney. She's since buried her face into her hands and is shaking like a leaf. I climb from Reese's legs, crawl over, and place a gentle hand on her knee.

Emma is rubbing her back with a worried expression on her face.

"Are you okay?" I keep my voice low and gentle not to disturb her.

"I-I'm sorry, I j-just don't like storms."

I peek at Sawyer, but he's gone. Seconds later, though, he comes back from the kitchen carrying two handfuls of shots. He slams them on the table, and Laney jumps. She lifts her head, and he points to the shots.

"Drink."

"I don't think—"

"Drink, Delaney."

I'm not sure even I would argue with that tone, and I'm not into this man. Emma tries to defend her friend, but Laney assures her it's okay. Gosh, I don't know how Emma is around them all the time and misses that her best friend and brother totally want each other. I guess it would be the same for Elijah.

"It's fine. Maybe the alcohol will settle my nerves."

I reach for a shot and pass it to Laney. Her hands are shaky, but she manages not to spill.

"There's one for everyone," he tells us while he grabs his.

Reese moves forward, taking his before passing me one.

I stare at it for a beat, but Laney nudges me. She points to the shot, and while Reese and Sawyer are distracted, we swap drinks and she throws it back.

I need to tell Reese soon, or poor Laney is going to be shit-faced by the end of the night.

Reese

"Never have I ever sucked dick." Beckett smirks like he's the king of comedy.

Three out of four girls lift their drinks, and I smile proudly knowing I'm responsible for one of them.

"Fuck, Emma, really?"

"Look, it was after prom and—"

Sawyer throws his hand to his ears, but she continues with a shitty smile on her face, telling us all about how her date was hot and that was her only reason, really.

"Okay, new game," Sawyer grumbles. "I'm tired of hearing everything my sister has done sexually."

"Ooh, what about karaoke?" Laney is definitely smashed. Her words are slurred and her movements sloppy. We've only been drinking for a little over an hour, and I haven't seen her get up and refill her cup once, but I guess she is small.

As if God thinks that's an awful idea as well, the power cuts out. Laney, or maybe Emma, screams as the apartment goes dark.

"Fuck. You got flashlights at your place?"

"Let me go look."

Winnie climbs up after me, but I quickly add, "You can stay, I'll be right back."

Instead of sitting back down, she steps closer and drops her voice. "I was thinking I could up my chances at never have I ever."

My eyes widen with a mixture of shock and excitement. I scan hers to make sure I understand what she's hinting at. When I'm positive, I grip her hand and begin dragging a giggling Winnie from the apartment.

"We will be back."

"Bring those fucking flashlights over first!"

Yeah, no fucking way am I doing that.

I don't stop until we are in my room. It's dark, but I have a battery-operated lamp I flick on. I turn, breathing hard as I lift a questioning eyebrow. Winnie's chocolate eyes roam down my body and back up. She bites her lip, and any reserve I was holding disappears. I all but pounce on her. Grabbing her around her slim waist, I lift. She wraps her legs around my hips, and I lead her to my bed.

Dropping her onto my bed, I grip her leggings and thong and tear them down her body in one smooth movement. She pulls her top off next and then leans up on her elbows to look down at me, watching as I enjoy her body in the most organic way.

"You look so beau—"

"I'm pregnant."

31

Reese

You ever have those moments when the world stops? This is one of those moments for me.

I stare at Winnie, and she stares back, anticipation blowing her pupils wide. She worries her lips, waiting for me to respond, but all words are lost. My tongue is heavy in my mouth and not willing to let me reply with anything logical.

"Reese? Did you hear me? Well, I'm guessing you heard me, but... aren't you going to say anything?"

What do you say to your dream woman when she gives you the best possible news you've ever heard?

"You're pregnant?" Apparently, you repeat the same words back.

Winnie blinks and eventually nods. "I wanted to wait until the weekend was over, but I couldn't hold it in any longer."

"How long have you known?"

Winnie lowers her eyes to her hands on her lap and twists her fingers together. It might be easier to have this conversation with her if she wasn't naked.

"I took the tests a few days ago."

I wish she would have let me be there with her, but I understand why she didn't. This isn't just a big moment for me, it's a huge moment for Winnie. She's the one with a baby inside her. Not just a baby, but my baby. *Our* baby.

"Reese, you're worrying me. I can't tell if you're happy or not."

I can't have her thinking I'm anything but ecstatic. I tug my shirt over my head and drop my sweats to the ground, and she shifts eagerly. Winnie lowers herself onto the bed, and I crawl over her, hovering and looking into the eyes of the woman I love.

"There's nothing you could have told me that would have made me any happier than I am right now."

Her chest caves with what sounds like a relieved breath. I press my lips to hers, soaking in the moment. Bringing my hand up, I lay it on her slightly swollen stomach. It's not big enough for me to have noticed it before, but now knowing my child is growing inside her, I can feel the smallest difference from before. Or maybe I just want to think I can.

I shift down the bed and chuckle when she lets out a desperate sigh.

"Hi, baby. It's your dad." I flick a look up to Winnie and grin. "Your mom looks so fucking pretty right now."

"Reese," Winnie warns, still smiling.

"Shit—shoot. Damn, this is going to be hard. But I have nine months to practice."

Winnie threads her fingers through my hair. "More like seven or eight."

Oh, shit, that's right. I drop my forehead to the smooth plane of her stomach and press a gentle kiss just under her belly button. "I love you."

"I love you too."

My heart thunders as I meet Winnie's watery chocolate eyes. "You mean that?"

She nods quickly. "I always have, Reese. I'm scared of what's to come, especially telling my brother, but as long as we're together, everything will be okay."

God, this girl.

I press another kiss to her stomach, then trail my lips up her body. Hard, pointed pink nipples call my name, and I suck one into my mouth and swirl my tongue around it. Winnie whimpers, and my partially stiff dick fully erects. I'm too desperate for her to mess around with any foreplay, so I slip between her legs, line myself up, and slide into her with ease. She's still unbelievably tight and strangles my dick in the best way.

Wrapping her arms around my neck, she pulls me on top of her, but I'm hesitant, wanting to protect her and our baby from my weight.

"You're not going to hurt them, Reese. Fuck me properly."

"Your wish is my command."

Winnie

Watching Reese do his best not to explode with the news is equally hilarious and heartwarming. He's nearly bouncing, and anytime he opens his mouth, I'm sure it's going to pour out. But we've been sitting with his friends for a good hour, and he's held it back thus far.

We agreed—well, I decided, and Reese reluctantly agreed—that we should keep it to ourselves for the time being. I said at least until after the doctor's appointment he plans on scheduling for me after the weekend, but I'm thinking until I can tell my brother. Which I'm still unsure how I'm going to do in a way everyone stays alive.

I don't know why I was ever nervous to tell Reese. I should have known how thrilled he would be, but maybe that's why. Thankful doesn't even begin to describe how I feel that Reese is the way he is and couldn't be more excited about having a surprise baby, but it only reminds me how scared and nervous I am.

There are so many variables; ages and life situations are only the tip of the iceberg. I don't think he has thought about any of that, though, which is one of the many reasons I love him. He's such an in-the-moment kind of guy, but it's doing nothing to calm my nerves. After my appointment, I'm going to call my mom, and hopefully, she can talk me through all this. I mean, she's done this two times, even if the last time was almost nineteen years ago.

"Wiiiiiinnnniieeee!" Laney falls next to me on the couch, a sloppy smile on her face.

I giggle into my hand at her obvious drunkenness. She's gotten worse as the day's gone on, and not because of me. After I told Reese, he's done his part keeping the alcohol from me, but not by drinking it like she was, thankfully. Lugging around a drunk Reese would be a lot harder than five-foot-nothing Laney. "Hey, Lane. How you feeling?"

"Good! Great. I've never felt betterrrr."

"Yeah, you seem like it."

The room is lit by the glow of a few candles, wanting to save the batteries on the flashlights Reese eventually ended up finding.

Emma steps in front of the room, holding the microphone connected to the battery-operated karaoke machine. The lyrics to "Like A Virgin" slide across the little screen, and Sawyer uses that time to excuse himself to the bathroom. Apparently, listening to your sister sing about being touched like a virgin isn't something you want to listen to. Who knew?

Emma finishes, and we erupt into a fit of clapping. To my surprise, Reese jumps up next.

He takes his time picking a song, and all I can do is sit back and smile. I've heard Reese sing before, but never in front of people. He's changed so much since he was a shy, brace-face teenager. I'm allowed to call him that because he called me "train tracks" when I got my retainer.

I've always found Reese handsome, but if someone had told me that tall, lanky, awkward kid would grow up to be this still-tall but confident, sexy man he is now, I would have believed them, but I know others wouldn't have. I definitely hit the lottery, and I know my baby is going to be beautiful with a dad like Reese—not just outside, but in too.

Reese stands, holding the microphone in his right hand and pointing to me with his left as "Juliet" by LMNT blares through the shitty speakers. He sings along, replacing Juliet with my name, and I'm giggling like a schoolgirl every time he does. He knows how much I love that song, and hearing my name in place of it is the cherry on top of a really good sundae.

Sawyer wanders in halfway through—suddenly shirtless—and drops into the empty seat on the other side of me.

"You really got him whipped."

I grin, because he's right. Maybe *whipped* isn't the right word, and it's not like I told Reese to sing this song for me or to replace the main name with mine; he just did it because he loves me. I'm glad Reese isn't shy of showing off his feelings for me. It makes me even more confident in my choice of a baby daddy than I already was.

I wasn't lying when I told him I loved him. It wasn't a midst-of-the-moment type of thing—maybe it was, but I meant it as well. I've loved Reese since before I even knew what that meant.

"You mean in love."

Sawyer snorts an ugly sound. "Sure."

I narrow my eyes. "One day love is going to bite you on the ass, and I can't wait to laugh at how big of an idiot it makes you."

Reese passes the microphone to an eager Laney before sauntering toward me with a crooked smile tugging on his lips.

"You like the show?"

"You know I did."

He squeezes behind me and pulls me to lay against his chest, then kisses my temple with a grin.

I recognize Shania Twain's "Man! I Feel Like a Woman" immediately and smile at a cheerful Laney. The others who have gone kind of sucked at singing. Laney, on the other hand, is great. Better than great; she's amazing. Even in the drunk state she's in. I would love to hear her sober because *wow*.

"She's amazing."

To see Sawyer's reaction, I glance to the side, only to find him with a harsh expression and a clamped jaw. "I know."

I can't get what Reese told me about them and their so-called history out of my head. They have obvious feelings for each other, so why don't they just date? Maybe that's a naive thought—that just because two people care for each other, they should date. But why not? Doesn't that make the most sense? Dating the person you're actually into instead of the one you're not. There's obviously more to that story, but it seems pretty cut and dry to me.

Especially when Laney walks over to us, looking to claim her seat, but instead stops in front of Sawyer. She sways a little, bites her lips, and eyes him not at all discreetly. It's a good thing Emma is busy picking out her next song and not watching her best friend and brother eye fuck each other.

"You're an amazing singer," Reese butts in, either not realizing what is happening or maybe attempting to save his best friend. From what? I don't know. I guess making a mistake he thinks Sawyer will regret.

Laney drags her dilated eyes to us, releasing her lip from her teeth, and offers a friendly smile that's more like the Laney I know as she blushes. "Thank you."

"Seriously, Lane. So amazing."

Her face reddens more. "Thank you, Winnie." She glances at Reese. "You're not bad yourself."

Reese snorts, and I can't help but giggle. He tugs me into his side and nips at my jaw, making me laugh harder. "Thanks, but you're drunk. If you heard me sober, you'd be laughing like this one."

He digs his fingers into my side, and I scream out another laugh mixed with a beg for him to stop.

He grunts and grips my hips instead of tickling, then leans in close to my ear. "Keep wiggling that ass on my dick, and that'll be the next virginity you lose."

I swallow hard, and my eyes round. He leans back, spreads his arms over the back of the couch, and cocks an eyebrow like a challenge.

"That baby is so lucky to have you two as parents."

Reese's smile falls, and he waits for me to catch up to what Laney just said, which, to be fair, takes me longer than it should.

I whip my head to the side, but she's already holding her mouth, apparently sober enough to know she let it slip. Aside from Reese, I asked Laney to keep it to herself until we were ready to tell people. I'm thinking the rest heard, considering all four guys are on their feet, eyes wide with disbelief.

Reese shifts under me.

"You're pregnant?" Sawyer is the first to break the ice.

I swallow hard.

"I'm so sorry, Winnie. Reese. I-I'm drunk. That's not a great excuse, but I promise normall—"

"It's okay." I place my hand on her leg, and her mouth snaps shut.

Tears form in her eyes as she murmurs, "I'm so, so sorry."

"So are you?" Sawyer barks out impatiently.

I angle to meet Reese's gaze. His eyes bounce from me to his friends as if he's asking permission. I wanted it kept a secret, but I know it would kill him to lie to them, and honestly, there is no point after Laney just made it very obvious.

I nod for him to tell them, and a weight lifts from his shoulders. He pulls me close and gets the biggest, cutest smile on his face. "We are."

We. I like that. Like no matter what I go through, it's not just going to be me. That's a really comforting feeling.

You wouldn't think a bunch of giant hockey players—and Schmidt—would care about something like this, but I've never seen them look so excited. Beckett tugs Reese from the couch, and I fall into his seat.

Schmidt holds up a bottle and a handful of shot glasses. "Celebratory shots are in order."

"Someone get some juice for the mama-to-be," Gavin orders, and Avery scurries to the kitchen. She comes back with a shot glass full of red liquid and passes it to me.

"Congratulations, Winnie."

Emma bounces into the seat next to me. "I cannot believe I'm going to be an aunt."

I giggle but don't deny her of her want. It's nice having people so excited for me. Especially Reese and his friends, and if I didn't know any better, I would say there are unshed tears in Sawyer's eyes.

He looks at me for a passing beat and offers a nod of approval. I lift my shot, and we tip them back together.

This morning I was so nervous about everything. Telling Reese, being a mom in general. While I'm still nervous about becoming a mom, it's really good to know the kind of support I'll have around me when I do.

32

Winnie

It's still dark out when my eyes flutter open with the need to pee, but before I move, I'm distracted by someone talking. Not just someone, but my boyfriend. I've never known Reese to talk in his sleep, but maybe it's a habit he's picked up over the years.

But when his fingers caress my abdomen, I realize he's not talking in his sleep—he's talking to *our baby*. His face is close to my stomach, and he's brushing soft, gentle circles across it. I stay still, hoping not to interrupt this moment for him.

"The whole not cussing thing is really fu-f-freaking hard, but I'll quit by the time you're born. At least I'm going to try really hard. For you. There's hardly anyone in this world I would change for, but you and your mama are at the top of that list. I want to be the best version of myself because you deserve that. My dad sucked, so I don't know how good I'll be, but I promise I will never fail you. I will hold you when you cry, change your diapers, feed you, teach you to ride a bike, and to skate better than your mom."

I have to stop myself from giggling, but the tears pouring down the side of my face are doing a pretty good job at stopping any giggles from breaking out.

"I'm going to be the best fucking dad."

Unable to help myself, I slip my hand into his hair. He jolts but quickly settles.

"You are going to be the best dad."

Reese is silent for a few moments before he whispers, "I'm scared, Win."

"You don't need to be, Reese. You are the best guy I know."

"Just not when I'm drunk, right?" He's trying to make a joke, but it falls flat.

"It was a bad night. That's all. I'm sorry I ever compared you to Robert. You are nothing like him, Reese. Nothing, okay?"

He kisses my stomach. "You have the best mom, kid." The mattress dips as he crawls his way up my body, settling to the side. It's dark, but I can just barely make out his sharp features.

"Did I wake you?"

Oh, shit. I totally forgot why I woke up, but now it hits me tenfold. I kick the blankets off my lower body and scurry from the bed.

"Win?"

"I have to pee!"

Reese's chuckles carry through the room while I do my business. He's waiting for me with open arms when I walk back into the room, and I crawl into them, settling beside him with my head, arm, and leg draped across his body.

I'm just drifting back to sleep when Reese mutters, "Thank you."

I tilt my head up to look at him. "For what? You're the one who put the baby inside me."

His teeth snap together, and I can imagine the biggest grin across his handsome face, and it makes me smile. "While that's very true and I am thankful for that. I meant thank you for coming back into my life. It was dark without you. Lonely. And I didn't realize it until you came back. So thank you."

"Me too." I curl into his side, and he kisses my forehead.

33

Reese

Coach: Get your boys ready to play.

Probably the best text to wake up to. After the storm two nights ago, it calmed down, but there was a lot to clean up, and we weren't sure our games were still on. But thank fuck they are. I've had the best couple of days with Winnie, and I'm looking forward to continuing the good times.

I shoot off a text, drop my phone, and roll over. The sun is starting to rise, and the golden glow shining against Winnie's exposed skin makes her look like some kind of Greek goddess. I tug the blanket lower to see the rest of her body. She mumbles a complaint but doesn't wake up, giving me time to take in the entirety of her.

"Stop staring at me."

I guess I did wake her after all.

Brown eyes flutter open, and she smiles sleepily at me.

I lean down and take her mouth with mine. She's informed me she doesn't enjoy kissing first thing in the morning, so I don't shove my tongue inside, even though I don't give a shit and want to do just that.

She pushes me away and scowls, but it's obviously forced. "Why are you up anyway?"

Oh, shit. That's right. This is the problem with Winnie being around; she fucks up my ability to focus on anything besides her.

"Coach texted me. We have games today."

"Really?" she cheers. "I'm excited now."

"Me too, and I need to go tell everyone else, but seeing your nipples hard and begging for my attention is making it quite difficult to get out of bed."

"My apologies." She tugs the blanket up and giggles. As much as I hate her covering her body, I know it's necessary if I want to make it to my games today.

Still, I groan and kiss her again, all the way down her neck until I reach the blanket flush to her skin. "We need to be there in two hours. You can use my bathroom to get ready, and I'll use the one in the hall."

Something like confusion tilts her face. "Why can't we use the same bathroom? We have been for two days, Reese."

I thrust my hips forward, letting her feel my hard dick against her bare thigh, and she giggles once more.

"Oh."

"Oh is right, and if I get in the shower with you, we will never make it. And then I'll lose my captain spot and my chance at going pro, and you'll be forced to sell your body to support us, and I'm simply not willing to let that happen."

"That's a pretty drastic turnout."

I nod while reluctantly slipping from the bed. Fuck, why does she have to look at my body like she's ready to devour me at any given moment. *Talk about fucking distracting.* "Sure is. Now get your pretty ass ready and remember, ice is cold."

I bend, grab another hockey sweatshirt since I knew the one I gave her before is probably still at her brother's, and toss it at her without looking back.

"What am I meant to do with this? Swim in it?"

I glance back and curse seeing her naked and standing in the middle of the room. She's holding my sweatshirt by her side, but it does nothing to hide her perfect body.

"Whatever you gotta do, just make sure that sweatshirt with my name and number is on your back."

Air sparks against my skin like a bunch of tiny needles as I bask in the game-day excitement. A sheet of glassy ice catches my attention on the way to the locker rooms, and I pause to stare at it. I fucking love hockey. Nothing pumps my heart quite the same. Except maybe when I'm balls deep in Winnie, but even that's not the same. I give Winnie my all when we fuck, or the "all" I'm willing to, anyway, but when it comes to hockey, I don't hold back on anything. I can slam into someone with my entire force, and I know they will mostly be okay and turn around and give me the same back. The same treatment with Winnie would not only be abuse but also not possible because she weighs, like, half of me.

No, this is where I leave it all.

I'm not complete without the two.

"No, don't smile. Brood."

I snap my head toward the direction of her voice. Winnie rolls her eyes at something Sawyer said, and I chuckle while hurrying forward to defuse the tension if necessary. These two are so similar, and they don't even see it.

"What the fuck does that mean?"

"It means keep that same exact face and walk toward me."

"Like a douche?" Sawyer asks, and a few of the guys around him laugh. I have to bite mine back to stay neutral.

"Like a sexy guy. Surely, you can pretend to be that for a single photo."

Sawyer's eyebrows drop, and he scowls like he's legitimately offended. And if I know Sawyer at all, he is. "I am a sexy guy."

"Prove it."

He heads toward me, but in the last moment, he turns, facing her, and trucks forward. A new kind of swagger in his walk.

"Perfect!" Winnie pulls the camera back to see what she got and grins. "Not half bad."

"Not half bad," he huffs, mocking her.

"Okay, my turn." I don't particularly enjoy her looking so intently at photos of other guys. I know it's her job and she probably looks at hundreds daily, but I'd prefer it wasn't in my face. Ignorance is bliss and all that.

Winnie looks up from her camera grinning, but I notice how her eyes rake down my suited body. Most teams only wear suits for home games, but Coach likes us to be our best dressed before every match. Right now, I'm fucking thankful he does because, with the way Winnie is looking at me, I'm tempted to sneak her away and impregnate her all over again.

"Alright, walk to me."

I do, and when I reach her, I tug her against me. She complains about the camera being crushed between us, but I kiss her anyway.

She pulls away, breathing hard and eyes wide, and looks around as a deep pink creeps up her throat. "You're not meant to kiss me at work, Reese."

"That's a dumb fucking rule. You're my girlfriend. I can kiss you wherever and whenever I want."

"Your girlfriend, eh? I don't remember you asking me out." She's teasing me, but she's not wrong. I step closer, and she lowers the camera to her side, giving me room to pull her flush to my front.

"I thought I made it clear when I was balls deep inside you, but in case not... yes, Winnie Lewis, you are my girlfriend. And no, I'm not fucking asking."

Winnie lets out the cutest sigh and grips my jacket, holding me close. "You look so hot right now."

I grin and lean down to take her lips again. This time, she doesn't hold back, slipping her hands up my body and wrapping them around my neck. She bumps my hat with her camera, but I don't care to fix it right now. It's taking everything inside me not to pin her against the wall and show her just how *mine* she is. She shoves her tongue in my mouth, and I gladly accept the invasion. A low groan rumbles from my chest when I drop my hands to her ass and she whimpers.

Suddenly, I'm tugged back, and I glare at my best friend with a harsh look. "Unless you want Coach to fire her for distracting you, get your ass to the locker room."

I glance around at several of my teammates watching us make out, then look back to Winnie. She couldn't look any more embarrassed if she tried, but I'm not embarrassed. I'm fucking horny and a little irritated there were other guys around to hear Winnie's whimpers for me.

I brush Sawyer off.

"Dude."

Ignoring him, I step forward, crowding Winnie but not touching.

She squeaks out a small "good luck," but she doesn't lift her eyes to look at me.

I tilt her chin and smile at her burning face and wild eyes. "Same to you."

Recognition hits her like she forgot what she's here for, and she gasps. "Go, go! I have to work."

I chuckle and step back, giving her space to adjust her camera to the right settings. She lifts it and snaps a few photos of the other guys, then glares at me and makes a motion as if to say *shoo*. She will pay for that later.

There's no other feeling like being in full uniform for the first time of the season. It's like I'm eight years old again and Mr. Lewis passed me my first-ever jersey.

Number seventeen, and it's been my number ever since. He mentioned one time how he gave me seventeen because it was the date of my birthday, but he missed a very important detail that it's also his daughter's birth date. He set our fate when he passed me that jersey.

I try not to think about Mr. Lewis often because it makes me feel like shit, but he was such a big part of my childhood. I mean, I wouldn't be standing here, ready to start my third college season, if it wasn't for him. If only he were here to see it. I know he would be so fucking excited for me, and maybe if he were still alive, his son would be lacing up with me.

Winnie doesn't want to tell people she's pregnant, and I do get why for the medical side of things, as a lot can happen in the first twelve weeks, but I also know that a lot of the reasoning has to do with her brother. He hates me, and knowing his baby sister is pregnant with my kid isn't going to warm him up at all.

We were best friends once; it would be nice if we could be even half as close as what we were. Maybe not even that, just be able to be in the same room without him wanting to kill me. I wonder if I spoke to him and he understood Winnie isn't just some kind of weird, unobtainable desire for me. She is everything. Elijah doesn't care about anyone more than he cares for his family, and I know if he saw how happy I make Winnie, he would begrudgingly accept us, but getting him to see that before he punches me is the problem.

"Larson," Coach barks, and I push everything else aside to focus on the game. Turning, I throw my hat off and slip into my green helmet. He nods approvingly. "Is your team ready?"

I glance around at the boys vibrating with the need to get on the ice. Dressed fully in white-and-green jerseys and matching green pants. Skates tight and ready to rock. Confidence hits me like a truck, and I straighten.

"We're ready."

"Good. Let's kick some ass."

The crowd cheers as both teams hit the ice, but that fades into the background; the only thing I hear is blood pumping through my ears and the sharp slice of my blades through the glassy ice.

I instruct my team through warm-ups like I've done a million times, and by the end, my heart is ramped up and ready to play. Winnie skates by me for the fifth or so time, and my eyes snag on her round ass. Coach agreed to let her on the ice while we warm up to get photos, but during the game, she will be safe behind the glass. Her being on the ice, now knowing what I do, doesn't sit well, but the guys make sure to watch for her, and she's pretty good about not getting in the way, having watched us warm up for a while now. I do worry about her being pregnant and skating, though. Maybe I should talk with her about staying off the ice.

I glance at Coach, but he's busy talking with some of the officials, so I skate over.

"Reese," she mutters, feeling my presence. She doesn't have to look behind her to know who it is, and it makes my heart fucking swell. She can sense me like I can her. "You shouldn't be over here."

Winnie lowers her camera and cocks a sharp eyebrow at me over her shoulder. I skate to her front so I'm gliding backward.

"I just want to make sure you're okay."

Her head tilts in that cute way she does every time she's confused. "Should I not be?"

"No, it's just…" I lick my lips and drop my eyes to her stomach, hidden behind my—now cut—sweatshirt. "You being on the ice now makes me nervous."

Winnie cups the side of my face. "I love that you care so deeply already, but I promise I'm—*we're* okay, alright?"

I sigh and sink into her hand, cupping it with mine. "There's no one I care about more than my girls."

Her eyes brighten. "Girls?"

I nod. "I'm guessing it's a girl."

"You are?" Her hand falls from my face, and she places it on her hip, grinning.

I match it with my own. "I am, and I have to admit I'm hardly ever wrong."

Winnie's lips purse. "Well, I guess we will just see about that, won't we?"

"We will, and when I'm right, you owe me something." I skate closer to her, and she gulps, looking up at me with excited eyes.

"What might that be?"

"Guess we will find out." I lean down and smack a quick kiss to her lips before skating away.

"What do I get if you're wrong?" she calls after me.

I look around and flash her a smirk so she knows exactly what I'm thinking. "It rhymes with *fussy fate*."

Winnie gasps and quickly turns away from me, but I don't need to see her to know her face probably matches the other team's jerseys.

I hate to say it and jinx anything, but life honestly couldn't be any better than it is right now. I just hope I didn't ruin our chances of winning today.

34

Winnie

I have a lot of favorite moments that I've captured on camera, but as I sit on my bed and look over all the photos from today, I think they might be in my top three. Photo after photo, each one better than the last. Full of pure joy as the guys jump all over each other, celebrating their win. After the game, there was a chaotic slew of interviews, which I didn't know happened in college hockey, but I stood corrected, and I decided to dip to the hotel to get working. Schmidt is amazing at running their social media account, and I'm so thankful for him because there's no way I would be able to do what he can. He uses my photos and runs with them. I can take the photos and edit them to perfection, but it's his witty captions that bring the people in. He's gained over ten thousand followers since we started working with the team, and Mr. Kinnon seems more than thrilled about that.

I pull out my phone and click on Schmidt's name. It rings a few times before he finally answers. Something loud crackles in the background, like a loud machine or something.

"What are you doing?"

The noise cuts out before he says, "Sorry, just in the studio. What's up?" Schmidt is an art major, and how he got roomed in the athletic hall, I'll never know. He doesn't play any sports, and when I asked Reese about it, he didn't know either. Apparently, he never thought to ask, but I digress.

"I am just going through the photos now. They are amazing."

"Sweet. I know people have been getting antsy to see game snapshots."

"Well, they aren't going to be disappointed, that's for sure. I'm going to spend the evening editing and should have a bunch to send you by morning."

"'Ight, cool."

A loud knock raps on my door, and I jump and scurry from the bed to see who it is. I have a pretty good idea, but just in case it's not, I look out the peephole first.

Reese stands on the other side, his hair wet from a shower but tucked under a backward cap, per usual. Gosh, he looks hot. I don't know if it's the pregnancy that is causing the high sex drive or if that's just Reese, but sheesh.

"Okay, I'll let you go. Just check your email in the morning."

"Sounds good. Later, Winnie."

I tug on the door while saying my goodbyes. Reese narrows his eyes at me as I toss my phone on the bed behind me. Silence rings between us as he scans lower, and his upper lip twitches when he sees my bare legs. I removed my pants when I got here—not to seduce him but because it's more comfortable being pantsless. However, the look Reese is giving me is merely an added bonus.

"Who were you talking to, pantsless, while your boyfriend stood in the hallway?"

He pushes through the door, and I back up, giving him room, but he follows me all the way to the bed. The back of my knees hit the mattress, and I fall onto my back.

"Schmidt."

Reese stands above me, his feet wide and chest heaving. A stance of power. Images from the game flick through my mind. Seeing The Rapture on video was hot, but witnessing it in person... that was a whole other level. If I'm being really honest, I took my pants off and changed my underwear because they were soaked from watching Reese. When he's off the ice, he's the sweetest guy, at least to me, but when he's on the ice, he's so... rough. A shiver racks through me, and he leans down.

"You weren't there when I got off the ice."

My throat bobs as I swallow hard. "I, uh, came back here to work on the photos."

"I was looking for you."

Oh. I didn't think he would notice my absence because he was so busy with everything else. We were meeting up for dinner later, and I knew he would most likely stop by my room when he got here. He's already moved his stuff in, thrilled we would have a room all to ourselves. I don't think that's what Coach Swanson and Miller were thinking when they booked me a room, but I won't be the one to get in trouble if he gets caught in here.

"I'm sorry." I keep my voice soft and extra sweet in hopes of ridding some of his irritation. When he doesn't budge, panic settles low in my stomach. I shift, biting my lip as my head scrambles to come up with something that will make him forgive me quickly. It doesn't take long for me to figure it out. I lift my hand, but he must be able to read my mind because he snatches both my wrists in one hand and lifts them above my head before I can touch him. His sweatshirt rises and flashes my panties, but they're not sexy. My white cotton granny panties are the opposite of attractive, but they are comfortable and what I wear when I'm alone.

Still, Reese's eyes blaze as if I'm in lingerie.

"Next time, wait for me. Unless there is an emergency, and in that case, have someone come get me. It fucked me up looking for you and not finding you,

Win. You're lucky I checked my phone and saw your text because I was ready to tear the building apart."

My chest caves with his words. "I didn't think you would notice. You were so busy. I'm really sorry, Reese. I didn't mean to worry you."

He drops his forehead to mine and blows a minty breath over my face. "There will never be a day when I won't notice your absence, Winnie. Ever."

Reese is tucked into my side, watching TV with his arm behind his head while I edit photos, and I can't help but love how natural this feels. Every so often, he makes a comment on a photo, and it warms my heart that he's interested in what I'm doing.

He absentmindedly drags his fingertips along my bare back under my shirt, and it's distracting, but in the best way.

We have to get ready for dinner soon, but I'm so content, I don't want to remind him. Unfortunately, someone knocks on the door to do just that. I let Reese answer it since I'm still pantsless. I've gotten a lot done in the last couple of hours, enough that I gather the finished photos and get an email going for Schmidt. I'll need to finish the rest later, but these should be good for now.

Reese throws open the door, and before a word can be uttered, ten hockey players wander into my room. I shift, pulling the blanket further up, just in case, and shoot a look to Reese, but he doesn't look any more pleased than I am by the intrusion.

"Get the fuck out."

They ignore him, finding a place to sit anywhere they can. A few even sit on the foot of the bed, and I wonder if Reese is going to lose his mind, but Sawyer grabs his attention first.

"The girls want Snaps."

Twenty-two eyes turn my way.

"What for?" Reese asks, because I can't seem to get a word out. I see these guys all the time, but I'm usually wearing pants. Mind you, they all have probably seen my ass—something I keep forgetting.

"How the fuck am I supposed to know? Amy mentioned something about picking outfits or some shit. I don't know, okay? I blacked out when they were talking."

Oh, right. I forgot Amy made the trip for the game. Apparently, that's what the call was about. She was planning on spending those few days before with Sawyer, but the storm made it impossible, and somehow that was Sawyer's fault. Honestly, I'm not interested in helping her pick outfits, but I am curious to meet the girl.

Reese leans against the wall and crosses his arms. He doesn't seem to care about being in his underwear in front of all these guys, but I suppose that's because they share a locker room and have probably seen more than his blue briefs. We didn't even have sex, though. He merely stripped before he crawled into bed. I wanted to, but I could tell he was tired, so I didn't push it. Besides, it was nice just being with him.

He looks at me like I'm the only person in the world, and it never fails to swell my heart. "You want to go? Feel free to say no. Amy is a bitch."

Sawyer scowls at his best friend, but he doesn't deny it. A few of the guys out of Sawyer's eyesight nod, agreeing with Reese as well.

"I guess," I say with a shrug. I mean, how bad can one person be? I've met Zoey, so can Amy really be worse?

"Who the hell are you?"

Okay, so not the best first impression. Amy throws her short bottle-blonde hair over her shoulder and glares at me.

"Hi, I'm Winnie. You must be Amy." *Based on the bitch-iness.*

Her thin eyebrows pinch together, and she purses her lips like she just tasted lemon. She holds it for so long I wonder if her face is permanently going to stay that way. "Winnie? Like my boyfriend?"

"Uh… no. Winnie as in, Winnie is my name, and his last name is Winnifred."

"How do you know his name?"

I stare at her with a blank face because what else am I meant to do? A sick thought occurs to me, and I'm tempted to tell her the story I told Elijah about how we slept together, but if she's going to be here all weekend, I really don't want to have to deal with it. How has Sawyer been dating her for years? It's only been five minutes since she opened the door to what I *thought* was Emma and Laney's room, and I'm already tempted to turn around.

"Amy, calm down. Winnie is dating Reese."

Amy settles a smidge as Emma steps to her side. She smiles at me, but it's obviously forced.

"So glad you could make it. Come in." She tugs on my arm, despite Amy's arguing behind us.

Laney sits on a chair in the corner of the room, hugging her legs. Her eyes brighten when she sees me, but the moment Amy walks into the room, she cowers again. What the hell is this girl's problem? I know what

Reese told me, and while I get Amy probably isn't happy about her boyfriend's obvious feelings for another girl, she should have some self-respect and break up with him, geesh.

"So, you're dating Reese Larson?"

"I am."

She eyes me skeptically. This girl has some serious issues if she hates someone without even knowing them. "What are you, like, a buckle bunny or something?"

Emma drops her head to her hands, and I have to hold back a laugh to not piss her off any more than she already is.

"I think you mean puck bunny. And no. I've been around hockey my whole life. My dad was a coach and coached Reese all throughout school. I also photograph the team for their social media page, the local newspaper, and recently got asked to photograph the individual and team photos for the Emerson U magazine."

"Did you?" Emma squeals.

I grin at her. "I did. Just got the email last week." It was surreal getting an email from someone so high up at my university, but I guess everyone is pleased with my work. Everyone but Amy, that is. Her face is pinched, but I'm starting to believe that's just her face at this point.

"So you're the one who makes those posts sexualizing *my* boyfriend?"

"Uh, no? I just take photos at practices and games. No sexualizing going on, and I'm not even the one who makes the posts. That's Reese's roommate, Schmidt. Whatever he posts with my photos is none of my business." But I know for a fact he doesn't post anything inappropriate, so I don't know what she is getting at.

Amy pulls her phone from her bra and scrolls for a minute, all while I'm glancing at Emma and Laney. They shrug, obviously not having a clue what is happening either.

After another minute, Amy whips her phone around, showing an Instagram feed. I lean closer, wanting to get a better look, then laugh. I don't mean to, but I laugh hard and loud at the Sawyer Winnifred fan page. It's not sexual, either. In fact, it looks like it was made by a twelve-year-old with a crush.

"Oh, you think this is funny? My boyfriend is being harassed and it's funny to you?"

"No, what I do think is funny is that you are threatened by some random fan page that looks to be made by a child."

"But those are your photos."

"Yeah, they are, but that's not my page, and I'm not into your boyfriend. In fact, I find him infuriating more times than not." And now I'm really starting to question his judge of character.

Amy's brown eyes blow wide as if I just said I was into her boyfriend. She stands, gets in my face, and snarls, "If I find out this is your page, I will make your life hell."

I push to my feet, forcing her back, even though she's taller than I am. "Don't fucking threaten me again."

Amy glares at me. She's a bitch and makes Zoey look like an angel. Okay, not that far, but pretty damn close. I'm not a fighter, but Elijah taught me how to punch. He said it was just in case, and if this girl keeps threatening me, it will become a just-in-case moment.

Emma steps between us and claps her hands with an awkward smile. "I need help deciding between two dresses and could really use opinions."

Amy continues her hateful stare, but I flick a friendly smile at Emma. "Sure thing."

Emma has more than two dresses to pick from; she has a total of *seven*, and none of us can agree. Well, Laney and I agree, but of course Amy doesn't, and I'm not saying she's the worst human ever, but she's totally telling Emma to pick the worst one on purpose. Thankfully, Emma isn't an idiot and doesn't listen to her.

"I think I'm going with the blue one."

Laney and I smile, nodding in agreeance.

Amy scoffs. "Okay, well, if you want to look washed out, whatever."

This girl isn't even upsetting me anymore, she's just annoying. I've been in this room for over forty minutes, and not once has one positive thing come out of her mouth.

"Okay, Laney's turn," Emma says, completely ignoring Amy, which seems to piss her off all over again. Or maybe it's the mention of Laney. She shoots dirty looks her way, but for the most part, she's ignored her existence altogether.

"Why does she need to dress up? Who is she trying to impress?" Amy is looking at Laney but asking the question like she's not talking to her.

Laney lowers her eyes to her hands and twirls her thumbs. I don't understand why she lets Amy speak to her this way.

"She can dress up for whoever she wants. Or maybe she just wants to dress up for herself," Emma snaps.

Amy rolls her eyes. If she continues to do that, I wouldn't be surprised if they rolled out of her head.

"I only brought one outfit, so no need to decide."

Emma groans. "Bor-inggg, but go put it on!" She spins to me. "What about you, Win?"

I tilt my head at the other dresses lying on her bed and study them for a hot second. I can see Emma grinning from the corner of my eye. She's tall, like her brother, and curvier than I am, but a few of the dresses were bodycon and would probably mold to my body as well, and the thought of Reese seeing me in something like that causes giddiness to run throughout my body.

"Well, I was just going to wear this. But would you want to lend me a dress for the night?"

She squeals and claps her hands. She picks up all the dresses from the bed and tosses them at me. They are heavier than I thought they'd be, and I grunt with a smile on my face.

"Go try them on!"

I don't know what we are dressing up for. As far as I know, we're simply going for a nice dinner. That's hardly the occasion for what I would classify as a going-out dress, but oh well.

I slip into the third dress and know this is the one. It's the tightest and the shortest, but I don't look like Reese paid me to be there. I look sexy. The red satin looks like melted rubies against my body. It brings out the warmth in my hair and eyes, and the freckles that cover my body. Yeah, this is the one.

I open the door, ready to defend this dress because I know Emma loved the first one and Laney liked the second. Amy doesn't like any, surprise, surprise.

"Okay, this is it. I know you guys liked the other ones, but I think I like this one."

I stop and look up to find their mouths open and Amy glaring at me.

"Yep, definitely that one," Emma comments, and Laney nods. "Boy, am I glad I don't have a boyfriend on the team knowing you look like that and are with them all the time."

Emma flicks her eyes to Amy, and I have to cover my chuckle with a cough behind my hand, knowing she's saying it on purpose to rile up Amy. And it works because she stands and storms from the room without another word.

I turn to the girls, and we laugh to ourselves. Emma links her arms in ours and tugs us close. "Let's go find dates for the sports ball."

I pause. "The what?"

Laney cranes her head around Emma's body. "The sports ball. It's like a big, fancy dance to raise money for the athletic departments and other charities."

"Hasn't Reese asked you?" Emma asks.

My heart sinks, and I shake my head. "Uh, no. He hasn't."

A beat of silence falls over us.

"Well, I'm sure he's going to." Laney is such a sunshine human, ready to brighten anyone's day.

"Yeah, it's not for, like, three weeks anyway."

Three weeks? That's it? Why wouldn't he ask me? I guess we only officially got together recently, but he hasn't even mentioned it. Does he not want to go with me? He has no issues being with me anywhere else, so why not at some fancy fundraiser thing? A dark thought clouds the back of my mind. In three weeks, I'll still be early in the pregnancy, but it's possible I could start showing...

Nope. Not doing that. Straightening, I swallow back everything I'm feeling. And not even a second later, my phone goes off like he knows what is running through my head. I read the text across the screen.

> **Reese:** Amy mentioned you wanting to meet us there. Is that true? We are in the lobby if not.

Of course she told him that. She really is insane, but oddly, I'm thankful for her insaneness right now. I need to straighten myself up before the dinner.

> **Me:** Yeah, running a little behind.

> **Reese:** I can wait.

> **Me:** No, you go. We will be there shortly.

I drop my hand with my phone in it and meet my friends' eyes. It's obvious they are worried.

"I'm fine."

"He probably just assumes you're going together. Maybe doesn't think asking is all that important," Laney tells me with a halfhearted smile.

Yeah, that actually sounds like something Reese would do. He demanded I be his girlfriend, didn't ask. So maybe he is thinking the same for the fundraiser.

Still, I can't help but wonder if maybe he's not as proud about becoming a dad as he seems to be, but that could just be my nerves about becoming a mom rearing their ugly head.

35

Reese

The first day I saw Winnie was not that day she got her first camera like she thinks. It was the day they moved in across the street. She was playing with her mom and caught my attention. That was also the first time Winnie smiled at me. I couldn't explain it back then—hell, I still don't really know how—but something clicked inside me that day, and I knew Winnie was special.

Now, looking at my girl walk in, that same feeling hits me like a fucking moving truck. That same feeling, along with a whole lot of horniness when I am able to move past her teasing smile to see what she's wearing. Instantly, my dick solidifies at the sexy red dress pasted to her like a second skin. It's long enough to be classy for the restaurant but short enough, with a little slit on one side, to drive me wild.

The room goes fucking silent at the girls walking in. Emma, Laney, and two others I don't bother to look at because they aren't next to Winnie, but I think they are girlfriends to the other players.

Forty Timberwolves look ready to strike and capture their dinner for the night. Lucky for me, I have a cub who willingly crawls into my cave. More puck bunnies file in behind the other girls, and the buzz in the room intensifies. My buddies shift, itching to claim the girl they want. This is how it's always been after games, but usually, I'm not a part of it. Now I get the best one. Except Winnie is hot *and* knows about hockey—the best of both worlds.

Slow and steady really does win the race.

I can't take my eyes off her the entire walk across the crowded restaurant, and I don't know what part to stare at. Her taunting smile is enough to make me want to lay her on the table and take her in front of everyone, let them know who she belongs to, but then there are her tits. Perfectly framed by the red satin. And dipping lower, my eyes snag on her stomach, and pride blooms inside my chest. My baby is in there. My favorite girl is growing my second favorite girl as we speak, and I'm so fucking lucky. Then her legs, fuck. Winnie has always had really nice legs, and the black heels are only making them look better.

No way I'm lasting all of dinner without taking her.

She slips next to me, her usually sweet scent even stronger than usual. I lean in, taking a deep smell of her throat, then kiss the same place as it bobs beneath my lips.

"Hi."

"Hey." I open my mouth and sink my teeth into the tender flesh, just until she wiggles with discomfort. Moving back to see my work, I smirk at the teeth prints that'll be there for a little while, letting whoever looks at her know she's taken.

Winnie's wild eyes bounce around the table, I'm sure looking at our audience, but I can't be bothered to pull my eyes from her.

"You look beautiful."

"Thank you." She turns her eyes back to me and looks down my torso. I'm not in a full suit, but I'm still wearing a white dress shirt, green tie, and gray slacks. "The hat really pulls it all together."

"I know."

She giggles and swats at my chest. "If we get married, are you going to wear a hat then, too?"

Her eyes round and her mouth falls open like she can't believe she just said that. I, on the other hand, can't believe she said *if*. As if there is any chance we don't end up married in the end. Silly girl.

I wrap my arm around her small waist and tug her tightly to my front, then lower my lips to her ear. She shivers, and her skin prickles with goosebumps.

"When, baby, and yes. I'll wear a hat because I know how wet it makes you when I do."

Winnie's eyes drop to my lips, and she leans forward. Our lips are centimeters away from meeting when Sawyer nudges me.

I shoot daggers in his direction for interrupting our moment. "What?"

"Amy has to pee again."

Of course she fucking does. Amy is already getting on my last nerve, and it started with her telling me Winnie said to go without her. I knew that was a lie right away. Amy might be able to manipulate Sawyer, but it's not going to work on me.

We step aside, and Amy brushes past. I don't miss how she looks at Winnie or the way Winnie gives her the fakest smile that falls as soon as she passes.

Looking back at Sawyer, Winnie asks, "Are you aware your girlfriend is actually the worst?"

He rolls his eyes, but his jaw is locked tight. "I'm aware."

"Good, because she's awful. Called me a puck bunny. Me!" Winnie tosses her arms up. She shoves by Sawyer and crawls onto the bench seat. I step right behind her because her dress is short, and I'm not letting anyone get a free show of my girl's ass. Again.

Sawyer drops into the end of the seat, pouting on his own. His eyes flick across the table, and he stiffens. Following his gaze, I find Laney talking with another guy on our team, Westen. He's a rookie and also a goalie, just like Sawyer. Nice enough kid, but it's obvious Sawyer isn't thinking about how nice he is right now.

I shake my head and turn to focus on my girl. One day Sawyer is going to realize.

Winnie has her back to me, chatting away with Gavin. I scowl, probably looking pretty similar to Sawyer right about now. The difference is, I slip my arm around her body and tug her to my chest. I can do that, and Sawyer can't.

Gavin cocks an eyebrow, and Winnie giggles against my chest, her whole body shaking.

"Gavin was telling me about the fundraiser in three weeks and how his date already got her dress because she was asked weeks ago." Winnie's eyes narrow, and I know I fucked up.

It's not that I wasn't going to ask her, but until three days ago, we weren't even speaking. The goal was always to go with her, but I was giving her time. The plan was to just show up at her house and kidnap her if necessary.

"Are you upset I didn't ask you, Win?"

She doesn't need to say anything; I see it all over her face.

I tug her into my body and drop my lips to the bend of her neck. She tilts her head, and I kiss my way up to her ear. Smelling Winnie so intently is making my cock fucking ache.

"Silly girl." I nip at her ear. "I fuck you. I talk my coach into hiring you just so I can be around you. I *tell* you that you're my girlfriend." I drag my hand from her thigh, teasing the inside with my fingertips, and then place it on her lower stomach. "And my baby is growing inside of you at this very moment."

"But you didn't ask." Her voice is breathy and blows across my face.

"It wasn't a question of whether you were coming with me, baby. Just like it's not *if* we are going to get married. It's a matter of when."

Winnie sags against my front and whimpers into my neck. "I thought maybe you didn't want me to go with you because I might be showing."

Oh, silly, naive girl.

I grip her wrist and drag her out of the booth, much to Amy's dismay, like she wasn't the one making us move five hundred times before. Winnie tugs on my arm behind me, but I ignore her.

Sawyer reaches out and grabs my free wrist to stop me. "Coach is going to be pissed if you make us wait to order."

"Get me the steak." I glance over my shoulder to Winnie. "Get her the lobster mac and cheese." I pause, remembering something about pregnant women not being allowed to eat seafood. I'll have to do more re-search on that later, but right now, I have one thing on my mind. "Actually, get her the same as me, but make hers medium."

He slaps my back, and I continue toward the bathrooms. I debate my options and push into the family one. It's just the hockey team here tonight, so this should be the safest bet.

I let go of Winnie and flick the lock on the door. Turning, I take in my girl nervously shifting across the room and the tight little number hugging her body. Her stomach is still flat, but the thought of her thinking I wouldn't want to be seen with her when she's showing is insane. If anything, I can't wait until she is showing so I can tell everyone it's mine.

"Lift up your dress."

"Reese, I—"

"Lift. It. Up."

To my surprise, she listens. So fucking slowly, she drags the soft material up her thighs until it's above her hips. My heart thunders seeing her perfect pussy—*bare*. As in nothing but the small landing strip of red hair covering it.

She's commando.

"Dirty fucking girl, Win."

"None of my underwear fit with this dress."

I stalk forward, and she backs into the wall. Silky skin kisses my palms as I place my hands on her thighs and drag up, loving how her smooth skin divots for my pleasure.

"Speaking of, whose dress is it?" The thin material is flimsy between my fingers. So easily, I could rip it.

"Emma's, so you can't rip it."

Smart girl. "I wouldn't anyway. No one gets to see you naked besides me."

She shudders when I press my lips against hers. They taste like strawberries from the gloss she's wearing, and I drag my tongue over them before deepening the kiss. Fuck, it feels good to be touching her how I want. Ever since she walked in, I've been ready to pounce, and now she can find out what she's been doing to me.

I step closer, slipping my leg between hers. She's soaked, and it's probably going to sink into my pants, but I don't give a fuck right now. I'll wear it with fucking pride.

"However—" She gasps at the pressure on her clit before continuing. "They have seen my ass, so—"

I smack her pussy, and Winnie's eyes round. Her mouth drops open, and I shove my tongue inside. She tastes like the strawberry lemonade she ordered, and I lap it up. This girl is like the best hit of ecstasy. If someone would have told me a year ago I wouldn't be able to control myself and would have to drag a girl away to fuck her during dinner, I would have brushed them off.

If they had told me that girl would be Winnie Lewis, though, I might have believed them. She's my exception. My favorite girl. My everything.

"Did you just smack my pussy?"

"I did, and I'll do it again if you keep talking about other guys seeing what's mine."

Winnie's eyebrows twitch, a conflict raging on her face. She wants me to smack her. I smirk, and she scowls.

"It was your fault they did." She attempts to cross her arms, but I move closer, blocking it and holding her eyes as I pull back and smack her pussy again. The sound is sinful and so fucking erotic. I glance down, knowing my dick is leaking, and if I don't pull it out soon, I'm going to have a mess in my pants.

"Take my dick out."

Winnie makes haste undoing my belt and unzipping my pants. She shoves her hand in my briefs and wraps it around my shaft. The sensation is overwhelming, and I grunt as my eyes threaten to close.

With my dick out, I shift closer and press myself against her stomach.

She looks up at me with big, hungry eyes, and I brush a piece of hair from her face. "If you think I'm not waiting for you to give me the go-ahead to shout our pregnancy from the rooftops, you haven't been listening." I cup her face and drag my finger across her lower lip.

"Our pregnancy?" she teases.

"Yes. Ours. I'm going to be here the entire time, Winnie. You're not going to go through a single moment alone."

She nestles against my hand and tugs on my shirt, pulling me closer. "Every day, you make me fall in love with you more than the day before. It really isn't fair."

I throw my head back with a chuckle. "That's always been the plan, baby. I'm glad you've finally caught up.

Winnie

"Harder, Reese."

He grunts and grips my hips painfully hard, but all I can do is grasp his shoulders and attempt to hold on as he fucks me against the bathroom wall.

This is by far the wildest thing I've ever done; I can't wait to do it again, and we're not even done this time.

Reese smacks his fingers against my pussy and massages my clit. My gasp echoes off the bathroom wall before I moan his name, begging him to let me finish.

My orgasm is cresting in the background, waiting to reach its peak.

"Again," I whimper, and he chuckles darkly, the sound shooting straight into my ear and tightening my nipples to a painful point. "Please, Reese. Please."

"Fuck! Keep begging."

I do. I beg until my throat is raw and tears burn my eyes. Reese continues his slow thrusts, each one harder than the last. One arm hooked under my ass and the other one gripping my hair. He tugs my head back, exposing my throat, and attacks it, sucking, licking, and biting.

"It'll never be enough with you, Winnie. Fuck, your pussy is too good."

"Make me come. Please, Reese."

He drops his hand from my hair and shoves it between us to my clit.

I gasp; being so full with his dick as his fingers massage my clit is too much. My mouth drops open, and Reese takes the opportunity to mash his lips to mine. Maybe to stop everyone from hearing me scream.

"Take what you need, baby. It's yours."

Reese's thrusts turn panicked, fast and hard as he slams into me, and all I can do is hold on, but it's not easy when my body feels like Jell-O. It only takes a few more pumps for him to shove deep inside me, shooting cum as deep as he can.

He collapses against me, crushing me to the wall and breathing hard. "Fuck, Winnie."

I couldn't have said it better.

"So, is this your way of asking me to the fundraiser? Because if so, I think my answer will be yes."

Reese grins against my shoulder and shakes his head slightly. "I wasn't asking, but I'm glad you said yes. Wouldn't want people asking about the rope burns when I had to tie you up and force you there."

I think he's joking, but there's a small part of me that feels like he's not. Reese doesn't take my no's lightly. In fact—he doesn't really accept them at all.

He's lucky I like that he doesn't.

36

Winnie

I stare down my lens, trying to get the perfect snapshot. Someone skates in front of me, but instead of moving out of the way, they stop right in front. I lower my camera and peer at the guy curiously.

"Can I help you?"

"You could give me your number."

I'll give it to blondie here. He has balls for outright asking. Or maybe he's a cocky douche; I'm leaning toward the latter.

"No, thank you."

I skate to the side and lift my camera, only for him to follow. He places a gloved hand on top of it, forcing it down, and I see red.

"You want to lose that hand? Don't touch my camera."

My words only egg the man on. He moves closer, forcing me toward the wall. I'm not that great on my skates, and the circumstance in front of me doesn't make me any better. He skates forward, and in my attempt to get away, my skate glides out from under me, and I fall to my ass.

The guy laughs, but I'm too focused on making sure my camera is okay to care about him.

Suddenly, he's gone from in front of me, crashing into the wall a foot away. I throw a hand to my mouth as Reese pounds on the guy's face.

Someone else lifts me by the elbows. Sawyer spins me, looking over my face.

"Are you okay?"

"Yeah, no. I'm fine. I just tripped."

"What really happened, Snaps?" His voice is hard, much like his sharp jaw right now.

I glance in the direction of Reese and the guys, tumbling on the ice as the refs simply watch. I know they typically allow the guys to throw a few punches before breaking it up, but the game hasn't even started yet.

"He was just being annoying, so I backed up and lost my balance. Really, that's all, Sawyer."

A whistle blows, and he curses. A second later, I'm being lifted into his bulky, padded arms, and he's skating across the rink.

Embarrassment burns like wildfire up my body.

"Put me down," I hiss.

"Reese is losing his fucking mind, Winnie. Just let me get you off the ice before something else happens."

"Your girlfriend is going to blow a gasket."

He shoots me a glare and clenches his jaw. "I know."

The refs eventually get the fight broken up. Reese yells something at the guy with a bloody face as the ref drags him away, but I can't hear what he said. Halfway across the rink, he turns, narrows in on me, and skates faster than I've ever seen him. He hops the wall and drops to the floor in front of me on his knees. He cups my face, even though I should be the one cupping his. He's bloody, but I'm not sure if it's his blood or that guy's.

"Are you okay?" He shoots a harsh look behind me and lowers his hands down my body, feeling all over. For what? Who knows. I've never seen Reese look so... out of it. He's like a wild animal right now.

"What the fuck happened?" he barks, but it's not aimed at me.

"Reese."

The guys around me mutter nonsense, but it does nothing to settle him. I call his name again, finally catching his attention. He presses a hand to my stomach, and his eyes flicker. "I'm going to fucking kill him if something is wrong."

My heart aches seeing Reese so worried. Logically, I know I'm fine. A stumble to my ass isn't a big deal, but Reese isn't thinking logically right now.

I cup his face, forcing his wild eyes to me. He breathes hard, a look of absolute desperation etched across his face.

"I'm fine. We are fine. Okay?"

He breathes out a shuddering breath. "Are you sure? How can you be sure?"

"Because it was just a small fall, Reese. I promise there's no need to worry, and no need to go to prison."

He winces, and I regret my words immediately.

"I will get an appointment tomorrow, and you'll see everything is okay."

That seems to calm him. His eyes close, and he goes to drop his forehead to my thigh but must remember his bloody face and stops.

"Seeing you on the ground." His body vibrates under my hands. "It fucked with my head, Win. Scared the shit out of me."

"We're okay." I'll repeat that as many times as it takes.

"Larson," Coach barks, and I jump.

Reese lifts his head and looks to his coach with a blank face. My lips tilt down. I don't like seeing Reese like this. I love that he cares so much, of course, but I don't want it to completely wreck him every time something not ideal happens. That fall was nothing; it didn't even hurt my butt, and I know he didn't see it, but still.

I've never seen Reese so untamed.

Reese kisses my forehead and wanders off with his coach, and all I can do is stare after him.

Sawyer nudges my arm and nods his head. "You can come get those shots in the locker room now. We're all dressed."

Oh, right. I forgot Schmidt had texted me asking for those.

I stand on shaky legs. Gavin and Beckett place my hands on their shoulders. They probably assume I'm shook up from the fall, but that's not it at all.

I'm worried about my boyfriend.

"Google says you should be okay, but it doesn't hurt to see a doctor."

"WebMD says falling can cause a detached placenta."

Sawyer smacks the back of Beckett's head. "The placenta isn't even fully formed yet. Don't scare her like that."

"I'm just telling you what it says!"

I giggle to myself. "Thank you, Beckett."

As soon as I finished with the photos, a handful of the guys pulled out their phones to google how falling can hurt pregnancies. I did the same but quickly exited out when I saw horror stories that were doing nothing but stressing me out.

Sawyer drops his phone, and the others follow.

"You think they are going to let Larsy play?" someone asks.

My stomach sinks with worry. I know how much Reese hates riding the pine, and it would kill me to know it was my fault he ended up there.

Gavin shrugs. "They better. We need our captain."

"Hopefully." Sawyer flicks a look at me. "He needs to burn off some... emotions."

I lean against Reese's locker and close my eyes. Taking the photos was a nice distraction, but now my head is pounding.

Something next to me crashes, and I peek an eye open to see Reese's stick on the ground next to me. I reach down and grasp it, and the room goes silent.

I pause and look around, meeting roughly thirty sets of eyes filled with a mixture of shock and horror.

"What?"

One guy nudges another. "She touched his stick."

Beckett swallows hard. "Fuck."

Gavin runs a hand down his face, and my heart rate increases.

"Someone tell me what is happening?"

"Today of all fucking days," Sawyer grumbles and pushes to his feet. Gavin is right behind him.

"Reese is weird about no one touching his stick. Some kind of superstition."

Sawyer stops next to me, staring down at the stick in my hand like I'm holding a giant dildo. "It's a good thing you suck his dick, Snaps."

"Well, what the hell do I do?" I hiss. Reese is in the coaches' room right in front of us. He might even be able to hear everything being said right now. He is already in a bad headspace. So if he walks out and sees me holding the stick—

"Should I drop it?"

"Nah, he will know someone touched it," Tucker says. "One time I touched it, and he gave me a black eye."

A black eye? Reese would never hit me, but it doesn't mean he's not going to be pissed.

"Best to just accept your fate and deal with The Rapture, Snapshot." Gavin slaps my shoulder. I think it's meant to be comforting, but it's not.

"Yeah, maybe he won't be too rough on you." Brogan grins. "Or maybe he will." He winks.

My heart is about to drop out of my ass.

Then the door opens. Coach steps out, looks at me, and huffs. "You okay?"

"Yep." My voice is squeaky, and I clear it. "All good, Coach."

"Good. I don't want you on the ice for games anymore."

No problems there. I might not live to see the ice again.

Coach steps to the side, and my heart freezes altogether. Reese steps forward with puffy red eyes, but he forces a weak smile when he sees me. He hasn't looked at the stick in my hand, but he doesn't necessarily look angry as he walks to me. If this is how The Rapture looks on the ice, no wonder the guys always seem surprised when Reese rocks them.

He stops in front of me, and I swallow hard and smile because I know I won't be able to get a word out right now.

Being so much taller in his skates, he bends at the waist before he kisses my cheek. "Thanks for holding that, baby."

He grips the stick and gently takes it from my hand before turning and walking out of the room.

No one else moves. Even Coach is staring after him like he can't believe what just happened.

I let out a heavy breath and fall against his locker. "You assholes. I was pissing my pants."

The guys turn in my direction, confusion etched across each of their faces. Some shrug and head out after Reese, while others stay and stare at me.

"So he, like, *love* loves you," Gavin comments before heading for the door.

Sawyer is the last one, and he glares at me. "He doesn't even let me touch it."

I giggle, stand, and bounce past him, slapping his back. "Maybe you should try sucking his dick."

37

Winnie

"Okay, but don't forget Mom is going to be here later today. You promised her you'd be home for dinner, Elijah."

He huffs a breath in my ear through the speaker. "Yeah, I fucking know. I'll be there. Bye."

The phone beeps, letting me know the call ended, and I roll my eyes and lower it. A second later, a text comes through.

Elijah: I love you.

I lock my phone and drop it to the counter, only to pick it up and shoot off an I *love you too*. I don't get Elijah. He's not been home hardly at all, and when he is, he is constantly picking fights with me. I don't know what is going on, but he's pissing me off. Still, he always manages to tell me he loves me.

Sweet, but still a dick.

I'm in the middle of shoving a piece of toast into my mouth when a knock sounds on the door. I glance at the time on my phone and frown. Mom's not meant to be here for another few hours. She knocks again, and I hurry around the living room to pick up the pillows and blankets I was using. Swallowing the rest of that piece of toast, I grab the other and tear a bite off, carrying the rest to the door with me.

I'm breathing hard when I open the door. "Mom, you're early."

Stopping, I come face-to-face with a huge bouquet of flowers. I can't see who is holding them, but they're pretty.

"I think I'm going to have our daughter call me Dad, if that's okay with you."

I swat at Reese's arm and tug him inside. "What are you doing here?"

Reese and I agreed the only time he would come by my place is if he was picking me up or dropping me off. I can't have him sneaking around with the chance of Elijah coming home. I'm doing my best to warm Elijah up to the idea of Reese being in the picture again, and by warming him up, I mean asking him to come to a game with me and him saying fuck no. So it's not really working, and Reese definitely shouldn't be here right now.

But he walks across the room without a single care in the world. Carrying the flowers, he glances around, looking for a good spot before he sets them on the counter. "These are for your mom."

God, I love this man. "She's going to love them."

He spins to me, and my heart skips a beat. Like he can hear it, he smirks, and I wonder if I'll ever get used to how hot he is. I sort of hope not.

He saunters across the room and engulfs me in a tight hug, but not too tight because he's still so worried about hurting us. He calmed down after my first appointment last week, when the doctor said everything was okay, but he's definitely more cautious than he needs to be.

Reese kisses me, and I tug on the hair under his hat, holding his mouth to mine. He grins against my lips but doesn't pull away.

"I missed you too." He chuckles and lowers to his knees. The soft material of my shirt tickles against my skin as he drags it up and kisses my belly. "How are my girls today?"

"The same as this morning when you dropped us off."

Reese mutters something to my stomach about her mom being snippy. I push my shirt down while also tugging him to stand, which he does.

"I see you're eating, so you're probably not hungry. Are you tired? Thirsty?"

He turns, but I grab his arm.

"I'm fine, but why are you here? Elijah could be home any minute."

"My shower is busted. I was hoping to use yours."

I cross my arms and drop my weight to one hip. "You couldn't use the showers at practice?"

He drops his head and gives me a crooked smile. A look he knows I can't deny.

Rolling my eyes, I kick off and head for the bathroom. "Fine, but when Elijah kills you naked, I don't want to hear it."

I deny Reese when he asks me to shower with him, much to his displeasure, but I need to get the apartment clean. Thankfully, Mason went home for Thanksgiving and offered to let Mom use his bed. Elijah bought new sheets and a blanket just for her. We did offer to go home for Thanksgiving, but she insisted she wanted to come and check out our place. My FaceTime calls haven't been enough to satisfy her need to know everything going on in her children's lives. I still haven't told her about her grandchild growing inside me. After our first appointment and hearing the heartbeat, I got really excited and decided I wanted to tell her in a special way. So I made up one of those first-time grandma boxes to give her while she's here.

I fall onto the couch and let out a deep breath. Cleaning is exhausting, and I didn't even have to do a lot. I bet if I complain about my feet hurting, Reese would rub them. He's been at my beck and call since we got back from the games. It's nice, but he's also exhausting me by checking in every three minutes.

Closing my eyes, I drop my head to the back of the couch. It doesn't last long, though, because the door handle jingles. Shooting up from the couch, I stare at the handle for another second, making sure I didn't imagine it, but then it twists, and I take off for the bathroom.

I barge in and slam the door behind me, breathing hard as I flick the lock.

When I open my eyes, Reese is grinning at me, a cocky eyebrow arched in question.

"Work yourself up thinking about me in here alone?"

"Shh!" I rush forward to throw my hand over his stupid mouth. He grips my wrist and tugs me into the shower with him. I gasp but bite it back to not alert anyone, and he grins beneath my hand.

"Elijah came home, so you need to shut up."

"Win?" Elijah calls from the hallway. "How many times have I told you to put the peanut butter away when you're done. We're going to have ants."

I roll my eyes.

"He's right, you know?"

"Shut up," I hiss before yelling out to Elijah. "Okay, sorry!"

"Whose flowers are those?"

Reese smirks.

"Uh, Mom's. I had them delivered for her."

"Kissing ass already, eh?"

I roll my eyes and wait for him to walk away, but instead, he drums his fingers against the door and tests the handle. "Open up. I have to piss."

Is he fucking kidding me right now? Reese is grinning as he rinses the soap from his head, not at all fazed that my brother, who hates him, is home, and he's somehow going to have to sneak out without getting caught.

If I make Elijah wait, he's going to be standing there when I'm "done" and will for sure see Reese. If I let him come in to pee and can keep Reese quiet—task impossible—then maybe he will go to his room after and I can quickly shove Reese out.

"Uh, yeah, okay. Just unlock it and come in."

Reese's eyebrows fall, and he leans forward. I lower my hand from his mouth, trusting him to whisper.

"You realize I'm taller than your curtain, right?" He flicks his eyes to the rod, and I follow. Fuck, he's right. "He's going to see the top of my head."

The door clicks, and I know he's unlocked it.

"Coming in."

I shove on Reese's shoulders, but he doesn't move. "Get down," I hiss.

He rolls his eyes but lowers himself onto his knees, and I realize the mistake I've made as soon as he looks forward and his eyes blaze. I cross my legs and do my best to scowl, but it's a lost cause. I can't say no to Reese any more than I can say no to mint chocolate chip ice cream. Which I've convinced Reese is my craving, and he has a tub delivered every few days. I don't think cravings happen this early, but the less he knows.

"Mom called. She should be here soon."

Oh, great. Even more people to hide Reese from. I think Mom is actually going to be rather excited about us, but it's only going to make it harder to tell Elijah. I'm hoping Mom can help dampen the blow by telling him with me. I know he will feel betrayed if everyone else knows besides him, and right now, pretty much everyone does. Reese is lucky Elijah doesn't run in the same circle as him because he can't keep his big mouth shut.

Reese leans forward, nudging his nose against my center. I gasp but am quick to cover my mouth. He grins and looks up with fake innocence, then hooks his fingers into my leggings, and for whatever reason, I don't stop him from pulling them down my legs.

The toilet flushes as Reese lifts one of my legs, draping it over his shoulder, but he hesitates, I assume waiting for the door.

"Winnie," Elijah growls. "I told you to stop fucking wearing my clothes. If you can't fit in your own, that's not my problem. Lay off the ice cream."

Then the door slams.

Reese blows a sharp breath against my pussy, and I shiver. "He took my clothes, didn't he?"

I peek outside and slap a hand to my face. "He did."

"Fuck."

Fuck is right—my hand comes down hard on top of Reese's head, but he doesn't seem to notice. His eyes are closed, and he laps at my pussy like a starving man, not wasting another second.

"Reese," I whisper-moan. My hips start to buck, but he pulls off to lick two fingers and then shoves them inside me. For Reese not having experience outside of me, he's so damn talented with his fingers. And tongue. And dick. He's just overall sexually talented.

He brings me to the hilt, sucking, some biting, and fucking me with his fingers. All I can do is hold on to him and the wall and pray I don't fall, which Reese would never let happen, anyway.

He groans, and I swear he pushes even deeper. "Fuck, Winnie."

Slapping a hand to my mouth, I mask any noise that might come out as my climax takes me to ecstasy. Wave after wave of pure bliss crashes over my body, leaving me weak and boneless.

I fall against the wall and sigh, and Reese chuckles, climbing up my body before pressing a deep kiss to my lips. I'm too tired to kiss him back, but he doesn't seem to mind and kisses me enough for the both of us.

"How I missed hearing you come."

"You heard me come yesterday after practice, Reese."

387

"Still."

Right, *still*.

"I'll check the coast, but you need to sprint to my room."

"Aye, aye." Reese makes a little salute, and I swat him. "It's not time for jokes, Reese Abraham Larson."

He narrows his eyes at the mention of the middle name he hates.

"Whatever you say, Winnie Rue Lewis."

Asshole.

I crack the door open and stick my ear out. The TV blasts from the living room. I wait for another moment, then quietly close the door.

"He's playing a game, so we should be good. Just head right to my room."

"Oh, what game?" He grips the handle but I shove him off before he can open it.

"Stop it. It's not like he's going to invite you to play."

He rolls his eyes and brushes by me and walks right out the door without even looking. I could thump him for that, but there's no yelling, no one screaming from a broken bone, so I guess it's fine.

I look out, just in case he's walking by, and when I don't see anything, I slip from the bathroom, towel tight under my arms and my wet clothes tucked under.

Leaning against my closed door, I breathe out a long, relieved sigh. Reese is on me instantly, inhaling my air and eating at my lips a second later. He drags his hand up my thigh, over the towel, and pauses when he hits the bump from my clothes. He steps back and gazes at me, tilting his head. He scans all over my body with an expression I can't get a read on.

"Fuck, I can't wait for you to get bigger."

My eyebrows shoot up my forehead. I look down at what he's seeing, noticing the clothes look an awfully lot like a pregnant belly.

"Yeah?" I ask, sort of embarrassed.

He steps closer, drags his nose up my jaw, and nods. "Mm-hmm. Maybe after this one, I'll pump you full of my cum until another one pops out."

I shouldn't like what he's saying as much as I do. "How many kids do you want?"

"I don't know. A lot."

A lot. What the hell could that mean? A lot to me is, like, four. That would be a lot, but I think I could do four. Especially since I'm starting a lot earlier than I thought I would be.

"Like, uh, four?" I ask, hopeful he doesn't say something crazy like eight or more.

Reese snorts and kisses my jaw before pulling back to grin at me. "I'm just playing, Win. Not about you being pregnant. I would love to see you swollen with my babies all the time, but I know it's not easy on your body. I want as many kids as you will and can give me."

I smile, and he brushes his fingers over my cheek. "But it doesn't mean I'm not going to be pumping you full of my cum any chance I can."

"I would expect nothing less."

Reese is lucky I like my lounge clothes oversized and I still have a pair of his briefs he sent me home with that first night. My biggest pair of sweatpants are still way too short, but at least they fit around his hips. I still have his sweatshirt, which I don't like lending, but he promises I'll get it back.

He falls to my bed, and I groan. "Reese, you have to go home."

He grabs my pillow and curls into it. I think he's trying to give me puppy-dog eyes, but it's not working in his favor. At all. "Let me stay. I'll be very quiet and no one will know I'm here. Just bring me a plate of dinner when you come to bed."

As tempting as that is—and it is because I much prefer sleeping with Reese than sleeping without him—I know my mom is going to want to see my room, and if she finds Reese lying on my bed, she's going to flip, which will in turn alert Elijah, and tomorrow is Thanksgiving. I don't want to spend it in jail or the hospital.

I open my mouth but am cut off when Elijah calls for me, followed by, "Mom's here!"

Fuck.

Reese smiles like he just won the lottery.

"You need to be quiet. Okay?"

He makes a motion of zipping his lips and falls back, tucking both arms under his head as he closes his eyes.

"Winnie!" My mom's sweet voice singsongs, and my stomach pinches.

Here goes nothing. Let's see if my poker face has gotten any better.

38

Reese

"I'm not playing house. This is stupid."

Winnie scowls at me and her brother. "I do everything you guys want. I just want to play with my new baby dolls, and I have no other friends to play with."

She puffs her bottom lip out, and Elijah and I take turns groaning because we know we are going to give in to her pouts like we always do.

"Okay, how do we play?"

Winnie bounces around, grabbing various items from her messy room. She thrusts a baby at me and a toy car at her brother. My eyebrows pinch, and he chuckles.

"Why do I get a baby and he gets a car?"

"Because you're the dad and he's the brother."

"Well, I don't want to be the brother." Elijah drops the car and crosses his arms over his chest. "I want to be the dad so I can boss you two around."

Winnie rolls her eyes as if that's the dumbest thing she's ever heard.

"You can't be the dad. I'm the mom, and we are brother and sister. That would be weird."

Elijah ponders that thought, tapping his finger to his chin. He looks at me, and I shrug. I'm not in charge of this game.

"Well, it's weird for you two to play Mom and Dad too. He's like your brother."

"Yeah, but no blood relation. Now shush or you get to clean the toilets."

I bite back a laugh because Winnie really does sound like a mom, specifically her mom. I've heard Mrs. Lewis say that exact thing when Winnie and Elijah are fighting.

Playing house is actually kind of fun, but I'd never admit that out loud. Because I'm the dad, I'm in charge of the house. Even Elijah gave in to the part when I told him if he cleaned his "room," he could play games. His room being a corner in Winnie's room, but he really did disappear to play games.

Winnie hums across the room. I think she's pretending her bed is the kitchen and she's making dinner. I place the baby doll in its crib and wander toward her.

"Is the baby asleep?"

"Yep."

She eyes me and smiles. "Good, you can help make dinner."

Oh, great.

"Okay, what are we making?"

She falls out of character and whispers, "What's your favorite food?"

"Uh, I like spaghetti, I guess." Her mom made that for dinner last week, and it was the best food I've ever had, so I guess that works.

"We're having spaghetti."

I grin. "My favorite."

Winnie giggles. "I know."

I set Winnie's tiny table with plastic plates while she goes and gets her brother—er, son, I guess right now.

To my surprise, Elijah behaves himself at the fake dinner, and it's actually a nice time. I wonder if we will ever have dinner together like this when we're bigger.

I hope so.

39

Reese

Winnie is a closet hoarder. She's not even been at college long and yet her closet is full of the most random shit; I found the skateboard she swore she was going to use and begged her parents for on her tenth birthday. I've never seen her skateboard a day in her life.

She has photo album upon photo album. Some with pictures from before she was even born that her parents must have taken, and others that she put together. I'm in a lot of those ones. I fucking love that most of her childhood memories involve me, and I'm equally thankful mine involve her.

I don't know where I would be without Winnie.

As I'm flipping through the final photo album, I stop on a photo of all four Lewises and me. I think it was taken on Thanksgiving, based on Mr. Lewis's turkey sweater. I run my finger over the photo, and my heart clenches. Every time I think about Mr. Lewis, I can't help but think about how proud he would be of both his kids, and how much his son needs him.

Elijah is lost, and I know Winnie worries about her brother more than she lets on. That's why she doesn't want to tell him about us or our baby. He's already on the edge, and she knows that would push him over. I can appreciate Winnie looking out for him, but what's the cost? Not being able to live her life how she wants, or live it in secret? Sneaking around. If he knew, I could be eating dinner with them right now instead of stuck in her room.

I won't pressure Winnie to tell him. But boy, I can't wait. I miss Mrs. Lewis and her infectious laugh. She was the mom I never had and always wanted. When she could have hated me and pushed me out of their life for what my dad did, she pulled me closer, and I'll forever be grateful for her. Even after Elijah cut me out, Mrs. Lewis checked in on me every holiday, birthday, and the months in between. I've never told Winnie that, and I won't, but her mom was the one who kept me updated on her. I don't remember how I got to that point, but there was a night last year when I called her and spilled everything—besides me actually fucking her daughter when I did. Even drunk Reese knew better than to tell her that much. However, I did tell her how much I missed Winnie and how Elijah being cold to me fucking sucked. Not my proudest moment, but the next day, I woke up to a package of Tylenol and beef jerky on my doorstep.

She gets me a gift for my birthday and Christmas every year, and I do the same for her, and I know if Winnie were to tell her about us, she'd be so fucking happy for us. Winnie needs to see that it's okay to be with me.

Which is why I stay seated on the bed when Winnie texts me a very panicked *hide!*

"Okay, Mom. I'll show you my room!"

Winnie needs to take up acting lessons if she's going to continue this charade because *ouch*, her acting is painful.

Something slams into the door, and Winnie laughs. "I'm just so clumsy. Okay, let's go inside."

Oh my God.

The door creaks open, and Winnie sticks her head in first, her eyes rounding when she sees me sitting on her bed like it's the most normal thing, and to me, it is. I've been sitting on Winnie Lewis's bed for ages. Even if we weren't together right now, this wouldn't be that big of a deal. At least to her mom, and thank fuck it's only her mom who walks through the door.

Her eyebrows shoot up her forehead much like her daughter's. She glances behind her and closes the door. A cheeky smile splits her face as she looks from her daughter to me.

"Reese Larson." She tsks. "Thought I was past finding you sneaking around my daughter's room. Get over here and give me a hug."

Winnie's mouth drops. I pull Mrs. Lewis in for a hug, or more so she pulls me in like I'm a little boy and not a good several inches taller than her. Her soft body is like a hit of comfort that I haven't had in a while.

"What the hell are you doing?" Winnie hisses.

"Winnie Lewis." Her mom scolds, and I stick out my tongue at her. It really is like we are kids when her mom is around.

I drape my arm over Mrs. Lewis's shoulders and place my hand on my hip much like her mom is doing.

"You have a lot to tell me, sweetheart."

Winnie smacks her hand to her face and grumbles under her breath. I'm sure cursing my name in the mix of things.

Mrs. Lewis smiles at me and lifts an eyebrow. "You treating my daughter well?"

"I'd dream of nothing else."

She pinches my cheeks. "I know you wouldn't. Such a nice boy."

Damn straight, I'm a nice boy.

Winnie groans like an embarrassed teen, and I give in trying to prove her wrong. I let go of her mom to wrap her into my hold instead. I kiss the top of her head, and her mom squeals. This is exactly what Winnie needed to see—someone who would be happy for us—and now she has, so I'm not sorry at all. She might be mad at me, but I know what's good for her.

"I take it Elijah isn't aware, and that's why you are hiding out back here?"

I nod.

"Mm-hmm, well. I'm certainly not going to tell him, but you should, sweetheart." She takes her daughter's hands, forcing Winnie to look at her. The love that flows from these two is everything I want for our daughter and any future kids, and I know it's everything they will get. Winnie loves harder than anyone I know. "Elijah loves you."

"I know, but he hates Reese."

Ouch, but she's not wrong.

"Yes, well, he's going to have to get over it eventually, isn't he?"

God, I love Mrs. Lewis.

The past few Thanksgivings have been spent alone, and it's not really bothered me. This time, though, it fucking sucks. Mrs. Lewis texted me, inviting me to join them, but I politely declined. Winnie isn't ready for that just yet, and I don't want to ruin her holiday. I told her and

Winnie I was thinking about heading to see my mom, but I'm definitely not going to be doing that. I haven't spoken to my mom in months, and the last time was for her to tell me she needed her lawn mowed. Something I can't do from three hours away, but she wasn't asking me to do it. She was asking me to pay to have it done. Which I did.

I pull my stick back and bring it forward, sending the puck sailing right into the net.

Coach gave me a key to the rink after I became captain, and when I'm avoiding my problems, this is where I come to clear my head.

Slap shot after slap shot, but I swear time hardly ticks by. There's so much going on in my life, but it feels like not enough. My girlfriend is pregnant, due in seven short months that I know will fly by, and we've not talked about anything that comes with that. Where we are going to live since I refuse to live apart. Winnie is going to need help, and I'll be damned if I'm not that help. The baby is half mine. I'm going to do my part.

Ideally, I'd like to marry Winnie—not for the traditional aspect but because a lot comes with marriage. My life insurance, my savings, my last name. She's not mentioned what name she plans on giving our daughter, but I really hope it's mine—the name she will one day share. If she wants to hyphenate, that's fine, I just want to be involved.

Winnie giggles every time I say daughter, and I don't know how I know, but I just know that baby inside of her is my little girl. I can feel it.

What names does Winnie like? Honestly, I've not even thought about names, but that's something I want to do with my girlfriend. Unfortunately, we never get the time to. I see her at practice, she comes over when she can, and we talk on the phone, but it's not enough time to discuss everything.

Maybe it would be if every time I got her in my room I didn't shove my dick into her immediately, but fuck if it's not hard. She's just starting to show now, and every time I see her swollen stomach, it cranks me, hard. Plus, I don't know if it's the pregnancy or what, but Winnie is nearly panting when practice ends. Last weekend I had to fuck her in an abandoned closet after the game because she looked ready to burst, and fuck if I'm not going to satisfy my girl when she needs it.

Then there's the part I would never weigh Winnie down with, but my dad pops into my head every time I think of myself being a father. Winnie said I've proved that I'm nothing like him already, and she's right, but it doesn't make that fear of what I can become go away. When that guy knocked my girl over, everything besides making him bleed left my head. I've woken up in the middle of a nightmare a few times, where the refs didn't pull me off and I killed him. As much as I would have liked to in that moment, what would that say about me? Nothing good. What kind of dad kills people?

My father, that's who.

I pull my stick back, but instead of making another shot, I break it over my knee and chuck the pieces across the ice.

I hate who I share blood with, and there's nothing I can do about it.

The thought of my kids growing up to hate me the way I hate my blood is crippling. This isn't something I can share with Winnie, though, because she would simply assure me I'm nothing like him.

Winnie sees the best in me. I'm sure my mom saw the good in my dad at one point too.

I skate over to the bench and drop onto it, then lower my head to my hands.

"What a way to spend Thanksgiving."

I jump at the voice, looking up at Winnie standing in the doorway. Relief floods through me like it does every time she's around.

Winnie is my home. Safe, welcoming, and mine.

I open my arms, and she walks my way on shaky legs. She straddles me, and I bury my face into her warm neck.

"How did you know where to find me?"

"Sawyer."

She pushes back and nods, and I follow and find Sawyer, Laney, Emma, and Schmidt leaning against the wall.

"What are they doing here?"

Winnie shrugs. "Sawyer and Emma's parents are on some kind of vacation." Like usual. "Schmidt snuck away from his family, and I don't know about Laney, but they were all at the apartments when I went there."

"You went looking for me?"

She blows out a shallow breath. "Yeah. I feel like the worst girlfriend ever, leaving you to celebrate on your own. I knew you were lying when you said you might go see your mom, and it ate at me all day."

"You don't need to apologize, Win. I know you're in a tough spot."

She shakes her head. "Not tough enough to have my boyfriend spend his favorite holiday alone."

"You remember." A grin tugs on my lips, and it's funny how ten minutes ago, I didn't feel like smiling at all, but two minutes around Winnie, and here we are.

"Of course I remember." Winnie frowns. She sinks her fingers through my hair and tugs my lips to hers. "I remember everything about you, Reese Larson."

I only get a small kiss, and then she pushes away, but I don't think she wanted to.

"I'm going to tell Elijah soon."

My eyebrows raise.

"But," she adds, "I'm afraid he might kick me out. I've already talked to Laney and Emma, and they said I could stay with them."

"No." I shake my head. "You can come live with me."

"I don't play sports."

"Neither does Schmidt." Which I am still curious about how he ended up in my apartment, but whatever.

"Still, it wouldn't be fair for your roommates."

"Then we can start looking for our own place." In fact, why hadn't I thought about that sooner? We don't have to live at the dorms after sophomore year, but there was no point in getting my own place and paying before. Things are different now, though.

"We can after the school year."

"Winnie—"

She places a finger over my lips and giggles the sweetest sound I've ever heard. "Just listen. I'll live with Emma and Laney, they will have a whole extra room here soon because their third roommate is transferring next semester. After finals, we will start looking, and I'm sure something will come up shortly because of people moving out."

She's forgotten one big detail. "You are due in June, Winnie."

"I know. That's why after the year, I'm going to move home with Mom."

I open my mouth, but she is quick to cover it with both hands. "Only until we get a place. I told Mom today, and she's so excited. She will love me and our daughter being there."

"Daughter?" I mumble against her hands.

She smirks. "I decided to give in and listen to you."

Finally.

She lowers her hands, and I suck in a breath.

"I love that you have thought everything through, but you forgot one thing."

She tilts her head in the cutest way.

"How stubborn your boyfriend is. I refuse to live apart. The guys love you and will have no issues with you being around. If you want to live with Laney and Emma for a few months—until I get us a place and *before* school ends—fine, but I want your phone on you at all times and your location in case you need me so I can be there. Your mom can come stay the summer, hell she can move in with us, but Winnie, I swear to fuck, no one can keep me from being with you and our baby."

Winnie sniffles, and before I know it, she bursts into tears. She throws her arms around me, and I squeeze her, but I'm not sure why she's crying.

Eventually, she pulls away with red eyes and a quivering lip. "I'm sorry, I'm a mess."

"You're pregnant."

"Yeah." She sniffles again. "I spent all day trying to come up with the perfect plan that didn't require your life to change much."

Silly girl.

"I *want* my life to change, Winnie. Maybe other guys would feel differently, but I couldn't be more excited to be a dad and play house with you."

She groans and drops her forehead to my chest. "I can't believe *you* remember *that*."

"I remember everything."

Winnie curls into my chest and places a chaste kiss on my throat just under my Adam's apple. "I can't wait to play house with you either, Reese."

40

Reese

FLASHBACK

"Where the fuck is my sister? We are going to be late."

I shrug, not having the answer either. Winnie never takes a long time to get ready, but I guess tonight is a special occasion. I didn't go to my freshman homecoming. Actually, this is the first time I'm going too. Elijah has gone the past two years, but he always brings a date, and I don't feel like being uncomfortable in dress clothes and a third wheel all night. With Winnie not having a date, at least I'll have someone to chill with.

Another ten minutes pass, and with each one, Elijah grows more impatient. In my opinion, the longer she takes, the less time we will have to be there.

"'Bout fucking time."

I turn my attention to the front door, and my mouth drops. That's Winnie? Looks like her, but doesn't. Her long ginger hair is curled and pinned in various places. I've *never seen her wear makeup before, but she is now. Holy fuck, she looks so... different.*

"No fucking way my dad is letting her wear *that*." Elijah throws his door open, and I do the same.

I hadn't even looked at her dress, too distracted by the rest of her, but he's right. What the hell is she wearing? The dark-green dress complements her hair, at least that's what I heard her mom and aunt say. It's short, hits midthigh, and small spaghetti straps hold up a top that shows an uncomfortable amount of cleavage. It's not even a lot. Girls at school show more on the daily, but this is Winnie. It's not that the dress is inappropriate, per se. But it shows way more of her than I'm used to seeing. When did she grow up? I swear just yesterday, Winnie looked like the same pip-squeak as always, all legs and arms. Awkward and boney, but now... well, she looks like a young woman. I don't like it, and I definitely don't like that other guys will be seeing her like this. We have most of the guys in school too scared to even look her way, but I worry this night may change that.

"She's not wearing that!"

"Oh, stop it." Mrs. Lewis chuckles while scolding her son. "Your sister looks beautiful."

"Sure, but—"

"But nothing." Mr. Lewis wraps a loving arm around his daughter and squeezes.

Elijah and I stop at the bottom of the steps. My mouth is dry, not having anything to say, but I can't take my eyes off her. I can't believe this is the same girl who spit on my face two days ago. She technically didn't mean to, but still. She had spit hanging from her mouth, Elijah laughed and startled her, and it dropped on my forehead.

And now here she stands, looking nothing like that girl but so much like her at the same time. It's confusing.

"I'll be right back." Elijah slaps my chest and wiggles his eyebrows. He mentioned maybe getting a quickie in before the dance since his date's parents are gone all weekend.

"Yeah, sure."

He laughs, and the door slams behind him. The radio croons one of Winnie's favorite songs, and I turn it up and glance back at her. She's been quiet since we got into the car after the photos her parents insisted on at her house.

"You're not singing," I comment. She flicks a blank look my way but goes back to looking out the window like the moody teenager she normally isn't.

"Win." I reach back and shake her knee. Something I've done a million times, but normally, she's not in a short dress. Thank fuck I didn't see anything. It's already

*awkward enough, and the weirdest part is I don't know
why it's awkward, but I don't like it.* "What's wrong?"

She shrugs.

I pinch the bridge of my nose and sigh. "Come on, Win.
You know I hate the silent treatment."

"Do you think I look weird?" *The vulnerability in her
voice is enough to make me feel like a pile of shit. If I didn't
know any better, I'd swear her eyes are watery, too. Fuck.*

"It's not that you look weird. It's just different, I guess.
You know, we're just not used to seeing you look like that."

She scoffs and crosses her arms. "What? Like a girl?"

"Yeah," I deadpan. "Exactly."

"Well, I'm glad you and my brother finally see it because
I am a girl, Reese."

*My eyebrows bunch, and I turn back to the front. I
mean, I always knew Winnie was a girl, but she's like a
girl now. Whatever the fuck that means, because I don't
know. All I do know is it's weird, and I don't know if I like
it.*

"Maybe a guy will finally ask me out."

*My fists clench automatically at the thought. I know
how high school guys are, and I don't want that for Winnie. I want better for her.*

"Yeah, maybe," *I grumble.*

*Thank fuck Elijah and his date come out not too long
after. The air in the Bronco is thick with tension, and I'm
gritting my teeth so hard they ache, still thinking about*

Winnie going out with some random guy. I was worried before she said anything, and then she mentioned wanting to get asked out. *Why would she want that? I've been single my entire high school career, and it's great. No drama, I'm free to do whatever I want on the weekends. I don't know why she would want to have the worry about a boyfriend at her age. She's still so young, despite how she looks tonight.*

I could tell Elijah what she said, but I don't think him biting her head off would fix anything. If anything, it would probably make things worse. It seems Winnie is pissed right now, and I think fighting with her would send her further down that path, and we don't want that.

Elijah pulls the door behind me open, letting Calie climb in.

"Hey, guys!"

Calie is Elijah's flavor of the week. Unlike his sister, Elijah dates a lot. This week it's Calie Jones. Actually, he's been dating her for a month now, I think, but I'm sure their course is almost up. She's nice enough, I guess, but Elijah doesn't like to stick to the same girl for long, so I don't get too close.

"Hey, Calie." I glance back but catch on Winnie instead. She eyes Calie with furrowed brows. Moving my eyes to Calie, I don't understand what the look is for. She looks the same as she always does.

"Hey, Winnie. You look gorg!"

Winnie's smile is the most forced I've ever seen from her. "Thanks, Calie. So do you. I love your dress."

"Oh my gosh, thanks. They didn't have my size, so it's a tad small, but I made it work."

"Yeah, she did." Elijah pumps his eyebrows twice at me like his girlfriend isn't currently giving his not even fifteen-year-old sister tips on how to make her tits look bigger.

I'm going to fucking stroke out by the end of the night.

High school dances are exactly what I thought they would be like. A bunch of girls trying to get guys' attention, and guys doing their best to hide their boners as they grind against their date. I don't know why I'm not like the other guys in my grade. It's not like my dick is broken. I jack off like every other hormonal teenager, but the girls here don't interest me.

Well, besides one. Fuck, no, I'm not into Winnie like that. Holy shit, but she does interest me in the way that she's the only one I enjoy being around for more than a class period.

The only one I would choose to spend my time with. Maybe that's why I'm not like the other guys; I spend too much time with Winnie and not enough trying to get to know my peers.

Speak of the devil.

Winnie drops into the chair next to me after returning from grabbing more punch. She plops her elbow on the table and her chin on her hand and sighs. We've hardly moved from these spots, other than to refill our punch. I can tell she's itching to dance, she just doesn't have anyone to dance with since her brother is too busy making out with Calie in the back of the cafeteria.

"This blows."

"Yup."

She falls back in her chair and sighs even louder this time. "I wish you drove, at least then we could do something fun."

Actually, that's not a bad idea. "I'll be right back." I push to my feet and glance around, making sure some guy isn't waiting to pounce on Winnie the moment she's alone. When the coast looks clear, I hurry across the room. Interrupting my best friend, who looks like he's about to fuck in front of everyone, I tap on his shoulder.

"Dude."

"Huh? What?" He pulls away, breathing hard and covered in red lipstick.

"That's not your shade. But give me your keys."

"Dick, and why?"

I nod over my shoulder toward his sister, and he follows my gaze and frowns. "What's wrong?"

"Nothing, other than this is really fucking boring. I'm going to drive us around or some shit."

He takes a step out of Calie's arms and digs in his pocket before dropping his dad's keys in my hand. I forgot we took the Bronco tonight; I'll have to be extra careful. I know how much Mr. Lewis loves it.

"You break my dad's SUV, and I'm throwing you under the bus, no hesitation."

Calie tugs on Elijah's tie, dragging his attention back to her.

I ignore her, hoping my best friend can stay focused for five more seconds. "When should I pick you up?"

Elijah shrugs. "We can catch a ride to the party. You're coming to that, right?"

Shit, I totally forgot about the after-party. "I don't know. Maybe."

"Well if not, just drop the car at home and tell my parents where I am, would ya?"

"Yeah, later." I take a few steps and turn back to find them making out again. "Don't forget to wrap it!"

He flips me off without coming up for air, and I back away chuckling.

Turning, I knit my brow, not seeing Winnie at the table any longer. My blood pressure spikes as I look around the crowded room. Come on, Win, where the fuck are you?

I scan the room again, just in case I missed her, and I spot her walking back into the cafeteria. Finally.

"Where the hell have you been?" I snap as soon as I'm close enough.

Winnie's eyes blow wide, and she looks around like she's not sure who I'm talking to.

"You, Winnie, where have you been?"

"I went to the bathroom, Reese. Why, what's wrong?"

What is wrong? And why didn't the bathroom pop into my head? "Sorry." I let out another deep breath, hoping it eases some of the tension between my shoulders. Winnie watches me, a curious and confused look on her face. "I'm just tense."

"I've noticed. You have been all night."

Yeah, but I don't know why.

"Are you ready to go? Eli gave me the keys. I figure we can run through the Scoop and get some ice cream."

Her eyes brighten, and I grin as I throw my arm over her shoulder and lead her outside.

"Double mint chip in a waffle bowl and a double rocky road in a waffle cone, please." I pass the employee my card, and she takes it, disappearing through the little window. The Scoop isn't a walk-in place, it's only drive-through, but they have the best ice cream, and their parking lot overlooks the bay.

Winnie has been quiet since we got into the car and only mumbles a small "thank you" when I pass her the ice cream. I'm halfway through my cone when the silence makes me snap.

"What's wrong?"

She shifts awkwardly, surprised by my tone, I'm guessing. But she has to know her being this quiet is bothering me. It's not normal. Winnie usually never shuts up. Her dad often jokes that she was born talking.

"Nothing."

"Come on, Win. You're killing me here."

She blows out a harsh breath. "I'm just tired of being different."

Different? "What do you mean?"

She drops her bowl onto the dash and brings her knees up to her chest. I don't have the heart to tell her she maybe shouldn't do that in a dress, but I just won't look.

"All my classmates had dates tonight." That's what is bothering her? Honestly, I expected more, but I can kind of understand.

"Do I not make a good date?" I gently nudge her knee, and she groans. Okay, not a joking time, apparently.

"I didn't even get to dance."

Ahh. That makes more sense now. Winnie loves to dance. She's not really good at it, but she likes it.

I lean back in my seat and finish the rest of my cone. I'm looking around for a way to cheer Winnie up when I spot the radio and an idea pops into my head. I grab her phone and scroll to her music. It takes a while, but eventually, I land on "Sorry" by Buckcherry. A popular slow dance song, but it's just a great song in general.

I turn up the volume as high as it will go, roll down all the windows, and jump down, heading around to grab her.

"What are you doing?"

I tug open her door and lift my hand. "May I have this dance?"

Winnie glances at the phone, and then her face lights up as she laughs. She presses play and grabs my hand.

"I'd be honored."

I help her to the ground and lead her a few feet from the truck. Spinning, I'm hesitant to place my hand on her hips, but she's not hesitant at all to wrap hers around the back of my neck. As much as she can with her height, anyway. I hit my growth spurt this past summer, but I don't think the same can be said for Winnie.

"I'm not very good at this," I admit. We're just shifting back and forth, nothing like those movies Winnie and her mom watch.

"I don't care." Winnie rests her head against my chest. "This is the nicest thing anyone has ever done for me, Reese. Thank you."

Hinder comes on next, another favorite. "This is a good playlist, Win."

417

She giggles, and it shakes my chest. "Well, this is my Reese playlist, so I'm not surprised you think that."

Her Reese playlist? "You have a whole playlist dedicated to me?"

"Mm-hmm. I know my parents' oldies can get, well, old, for some people, so I made you a playlist to listen to when it is. It's songs I've heard you hum, play in your truck, or they just remind me of you."

"That's the nicest thing anyone has ever done for me."

Winnie pulls back and smiles at me. "I'm glad."

After another song, Winnie is shivering, so I help her back into the Bronco, roll up the windows, and crank the heat.

"Sorry, I didn't wear a jacket either."

"It's f-f-fine."

Damn, she's shivering. I swallow and lift my arm. She eyes the space I opened for her, and without another beat, she crawls over, and I lower my hand around her. We've sat like this before, but for some reason, it feels different now.

My stomach is fluttering like butterflies were released inside, but that makes no sense because this is Winnie.

I do my best to shake the feeling away and settle into the seat. Focusing on Nickelback playing low in the background. She really does know what I like.

"Thank you. For everything."

I drop a kiss to her forehead. Something I've done a million times as well. "Anytime, Win."

41

Winnie

"The team is on a roll. They are 5-0, with no signs of stopping anytime soon."

Mr. Hudson nods while looking over my shoulder at the photos on my computer. "These are incredible shots, Winnie. Professional level."

I wiggle in my seat, a beaming smile on my face. "Thank you. I really think I've found my thing, you know?"

He backs away, falling into the chair next to me, and crosses his hands, then places them over his knee. "I would agree."

"I can't thank you enough for allowing me this opportunity. I know Reese technically asked for it, but you didn't have to agree or bring it up to me at all."

Mr. Hudson tips his head, a knowing smirk on his face. "I take it you and the hotheaded hockey player worked things out?"

My cheeks bloom, and he chuckles.

"I see. Well, good. Despite his irrational anger for every male who walks into your viewpoint, he seems like a decent guy."

"He is."

"Good." He dips his chin and sighs. "Winnie, I meant it when I said these are professional level."

I glance back at the computer, eyeing the action shot of the guys celebrating a goal at the latest game. The photo is clear and a good angle. I happen to agree.

"It's a good shot."

"Yes, it is, but so are the rest. Shot after shot, all beautifully taken."

"Thank you, Mr. Hudson. That means a lot coming from you."

He stands and wanders in front of the classroom. It's empty because it's Saturday morning, but I've been wanting to show him my work, and he was busy last night, so he asked me to come in this morning.

"What's your goal, Winnie? In photography."

Didn't we already talk about this? "Uh, I'd like to eventually be a photographer for a professional team."

"Right." He stops and places his hands on the desk. "So, why aren't you?"

I blink, taken back by the question. "Um, because I'm eighteen and still in college?"

"What I'm getting at, Winnie, is you're good. Better than good. Hell, I bet you could teach me a thing or two about action shots."

"Oh, I highly doub—"

"I don't." He tugs his desk chair forward and places it in front of me. "What would you say to an interview with a professional sports team manager?"

"Like... like for a job?"

"Exactly for a job. I really think you have a gift. One that others cannot be taught in a classroom. I remember you mentioning your dad was a photographer. I'm guessing he taught you, and he taught you well."

At the mention of my dad, my eyes prick. "Thank you, he did."

Mr. Hudson leans back and grabs me a tissue. I pat my eyes of any unshed tears. "You are a great student, but I see how bored you are in class. Everything I'm teaching, you already know."

He notices that? "You're a great teacher," I offer, hoping that makes it better.

He laughs, so I'm guessing he's not that mad. "Don't apologize. I was the same way because I was too advanced for the class. Which is why I dropped out."

"You dropped your photography class?" My eyebrows shoot up my forehead.

"No."

Oh, well, that's good because I was—

"I dropped out of college."

"But you're a teacher."

He grins. "I am, but I only just got my teaching degree. I don't have a photography degree, Winnie, and not to brag, but look how successful my career has been. I don't *need* to teach, but it seems selfish not to share my knowledge with those eager to learn. Those who aren't like you with a natural eye."

"Are you telling me I should drop out of college?"

"No. I'm telling you, you have options. I know a few people. I could pull some strings and get you an interview with a professional team. It would be up to you to get hired, but I have no doubts you could."

Wow. I don't even know how to process what he is saying right now. That I don't need school, and he thinks I can get my dream job without it. That's, well, that's crazy. I never considered what I would do if I didn't go to college. That was always the plan, but what if he's right? I really love school, and I love learning, but to be able to get my dream career at just nineteen. My head is spinning.

It must show on my face. Mr. Hudson leans forward and places a steady hand on mine. "Just think about it, okay? But know that I will support whatever decision you make."

"Thank you, Mr. Hudson. Really, I'm... I'm at a loss for words, honestly."

He chuckles and retracts his hand. "It's overwhelming, but I feel I would be doing you a disservice if I didn't mention anything."

"I appreciate that, really. I'll think on it and let you know after the holidays, if that works?"

"Absolutely, as long as you need."

While I'm shutting down my computer, Mr. Hudson gathers his stuff, and he follows me out of the building. He tells me a little about his college days—before he dropped out. Apparently, he was a nerd. Which I can kind of see, but not the kind of nerd we see in movies. More like the kind we see in porn.

Holy hell, I can't believe I just thought that about my teacher.

He pushes open the door, and I step out into the frigid air. It's gotten significantly colder as the days go on. We got the first snowfall that I think is going to stick this morning.

Mr. Hudson is parked by me, so we head that way.

"Can I ask how your father died? He couldn't have been too old."

My throat tightens. It's not the first time I've been asked about my dad dying, and I know it's only natural curiosity, so I don't fault him for asking. Besides, he's right. My dad *was* young. "Drunk driver."

He curses. "Sorry, I just cannot stand drunk drivers."

"Me either," I murmur. He sets his stuff on top of his car and pulls me in for a hug. It's very innocent, like when Elijah hugs me, but that doesn't make it any less weird.

Especially when another car pulls up right in front of us.

"Hands off, Mr. Flirt, unless you want to be a stepdad."

My mouth drops, and so does Mr. Hudson's, but he recovers quicker than I do and snaps his shut. He eyes me, then my stomach, but it's not like he's going to see anything. I'm wearing three layers because of the weather.

"You're pregnant?"

I shoot a glare at my boyfriend, then sigh. "I am."

"Wow, I had no idea."

"Yeah," I grit. "We're not really telling people." At least I'm not.

Reese meets my harsh stare with his own.

Mr. Hudson clears his throat. "Well, congratulations, to both of you." He hurries around his car and pulls opens the driver's door, but he stops before dropping inside. "Remember what I said, Winnie. Please think about it." He glances at my stomach. *Once again, you're not going to find anything, buddy.* "Especially now."

And with that, he's in his car and speeding away.

I turn to Reese and place my hands on my hips. "Do you mind?"

"Do you?" He throws open his door and slams it behind him. His footsteps slap against the pavement as he stomps around his truck and stops in front of me, crossing his arms. "I pull up and see another man hugging my girlfriend."

"He was hugging me because I told him about my dad, Reese. It wasn't just a random goodbye hug. Besides, why are you here?"

He huffs but doesn't answer. Instead, he grips the passenger door to his truck and tugs it open. I can't see what he's grabbing until he turns, a flower corsage in one hand and a bag of my favorite candies in the other.

Oh, this *infuriating* man. *Why does he have to be so sweet?*

"These are for you." He passes me the chocolates, then the corsage. It's a white rose with a green ribbon to match my dress tonight.

I sigh while looking at the stuff, then slowly lift my eyes to meet his. "You're infuriatingly sweet."

Reese smirks. "That's my charm, baby."

I drop the stuff on top of the Bronco and walk into his open arms. "Thank you." I kiss his cheek.

He grips my ass and squeezes much harder than necessary. "Anything for you."

Like I said, infuriatingly sweet.

Reese

"Where the fuck is your sister?" I glance at the watch on my wrist for the tenth time.

"I don't fucking know, but if they don't hurry, I'm going in there." Sawyer drops his head back and runs a hand down his face. "Why did the guys have to ask them anyway. It's fucked, and if I see Tucker's hand drop lower than necessary, I'm going to kill him in front of everyone, and then we can auction off his organs."

Morbid, but I get it. Sawyer is not only pissy because his sister and the girl he denies feelings for got asked to the fundraiser, but Amy also canceled. She tried getting him to go visit her instead, but he said no, and he's been in a bad mood ever since she called this morning.

Another minute goes by, and I reach for the door. Hearing Sawyer curse, I pause and follow his stoic face.

My mouth drops.

Winnie steps out of Laney and Emma's apartment. A long dark-green dress hugs every part of her gorgeous body, as well as highlights the small bump she's sporting now.

Fuck me.

A slit on her left leg splits high on her thigh, showing off the black heels on her feet. The neckline is like a heart, and I zero in on her breasts. She swears they've gotten bigger, and now I see what she means. Her ginger hair is long, curly, and flowing around her shoulders with each step.

Don't even get me started on her smile. She knows she's got me with that mischievous grin gracing her beautiful face. I'm guessing Emma assisted in the dark eye makeup, and it looks beautiful, bringing out the warmth in her chocolatey browns.

"She looks—" I swallow hard as I unclip my seat belt.

"Yeah," Sawyer grunts. I flick a look his way, but it's not Winnie he's looking at.

Laney and Emma both look beautiful as well, and it seems Sawyer has noticed.

We climb from the limo, and Winnie walks right into my arms. I breathe in her sweet scent and tilt her chin with two fingers. "You look... *fuck*."

She giggles, and I grin, descending toward her lips, but I'm stopped by a hand pushing me back.

Emma wiggles her finger at me like a mom scolding a child. "I just fixed her makeup. No kissing until after the entry photos."

I narrow my eyes, but she simply rolls hers and shoves past me, climbing into the limo.

Sawyer shakes his head and shrugs, not knowing what to say about his pain-in-the-ass sister.

Laney crawls in after him, and when she's out of sight, Winnie smacks a quick kiss to my lips.

"You look 'fuck' too, by the way."

I smack her ass and push her toward the door while demanding, "You better make up for that fucking kiss later. If you can even call it that."

Winnie grins at me over her shoulder. "Of course."

42

Winnie

I knew this was some kind of big fundraiser, but no one told me it would be so official. I feel like I'm at the Met Gala or something. Not to mention we arrived in a limo. How fucking cool is that? It was pretty crowded after we picked everyone up, but it made it more fun because I was forced to sit on Reese's lap, and he would grunt anytime I moved. I half expected him to have a mess by the time we made it, he didn't, but the night is still young.

The inside of the ballroom is decorated with Christmas lights, giving it a romantic and intimate glow over the room.

Reese walks us up to the photo booth, and we pose for our pictures. Before we're even done, he is tugging me against his body and devouring my mouth. I think I see flashes going off behind my eyelids, but I can't be bothered to actually look as Reese backs me against the wall. He grips my ass and the back of my neck and kisses me to the point of pain, but I pull him closer—because it's never enough—and lift my free leg. *Thank you, slit.*

"Fuck, Winnie," he growls. Reese grips my leg and drags his palm up the smooth skin, but to my sur-prise—and utter disappointment—he pushes it down.

I frown.

"Don't give me that look." He groans. "It's killing me having to tell you no, but if we don't stop, I'm going to end up fucking you in front of everyone, and I worry I might not get scouted if I do that."

He never mentioned anything about scouts. "There are going to be scouts here?"

Reese nods. "Yeah. The board invites them to give the players the chance to schmooze. And because they are rich as fuck."

"I can't wait to see you schmooze."

He takes my hand and chuckles. "With you by my side, I'm not sure I'll have to do much before they are begging me to join their team just to see more of you."

Always with the charm. I swat his chest playfully. "Stop it. What team are you looking at?"

He gives me a sideways glance. "I haven't thought much about it."

I don't think I necessarily believe that, but I don't get the chance to ask before Reese is being approached. I knew he was a big deal, but we have been here fifty minutes and he's had someone to talk to the entire time. I'm not sure who all the people are, but I heard one of the women introduce themselves as a masseuse. She offered him her business card and everything. Despicable. I mean, I can't blame her because look at Reese, but still. The only reason she walked away is because he introduced me as his girlfriend.

"These women are *persistent*."

Reese squeezes my hand. "They are, but it's their job. They are here to try and get business. Unfortunately for her, I already have my own masseuse."

He kisses my knuckles and leads me through the crowd, and somehow we're able to get to our table without another distraction. Relief swirls through me seeing Laney sitting in the chair next to mine. I sink into it and nearly cry at how good it feels to be off my feet and these stupid shoes.

Reese notices it and chuckles. "I'm guessing I'll be the one massaging tonight?"

I flutter my eyelashes in his direction. "If you would be so kind."

Laney leans forward, grabbing our attention. "Where's Amy?"

"She canceled this morning."

Not even a little surprised.

Laney shakes her head and leans back. Her eyes track across the room, and I don't have to look to know she's staring at Sawyer. He's been at the bar since we got here.

"Where's Westen?" I ask.

Laney winces. "Apparently, his ex-girlfriend is here, and he disappeared with her a little over twenty minutes ago."

Reese curses, and I place my hand on top of hers. "I'm sorry. He's a dick."

She smiles, but it doesn't meet her eyes. "Thanks. I don't even know why I agreed to come."

I do. I glance over my shoulder at Sawyer. He's alone, sipping at a drink and looking like a lost puppy.

"Why don't you go check on Sawyer? He looks upset."

Reese whips around to see his best friend, and his brow furrows. "Yeah, maybe I—"

I grip his tie and tug him to sit back down, shooting him a look I hope he can read. And when his eyes flick to Laney and he settles, I know he can.

Laney hasn't taken her eyes off Sawyer, but she shakes her head. "Why would I need to check on him?"

"You're friends, right?"

She shifts and bites on her lip. "Sort of, I guess. I mean, we used to be."

"Then, there you go. It seems like he could use a friend."

It takes her a minute to agree, but eventually, she stands and wanders his way. She taps him on his shoulder, and I'm pleased to see how he brightens when he sees who is tapping him.

I settle back in my chair, a proud smile on my face.

"Are you playing cupid, Ms. Lewis?"

I grin. "I don't know what you're talking about."

He tugs my chair closer to his and presses a deep kiss to my cheek. "You do, and you just sent that poor lamb to the wolf's den."

I don't see anything wrong with that. It's obvious Sawyer and Laney are fighting things between them, and it would be much easier if they just gave in. Maybe some liquid courage will help Sawyer pull his head from his ass.

The night drifts on, and to my surprise, it's been a very pleasant event. The food was amazing, and even though Reese has to speak with a bunch of people, he always makes sure to include me in the conversation. Even if some of the people look miserable with me being there, it's still been nice.

Eventually, they announce that it's time for the DJ over the speakers. Reese stands and holds his hand out for me. "May I have this dance?"

"I would be so honored."

He snaps his teeth in a bright smile and leads me onto the dance floor. Memories flash by in my head of me being fourteen and dancing in that ice cream shop parking lot with him.

"Do you remember your first homecoming?"

Well, I'm glad I'm not the only one remembering that night. I pull back to see his face but keep my hands around his neck. "I do. I think that's the first night I caught feelings for you."

Reese levels his stare and lowers his voice. "Me too."

"Really?"

He shrugs against my hands. "I can't say for sure, and I'm not sure I should even if I could, but something changed that night."

I settle against his chest with a smile on my face.

I'm not sure life could be any better than it is right now. Everything is seemingly perfect, and I'm going to try not to think about how I probably just jinxed myself.

I've known Reese for a long time. During many stages, from little boy to awkward preteen, teenage Reese, and now adult Reese, and I think this might be my favorite version yet. I can't wait to meet Dad Reese.

He's so confident speaking with scouts, not at all awkward, and every word he says is said with a point. He's flawless. The scouts notice too; I see the way they eye him, like they are sizing up a future player who will represent their team.

Before now, he wasn't showing any outward interest, but when the scout from the professional hockey team from our state walks up, Reese stiffens. His movements aren't as confident, at least for the first minute, but the more they talk, the more he relaxes, so by the end of their conversation, they are laughing at something Reese said like long-lost friends. I wasn't paying attention, so I offer a fake laugh, but the scout wouldn't notice if I was laughing or not. He is drawn in by my boyfriend, just as he should be.

Why wouldn't Reese tell me he was interested in playing for the Beavers? Maybe he didn't want to get his hopes up or be embarrassed when they weren't interested back. Either way, I wish he would have told me.

"It was nice speaking with you, Reese Larson. I look forward to future conversations."

Reese shakes the guy's hand, a huge smile on his handsome face. "Me too, sir. Thank you for giving us your time."

As if the guy just now realized I was standing here too, he looks to me, and his face softens. "Yes, of course. I will keep an eye out for your work, Winnie Lewis."

I tilt my head, but the man offers no explanation. Instead, he shakes each of our hands and saunters away to the next player.

Reese leads me through the crowd and onto the dance floor, then pulls me against his chest. I rest my head against it, listening to his beating heart.

"So you want to be a Beaver?" I keep my voice level, hoping not to startle him in case he doesn't want to talk about it.

And for a passing moment of silence, I wonder if he doesn't, but eventually, he sighs. "Yeah. Sure, the mascot isn't as cool as the Timberwolves, but Beavers are cool too. They build dams."

I giggle into his chest and pull away to read his face. "Why didn't you tell me that when I asked?"

"In case I tanked the interview." *Like I thought.* "Or in case you don't want to stay in the state."

I've never really thought about where I wanted to live when I was older, but I wouldn't be upset staying in our home state. Especially now with a baby on the way.

"I wouldn't mind."

Reese's eyes bounce around my face. "You mean that?"

So silly of him to think I would ever want to be apart from him again. Sucking in a deep breath of his rich cologne, I lower my voice and pull his face close to mine. "I'll follow you anywhere, Reese Larson. Me, our daughter, and any future babies we might have."

43

Reese

I guess it's true what they say. What goes up, must come down.

My truck complains at the high speed, but I'm too fucking pissed to care right now. I shouldn't get woken up by my girlfriend crying on the phone because her brother freaked the fuck out on her.

The only reason I'm not heading to see Winnie right now is because Emma and Laney promised to keep her at their place until I can get to her.

Brakes squealing to a stop, I throw the truck in park and wait. I'm not going into The Underground tonight. I'm too fucking mad and would end up pissing off the wrong person, and I'm not trying to die tonight. But I will fight if it comes down to it.

A part of me hopes it doesn't, but the other, louder part right now wouldn't mind throwing a few punches into Elijah's face. Winnie didn't tell me everything he said, but from how hard she was crying, I know it couldn't have been good.

She had just texted me this morning, telling me how she was going to make dinner, ask him to watch a movie, and slowly break the news. Well, none of that worked because I fucking texted her and he saw my name on her phone.

I don't know if I'm more pissed because my ex-best friend can't get over his shit and let his sister be happy, or if I'm pissed because I'm the one who fucked everything up.

Going back, everything starts with me. I was always the one to invite Winnie to play with us. I felt bad that she never joined in, and I never saw her with friends, so it just made sense to me. Elijah never put up a fight. He and Winnie were mostly close. I was the one who hung out with her more than I should have. I vented to her like she was some kind of weird child therapist, and she listened. I was the one who let us get close enough to where she thought it would be okay to kiss me. I was the one who snuck into her room that night and didn't leave when I should have.

Me. I'm the problem, and yet I'm selfish enough to not let Winnie go.

"What's the plan?"

I shrug. I hadn't thought about a plan.

Sawyer offered to join, I think, more or less, to make sure no one dies. I've already warned him not to step in unless it looks like it's getting to that point. I don't want Elijah thinking he's being ganged up on.

Finally, I recognize the figure stalking through the large doors. I fist-bump Sawyer and jump from the truck.

"Eli," I shout.

"You have some fucking nerve showing your face here, Larson."

"Yeah? You have some fucking nerve making my girl-friend cry."

He bounds for me, but I duck out of the way, turn, and throw my fist in his direction. I end up hitting his cheek, but he doesn't even react. He throws three punches back, two I'm able to dodge, but the third hits me right in the nose. Blood immediately pours from it; I wipe, but I know it's no use.

"Don't fucking talk to me about my sister."

"Or what?" I move closer, getting right in his face.

It's so easy to feel the hatred burning off him, but it's not just hatred for me, it's hatred for everything.

"Or I'll put you in the fucking ground," he growls, moving closer so we are nearly nose-to-nose.

"I'd like to see you try."

And he does. Punch after punch, we go for it. Neither of us caring how badly we hurt the other, and honest-ly, it feels fucking good. Years of pent-up frustrations, anger, and hatred—from his side and now mine.

Somehow, we collapse to the ground, and he's on me, whaling at my head, and I'm able to block most of them. But eventually, I get sick of being hit and throw him off me with as much force as I can manage. Elijah's back hits the wall. He glares at me, breathing hard.

"You're a fucking piece of shit, Larson. You know that? Just like your good-for-nothing, murderer of a father."

"Say whatever the fuck you want, Elijah. Get it out because I'm not here to fight over that bullshit."

"Then why are you here?"

He still doesn't get it, and at this point, I wonder if he ever will or if he's so lost up his own ass and in his own misery that he will be blind to everything else forever. That would crush Winnie, so I really hope that's not the case.

"For your sister, my girlfriend." And soon to be my baby mama. Winnie didn't mention anything about her telling him that much, and I'm certainly not going to do it. My head is already throbbing.

"Stop. Fucking. Saying. That."

"Sure, but it doesn't make it any less real."

Elijah drops his head back against the wall. "Why did you have to do this to me?" His voice is so low I hardly hear it.

My eyebrows pinch, and on shaky arms and legs, I crawl to the lamppost nearest to me and lean against it. "What the fuck does me being with Winnie have to do with you?"

"You still don't get it, do you?"

"I can't get something you've never told me, E. You hated me because of who my dad is, which I fucking get, trust me—no one gets it more than me. But then it was because of fucking Zoey. Sure, it looked bad, but I was your best friend and you didn't even let me explain. Even after she told you nothing happened, that still wasn't good enough. Nothing I have ever done for you has been good enough, and I've accepted that. We're not friends, I've heard you loud and clear, but friends or not, I love your sister, and she loves me. I care about her more than anyone, and I'm sorry, but I'm not going anywhere. So either you accept it or you don't.

"But I would suggest accepting it because all you're doing is hurting your sister. I don't give a fuck if you hate me anymore, but Winnie does. And you don't see how much it hurts her knowing you hate me."

Elijah levels his stare, and for the first time in a long fucking time, it's not just hatred I see. It's betrayal and hurt.

"That's the problem," he grumbles, then forces himself to his feet. I climb to a stand after because, to my utter shock, I think we are getting somewhere.

"What is?"

He shakes his head, and I've had enough of these games. I'm tired, cold, and I just want to get to Winnie to make sure she's okay.

I storm over—well, as well as my achy body will let me—only stopping once I'm toe to toe with him.

"Tell me the fucking problem, Elijah."

"You always picked Winnie over me," he snaps, and then immediately looks like he regrets saying anything. "Just fucking never mind."

Elijah shoves past me, all while my head is spinning fifty miles a fucking second.

"You were my best friend."

He freezes, his back facing me, and shakes his head. "No I wasn't. I was the brother of your real best friend."

What the hell is he talking about?

"Don't play stupid, Reese. I know you would talk to Winnie about shit at home. You talked to her more than you ever talked to me. Time and time again, you picked her. Inviting her to always hang with us. She tagged along to everything because of you. Winnie never made her own friends because you were always there, and you took advantage of that."

No words come to mind because... he's right. I didn't do any of it on purpose, but it doesn't change the fact that he's right. I liked Winnie's company. She was easier to talk to than anyone else, but I never really tried with Elijah. I didn't want to look weak in front of another guy, but with Winnie... I don't know, everything was different. From the first moment her eyes landed on me, I never wanted to be anything other than what I was. Never had to pretend to be strong when I felt weak. She accepted me for who I was and was not.

"I didn't realize it bothered you."

He scoffs. "Of course you fucking didn't. Your head has been so far up Winnie's ass since day one, you didn't notice anything else."

"Eli—"

"I needed you." His voice shakes, and my heart stops. The world around me slows down, and a glimpse of the old Elijah punches me in the gut. "When my dad died, I needed my best friend."

"I didn't think you wanted me around."

"At first, I didn't, but you didn't even try. You walked away that night without a fucking word. You took my anger and just accepted it. Ten years of friendship down the drain."

This doesn't make sense to me. In fact, it really kind of pisses me off that he is blaming me. "I did try." My voice is tight. "I came by the house every day, and *you* shut me out."

"I shut you out because you came by the house every *day*, but whose room were you in every *night*?"

"That's not fair," I bite out.

"No, of course it's not fucking fair. I was in my room self-destructing while you comforted my sister. I had no one, Reese. Fucking no one."

"What about your mom?"

Elijah turns his head to the side, his bruised and bloody face lit by the streetlamp, and his short dark hair plastered to his head, I'm not sure from sweat or blood.

"It was never about your dad being a piece of shit or you fucking—or not fucking—Zoey. It was about you being a shitty friend."

Elijah storms away, and I do the same. There's nothing I could say right now to make things better because I don't know what to fucking say. All these years, I blamed him for ruining our friendship. I blamed my dad, Zoey. I blamed everyone besides who actually did it.

Me.

I believed Elijah was blind to how close I was to Winnie, but it seems no one was as blind as I thought. I'm not sorry for how close I was to Winnie, but I am sorry for how he feels. I never wanted to abandon him. When I found out it was my dad who killed his, I felt a lot of things. Embarrassment, guilt, anger. They were all there. Elijah lashed out at me. I knew how he felt, and I was selfish and didn't want to be around someone who was mad at me. Winnie was never angry with me. Now I know Elijah wasn't either—not for *that* reason. I should have been his punching bag, let him get whatever he needed to off his chest, but instead, I cowered away, protected myself, and let him flounder.

Fuck.

I pull open the driver's door to find Sawyer sitting in it.

"I figure you're not in the place to drive."

He figures right. I slam the door and limp over to the passenger seat. The weight of the fight and knowledge is like a fucking house on my back.

Elijah was right about one thing. I'd pick Winnie every time, and that's something I'll never apologize for.

Winnie runs out of the place as soon as we pull up, like she was waiting by the window. She pulls open the door and gasps.

"Oh my—did Elijah do this to you? Of course he did. I—"

I pull her into my arms and kiss her. My lips must be split because it fucking hurts, but I push past it.

She pulls away, breathing hard, and cups my face. "Are you okay?"

"You should see the other guy." It's a bad joke, especially since the other guy is her brother, and she winces before I add, "He's fine, Win. We both are." *Physically.*

She eyes me skeptically, twisting her mouth and looking over me from head to toe. "You look awful, Reese."

I feel it too.

"I'll be good in the morning."

She doesn't believe that, and I can't blame her. I've seen dudes after fighting Elijah, and if I look anything like that right now, it must be rough. Winnie drags me from the truck with the help of Sawyer.

It occurs to me then that I have these guys, but who does Elijah have?

44

Winnie

Reese has been off since the fight with Elijah. He's as loving as ever, and I can't place a finger on what's different, but something definitely is. I've not been home since the fight a week ago. I'll have to go before we leave for Christmas break in a few days, but I'm not looking forward to seeing my brother. Reese still hasn't told me what was all said between them, but Elijah really hurt my feelings with what he said to me. He didn't give me a chance to explain anything, and he kept going on about how everyone in his life is a liar and a snake. He didn't particularly kick me out, but it was obvious I wasn't welcome there anymore.

As far as I know, Elijah is going home for Christmas too, so I'll have to see him. Mom is aware of everything, and I know it breaks her heart that her kids are fighting, but it's on Elijah to make the first move because I know if I try and apologize, he's just going to blow up. I've texted him, asking to meet for lunch to talk, but he never replied. The only way I know he's alive is because

I saw him on campus during the week. He didn't look at me, but I at least saw him.

I should be more sorry for getting with his best friend, but truthfully, I'm not. Reese is the best guy I know. Elijah should want us together.

Everything that's happened lately is starting to weigh on me and my body. I've been having cramps since before things with Elijah, but they definitely got worse after. Which is why I'm sitting in the doctor's office.

Reese knows I'm at the hospital, but he doesn't know why. It would only freak him out, and with a big game tomorrow, I don't want to throw him off any more than he already is. He doesn't let me out of his sight, and he has my location, so I told him Laney needed me to come with her to get birth control. Sawyer overheard me say that, and I thought for sure he was going to throw his fist through a wall.

Those two are enough to make me want to rip my hair out. Something happened at the fundraiser. I don't know what, but ever since then, they both have been weird—more than normal.

I wish everyone would just chill out.

"Winnie?" a young nurse calls. I grab my jacket and follow her back with Laney in tow. I'm surprised at how close I feel with Emma and Laney after such a short amount of time, but I'm forever grateful for both of them.

The nurse leads us into a room and does all the normal things—blood pressure, height, and weight. She asks me to lie on the table and wait for the doctor before disappearing out the door.

"Wait until you see my doctor." I grin and turn my head Laney's way. "Reese hates him, but he's rated the best, so he puts it aside."

"Why does he—"

A knock on the door interrupts her, and Laney's mouth drops when it swings open. I don't know what it is with the people in this town, but they all look like they belong in modeling. Dr. Alvarez is the definition of tall, dark, and handsome. He also has a slight Columbian accent that hits the ears just right. He's a total dreamboat, and it's obvious Laney thinks so too. She's since closed her mouth, but her eyes haven't gone down in size.

"How's it going today, boss?"

Also, I really like when he calls me boss.

"All good. Just some cramping here and there I wanted to be seen for."

He takes his time washing and drying his hands, then grabs the gloves from the wall and turns to face me with a bright smile. Honestly, panty wetting.

His eyes flick to Laney. "I don't believe we've met?"

"Uh..."

I bite back my laugh. "Dr. A, this is Laney, one of my best friends."

"Laney, beautiful name."

"Thanks," she squeaks.

He turns his back, and she shoots me a look as if saying *Are you kidding me? Look how hot he is.* At least, that's what I imagine she's saying.

Dr. A is great for a lot of reasons, not just because he's extremely handsome, but he really knows how to handle patients and make them feel relaxed. He pokes and measures, pushes, then pulls out the heartbeat monitor. This is the part I wish Reese was here for. He cried when we first heard the heartbeat. It was so faint the last time, but this time it sounds stronger. I am further along, right around thirteen weeks, I believe.

"Do you mind if I take a recording for Reese?"

"Ah, yes of course."

Laney passes me my phone, and Dr. A holds the machine in place. When I pass my phone back to Laney, she has tears in her eyes.

"Are you okay?"

She sniffles. "Yeah, sorry, there's just, like, a whole baby in there."

Dr. A and I fall into a fit of laughter.

"The baby is about three inches at this time of gestation." He points to a sheet on the wall showing the baby at all stages and comparing them to fruit. Right now, baby is about the size of a peach, according to the paper.

He cleans off my stomach and pulls me to sit up before taking a seat on his stool. "I want a urine sample and some blood drawn, but the heartbeat was strong. Cramping can be normal. Some women experience period like symptoms through all of pregnancy. That being said, if you notice any bleeding, please come in right away. If the cramping gets unbearable, come in. Basically, if you are at all worried, come in. We are here to ease your mind."

"Thank you, Dr. A."

He taps my leg. "You should start feeling flutters soon. That is the baby moving, and in seven weeks, we can look for the sex if you would like."

I can't believe how fast this pregnancy is going by. Besides being sick, it's been pretty nice, and I know I'm lucky because some women have an awful experience.

Reese is going to lose his mind when we find out the gender. He's already set on a girl, but I know he will love him or her no matter what.

"Excuse me for being extremely unprofessional." He swivels Laney's way, and her eyes widen. "Are you single?"

Holy. Shit. You know what, I'm holding out for Sawyer, but if he's going to drag his feet.

"Yes, she is."

Laney hasn't moved since he asked her, and I'm not going to let her miss out on being asked out by a *doctor*.

He glances my way, slight embarrassment darkening his face. "Here is my card." He leans forward and slips it into Laney's frozen hand. "If you are interested, Laney. Call me."

Dr. A writes me a prescription, which just says no stress and stay off my feet as much as possible. At least, that's what I think from the chicken scratch writing because he didn't really say anything after asking Laney out. He fled from the room, and the nurse brought by the note. With Christmas break next week, it shouldn't be an issue staying off my feet. I know Mom is just waiting to get me home so she can wait on me hand and foot, which I won't let her, but I will gladly accept some help and love you can only get from your mom.

"What just happened?" We step into the cold, and it must make Laney come to. She's been a robot since we left.

I giggle and do a little jig, excited for her. "Well, my hot baby doctor asked you out."

She nods and licks her lips. "Thought so."

I tug her forward, wanting to get to the truck and out of the bitter cold. "You have to call him, Laney. I don't care about you and Sawyer, you can go on one date with the hot doctor."

Laney stops, pulling me with her. Her eyes round, and she looks everywhere but at me. "What do you mean me and Sawyer? I'm not—I mean, he's—"

I grip her hands in mine. "Lane, calm down. It's so painfully obvious you guys are into each other."

She cringes. "Is it?"

"Well, to me and Reese. I think Emma is blind to it, although I don't know how."

Laney breathes out a sigh of relief. "Oh."

I tug her to walk again because it's freaking cold outside, but once again, we come to a stop. I groan inwardly but plaster a smile on the outside. "Zoey."

She pauses and nervously turns to us. "Oh, you. Hey."

So *kind*. "Hello to you too."

She rolls her eyes. "Sorry, I'm just kind of in a rush. I'm late."

I glance over my shoulder. This is the OBGYN and Gyno wing of the hospital. "Ah, yeah. Good luck." I take a step, and she calls after me.

"I'm just going for a pap smear. I don't have any STDs."

What a weird thing to say. I wasn't even thinking that. "Okay."

"Although you might. Have you been checked since getting with Reese? Those hockey guys are known for getting around, you know?"

Laney squeezes my arm. "She's just trying to get to you."

"Well, it worked."

I spin and hear Laney mutter something behind me as she jogs to keep up. I stop just in front of Zoey and her stupid smirk like she won.

"No, haven't had time to get checked..." I tug up my shirt to expose my stomach. "You know, been kind of busy."

Zoey's eyes widen at the sight of my hardly swollen stomach. "You're pregnant?"

I drop my shirt. "Yep. Have a great pap smear."

Reese

"I know we have a break after today, but I don't want you lazy asses sitting around the whole time. I want you on the ice, running, something to keep you in shape because when you're back is when the real season begins, you hear me?"

"Yes, Coach."

"Good. Now get out there and let's make this 8-0."

Tucker calls us into a huddle and starts our game-day ritual of praying. There's a reason we call him Priest, and it's not because his last name is Lamb.

We break, and Sawyer tugs me to the side. He waits for most of the guys to clear before stating, "We need our captain on his game tonight."

"I'm right here." I take a step, but he grips my arm.

"Seriously, Reese. You've not been good since whatever went down with Elijah."

I cringe at the mention of his name, and Sawyer notices, his eyebrows falling.

"Whatever it is, I need you to leave it behind until after. We are on a winning streak, and I don't want to lose that."

"We're not going to lose anything. You know how I am. Forget everything and play."

Sawyer frowns, obviously not thrilled about my answer, but it's the truth. Hockey is my escape.

"I'm here when you want to talk. You know that, yeah?"

I force a smile and slap his shoulder pad. "I know, man. Now let's go."

He lets me go, and we head for the door.

"Are you ever going to let me touch your stick?"

I side-eye him and cock an eyebrow. "I hope you're talking about this stick"—I hold it up—"and not my dick, but the answer is no. Never. For both."

He grumbles under his breath, and I push through the door chuckling. My eyes land on Winnie immediately, and she offers a weak smile. She looks behind me to Sawyer and tilts her head.

"All good, baby." I smack a kiss to her forehead.

She calls after us for a picture, and Sawyer and I turn and pose.

"Come on, boys, smile while you still got all your teeth."

One day she's going to jinx me with that shit.

45

Reese

Stepping into my childhood home is like a bad dream. Nothing has changed from when I walked out of here three years ago. It's like a time machine taking me back to a place I don't want to be in. There are still holes in the walls from where my dad punched through. I can picture him sitting in the nasty old chair in the living room that still probably smells like BO and beer. See Mom crying on the steps.

I popped into the Lewises' quick enough to help Winnie get her bags to her room and eat a plate of Mrs. Lewis's tater tot casserole, a midwestern classic. Their house smells like vanilla and warm food and is decorated to the nines for Christmas.

My house—or my mom's—smells like stale bread, and there's not a single sign of the up-and-coming holiday.

I don't blame my mom. Not really. She was abused for years, leaving a shell of the woman she once was. The woman I only caught small glimpses of over the years, but it doesn't mean it's not disappointing.

Winnie was going to lie down, tired from the trip, even though she slept most of the way. While she does that, I dig around for cleaning supplies. There's a thick layer of dust on everything, and I'm not sure the last time the fridge has been gone through. It's no way for anyone to live, especially my mom.

Two hours go by before I even realize what time it is. I'm blasting music, so I don't hear anyone knock on the door or walk up the steps.

I jump when I spot Winnie leaning against the bathroom door, watching me scrub the tub.

"Holy fuck, Win."

"You look so sexy cleaning."

I lift an eyebrow. "Yeah?" I make a show of dragging the sponge over the tub edge. "You like this?"

"Mm-hmm, really gets me going."

I can't tell if she's joking, but it's not like I'm going to wait around and find out. I stand and rip the gloves from my hands, and Winnie waits patiently for me to wash them.

She backs away toward my room, and I stalk after her like a hungry wolf.

Winnie squeals and darts into my childhood bedroom. She spins, looking around at the posters of Playboy Bunnies, and scowls at me.

I grin, scratch the back of my neck, and watch her walk over and tear them off the walls.

"I'm not fucking you in a room full of other women."

Like I would be looking at them when she's right here, but I let her do what she needs. Only after all sixteen posters are on the ground does she turn to me. Her hunger turned to anger.

"Feel better?"

"No." She crosses her arms.

I kick off from the door, holding back my laugh, and scoop her into my arms. She's a bit heavier than she was, but nothing I can't handle. I force her to wrap her legs around me and move onto my bed. Letting her straddle me. Now that her stomach is growing, I don't particularly enjoy lying on top of her. Plus, her riding me feels fucking amazing.

"Does it help knowing you're the only girl I jack off to anymore?"

"No." She leans down and brushes her lips over mine. "Maybe a little."

I cup her face and take her lips. Her chest brushes against mine as she sighs and sinks into me. Her tits have gotten bigger, and when they push against my chest, it's the best fucking feeling. As well as her swollen stomach.

God, this girl has no idea what she does to me.

Winnie wastes no time pulling her shirt off, and I'm right behind her, tugging mine over my head. It feels like I'm sixteen again, except the only girl I ever had in my room was Winnie, and we definitely weren't doing this back then.

Her tits bounce free, her little red nipples already tight and begging for my mouth. I don't even have to pull her to me, she does it on her own.

"Horny, baby?"

"Yes," she pants, then gasps when I tease the peak with my tongue. "I had a sex dream about you during my nap."

"Mmm. What was it?"

"You," she breathes. I nip at her nipple, and she arches. She's so fucking responsive to me, it drives me mad. "You bent me over and fucked me from behind."

Fuuuuck. I've not taken Winnie from behind yet, simply because I like the way her small tits bounce and love seeing her expressions. That being said, if my girl wants to be bent over, damn me to hell if I don't give her what she wants.

"On your knees, baby. Stick your ass nice and high for me."

Winnie shudders and scrambles to climb off, moving to the end of the bed. I don't have a bedframe, so there's nothing to hold on to, but it's fine because I don't plan on letting her go.

I slip my hands in her leggings and peel them and the thong down her ass, exposing the most intimate part of her to the room. Fuck. Me.

Puckered and tight. I can't wait to get my dick in there one day.

I finish tugging her leggings off and drop them to my floor. My shorts are the next to go, joining hers. Lining up behind her, I tease her, dragging my head up and down her slit. She's already soaked from her dream, but I drop some spit down her crack anyway. She tenses when I thumb over her ass.

"One day," I mutter.

Winnie shivers, and her back arches. I bite my fist and use the other hand to line my dick up with her opening. She's still tight as can be, but it's easier to slip in than the first time. Especially from this angle.

I love sex with Winnie at all angles, but fuck if this one doesn't hit in a different way.

"Oh, Reese."

"That's it, baby. Say my name. Tell me how much you love being fucked from behind."

"So good."

Yeah, it is. I pick up the pace. My hips slapping against her ass, and it's fucking sinful how her cheeks bounce.

It takes no time at all for my balls to tighten. I need Winnie to come first, though. Leaning down, I wrap my hand around her front and find her clit. She bucks, but I hold there, massaging just how I know she likes.

Her moans turn to whimpers, then cries. She begs me to come, and I can do nothing but oblige.

I grind into her clit and fuck her like my fucking life depends on it.

"Come for me. Soak my dick like I know you can."

I clamp down on her shoulder, and she screams out my name. Her pussy fluttering around my dick has my balls drawing up, so I push until we are flush and let go. I chant her name like a prayer in her ear, and she wiggles, milking me of every last drop.

When my balls are empty and her pussy is full, I kiss her back and fall to my heels.

It takes a few beats for Winnie to move, but she groans and falls to her back, probably dripping cum onto my bed, but I couldn't care right now if I wanted to.

"So, did that live up to dream Reese?" I shouldn't have to compete with myself, but I'm willing to do it if it ends like that every time.

Winnie twists her lips and her cheeks pinken. "Mm-hmm."

"That's all? *Mm-hmm.*"

Winnie nods quickly, then rolls off my bed and stands. "Yep."

What the fuck? I catch Winnie around the wrist and drag her back to the bed. Pinning her under me, I hold her arms above her head so she can't get out.

"What aren't you telling me?"

A nervous giggle bursts through her lips. "In my dream, we were, uh... in public when you did *that*."

Ahh. My girl's a bit of an exhibitionist, is she. That should come in handy later.

I fall to her side, and she buries her face into my neck.

"You're a dirty girl, Winnie Lewis."

She gasps, offended by my tease. "You made me this way! I haven't been able to get that time in the bathroom out of my head."

I grin and drop a kiss to her cheek. "And I fucking love it."

46

Winnie

Dr. A said if I started cramping again I should take it easy. Well, there's nothing easier than lying on the couch and watching your boyfriend and Mom play checkers, with soft Christmas music on in the background.

Reese smiles at me and rubs a hand over my belly. I do my best not to wince, but it hurts. Like period pains but worse. Is this how birth is going to be? Is it worse? Man, I should have thought about these things before we had sex without a condom. They warn you about pregnancy in sex-ed, but no one warns you about how scary it actually is when you are pregnant.

The timer in the kitchen goes off, and Mom bounces up. Ready to get dinner from the oven. I want to offer to help, but I can't. Reese does, however, and she shuts him down immediately.

He leans over and pulls my shirt up enough to expose my stomach. Warmth spreads across my abdomen as he places his hands across my belly, and honestly, it feels amazing.

I let out a long sigh. "That feels good."

Reese leans down and kisses just below my belly button. "Hi, baby. It's Dad." He glances up at me. "Once again, your mom looks beautiful."

I smile and thread my fingers through his hair.

"It's almost Christmas, and we are hanging out with your grandma. You're not even here yet and you still have presents under the tree."

Mom insisted on buying us our first baby gifts, but not only did she buy the first, she bought the first through the fifth. This little girl is going to be spoiled rotten.

"She is going to love you so much. Not as much as me or your mom, but close."

My eyes drift closed, and Reese presses another kiss to my stomach and continues his one-sided conversation.

A flash goes off behind my closed lids, and I peek an eye open. Mom stands in front of us with tears in her eyes and Dad's Polaroid camera in her hands. The photo prints out, and she waves it before looking. Big tears fall down her cheeks, and I smile. She really is going to love this baby so much. I know not many people are so lucky to have a mom who would be as supportive as mine, and I'm so thankful.

She passes us the photo of Reese kissing my stomach, and my heart skips a beat as my eyes burn with tears.

When I look at Reese, he is dragging his hand under his eyes as well.

Pregnancy might be hard, but it's so worth it.

Someone gently moving my legs startles me from a peaceful sleep. Assuming it's Reese, I reach a hand down and grip his arm.

"Before you do something we'll both regret. You should know I'm not Reese."

My eyes fly open, finding Elijah sitting under my feet, a weary smile on his face. I sit up too quickly, and my head spins.

"You're home."

"Don't seem too excited about it."

Mom and Reese stand in the doorway to the living room. Mom looks pleased, but Reese is obviously on edge.

"I am, sorry. I'm just not feeling well."

"What's wrong?" Reese and Elijah ask at the same time, then cringe.

This room couldn't possibly be any more awkward than it is right now. You could cut the tension with a spoon. Elijah and Reese share not quite a glare, but something similar.

"Just tired, I guess." I shrug. The pain in my stomach has mostly gone away, so I'm not really lying.

Elijah lowers his eyes. "I'm sorry, Win."

Well, I can honestly say I never expected those words from my brother's mouth. In all the years I've been alive, not once have I ever heard him apologize. To be fair, I don't usually either when it comes to him. We have our fights, and then we move on. I think we both knew our last fight wasn't one we could just move on from, though.

"Me too."

He flicks a look my way and frowns. "Why?"

"Because I lied to you. Repeatedly. I should have just told you from the beginning."

"It's not like I made you feel comfortable enough to tell me."

True. "But still."

He curves his head toward Reese. "I'm sorry to you too. For everything."

Whatever that *everything* is seems pretty heavy, more than what I'm aware of. I've still not been able to get Reese to tell me what happened that night he showed up bruised and bloody.

Reese walks forward and sticks a hand out for Elijah. "I'm sorry for not being there. I should have tried harder."

Elijah slaps his hand away and, to my utter shock, stands and hugs Reese. Mom cries softly across the room, but I can't manage to do anything but stare. Even Reese is surprised, but he quickly recovers by hugging him back. They slap each other's backs in such a man way, harder than I think necessary, but what do I know?

"Brothers?" Reese mutters.

Elijah sighs, but he nods his head. "Brothers."

"Guess this is that big thing, eh?"

Elijah narrows his gaze, confused as I am, but he rolls his eyes a second later, seemingly catching on to what Reese is getting at. "Don't even think this is the same thing as a birthday present."

Reese grins. "And Christmas, don't forget."

While I'm still confused on what they are talking about, I butt in, no longer wanting to feel left out. "So, are we one big happy family again?"

Elijah rolls his eyes, grabs my wrist, and tugs me from the couch. A sharp pain shoots throughout my body, but he's squeezing me before I can say anything.

"If we are family, you two would be in prison."

I giggle into my brother's chest. "Yeah, yeah." I shove him off. "You reek like smoke. I thought you quit."

"You smoke?" Mom's voice carries through the house. "Elijah Anthony Lewis, I raised you better than that."

"You're such a pain in my ass," he grumbles before stalking toward the kitchen, probably to soothe our mother.

Reese slides behind me and wraps his arms around my body. A shiver darts down my spine as he kisses my neck. "We are a big happy family."

He places a hand over my stomach, and I relax into his chest.

"Your mom told me I need to invite my mom to dinner. She should be home any minute, so I'm going to head that way so I'm there when she gets home."

Another pain shoots through my body, and the urge to pee hits me out of nowhere.

"Okay," I say quickly and pull from his arms. "I have to pee!"

His chuckle echoes from behind me. When I get to the bathroom, I rip my pants down and gasp at the sight of blood. Not a little, either. A *lot*. My legs are covered in it.

"Reese!" *Please still be here.*

"He left. What do you need?"

"Elijah, get Mom," I order, but he doesn't move. "Now!"

The bathroom door flies open, and his eyes fill with horror. "What the fuck is wrong?"

More pain. More blood. My knees give out, but Elijah catches me.

"Mom," he shouts while carrying me through the house. "What the fuck, Winnie, why are you bleeding?"

Mom rounds the corner and gasps. "Oh, Winnie."

Tears roll down my cheeks, and I know from Mom's face this isn't "normal" bleeding.

"Put me down," I beg, as my stomach turns.

Elijah lays me on the rug in the living room but doesn't leave my side. He's panicking, ripping his hand through his dark hair as he looks over my body for a reason I would be bleeding this much.

I can't manage to open my mouth and tell him, though.

Mom rushes in and drops to my other side. "The ambulance is on the way, Winnie. Okay?"

But it already feels too late. I know this isn't normal. I can feel it deep down that something is wrong.

"Someone fucking—" Elijah cuts off as he reaches for something on the table next to him. His hands shake as he holds up the photo, so many emotions covering his face. He falls back, further away from me, and in a harsh tone says, "You're fucking pregnant?"

"Elijah," Mom hisses.

"Are you?" he demands, eyeing me with so much disgust.

I turn my head away and close my eyes. The pain and nausea are getting worse.

I *hope*.

47

Reese

Mom is running late, but I'm not surprised. She never was great about being home on time. It's one of the things that pissed Dad off the most. What he didn't realize was she didn't come home on time because of him. He's not here, but I guess old habits die hard.

I wander to the kitchen to grab some water, something to pass the time. I don't know why Mrs. Lewis wants my mom over for dinner anyway. No, I do know, and it's because Mrs. Lewis is a saint. I have no doubt the dishes I found in the fridge, piled with food, are from her. I know they can't be Mom's—the dishes are too nice. I grab the plates from the dish drainer and stack them, ready to bring them over when she gets home.

Another ten minutes go by, and I'm getting annoyed. Whatever, I'll come back when she gets home. Not like it's a far walk. I pull my hood over my hat and grab the dishes before heading for the front door. It isn't even fully open before the distant jingle of sirens fills the air. It occurs to me they could be for my mom, but I shake it away and step out, not bothering to lock the door.

Not like there's anything anyone would want to steal anyway.

The December air is bitter and bites right through my sweatshirt.

I squint against the snowy air. The sirens don't fade, they grow closer, and I stop and watch which way they go. They don't speed by like I expect. Instead, they turn. My heart skips, waiting to see which neighbors' house they stop at. The road is full of elderly people, but what a shitty time to need an ambulance.

Dread fills me when they come to a screeching halt right across from me, and my heart stops altogether when the door flies open and Elijah is carrying Winnie.

The plates fall from my grasp, crashing to the icy ground with a loud clatter. I hardly notice it, halfway across the road already.

No, no, *no*. What the fuck happened in the fifteen minutes I've been gone?

"What happened?" I bark when I'm close enough.

Elijah is shaking, looking at his sister, and Mrs. Lewis is behind him holding her mouth and crying. The paramedics are in my way, so I can't see her.

"Sir, you need to back off." One of them places his hands on my chest, shoving me away.

"What happened? Is she okay?"

"Are you related?" another asks.

"He is," Elijah growls. "Let him through."

My head is spinning with what could be wrong. There's a pit that tells me I might know, but I ignore it because I refuse to think about it.

The paramedic steps aside, and I move to Winnie's side. They load her into the back, and I follow. Looking her over, I don't see much, but they have a blanket over most of her body. Her eyes are closed, and there's O2 being fed into her nose.

My eyes fly to Mrs. Lewis and Elijah.

"We will meet you there," she tells me, with a wannabe-okay voice, but I see right through it.

I dig under the blanket and grab Winnie's freezing hand. Pulling it to my mouth, I kiss her knuckles. "I'm here."

She rolls her head my way, and her eyes flutter open. I blow out a relieved breath seeing her chocolate eyes.

"What happened, baby?"

Winnie's lips wobble, and her voice is weak. "I'm so sorry."

Sorry? What could she possibly be sorry for?

She's closed her eyes again, and it's obvious she's not completely in it. I drop my head to her hand, but my focus catches on something on her fingers, and pulling back, I spot the red. She's bleeding, but where? I reluctantly drag my gaze down her body and land on the blanket molded to her lower half. I swallow hard and lift the blanket, and everything in my body goes cold.

The rest of the ride to the hospital is a blur. Winnie hasn't opened her eyes, but she's breathing. The paramedics are doing what they need to, and when they lift the blanket, I look away.

It hurts.

Everything fucking hurts.

My baby.

I don't need to be a doctor to know all that blood isn't good.

We come to a stop, and so much happens all at once. The doors fly open, and Winnie is dragged away. I rush after, but when we hit the doors, two nurses turn and stop me from going any further.

"Sorry, sir, we can't let you go back."

"What the fuck do you mean you can't let me? I'm her boyfriend. I'm the fucking dad to that baby inside her."

They swap faces, but they don't budge.

"I'm the fucking dad! She needs me there."

"I assure you she's in trusted hands."

Trusted hands, maybe, but not my hands.

"You're not listening." I get in one of the nurses' faces. If she were a dude, I would throw a punch. "That's my baby in there. I want to be with my girlfriend."

"Sir," a deep voice sounds behind me. I don't have to look to know it's security.

"Please." I lower my voice and take a step back. "I'm the dad."

"Sir, back up, or we're going to have to physically remove you."

Fuck hospitals. Fuck everything.

I turn away but keep the nurses in my peripheral, and when they move from the door, I take off. They shout behind me, and it takes longer than I'd like to find Winnie. As I'm not completely a dick, I wait until I hear her cries before throwing open the curtain. The security is on me, holding me back and keeping me from getting to my girl.

"Reese." Winnie's voice is weak.

"I'm here. Are you okay? Is—" I cut off, unable to utter the words.

Her head shakes. My knees buckle, and it gives security the upper hand to drag me away.

"I'm the dad! That's my girlfriend. She needs me!" No matter what I scream, they don't stop. They drag me all the way outside, fighting the entire time, and drop me to the ground.

I can't stand. I can't fucking feel *anything*.

"Stay there until you can calm down."

It's not like I can do anything else.

You ever have those moments when the world stops? This is one of those moments for me.

48

Winnie

"Number seventeen, Reese Larson, is still on one, Rick. Don't you think?"

"Yeah, Chad, whatever has gotten into him has made him a machine. One that seemingly can't be stopped."

Mom turns the radio down and takes a seat across the table from me. She slides a cup of tea my way.

"Extra honey, just as you like."

"Thank you."

Mom nods to the radio playing Reese's game. "They talk about him like he's not a human."

"Well, right now, he hardly is."

Mom taps my hand lovingly. "It will take some time, but you both will eventually be better."

Why doesn't it feel like it, then? My entire world changed two weeks ago. I lost my baby, and that same day, I lost my boyfriend. At least the version of him he was before.

We're still together, technically, but I've been living with my mom, and he's back at college. He offered to stay back, but I could tell being around me was hurting him more than helping. I can avoid looking in the mirror, though I can't avoid feeling my now-flat stomach, but Reese cringed every time he saw me change. He didn't mean to, I don't think, but I saw the way his eyes shifted away anytime I was shirtless.

We talk on the phone—sometimes, but our conversations are empty.

This is all a part of the grief process, according to the therapist Mom found for me, but it hurts.

I want him to hold me, promise me everything is going to be okay like he did when my dad died, but it's not the same because now he's grieving a loss too.

"I think I'm going to go lie down." I keep my head down, avoiding the look on Mom's face. She's been great, but I know it hurts her to see me so upset. Everyone around me is hurting, and it's all my fault.

As I'm padding down the hallway, I pause outside the closet under the stairs. Knowing what's inside causes a shudder to rake down my spine and my eyes to burn. I've cried more in these last two weeks than I have since my dad passed.

The floor creaks behind me, but I bolt for the stairs before Mom notices me looking at the closet with my baby's stuff inside.

My bed is as soft as ever, and I will sleep to come, but of course it doesn't. It never does. Sleep isn't common for me anymore. Every time I close my eyes, I see that hospital room. The one where they removed the baby from my body like it meant nothing. Hear Reese's cries as they did.

Rolling to my back, I stare at my ceiling and watch the fan spin above. Anything to distract me from reliving that night.

It spins roughly thirty-two times a minute on the setting I have it switched to.

I know a while has passed when my phone jingles with a text. I reach for it and pull it in front of my face to read the message, even though I know exactly what it will say because it says the same thing every time.

Reese: Game's over, we won. Call you later. I love you.

And I'll reply with the same message that I always do.

Me: I heard. Congratulations. I love you too.

He won't call me later. He says he will, but he won't. I'll text him around nine, and he will have some excuse as to why he can't talk. It never fails.

Unlike us.

I've never been a bath girl, but lately it's the only way I can manage to clean myself. The bubbles hide me from seeing things I don't enjoy looking at right now. Like a flat stomach where my baby should be.

I drop my head back and focus on the small TV Mom placed in the bathroom for me. I started spending so much time in here, she went up to the attic and dug it out. Along with the DVD player so I can watch *Friends*.

I jolt when a sudden knock raps on the door. "Yeah?"

"It's me."

Elijah? What is he doing here?

"I want to talk. Just come out whenever you're ready."

My heart skips a beat, but I mumble some kind of reply he must hear because his heavy footsteps fade away. I haven't seen Elijah since that night after he kind of just disappeared. Mom said he wanted to give Reese and me time, but I was sad my brother left me after that. He's never been the type to comfort, though, so I wasn't surprised either.

I'm just not sure why he's here now. Especially since it's nearly one a.m.

The water has dropped below room temperature by the time I pull myself from the tub. Not just because I want to stall whatever it is Elijah wants to talk about, but... well, yeah, mostly that.

Reese's shirt hangs from my body, and I tug up a pair of sleep shorts for bottoms. The cool air wraps around me, and a chill runs up my bare legs. I reach for one of Mom's robes on the back of the door, but instead, my fingers grip a long brown one. *Dad's*. The lump that's been in my throat for two weeks grows three sizes. The robe is somehow warm as I wrap it around my chilled body, even though it's not been worn in three years.

I pause outside Elijah's room, unsure if I'm ready to go in. I'm not sure what is holding me back so much from seeing my brother. We made up regarding Reese, so I'm not sure what it could be. My knock is quiet, but he calls for me to come in.

Pushing open his door, I'm surprised to see his room so clean. I guess I haven't been in here in a while, but growing up, Elijah wasn't the cleanest of people. Me either, so I can't say much, but I remember Mom having to get after him about food wrappers and glasses constantly. There aren't any wrappers on the floor, but there are three glasses on his bedside table that make me want to smile. I guess some things never change, like the half-naked photos of women on his walls.

"Teenage boys really are so gross," I comment while stepping further into his room and closing the door behind me.

He's leaning back on his bed, with his arm behind his head and his feet crossed. In pajama pants and an old high school shirt, he looks so much like a younger, happier version of Elijah. Except he's covered in tattoos now. The black ink seeps from under his shirt, bleeding onto all the exposed parts of his skin. I've seen him shirtless a few times since we lived together, so I know they don't stop on his arms and neck. His whole torso is mostly covered as well. I also know he has a tattoo of Dad's face over his heart. My chest tightens at the thought.

Elijah smirks, but it doesn't quite meet his eyes. "I was just thinking how my walls at school are looking a little bare."

I choke back a laugh, and oddly, it feels good. He taps the bed next to him, and I wearily wander over and sit down. Surprised to find his bed is harder than mine.

"Geesh, your bed is like a rock."

"I didn't have someone breaking in the side I don't use on a regular basis." He cocks an eyebrow, and heat floods up my neck. "Just saying."

"You wanted to talk?" Anything to get the topic off Reese sneaking into my room at night.

Seconds pass, and Elijah doesn't speak. The side of my face burns each time he flicks a look my way, and the tightness in my chest heightens with each passing beat.

"Is that Dad's robe?" His voice is soft, as if he's afraid of the words he's speaking.

"Yeah," I say, dragging my fingers over the fluffy material.

"Mom said he would love it, but I didn't believe her. I mean, who wants a robe for their birthday?"

I shoot my eyes in his direction. "You got him this?"

He nods, and even though his face is bunched the same way it is when he's angry, I know it's not what's pinching his face. His eyes are soft, full of emotion as they soak in the brown material.

"You can take it with you when you go. I don't use it a lot, just happened to grab it tonight." I tug it up to my nose and suck in a deep breath. "It still kinda smells like him."

Elijah leans closer, sniffs the collar of the robe, and nods. "It does."

Silence rings between us like a pendulum hanging over our heads, waiting for the hour to hit. I move down and place my head on his flat-ass pillow, then tug the robe up to my nose and let my eyes close. Over these last few weeks, I've been wishing Dad were here. For some reason, I think he would know what to say. He wouldn't, because nothing anyone can say will help, but he was my dad. The person I went to for everything. I love my mom so much, but I was always a daddy's girl at heart.

"I miss him." Elijah's voice comes so suddenly and closer than I expect that I freeze. My eyes pop open, and I turn to find him with his eyes lowered and his fingers stroking the robe tie that's lying next to him.

"Me too," I choke back.

Elijah moves closer and wraps a brotherly arm around me, tugging me closer. "I'm sorry I killed your baby, Win."

Pain sears through me like a hot knife, and I shove him away from me. He meets my eyes, and although he might not be crying like I now am, he looks to be in the same amount of pain.

"I don't ever want to hear you say that again."

"It's true. I caused you unnecessary stress. I was pulling you, squeezing you, and messing with you that day. You looked sick, and I still…" He trails off, and a sob rips through me. "Please don't cry, sis."

His beg is enough for the dam to break, and everything I've been holding back floods to the surface. He tugs me against his body, burying my face into his strong chest.

"I've been a shit brother. Not just lately, but for years. I should have been the one comforting you. Holding you when our dad died. I should have been there, but I wasn't, and I'm so fucking sorry, Win."

"You were grieving too, E."

He shakes his head against the top of mine. "I'm the big brother."

As if that keeps you from being sad when your dad dies. "If you are blaming yourself for me and Reese, don't. That would have happened with or without you. It's fate."

He makes a noise in his throat that I don't think he expected me to hear because it sounds an awful lot like a scoff. "That's not what I mean—for once. I'm saying I should have been a better brother. Not to stop you and Reese, not for any other reason than the basic one. I'm the big brother. Dad trusted me to look out for you no matter what, and I didn't. I'm the reason you lost your baby, Win." He pauses ever so slightly, and I peek up but quickly look away when I see his jaw locked tight and his red-rimmed eyes peering down at me. "And I'm so fucking sorry."

I shake my head but can't get my jaw to move. Not because I agree with him, but because I can't believe the guilt he holds. I never resented him for not being more involved after Dad died. As far as I was concerned, Elijah was grieving the same as me, but in his own way. Big brother or not, we both lost someone that day.

"Please don't apologize." I lick my dry lips and lower my eyes to the baseball logo across his chest.

What a morbid fucking thought that no one should carry. Including me. I've blamed myself for weeks. Things I could have done differently—maybe if I had done *this*, it wouldn't have happened. Maybe if I would have done *that*.

It's gotten me nowhere.

"I can't stand you even thinking it's your fault." I shove him back so I can see his face. He refuses to meet my eyes, but I know why and allow him the freedom of coming to me instead of forcing him. "Because I know what it feels like, and it's suffocating. Eventually, it'll grab ahold of you and drag you under its unforgiving grip." *Unless someone saves you.* I'm in no position to save anyone. I can hardly keep myself afloat. But knowing why Elijah has avoided me—because he has it in his head that he's the reason I lost my baby that night—is enough to make me want to try.

"It's not your fault, Win. I don't know why bad things happen to good people, and I promise before I sink to the pits of hell, I'm going to find out from the big guy upstairs, because it's fucking bullshit."

My stomach shakes with a small laugh, and I curl into his side and roll to my back to stare at the ceiling as if I'm going to see what I'm looking for. "Sometimes I like to pretend that Dad is up there holding my baby." I've never been religious. We went to church on special holidays when growing up, but I never really thought much past it. I don't know what's true or not, but I know thinking that my baby is with my dad helps the pain. Not much, but a small amount.

Elijah is quiet, probably wondering if his sister has officially lost her mind.

"That's a nice thought."

"Beats the others I have as of late," I joke halfheartedly.

He grips my hand, and his voice drops an octave. "Reese isn't doing good, Win. I've been checking on him, from a distance." *Of course.* "He's... I don't know. Like, lost."

My stomach clenches, and I drop my head the opposite way of Elijah as tears drip down the side of my face. Him and me both. Knowing Reese is struggling hurts more than I could ever explain. Like a weight is just about to crush my heart into a million pieces. The worst part is I have no clue how to help him when I can't even help myself.

Reese was always there for me growing up, and I was there for him, even when I didn't know how to be, but things are different now. He's hurting because of me. Maybe in a roundabout way, but it's my body that rejected our baby like—

"I think he needs you, Win. I haven't seen him this lost since I ran into him at the library the first week back after Thanksgiving freshman year. He was just sitting at a table, staring at a wall. My ego always let me believe it was me he was hurting from, and I relished in that, but I don't think it was me. I think it was the lack of *you*. He's not good without you."

"He can't even look at me, Elijah." My voice is soft but might as well be a scream for how bad it hurts to say out loud. Thinking it is one thing, but admitting it out loud hurts like a knife in the side.

"I'm not saying it's going to be easy. It's going to fucking hurt, and you guys are going to mourn what could have been, probably forever. But hurt together, not apart. You can't have Reese without Winnie. It's like Pooh Bear without *hunny*."

I turn my head to meet Elijah's eyes. They are soft, a look he doesn't give often anymore. "You're turning into Dad at the old age of twenty-one."

He drops my hand and uses that same one to shove my shoulder lightly. I giggle, and he follows with a chuckle until, eventually, they fade and he sighs. "Just think about it. I'm not trying to pressure you, but I saw him walking a turtle with a leash the other day, so maybe hurry with your decision."

49

Reese

"Do I look fucking interested?"

The girl who hasn't fucking shut up snaps her tiny mouth closed. *Finally*. "Well, uh—"

"Well, uh, nothing. Go away. I'm not interested in whatever you fucking want from me."

Some fucking people don't know how to leave others alone. Just because I'm sitting alone at a bar doesn't mean I want company. Maybe I just want to fucking be alone. Wild idea to some people, and apparently impossible to others. Fuck.

I push from the bar and stalk from the hotel lounge. Exhaustion hits me like a brick, but I slam a fist into the elevator button, praying I hit the right one. It's a little foggy right now.

Finally, the ding sounds, and the door eventually pops open. I stumble inside and lean against the wall, closing my eyes and dropping my head to it at the same time. I should have taken the stairs, but I'm not sure I would have made it up them, and the last time Coach found me passed out someplace that wasn't my room, he threatened to bench me. He wouldn't have done it with how good I've been playing, but the threat was more about me respecting his wishes than the threat itself.

"Alcohol only masks what you are feeling for a short period."

I shrug, not bothering to look at Coach Miller. "Temporary relief is better than no relief."

"True." He punches a button with a thud, and I can only hope it's my floor because my limbs are heavy. I should have quit after the... whatever drink number was before the last.

"Me and my wife lost a baby when Zoey was four. He was three months old, and one morning, he just didn't wake up."

"I don't want to hear this," I ground out, feeling that same pressure rising, ready to wrap around my neck and choke me until I can no longer breathe.

"Sometimes you need to hear things you don't want to," he tells me, sounding so fatherly I want to punch him. "The grief was heavy, as you know. It destroyed my family. Part of me believes that's why Zoey is..."

A *whore*? I almost say, but even in my drunk state, I keep my mouth shut.

"Well, you know." *Unfortunately*. "We didn't mean to, but I think we neglected our daughters because of the grief. Eventually, I surfaced, but by then, it was too late. My wife, however..." He trails off, and I pop an eye open.

Squinting against the bright light of the metal elevator. "She never really did. We were officially divorced a few years later."

"That's shitty." But what the hell does this have to do with me?

"It was. She let it change her into a woman I no longer knew. My last straw was when she drained my account and left on a holiday I had planned for the family, alone. The men she hooked up with on the trip weren't even an issue since I was already in contact with a divorce lawyer. I served her the moment she walked in the door, and she didn't even blink as she signed the papers. She was gone a week later, without even a goodbye to the girls."

Confusion hits me, and I pinch my eyebrows. "Zoey has talked about her mom. She's married to a cop or something. In fact, it's you she never mentioned."

His face stiffens and his lips flatten. "Yes. That's because a year or so after Lindsay left, she came back wanting partial custody of the girls. Zoey was young, missed her mom, and was eager to jump at the opportunity. It wasn't long before Lindsay had her convinced I was the problem, and when she came of age and was able to pick where she wanted to live, she chose her mom and her rich boyfriend. I can't blame her. They were buying her everything she wanted, and I was still recovering from the divorce."

"No offense, but I don't really care about this."

"I know. I'm not telling you this for any other reason than one. Lindsay was the love of my life before she let grief change her."

All at once, recognition settles as anger bubbles inside me. "Are you comparing my Winnie to your ex-wife?"

"No." He shakes his head, and he's lucky because I'm drunk enough and stupid enough to throw a punch at one of my coaches for comparing my sweet girl to his bitch of an ex. "But grief can change people more than you ever thought possible."

"Or it brings out their true self."

He shrugs and lifts a palm up in my direction. "Is this your true self?"

I scowl and cross my arms over my chest. I'm aware of how childish I look right now, but he's purposely trying to piss me off. It's working.

"I didn't think so. My advice? Go be with your girl. Hold her, and grieve together."

He has no idea how many times I've thought about driving to Winnie's and pulling her into my arms, doing just that. But I'm a pussy.

I push off the wall when the doors open. Before stepping out, I glance over my shoulder. "I'm sorry for your loss and everything that came after it."

Normally when I drink as much as I did, I pass out as soon as my head hits the pillow, but it's almost as if that conversation with Miller sobered me. Mostly. Brushing my teeth was interesting, as there were two of me in the mirror, but lying in the dark hotel room, my mind is swimming with everything.

Which is why I don't notice when the door opens. Not until Sawyer's big body drops onto his bed next to mine with a thud. He throws an arm over his eyes and sighs. "Why are women so fucking complicated?"

"I think they say the same about us," I mutter, barely coherently.

"Yeah, well. Amy wanted me home for the weekend, and I said fine, but I'd have to leave after the games. Well, she changed her mind and said never mind."

I sit up and cock an eyebrow. "And you believed her?"

"She fucking said it was no big deal, so yeah, I believed her." *Idiot.* "But what does she want me to do? Skip the games? This from the same girl who has been pushing for me to go pro since she found out how much pro goalies can make."

"Well, it's Amy. I don't think she even knows what she wants most of the time, but rule one for girls, never trust what they say, but how they say it." I found that very early on with Winnie. She would say one thing, but her body language would say a whole other thing. Confusing as fuck, but I think it's programmed in them to beat around the bush or something.

He grumbles under his breath, and I drop back to the bed with a sigh. "Coach Miller called me out for not being with Winnie."

Sawyer is quiet for a beat. He's really been the only one I've spoken to about anything, but still, it's not been much. He just happened to be the one to find me crumpled in my shower after a panic attack when I got back to school.

"Why *aren't* you with Winnie?"

"I'm scared." This is the first time I've admitted it out loud, and it feels good. "I'm scared that seeing Winnie is going to bring back all the hurt. The memories."

"You mean the hurt and memories she has to deal with daily?"

I flick a look his way.

"I'm not trying to piss you off, man, but you can pretend to hide from it. She can't. Every time she changes, she sees—or doesn't see—what should be there. What they did to her after..." He trails off, and I'm glad. I never want to think about that ever again. I'm not sure how I managed to explain it to him in the first place. "These are all things that probably haunt her daily. Alone."

"She's not alone," I mumble. "Her mom is home more than not."

He shakes his head. "Nah, that's not what I mean. You guys made the baby together. Don't you think you should be grieving the loss together?"

The pain of losing our baby is nearly unbearable, but the pain of knowing Winnie is suffering alone because I've been selfish is soul-crushing. Sawyer's right. I've been avoiding my feelings, lost in hockey and the bottom of a bottle, anything to keep my mind off the grief. But Winnie doesn't have that privilege.

My goal was never to make her feel worse. I just knew that, this time, I couldn't slip into her room, pull her against me, and promise everything would be okay. Winnie was always the person to hold me when I cried. It feels wrong making her do the same now, but maybe it's not about me holding her, or her holding me, but us holding each other.

50

Winnie

"You ready?"

I glance in my brother's direction from the front of the hotel and shake my head. "No, but I miss him."

He cups my shoulders and offers me a forced smile. I think it's meant to be comforting. "I'm ready to stop being your relationship counselor, so let's go."

The desk lady was not willing to give me Reese's hotel number, but after approximately three minutes of Elijah turning on his charm, she sang like a canary.

"It's gross how easily she gave in to you. She would have sent me on my way without a second thought."

He flashes me a smirk, much the same as the one he gave her, and I crinkle my nose.

"You'd be surprised what I can make women do with just a look, sis."

"Surprised and utterly disgusted, now knock it off."

He slams a fist into the elevator button, and when it dings, we step in. Nerves crowd my entire body like a weighted blanket.

"You're thinking too much, Win. Reese is going to be happy to see you."

I dip my chin; I know he's right. Mostly. There's a small part of me that worries about the memories seeing me will bring up. If it'll be too much for him. He's avoided me, and I can't blame him, but I hope he is as ready to see me as I am him. Or he could turn me away. Say it's too much, and he can't get past the grief. If so, I couldn't even be upset, but I can't afford to lose Reese too.

"What if it's too much?"

He wraps an arm around my shoulders and presses a kiss to my temple. "Then I'll break his kneecaps."

Somehow, I believe him.

The elevator doors slide open, and my stomach drops. My feet are heavy, and it's hard to take a step, but there is a young dad with a toddler waiting to get on, and I know he wouldn't appreciate me just standing here while his son cries for food. I don't look at the toddler as I step by them, and when the doors shut, I suck in a much-needed breath. Elijah eyes me cautiously, but I do my best not to let anything I'm feeling show.

Eventually, I glance around at the numbers and head in the direction of Reese's. My lungs are begging to suck in a breath only he can provide. It's like only when we are together do I fully get to breathe.

As I round the corner, I pause for a moment, recognizing the two girls walking in the same direction as me.

Emma's eyes pop open, and she takes off in my direction. Laney is right behind her. The three of us come together in a warm embrace, and even when I'm ready to let go, they hold on. I didn't realize how much I missed their faces until just now. Emotion crowds my throat, and tears burn my eyes.

"I didn't know you were going to be here," Emma cheers while pulling away and wiping her face. Her voice is low since it's only eight in the morning, not wanting to wake the people around us. Most likely grumpy Timberwolves.

"Me either." I laugh awkwardly while patting my eyes of any unshed tears.

Laney's lip wobbles, but she doesn't say anything, and she doesn't need to. They both have been checking on me regularly through texts, so I know everything they want to say but can't.

For so long, I wanted friends, and it's incredible to finally have them with these two girls.

"Are you here for Reese?" Emma asks.

I nod and swallow the lump in my throat.

"We are just coming to wake the boys for breakfast. I assume Reese will be too busy eating something else, though." Emma nudges me but giggles when Elijah huffs a breath.

I flick a look at my brother, who is making it a point to not return it.

"Just knock on the fucking door," he grumbles, and I grin at my friends.

They all take a step back, leaving me in front to be the one to knock. The door isn't abnormal, but it feels like I'm getting ready to go to battle with how my heart is beating. I want to prep my heart for heartbreak. But I can't when I'm just too excited to finally be in Reese's arms again.

Sighing, I raise my fist with the intent to knock, but the door swings open instead.

Sawyer stands on the other side, eyeing me, then my fist, and lifting an eyebrow. "You going to use that on me, Snaps?"

"Depends, is it deserved?"

He smirks before throwing his arms around me and squeezing tighter than anyone has been willing to squeeze me in weeks.

"*We've* missed you."

I don't miss the emphasis on *we've*, and my heart flutters. Maybe Reese will be excited to see me after all.

Sawyer's body is warm, and he looks like he just rolled out of bed. His blond hair is a mess, and sleep still coats his eyes. He squeezes me another time, then pulls away, but he keeps his hands on my shoulders.

"You look good, Win."

Someone behind me clears their throat, but I don't have to look to know it was my brother.

Sawyer flicks a look up, and his face hardens. "Elijah."

"Sawyer," he replies, then sighs a beat later. "I suppose this is when I apologize for punching you in the face when I thought you slept with Winnie."

Sawyer's hands fall from my shoulders, and he crosses them over his broad chest. He leans against the doorframe and cocks an eyebrow at me. Heat burns up my neck, and I can't help but laugh.

"Sorry about that, by the way."

"*By the way*," he mutters, mocking me. "Probably." He glances at Elijah. "But we both know you won't."

"You're right," Elijah deadpans. "I'll offer to buy you breakfast, though."

Sawyer flattens his lips. "You're going to offer to buy me a free continental breakfast that is included with the room? How kind."

"I said offer."

They might be bickering, and Elijah might have given him a black eye, but I can see a friendship growing between the two assholes. Deep, *deep* down. Okay, maybe not friendship, but something close, anyhow.

"Fuck it. Let's go," Sawyers says, and steps out of the room. His arm snaps out, and he stops the door from closing, then lowers his eyes to me. They soften, and it surprises me to see how genuine Sawyer is being when we are usually butting heads.

"Go get your man, Snaps. And convince him to shower, because he fucking stinks."

"I will." My voice is soft, and I turn for the dark room.

"Call if you need me to break his kneecaps," Elijah says as he steps away.

Sawyer scowls at him but says nothing, and they disappear down the hall we just came from.

My heart is in my throat as I take the first step into the dark room. It's so dark that when the door closes, it's completely black inside, thanks to the blackout curtains.

Slowly, I maneuver forward with my hands out in front of me and my feet sliding against the carpet. I come up to a wall and flip the first switch I find. It turns on the bathroom lights, which brightens the rest of the room enough for me to see Reese lying in the bed closest to the window.

He groans and throws an arm over his scruffy face.

"Turn the fucking light off," he snaps.

Despite his sour tone, I smile. My chest warms and my hands itch to touch him.

"Sorry, I couldn't see where I was going."

He stiffens but doesn't look my way. "Win?" His voice sounds so broken that a shiver racks down my spine.

"It's me." A sob rips from my throat, and I throw a hand over my mouth to hopefully silence it. Crying wasn't the first thing I wanted to do when I saw him, but the emotions are too much for me to handle. It's overwhelming seeing him, even more so when he slowly and sloppily pushes onto his elbows and his tired eyes meet mine.

His jaw locks, but it doesn't stop his chest from caving and another sob from ripping through me.

"Please don't cry," he begs in a heartbreaking voice.

"I've j-just m-missed you."

His face pinches, and his eyes shoot to the window. "I've missed you too."

Unsure what I should do, I wrap my arms around myself but stay where I am. He doesn't seem happy—or unhappy—to see me, and I really don't know how to take this Reese. I can feel that he wants to cry; it's all over his face, and it's my fault.

I take a step back, ready to run from the room, but his eyes slice over to me and lock me in place.

I drop my face and stare at the ugly carpet under my shoes. "I don't know why I came."

"I do." The bed creaks as he moves to stand. He wobbles in my peripheral vision, but I keep my eyes on the ground, allowing the tears that broke free to drop freely below. The closer he gets, the tougher it is to breathe, and when he's standing in front of me, an arm's length away, I stop breathing altogether. "You're here because I'm fucking weak and couldn't come to you."

"You're not weak."

My body explodes when Reese touches my chin. A single finger lifts it so we are eye to eye once again. Seeing his red-rimmed eyes so close has the ache in my chest growing stronger, forcing my already uneasy breaths to skip.

"I am. And I'm so fucking sorry, baby."

51

Reese

I'm a fucking asshole. Now that Winnie is here, in front of me once again, I cannot figure out why I stayed away. On the off chance I didn't feel so relieved when I saw her? What a stupid fucking thought. Winnie is my home. My safe place and the one person I've always looked forward to seeing, even in our hardest moments. Like now.

The bed is soft beneath me but feels solid compared to the girl in my arms. She's straddling me, holding me just as tightly as I am her. Our combined cries are the only noise in the room, pouring out of us like the fucking dam just broke. My chest is soaked with her fallen tears, just as her hair is soaked with mine. It hurts. It's so fucking painful knowing what we lost, but the fact we are together reminds me that just maybe we can get through it. Together. Always together.

"I feel so guilty," Winnie whimpers sometime later.

I shake my head and bury my face deeper, breathing in her comforting scent. "Please. Don't."

"I can't help it, Reese. Every time I think back to that night, all I can see is you... a-and the doctors. What they did—"

My lips take hers forcefully without thinking too much about it. All I know is I can't bear her reliving that awful moment. She kisses me tenderly back, but her lips are unsure. I pull away and cup her damp face between my large hands.

"I love you, but I can't bear to think about what you went through, Win. I'm sorry."

Her lip wobbles, and my heart races, waiting for her to reply.

"You mean it?"

"Mean what?"

"You love me."

Silly, silly girl. For the first time in weeks, a smile tugs on my lips, and I let it. It's not big, but it feels good. "I've loved you since I laid eyes on you, Winnie Lewis. My love for you isn't conditional. It's forever, everlasting—through anything and everything we go through. This won't be the only hard thing we face, but as long as we are together, it's us against the world, baby."

I flick the shower on and adjust the temperature. I guess Sawyer was right; I stink. Even Winnie was crinkling her nose at me after a while. Glancing over my shoulder, I watch as Winnie hooks the bottom of her shirt. I'm tempted to look away and give her privacy, but then I remember I'm Reese fucking Larson, and I don't give Winnie Lewis privacy. Ever.

The shirt drops to the counter with a light thud, and then she hooks her pants. She must feel my stare because she looks up, meeting my gaze in the mirror in front of her. A deep blush creeps up her cheeks, but she doesn't smile. Instead, something like dread filters across her pretty face. Furrowing her brow, she reaches for the shirt, stumbling over an apology that rips my heart to shreds. My feet carry me to her faster than she can unscramble the shirt and slip it on, and I grab the soft material and toss it out of her reach.

Winnie drops her face to her hands, and her shoulders shake. I thought we had cried it all out, but I guess not.

I wrap my arms gently around her, and she turns and curls against my chest.

"Why are you hiding from me?"

Her sobs cut through me like a blade made of ice. "Because where our baby should be is nothing."

I squeeze her tightly and close my eyes, fighting the burn from turning into anything more. "It's not nothing," I say, probably way too late, but my voice is only seminormal. "Your stomach was our baby's home and will be the home of future babies if we so choose to try. And if not, it's a part of the woman I love, and that's not nothing to me. It's everything."

"I love you."

Instead of replying, I pull away and hook her pants, then peel them down her thighs. Dropping to my knees, I look up as I wrap my hands around her waist, placing my face at her navel.

Goosebumps spread over her body, pricking the skin under my hands. She shivers, but it's not because it's cold, as steam fills the small bathroom from the hot shower running behind me.

My hands threaten to start shaking, but her eyes fill with tears, and I know what she needs right now is for me to not lose my control.

I drop my gaze over her perfect tits and down to her navel. Although I just saw her naked abdomen, being so close surfaces emotions I can't push away. Leaning forward, I press my lips firmly against her soft skin and let my eyelids drift closed. The photo of me kissing Winnie's belly where our baby laid is in my wallet with the other snapshot of us. I've not looked at it since I placed it in there, but it's constantly burning a hole in my pocket.

Winnie slips her hand into my hair, and an unwelcome noise erupts from my throat. Her hand tightens.

"I'm sorry." I choke on the words.

"I don't need you strong, Reese. I just need *you*."

That's been the issue all along. I thought I needed to heal before I faced Winnie again. Ready to take all her tears and hold her as long as she needed while being strong for both of us, but that's not the case at all. This isn't a process we face alone and come together when we are mostly okay again. Because, truthfully, I don't know when I will be okay.

"I'm here," I whisper against her soft skin and say a silent prayer to our baby before pulling away and meeting the eyes of the woman I love. They shine from unshed tears, but her lips that I love so much flick up in a soft smile that lets me know everything will be okay. Not today, or tomorrow, but eventually.

epilogue

Reese

FIVE MONTHS LATER...

I gasp awake. Slipping my hand into her hair, I grip and growl, "Winnie."

She pops off and flips the covers back to expose her smiling face. "Good morning."

"I told you, you can't suck me off anymore if you won't let me touch you."

She pouts, and it's the cutest fucking look, so I have to close my eyes.

Winnie hasn't let me touch her pussy since we lost our baby, and I get it, but she insists on waking me up with a blowjob more often than not, and it makes me feel like the biggest piece of shit for being the only one coming between us.

"I was thinking..." She twists her lips, a mischievous smile growing in place. "That maybe I let you touch me."

"If you say psych right now, I'm going to fucking die, Winnie Lewis."

She giggles the sweetest sound, but I'm serious. The window across my room is four levels off the ground, and I will jump.

"I don't know if I'm ready for sex, but maybe oral?"

Yes, fuck. I'll take anything. "Get on my face."

She takes too long, and I lean forward and lift her petite body on top of my face. She hesitates, but I grip her hips and shove her down on my tongue and suck in the sweet, sweet relief.

Winnie falls forward, I think meaning to go for my dick, but I'm a starved man, ravished for his girl, and it's the first time she's given me the chance in too fucking long.

I sit up, still holding her waist, and drop her on the bed. She doesn't get a word out before I'm diving back in for her pussy, lick after lick. She's gasping, gripping my hair, and riding my face.

I'm going to remind her how good it feels to come whether it kills us both or not.

Winnie screams my name, for sure waking the guys, but that's not my fucking problem.

I bring my fingers up now, watching her, but her eyes are closed. I drag them through her slit, teasing her pussy. While not pushing me away, she's tense, but that's expected.

The tip of one finger slips in, and she groans, withering with pleasure, so I push farther. Her hips rock, taking my finger deeper.

There's my good girl.

I lap at her pussy and let her ride my fingers as fast and hard as she wants until another orgasm overtakes her body. She thrashes, and I have to flatten my other hand on her stomach to hold her in place.

When she's done, she tugs on my hair, pulling me up her body.

"That was…"

"I know."

She blows out a sweet breath. "I'm sorry I've been holding back."

"Don't apologize. I know why."

Pain flashes through her eyes, a look I see often, and I know she sees the same from me, but we are working through it.

Together.

"We need to get ready."

"I don't want you coming, Win. I told you this." I slip from the bed and wander to the bathroom. Praying she doesn't follow. This is one thing I'm not caving on.

When my mom called me a few weeks ago, telling me my dad was dying, I didn't even blink. To me, the man who took part in creating me is dead. Whether he's walking around earth or not. I didn't plan on going to any kind of service they had for him, but Winnie mentioned how there probably won't be many people, and for whatever fucking reason, my mom is sad. Basically, she guilted me into going, but I made it clear she was not.

How fucking sick would it be for Winnie to go to the funeral of the man who killed her dad? Pretty fucking sick.

"Well, it's a good thing I'm a grown-ass woman, then."

Yeah, a grown-ass woman and a pain in my ass. I spin, ready to argue, but come up short when I find her naked. *Dirty game, Winnie.* And she damn well knows it.

She pads by me and makes sure to brush my dick with her hip as she does.

I narrow in on her ass, and a growl tumbles from me.

Water pelts against tile as I flick the shower on, grab her wrist, and pull her under the cold water with me.

"*Reese*," she screeches right in my ear, but I don't let up.

"You need a cold shower. Playing these teasing games like I'm not five seconds away from pinning you against the wall and fucking you senseless at all times. I'm really trying to respect your wishes, Winnie." I tighten my arms around her. "But you don't realize how close I am to snapping."

"I wish you would." Her voice is so small, so quiet, it hardly reaches my ear, but it does, and my flaccid dick stiffens.

"Tell me what you want, Winnie. I want words."

She turns in my arms, tears in her eyes, but a look of defiance on her face. "I want to be fucked. I *want* you to pin me to the wall and fuck me like you mean it. I don't want gentle. I want *The Rapture*."

She has no clue what she's asked for.

"Are you sure?" My restraint is snapping by the fucking millisecond.

"Yes."

If my girl wants The Rapture, I'll fucking give her The Rapture.

"You didn't come in me."

"I know. I figure we're not ready."

Winnie steps behind me and kisses between my damp shoulder blades. "Thank you for always knowing what I need."

"I do my best."

Her heat leaves my body, and I look back, watching her shimmy from the room. "You do a pretty good job, Reese Larson."

How do you say goodbye to someone you spent most of your life hating? Death is hard, but my dad's death is complicated. Our last conversation weighs heavy in my mind. It was months ago, right after Winnie moved to town and right after I found out she called me his name. I wanted to speak with him and make sure I was actually nothing like the man. He was so apologetic, but it doesn't take back all the mistakes he made. The mistakes I paid for.

He might have gone to prison, but I'm the one who lost everything that mattered most to me.

I don't cry, because I won't miss him, but there is a weight of what could have been. If he was a good dad, or if he was the one to die in that accident instead of Mr. Lewis.

Soft footfalls stop at my side, and a gentle hand slips into mine. I look down, expecting my mom, but she doesn't have ginger hair.

My voice is hoarse as I mutter, "I thought I told you to stay home."

Winnie flicks a warm look up to me. "You held my hand when I had to bury my dad. It's only fair I'm here when you do."

I tug her against my chest and wrap my arms around her front. "I fucking love you."

"I fucking love you too."

I grin into her neck and place a chaste kiss on her soft skin. She smells edible, but it's not the time to get a boner.

"I didn't come alone, though." Winnie points around my arm, behind us.

Sure enough, Sawyer, Emma, Laney, Schmidt, and... *Elijah* stalk forward.

They take turns offering their condolences, and I'm sure they are probably wondering why I'm not more upset.

Elijah stops by my side. He glances at his sister, then at me, and he sighs and looks to the grave. "Your dad was a piece of shit."

Someone gasps on the other side of me. I'm guessing Laney or Emma since Elijah is keeping his voice low enough my mom shouldn't have heard. Not that she isn't fully aware of that herself.

"I know. Thanks for coming, though, man." I know Winnie dragged him, but Elijah doesn't get dragged into anything he doesn't want to do, so him being here says a lot.

"You weren't the cause of my dad's death, but I was the cause of your baby's."

Both Winnie and I wince. We went through a time blaming ourselves, and it was a very dark time for both of us.

I clear my throat. "Don't say that."

"It's true." His jaw is locked, but he turns sorrowful eyes my way. "Anyway, your dad was a piece of shit. But it doesn't mean you are. I'm still not happy you fucked my sister, but that's life."

"It is."

There's a beat of calm silence before I pull my hand from Winnie's and angle it in Elijah's direction. "Brothers?"

He takes my hand, squeezing harder than necessary. "Brothers."

His voice is mocking, but I'll take it.

"Eventually brothers-in-law," Winnie adds enthusiastically.

Elijah drops my hand and grumbles under his breath.

I chuckle and drop a kiss to the top of Winnie's head. "My wife. I like the sound of that."

Her small body wiggles in front of me with her version of a happy dance. "Just say the words, baby. We could be married today."

Actually, that's not a bad idea.

Winnie

"Where are we going?" A laugh tumbles from me, but not easily. I haven't been able to catch my breath since Reese hasn't stopped tugging on my arm. The service finished, and I stepped aside to let him say his goodbyes and talk to his mom, and ever since, he's had this crazy excitement about him.

He's planning something, but I don't know what.

Reese reaches into my pocket and grabs my keys. There was hardly any room with the people I brought, but if we add another body to the pack, there's going to be no room at all. Ignoring that, though, he tosses my keys to Sawyer.

Reese throws open the back door and hops inside, then pulls me onto his lap and dives for my mouth.

My head is spinning with everything going on, but you'll never see me turning down a kiss from Reese Larson.

"Did you mean it?"

I'm breathing hard and am confused. He can't kiss me like his life depends on it and then ask me a question. "What?"

"About marrying me. Did you mean it?"

Is that what has him so excited? I giggle because this is silly. "Yes, I've said it a few times now. Why, are you asking me?"

"Nope." He pops the P, then leans forward. "E, throw on some fitting music."

"Yup."

"Will someone tell me what is happening?"

Emma and Laney squeal with excitement, and then the music plays. "I love spur of the moment, but you will owe us a real wedding eventually."

I tilt my head at Emma. "What do you mean?"

"Going to the Chapel" by The Dixie Cups starts blasting through the speakers, and my mouth falls.

Elijah glances back, his version of a grin coloring his face. "You always did love this song, eh, Win?"

I did, but...

I whip my head to Reese and stare into his wild, excited eyes. "You can't be serious. On the day your dad was buried? Right after his funeral?"

Reese waves me away. "Today is special for another reason, baby."

My eyebrows pinch, and I tilt my head.

"It's the seventeenth."

Oh. Right. I knew it was coming, but I didn't realize that was today.

Reese pulls me close to his body and kisses my head. "I've loved you forever, and I know you've loved me too. How could you not?"

He pumps his eyebrows, and I swat his chest as Elijah complains from the front.

Reese swipes away the stray tears from my cheeks with his thumbs and holds my face. "So, no, I'm not asking you. I'm telling you, baby." His eyes soften. "We need this, Win. A good thing to remember this day by."

Reese often says I stole his heart when we first met, but I think he stole mine the same day. From the broken boy across the street, to the strong man holding me in his arms right now, he has owned my heart the entire time. A love like ours isn't one that just goes away. I was silly for ever thinking Reese wasn't my end game. I could have fought it until I was blue in the face, but nothing would have changed. He still would have been there, waiting for me with open arms.

I stare into the hazel eyes of the only boy I've ever loved, allowing all the emotions I've always held for him to bubble to the surface. I choke on a sob and ask, "What are you saying?"

"We're getting married, Winnie Lewis. Today."

The End.

acknowledgements

I want to give a special mention to all the mom's that aren't able to hold their baby(ies). My heart aches with you.

To my editor, because she is AMAZING. Thank you for all your input and HEAPS of knowledge; I'm truly blown away at how stress free you made editing this book (who knew that was even possible?!) and how much I learned while doing it! This was a hard book for me to get through, dealing with my own pregnancy while writing about Winnie losing hers, it hurt. A lot. So thank you for being overly patient with me during this entire (very long) process.

To my husband, I have no words for you. You're my best friend, my rock, my everything. Each book I pour a little of us in every character(s) I write because you are a love story come to life. I can only hope everyone gets to experience something similar to the love we share. (Not with you, though, you're mine.)

To my babies, I pray you'll always know how loved you are.

My friends/support group (lol) each book I write I swear I'm going to quit. I'd say thank you for encouraging me not to, but that's not really what we do. So, thanks for listening to me bitch constantly.

And lastly, to my readers! Without you and your support I wouldn't be able to do what I do. So from the bottom of my heart, thank you for letting me word vomit all my thoughts on a page and call it a book.

also by

standalones:

- **Reap3r**

- **Him For Christmas**

series:

Broken Series
- **Break For You** (Book one)

- **Leave Me Broken** (Book two)

- **Heal For Me** (Book three)

Emerson University
- **Snapshot**

- **The Long Shot (coming 2025)**

about the author

I know these are meant to be in third person, but I loathe third person. So, I live in the USA. Specifically the mid-west so that means I love ranch and say "ope" when I bump into someone. I'm married to the love of my life and together we have created a life I only ever dreamed of having. Books are a huge part of my identity and one day I decided I wanna do that (meaning write a book) and, well... here we are. Romance is my favorite genre and I don't ever see myself veering from that. We all deserve a happy ending, even if it's only fictional.

Peace!

Printed in Great Britain
by Amazon

41773442R00303